FAEBOUND

Also by Saara El-Arifi

The Final Strife
The Battle Drum

FAEBOUND

SAARA EL-ARIFI

HARPER
Voyager

Harper *Voyager*
An imprint of
HarperCollins *Publishers* Ltd
1 London Bridge Street
London SE1 9GF

www.harpercollins.co.uk

HarperCollins *Publishers*
Macken House,
39/40 Mayor Street Upper,
Dublin 1
D01 C9W8
Ireland

First published by HarperCollins *Publishers* 2024

1

ISBN: 978-0-00-859696-5 (HB)
ISBN: 978-0-00-859697-2 (TPB)

Typeset in Scala Pro by Palimpsest Book Production Ltd, Falkirk, Stirlingshire

Printed and bound in the UK using 100% renewable electricity
by CPI Group (UK) Ltd

MIX
Paper | Supporting
responsible forestry
FSC™ C007454

For my sister, Sally

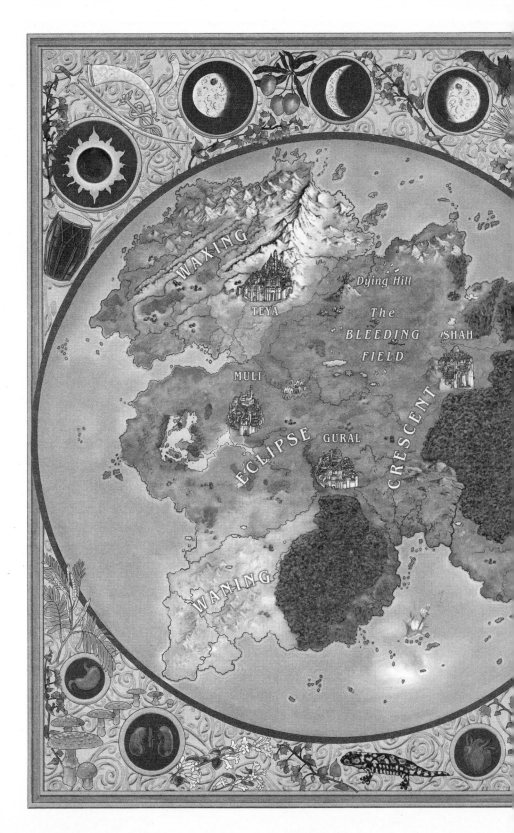

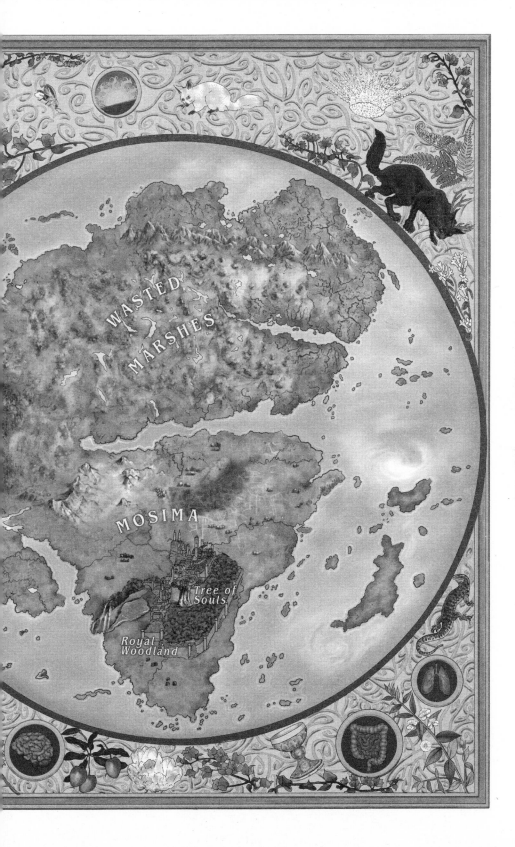

WASTED MARSHES

MOSIMA

Tree of Souls

Royal Woodland

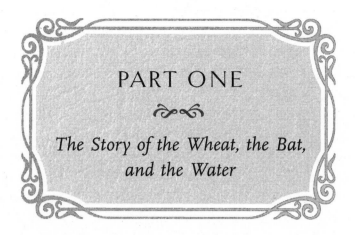

PART ONE

❦❧

*The Story of the Wheat, the Bat,
and the Water*

In the beginning there were three gods.

The god Asase came to being as a grain of wheat. A single particle that bloomed into life. As Asase grew, their roots became mountainsides and their leaves blossomed into forests. Valleys formed in the gaps of Asase's branches and the knots in their bark became canyons.

And so, the earth was born.

The god Ewia flew in on wings of darkness to bring day and night to the world. As a bat with two heads they found their place in the sky above their sibling. When one face looked to the earth there was light, and when the other turned their gaze downwards there was darkness.

And so, the sun was born.

The last god to appear in the universe was Bosome. They moved through Asase's roots creating rivers and seas before residing next to Ewia, a silver droplet of water in the sky that ebbed and flowed with the turning of tides.

And so, the moon was born.

The three gods lived happily for many years until one day Asase said, 'I wish for a child. I shall create one.'

From the seeds of the earth Asase made humans. Sprigs became bones and flowers sprouted smiles.

Ewia, seeing their sibling so happy with their children, said, 'I too wish for a child. I shall create one.'

And so, from the skin of their wings, Ewia made fae with pointed teeth and ears like bats.

Centuries passed and Bosome watched both their siblings in their happiness but saw their children's faults. Humans were too fragile to survive long, and fae too arrogant to care much for their parents. So Bosome made the elves out of the waters of the world with the pointed ears of fae, but with the humble nature of the humans.

And for a time, all was well. But no matter how much the gods wished for peace, they had given their children the one thing that would never ensure it.

Free will.

CHAPTER ONE

Yeeran

Yeeran was born on the battlefield, lived on the battlefield, and one day, she knew, she'd die on the battlefield.

Her first breaths were tinged with the smoke and ash of her mother's dying enemies. And when Yeeran screamed, she joined the rallying cry of her tribe as they rode into battle. Soldiers giving birth on the front line wasn't uncommon. If you could hold a drum, you could fight.

And yet we still don't have enough soldiers.

Yeeran let out a heavy sigh as she surveyed the war map in front of her. Each valley and hill had been etched into the slab of oak by skilled cartographers. An expensive piece of craftmanship to have in a bedchamber, but Yeeran's lover had never been called frugal.

The moonlight cast a shard of silver over the centre of the table where the four districts of the Elven Lands converged on the Bleeding Field, the front line of battle. She ran her gaze over the four quadrants of the map: Waxing, Crescent, Eclipse and finally her own elven tribe, Waning.

Her hand curled around the edge of the table, her nails making fine dents in the grain of the wood as she scrutinised the battlefield formations. White tokens tracked the locations of troops under her army's direction.

Yeeran's eyes homed in on one regiment that lay in wait by the eastern tower of the garrison. Hers.

'Yeery,' the nickname was breathed into the silence. Salawa's quiet steps had brought her to Yeeran's side. 'Come back to bed.' Her breath was hot as she brushed her lips against the shaved sides of Yeeran's head towards the pointed tips of her ears.

Yeeran's hand slid up Salawa's back and tangled her fingers in the edges of the woman's braids. They hung heavy against her naked skin, weighed down with beads and gemstones.

'I can't sleep.'

Salawa didn't respond for a time. Yeeran liked that about her lover, that each second was considered, every thought knitted together, before she spoke.

'Twenty years you have waited to be promoted to colonel. Few thought you'd do it before your thirty-fifth birthday, yet here you are, the youngest colonel the Waning Army has ever had—'

'Not until tomorrow.'

Salawa inhaled sharply. She didn't like to be interrupted. Yeeran's hand slipped up from Salawa's clavicle until it rested against her cheek. It was only then that Salawa softened enough to continue.

'Sleep will not take this moment away from you. Your new regiment will be there in the morning.'

Salawa looked to the window where the city of Gural pulsed as the heartbeat of the Waning district. Yeeran followed the direction of her gaze.

Chimneys thrust up from domed roofs puffing smoke into the star-speckled sky. Yeeran knew that the taverns would be teeming with soldiers made merry by spiced rum. For the bakeries it wasn't late night, it was early morning, and the aroma of their ovens seasoned the light wind.

Yeeran watched the tenderness in Salawa's face harden as she looked further, towards the Bleeding Field. Battle fire lit her green irises hazel and Yeeran felt herself burning from the flame reflected there.

'I got you something, to celebrate your new title,' Salawa said quietly.

Yeeran's hand dropped from Salawa's cheek. Her lover's gifts were always ostentatious and gaudy. Yeeran didn't wear jewellery or care for fine dresses. Neither helped her in combat.

The only thing she did keep on her was a small gold ring sewn into the lining of her uniform. It had no sentimental value for her, but she knew that, should she fall in battle, the ring would be rightfully claimed by the young children who made a living scavenging from the corpses of the army. With that ring, the children would be able to feed themselves for a year. Yeeran had spent many years of her childhood hoping to find such a boon.

'I think you'll really like this gift,' Salawa said as she padded away to retrieve something from under her four-poster bed.

Yeeran gave her a tentative smile and Salawa laughed knowingly as she withdrew a large circular object wrapped in a leather sling.

It took Yeeran less than three steps to cross the room. She lifted the gift from Salawa's outstretched hands and peeled back the grain of the leather to find the present within.

The drum was exquisitely crafted. The outer shell hewn in mahogany, making the barrel shine a deep crimson like fresh blood. The casing and hoop were gold and studded with sapphires. Beading threaded down the bowl of the drum, more for decoration than for sound. But the most beautiful thing by far was the black drumskin.

'From an obeah elder?' Yeeran murmured, her hand running over the stretched leather.

Obeah were the only creatures imbued with magic in the realm. The animals had once been as common as deer, roaming in packs across the Elven Lands. Yeeran's sight went inwards as she imagined the creatures thundering through the forest, their white horns slicing through the foliage, their feline forms slipping past trees with the ease of ink on paper.

But now the ink had all but dried up, as they had been hunted to near extinction for their magic.

Magic for weapons like these. Yeeran's fingers prickled where they rested on the drumskin.

Salawa grinned and clasped her hands under her chin.

'Yes, this was made from one of the oldest obeah our hunters have ever caught.'

As an obeah aged its skin colour deepened, making the creature's magic more potent, and its skin even more coveted for crafting powerful objects. Unfortunately, elder obeah were also more intelligent, so hunting them was near impossible. Salawa's gift was something rare and precious.

Yeeran could feel the magic emanating from the skin. She tapped her fingers across it and directed the vibrations of the drumbeat with purpose, knitting them together in her mind to form a small projectile. It was like weaponising sound. The invisible force struck a white token in the centre of the map ten feet away.

She'd always been good at drumfire. Having a clear intention was the key, but the clarity of the note and strength of magic in the obeah elder skin made her skills unmatchable. If her enemies had thought she was dangerous before, they would soon see how deadly she could be.

Salawa clapped.

'Now the greatest colonel of the Waning Army has the greatest weapon.'

Yeeran carefully sheathed the drum back in its case and went to Salawa. She folded her into her arms and rested her chin against her hair.

'Thank you, I will treasure this gift for the rest of my life.'

'Now can we go back to sleep? Tomorrow will come soon enough,' Salawa murmured.

Yeeran released a breath of assent and let herself be led back towards Salawa's bed. She slipped beneath the silk sheets, and Salawa moulded herself into the contours of Yeeran's body. She lay her head on the soft skin between Yeeran's shoulder and breast and let out a contented sigh.

Salawa's breathing elongated as she fell into a deep slumber. Yeeran watched as the fraedia beads in her hair began to softly gleam with the oncoming dawn. The crystal had the same properties as the sun and could be used to grow crops or warm homes in winter.

She reached out and gently moved one of the beads away from Salawa's face, lest the brightness wake her. She cradled the gemstone for a second, marvelling at its warmth. This small deposit could help grow a plant for its entire lifecycle. Could help feed a family.

She let the bead fall.

If only we had more of it.

For fraedia was the currency of the war.

Beneath the bloodied soil of the Bleeding Field were untapped mines of the valuable crystal. And where there is value, there is power, and where there is power, violence will always brew.

So, the Forever War came to be.

Yeeran found herself wondering how many soldiers had died for this small yield of fraedia in Salawa's hair. It cast her black skin, darker than Yeeran's soft umber complexion, in a warm saffron glow.

Though all elves looked different, the only difference that mattered was which tribe had your allegiance. And Yeeran was Waning, and Waning was Yeeran. There was no separating her from her tribe. To lead was to be one and the same.

Salawa had shown her that.

Sun sins, she is beautiful. Beautiful in dreams and fierce in waking.

Sleep didn't come for Yeeran, but nor did she seek it. Instead, she lay there watching the dawn break against her lover's skin, her mind alight with glory and power and death.

The next morning Yeeran slipped out of Salawa's bedchamber while she was still asleep and made her way across the city. The sound of warfare grew louder the closer she got to the Bleeding Field, the echo of drumfire was as soothing as it was exhilarating.

Today she was a *colonel*.

As she neared the training grounds, she heard the familiar lilt of a nursery rhyme.

One, two, three, four: the elven tribes,
Waning, Waxing, Crescent, Eclipse,
Made by the moon, made to persist.

From a distance it was easy to mistake the youthful voices for a group of children in a playground. But Yeeran knew that she wouldn't find schoolchildren when she turned the corner.

Three gods, three peoples, there were before,
Now only elves: one, two, three, four.

No, these soldiers had long stopped being children. They marched woodenly in time with their chanting, their expressions grim. Yeeran watched the boy closest to her spin on his heel, his small head rattling against his large helmet like an acorn in a barrel.

He can't be more than nine years old.

'Colonel Yeeran Teila.' The lieutenant overseeing the drills had spotted her.

Yeeran winced, she'd hoped to slip by without being spotted.

'Lieutenant Fadel.' She returned the lieutenant's salute.

'Are you here to select your next drum-bearer?'

The role was given to the youngest recruits of the army. Yeeran had always thought the title an odd one, as she never relinquished her drum's maintenance to anyone. Every night she would spend an hour cleaning the barrel of enemy blood and carefully oiling the drumskin.

Not that this drum would need as much maintenance.

It hung from her shoulder now, a reminder of Salawa's love resting against her hip. Heavy and ever-present.

'No, I have no need of a drum-bearer,' Yeeran said, shaking her head sharply.

Fadel frowned but then smoothed his expression into one of earnestness.

'What about Officer Hana? She is our very best.' He gave a signal and a girl, slightly taller than her peers, stepped forward.

Her uniform hung off her frame like a flag on a pole. Her stomach, though, swelled from malnutrition, and Yeeran felt her own abdomen prickle with the memory.

The child's dirty fingers curled into a tight fist as she pounded her frail chest in salute. The harder the drumbeat, the more respect the salute afforded, and this girl beat her chest so hard she was ready to knock the ribs from her breast.

Yeeran lowered herself to the girl's height, dropping all pretence of formality. Hana gave her lieutenant a worried look, but Yeeran drew her gaze back to her with a smile.

'It's OK.' Yeeran reached into her pocket and withdrew a single gold coin. 'Make sure you get a proper meal tonight, not the gruel they give you in the barracks. All right?'

The child stood still, awestruck by the gold coin in her hand. Then she said the most unexpected thing. 'They sold me for less than this.'

Yeeran felt a gasp reflexively escape her lips.

A few years ago, the chieftain had introduced a new programme: children could be sold directly to the Waning Army for half a silver. The child then became a ward of the district, their fellow soldiers their only family.

It made procreation a profitable business.

'War plays by no rules. There are only fighters and failures,' the chieftain had said when announcing the programme.

Looking at Hana, Yeeran wasn't sure she agreed.

She straightened before striding away from the girl and the open mouth of Lieutenant Fadel.

Yeeran told herself that her hurried steps were driven by the anticipation of meeting her new regiment. But really she was running from the sight of the child soldiers and her own memories of an aching hunger that had never truly gone away.

CHAPTER TWO

Yeeran

Yeeran pushed her camel into a canter as she surveyed the front line of her new regiment. Five hundred infantry, three hundred cavalry and a hundred archers. A sea of soldiers at her command.

It felt damn good.

Sweat trickled down her back despite the mildness of the weather. The sun had burned off the humidity of the morning, leaving the sky clear and the wind brisk, moving in a north-easterly direction.

Perfect weather to guide my archers' arrows true.

'Colonel.' One of her captains drew level with Yeeran and saluted from her saddle. 'General Motogo has been spotted on the western front. They are heading this way.'

Yeeran looked to the sun. It was nearly at its zenith. She'd be marching into battle soon.

'I will receive them in my command tent. I don't want to be disturbed. The regiment is under your leadership until I return.'

The captain nodded her assent and rode off, barking her own orders to her subordinates.

Yeeran jumped down from her camel and strode across her line of troops to her command tent. Though it was called a 'tent', the military encampments had so long become a fixture of the Bleeding Field that the tribes had built permanent structures. The bronze doorway was circled by bright pink bougainvillea flowers that grew in abundance across the Waning district.

'To help mask the scent of the battlefield,' the chieftain had said when the flowers were planted.

But it's impossible to mask the aroma of a thousand-year war. It lived in the air, in the skin, in the very bones of the earth.

Yeeran entered the circular room and stepped into the pool of sunlight that shone through the wide windows. The Bleeding Field stretched out for as far as she could see.

In the centre of the room she found Captain Rayan frowning over a letter. He looked up as she entered and smiled.

'Good morning, *Colonel.*' He said her title with a touch too much reverence and it drew out a laugh from her, which was exactly what he intended.

They had known each other a long time. She'd once been his lieutenant but had outgrown her rank long before he outgrew his. Her success had never bothered him, rather it had deepened his loyalty to her, grounding their roles in true friendship.

'How goes it?' Yeeran asked, peering over the letter he was reading. It was grubby and worn from being folded and opened too many times.

Rayan ran a tired hand over his shaved head.

'This is the last message I received from my scouts. That was four days ago. They were due to return back to camp yesterday.'

Yeeran frowned.

'Yesterday?'

'Yes.'

It wasn't unusual for scouts to be waylaid by unexpected enemy movement.

'They might have had to change their route,' she said.

'Maybe.' Rayan didn't sound convinced.

'Protocol requires they be missing for five days before we send in troops. We'll give them until tomorrow before I report it.'

Rayan nodded, but his lips were pinched with concern.

'Colonel Yeeran.' General Motogo's booming voice entered the room first, their body second. Like many elves, Motogo's gender was as flexible as the weather, accepted like the fall of rain, and change welcomed like the turns of seasons.

Yeeran signalled for Rayan to leave; he did so with a grateful glance. Motogo was known to ensnare people in long conversations.

'General Motogo, how fares the battleground beneath your feet?' Yeeran said, using the formal greeting reserved for respected elders.

'Well fed with the blood of my enemies,' Motogo replied as was customary. They kept their greying hair in short knots that made it clear that they rarely wore a helmet any more. Yeeran couldn't imagine ever wanting to stop combat.

'Now to the heart of the matter. I came to confirm your orders – oh, I see you have a new weapon . . .' Motogo had spotted the black skin of her drum in its sling.

'That looks like a fine specimen, one to be jealous of I'm sure,' they continued, their nostrils flaring with envy. 'Not that I partake in drumfire any more, I leave that to the young ones.'

Drumfire didn't physically drain you, but the intention required to focus took its toll mentally. And the general was at least a hundred years old, though Yeeran had known elves on the battlefield who'd made it to a hundred and twenty, the very end of an elf's expected lifespan. She intended to be one of them.

'Yes, the drum was a gift.'

'Very fine. Very fine.' Still their eyes lingered on the richness of the obeah skin.

'Was there something you wanted to mention about my orders today?'

'Ah yes. Given it's your first day in command of such a large cohort of troops, I wanted to confirm your position for today. You are to patrol the western bank up to the Dying Hill in the second quadrant. Our scouts have reported one or two scouting platoons sent over from Crescent. Eliminate the enemy you find there and return to camp. It should be a routine sweep. No offensive against the main line. You hear?'

'I hear, General,' Yeeran said, a little irritated. She knew how to follow orders. You didn't get far in the Waning Army if you couldn't.

Motogo nodded before reaching into their bag and withdrawing a freshly pressed uniform.

'Time to upgrade from your captain's attire, Colonel.'

Yeeran reached for the new clothing with gratitude. It was a deeper blue than her captain's uniform, like a storm-darkened sky.

'Good luck out there today,' Motogo continued. 'May the three gods protect you.'

They invoked the gods without meaning. No one believed in them any more except diviners like her sister. Still, she acknowledged the sentiment, empty as it was.

'And you, General.'

Yeeran watched them leave before letting out a heavy breath.

Her orders weren't what she'd had in mind for her first day as colonel. Sweeps were mundane and she'd be lucky if they encountered any of the Crescent tribe at all. She rubbed her thumb along the casing of her drum. She'd been looking forward to spilling first blood with it.

There was a sound at the window and the flicker of a shadow. Yeeran swung her drum out of its sling with practised efficiency. Perhaps she'd get a chance to use her new weapon after all.

Fingers slipped under the open window and curled over the frame. The intruder was breathing heavily as they pulled themselves up through the opening.

'Moon's mercy,' they cursed before climbing through and falling with a thud onto the floor.

Yeeran swung her drum behind her back and rubbed her brow.

'Lettle, what are you doing?'

Her sister's eyes flashed with annoyance.

'Coming to see you, of course.'

She gathered her limbs and stood with the regal manner of a

chieftain. The lilac dress she was wearing had tangled around her legs, but not an ounce of dignity was lost as she rearranged it.

'Couldn't you have used the door?' Yeeran said.

Lettle met her gaze steadily. The skin around her forehead was pulled taut by the cornrows that ran the length of her head, ending in plaits by her waist.

'Why yes, Yeeran, I would have liked to use the door. But some idiot at the front said you weren't to be disturbed and wouldn't let me past.'

Yeeran took pride in the fact her captains were loyal to a fault.

'And so, you climbed through the window.'

'I did.' Lettle folded her arms across her chest and waited for Yeeran to challenge her.

Yeeran watched her younger sister for a moment before letting out a laugh.

'You do know how to get your way.'

An unexpected smile broke across Lettle's face like sun escaping through rainclouds.

'I do.'

Yeeran turned to the decanter of juice on her desk and offered Lettle a glass, but her sister shook her head.

So Yeeran waited. Lettle never visited Yeeran without a reason.

'I went to the abattoir this morning.'

Yeeran tried to stifle her groan. Lettle had been training to be a diviner for years. The practice required the entrails of an obeah in order to read the magic that pooled there. A trip to the abattoir normally meant Lettle was out of money. Again.

'I'll have a messenger send over some coins later, Lettle.'

Lettle's eyes blazed like white coals.

'I don't need money,' she said through clenched teeth. Yeeran knew how much it galled Lettle to rely on her.

Lettle didn't work any more. When she had come to Gural after their father died, she had done her two years' conscription. But unlike Yeeran, she hadn't stayed on and worked her way up the army ranks.

Instead, her passion lay in divination. A petty skill of prophecy rarely used by elves any more. Rarely used meant rarely paid for.

'What is it then?'

Lettle's anger cooled as quickly as it had come. 'Today's prophecy was about you.'

Yeeran looked at the clock on the wall. She had just a few minutes before she was expected to march out with her regiment. She was about to tell Lettle as such, but the sincerity of her sister's gaze made her hold her tongue. This meant something to Lettle.

Yeeran turned to the new uniform Motogo had given her.

'Tell me about my reading as I change.'

Lettle shot her a brief grin before launching into her story.

'Like I said, I went to the abattoir this morning before they skinned the beasts. There were other diviners bidding on the entrails, but I knew this was your first day in command of your regiment. So, I bid the most. Even then they only gave me five minutes with the creature. And, Yeeran' – she always clipped the 'n' in her name like the letter was an inconvenience – 'you should have seen the sorry state of the place. We should send some money to the workers there . . .'

Yeeran nodded absently.

'I'll try and arrange it. Help me with this clasp, please.' Unlike her captain's uniform, Yeeran's colonel coat was trimmed with thicker obeah fur. Though the skin was the most potent part of an obeah, the black mane around the creature's neck also emanated pulses of magic that Yeeran could harness if needed.

The jacket was stiffly starched with a wide collar and epaulettes in the shape of the waning moon, the symbol of her tribe. On the back was yet another reminder of where she came from: three waning moons stitched into the centre of the jacket.

Yeeran didn't mind. She was proud to wear her tribal sigil many times over.

Lettle let out a small sound of annoyance and muttered, 'No client would ask for a diviner to help dress them in the middle of a reading.'

Yeeran wanted to retort that it would be difficult for any of her clients to ask as they were non-existent. But the words would hurt Lettle more than they'd satisfy Yeeran. Besides, her sister *was* helping as she spoke.

'There, done. Don't you look smart,' Lettle said.

Yeeran peered into the gilded mirror that hung on the wall. Broad in the shoulder and over six foot in height, her body was all angles where her face was soft. A wide nose and full, purple-tinged lips sat beneath deep-set eyes. Her violet irises were dulled with fatigue; the colour, rare for an elf, made her instantly recognisable.

Colonel Yeeran Teila of the Waning Army, she thought to herself, and a small smile spread across her face.

Lettle pursed her lips. 'Now to your reading. The Fates were clear, Yeeran: *your glory lies to the east.*'

Yeeran felt the corners of her lips crease as a precursor for laughter, but she swallowed it when she saw the earnestness on Lettle's face. Divination was never a precise art, but Yeeran knew Lettle was being trained to one day supersede the leader of her sect. She should give her sister's talents more credence.

'Thank you for the reading, Lettle,' she said with as much warmth as she could muster. 'I will be sure to keep my wits about me on the battlefield today. Crescent tribe moved half their infantry back from the western bank, so we'll just be running down the stragglers, it's a simple operation.'

Lettle stepped into the space between them and clasped onto Yeeran's wrist, nails first.

'Remember: *Seek your glory to the east.*'

Lettle was at least a foot smaller than Yeeran. Her left arm was shorter, the outer muscle atrophied from the wasting pox. The illness had ravaged their village, but they'd been too poor to afford the medicine to treat Lettle. Yeeran still felt guilty when she stood this close to her.

When they'd finally had enough money to pay a doctor for a check-up, they confirmed that Lettle's small stature and damaged arm was due to the prolonged effects of the pox. Yeeran should have worked harder to save the money for the medicine.

She laid a hand on Lettle's.

'Father would be proud of the work you've put into divination,' she said.

Lettle's grip turned limp, and she spun away.

They rarely spoke of Father. Though he wasn't the one to have fathered Yeeran – her biological father had died on the battlefield when she was a baby – he was the only parent she had ever known. Six years after her mother married him, Lettle was born.

Then an arrow through the heart had taken their mother as well, too young to leave her daughters with many memories.

With Father, memories were all they had. Even though they seldom spoke of him, it was clear that in every half-smile they gave each other, in every softly spoken compliment, he lived in their minds like a hero from a beloved faerytale.

But those heroes were never thieves.

After losing his wife to the bloodshed of the battlefield, their father had left the army and had retrained as an obeah hunter. But the older he got the harder it was to sustain the physical demands of hunting. Especially as obeah became rarer and rarer. Soon the family had to turn to pickpocketing and scavenging to get by.

'He'd be proud of you too, Yeeran.' Lettle didn't look at Yeeran as she spoke. It would have given away the lie.

They both knew Father would not have been proud of Yeeran's achievements. His grief had corrupted his views on the war, and he condemned any participation in it. When Yeeran had told him she had decided to travel to Gural to join the Waning Army, they had parted in anger. It was the last time they spoke. Father died soon after.

'I should go,' Yeeran said.

'Good luck out there.' Lettle reached for her hand and squeezed it.

Yeeran closed her eyes, taking comfort in her sister's support. No matter their differences, they had always faced the world together.

Today would be no different. Though Yeeran headed to the battlefield and Lettle to her books, she would carry her sister with her. Always.

The scars of their life had fused them together.

Lettle nodded as if she knew what Yeeran was thinking. Her violet eyes were a similar colour to Yeeran's, but their depths were unfathomable, as if Lettle saw the world in its entirety, and Yeeran viewed just a piece.

She gave Yeeran a small smile.

'Your regiment awaits. Remember what I said.'

CHAPTER THREE

Yeeran

The infantry marched in the centre of the formation with the cavalry flanking the sides and the archers bringing up the rear. Yeeran and her four captains rode at the front. The ranking officers and the cavalry were the only soldiers equipped with drumfire; obeah drums were a scarce commodity.

Obeah hunters were paid handsomely across the Elven Lands. If only Yeeran's father hadn't given up on his profession, they might have never known the gnawing hunger of true starvation.

She kicked her camel into a canter. The terrain was pockmarked from hoofprints and combat. Red puddles of blood from the previous campaign had soaked into the soil, leaving soggy, dark patches.

They crested the Dying Hill, named after the slaughter of a hundred civilians at the hands of the Two-Bladed Tyrant, a nickname he had garnered in the act. He'd had another name before that – Chieftain Akomido of the Crescent tribe.

As her camel's hooves pounded the wet earth, Yeeran was reminded of the riches beneath their feet: a fraedia mine large enough to eradicate poverty altogether. One crystal would be sufficient for a household to grow their own food and warm their homes for a year, maybe more.

If they could only secure the mine, no more children would go hungry.

Yeeran thought of the drum-bearer, Hana, and realised why the sight of her had pained her so.

She reminded me of Lettle as a child. The distended stomach, the painfully thin arms, the haunting helplessness that hung heavy in her expression. Yeeran swallowed the memory with a shudder.

'They're gone. Not a Crescent soldier in sight,' Rayan muttered as he drew level with her, pulling her from her thoughts. His brown eyes flashed with something hotter than anger – the dissatisfaction of a battle unfulfilled.

He was right. From this vantage point Yeeran could see the expanse of the first quadrant and there were no signs of the Crescent soldiers.

She felt the bitterness of disappointment in the back of her throat.

'Colonel? Do we proceed?' Rayan asked.

'Proceed where? The soldiers would have made it back to the enemy line by now and we're not to engage with the full might of the Crescent tribe. We're only one regiment.'

What a great first day, Yeeran thought sourly.

'We could sweep round to the east on our return and see if they turned off course?' Rayan asked.

Yeeran shook her head. 'That would be going against orders.'

Rayan shrugged. 'But there's a chance the enemy haven't made it back to the front line, and if so, shouldn't we take the opportunity to catch them?' He was as primed for a fight as she was.

'We can't, Captain.'

Rayan's jaw clenched but he didn't press further. Though the expression in his face was enough to do the speaking for him. He was never insubordinate but was always ready to speak his mind if she asked. It was what she liked most about him.

Yeeran was about to steer her camel back to camp when it dawned on her: *Seek your glory to the east.*

Lettle had read those words in the entrails of the obeah.

She hesitated. It was true that Lettle's predictions sometimes came true. Once she had foretold that Yeeran's roof would cave in from torrential rain. Though it had taken a year for the prophecy to be fulfilled, when the roof finally did cave in, Yeeran had already bought the supplies to fix it.

And perhaps Yeeran wanted this foretelling to come to fruition, so she took even more stock in it than she would ordinarily have.

She nodded slowly.

'Yes, I think we may find a few enemies to the east.' Then Yeeran raised her voice so the other captains could hear. 'Each of you let your squadron know. We move out to the eastern bank in five minutes.'

Yeeran had never disobeyed an order. But this wasn't disobeying an order exactly, it was more like stretching it. Yeeran had received intelligence that there were enemy soldiers to the east. Just because that intelligence was based on divination didn't make it any less valid.

Right?

Too late now. She grimaced.

They set off across the Bleeding Field, the sun hot on their backs. Yeeran's new jacket was soon sodden with sweat, but she didn't notice. Her blood pumped with the anticipation of battle.

They were nearly at the second quadrant to the east of her assigned battlefield when Rayan called, 'Colonel, bodies ahead.'

She didn't need Rayan to tell her, she could *smell* them. There were twelve in total, putrid and bloated from the afternoon sun.

'The scouting party.' Rayan's voice was strained behind his helmet.

Yeeran sent up a signal to the advancing infantry.

Their footsteps stuttered to a stop.

Too slow, I will have to train them out of that.

Rayan jumped down from his camel and began to approach the bodies. They wore the mark of the Waning tribe on the back of their uniform.

'Definitely our scouts,' Rayan confirmed, his expression taut.

Yeeran swung her leg over the saddle and leapt down. Her camel grumbled and she gave it a tenderless pat. She couldn't even remember the beast's name . . . Baul? Boro? Brado?

She found it easier not to grow too attached to her steeds, as they rarely survived long.

Yeeran walked towards the prostrate bodies. Her other captains followed her, some of them stuttering over the smell.

They weren't used to the odour of stagnant death. They only knew the quick kind that smelled of blood and sweat and urine too; iron, salt, ammonia. They knew nothing of a corpse left to fester, of the cloying aroma of liquefying organs.

But Yeeran knew death intimately. She knew what it felt like to search the jacket of a bloated corpse as gas leaked from seams in its flesh. She had rubbed against the shit of others as she pilfered back pockets. Or plucked earrings from ears blasted from faces five feet away. As a child, she had done what she had to do to survive. This was no different.

Yeeran knelt beside Rayan.

'They must have been killed by the Crescent platoon,' he said.

'Yes, those stragglers we've been chasing.'

'What's that?'

Rayan followed Yeeran's gaze.

There, in the dirt, was a shorn piece of the scout's obeah fur collar. Finding a torn collar wasn't unusual in itself – worse things had been torn in combat – but it looked like it had been dragged through the earth in the opposite direction of the scout.

Yeeran looked at the body again. The Crescent soldiers had left gaping wounds in the corpses where their blades had thrust through flesh. But from the discoloration of the ground, it looked like the scout had died from blood loss sometime later. The corpse's head was tilted backwards, its unseeing eyes fixed on the fur with concentration.

Not concentration, *intention*. The scout had used the dregs of magic in the obeah fur to push the collar forward through the dirt. The strength of mind to manipulate something that weak in magic was impressive, impossible almost.

The scout must have been truly determined.

Yeeran cocked her head. *But why?*

She followed the direction of the line the collar had made.

A copse of trees shifted in the breeze half a league away.

One of the branches moved.

'Does it look like an arrow to you? Like the fur is pointing to something?' Rayan said behind her.

But Yeeran wasn't listening. *Because that wasn't a branch.*

'Ambush!' Yeeran barked. 'Formation three, formation three.'

The collar had been pointing to the hidden Crescent soldiers. A warning Yeeran had seen too late.

The Bleeding Field thundered with the sound of running feet as the rival tribe advanced in their direction.

Yeeran swung into her saddle. The camel sprang quickly to standing, its muscles tightening as it sensed the oncoming danger, but it didn't baulk.

The enemy drew closer with every blink. There were over two thousand of them, more than double Yeeran's regiment.

'We need to retreat, find higher ground,' Rayan shouted.

'No.' Yeeran would not retreat on her first day as colonel. She would not be a failure. She ran her thumb over the lip of her drum and surveyed the battlefield.

She let out a breath of relief. The enemy didn't have archers, and her soldiers did. Her regiment could take out at least a third of the oncoming attack with their arrows.

'Archers, release.' Her command was accompanied by a hand signal. A few seconds later it was raining arrows.

Yeeran smiled, enjoying the sight of it. This was the drug she lived for. The knowing deep down in her gut that she would survive this. And perhaps the knowing that one day she would not.

The arrows fell from the sky across the enemy line and Yeeran held her breath as she waited for the soldiers to fall too.

But they didn't.

'What? That doesn't make sense—' Rayan's voice stuttered to a stop. Like her, he was struggling to comprehend what had just happened.

Not one Crescent soldier had fallen. It was as if the arrows had hit an invisible barrier around the elves. It was magic that Yeeran had never seen before. Intention only drove physical forces, and divination was an art based on reading the Fates. Neither type of magic could do something like this, on this *scale*.

'Colonel, what do we do?' Rayan asked. 'Contact in three hundred and fifty feet . . . three hundred and forty . . .'

Yeeran knew the answer. The magical shield made this fight impossible.

She cleared her throat, so her words wouldn't get stuck there. 'Retreat, call the retreat.'

But it was too late to retreat successfully. The enemy infantry was too close, close enough for Yeeran to see the bloodthirsty look in their eyes.

Her soldiers began to break ranks, fear sweeping over them even as the signal to withdraw was sounded.

They needed more time to get to safety.

Yeeran pulled on her drum sling, spinning the weapon to between her thighs.

'Colonel, what are you doing? We need to go, *now*. Yeeran!'

Then Yeeran began to drum.

The chaos around her melted away as her fingers brushed the black skin. Magic thrummed up her bones towards her elbows, a feeling more akin to pain than pleasure. She started with a slow bass tone created by a flat palm across the centre of the drum. It was an easier type of beat to hone her intention around. Though the note was less precise and the vibrations of magic wider than an open tone, the strands of magic were softer to mould.

And mould it she did. Each force of magic becoming a deadly bullet as she beat the drum faster and faster. She didn't look behind her to see if her regiment was retreating. She focused in on the moment, using the drumfire to delay the oncoming attack as much as she could.

Dum—bara—dum—bara—dum—

Just like the arrows, the drumfire didn't penetrate the magical shield protecting the Crescent elves. So instead she shot the magical projectiles at the ground by their feet, blowing up dust and causing a few ranks to stumble.

Still, the enemy kept coming.

'Two hundred feet, a hundred and ninety feet,' Rayan screamed next to her. 'Yeeran, come on, we need to leave *now*.'

But Yeeran wasn't finished yet. She needed to give her soldiers more time.

She was lurched backwards in her saddle as large arms wrapped around her waist. Rayan had joined her on her camel and was reaching for the reins.

Dum—bara—dum—bara—dum—

Then she was swung to the left, her drumfire dispelling as her intention faltered. She hadn't delayed the enemy attack by more than a minute or two. It wasn't enough.

Rayan kicked the camel into a fast canter, taking them further and further away from the battlefield. And further away from her infantry who were still running for their lives.

CHAPTER FOUR

Yeeran

'Three hundred and seventy-six casualties.'

The number was announced like a death sentence and felt like a noose around Yeeran's neck. She couldn't look the chieftain in the eye. Instead, she squared her shoulders and fixed her gaze on the tapestry that hung next to the throne.

The edges were fraying, the colours fading to a dull grey, but the scene was clear. It depicted the three beings: human, fae and elf. The fae, identifiable by their sharpened canines, held the human's throat between their jaws. The human with their rounded ears, their mouth open in a silent scream, reached for the elf on the far corner of the tapestry. The elf held a bloody sword, though it wasn't clear whose blood ran to the tip, fae or human.

The tapestry immortalised the horrors of the fae who, along with humans, only lived in history now. Even that history had eroded to mere myths and legends. After all, it had been over a millennium since fae and humans had walked the earth. Some faerytales claimed that the fae killed all the humans and were then cursed by the gods. But more likely disease had simply struck them both and wiped them all out. Either way, Yeeran had never cared for stories of the monstrous fae.

Now she wondered if it wasn't because she was a monster herself.

Yeeran dragged her eyes back to the throne. The chieftain sat with her legs folded beneath her and an arm draped over an armrest.

The throne itself was polished white obeah horn, thrumming with enough magical energy to strike Yeeran down should her leader so choose.

The chieftain felt Yeeran's eyes on hers and sat up, the fraedia beads in her braids tinkling.

'Colonel Yeeran, you disobeyed orders. I suspect you know the punishment for insubordination?'

'Dismissal from the army.' Yeeran was pleased her voice didn't shake as she spoke.

'Indeed. But insubordination is just one of your crimes. The manslaughter of three hundred and seventy-six soldiers, that, by your own admission, you caused. Though we have also received a statement from one Captain Rayan who has claimed partial responsibility—'

'It was my decision, my choice. No one else's,' Yeeran cut in.

There was a sharp intake of breath. You did not interrupt the chieftain.

'I see insubordination is a pattern.' The chieftain's tone was dry.

Yeeran heard General Motogo scoff behind her, but she didn't turn her head. Their displeasure was already palpable without seeing the scorn to match.

It probably looked a lot like the chieftain's right now.

'May I have the room? I would like to talk to the colonel alone.'

There was shuffling as all the high-ranking officials who were present for her sentencing left the throne room. Yeeran kept her head lowered as the chieftain approached. She paused a step away from Yeeran and lifted her chin with gentle fingers.

Yeeran looked into the sad eyes of her lover.

'Salawa.' The name was a tortured sound on her lips.

'Oh, Yeery.'

Then Yeeran was in her arms. Neither of them cried though they clutched each other tight.

'You need to sign my execution order,' Yeeran said, her mouth pressed against Salawa's hair, her voice muffled.

'No.'

'You must. It's what you'd do if I was anyone else. You can't trust me.'

Salawa stepped out of Yeeran's embrace and gave her a guarded look.

'Can't I?'

'You can't be *seen* to trust me. "No favours, no special treatment", that's what we said all those years ago.'

It had been nearly fifteen years since they had first met. Yeeran's eyelashes fluttered, and she saw the memory there, just beneath the membrane of her eyelids.

Yeeran had been standing by the fountains in Gural square. Her hands were jammed in her pockets, on one side she spun a flip knife, in the other she clutched a letter.

'Are you all right?' Salawa's voice had always been rich with authority, even back then.

Yeeran looked up at the newcomer through her tears. She wore the clothes of a civilian, a cluster of leaflets in her hand.

'I-I . . . my father has died.' Yeeran had just received a message from Lettle, who was on her way to Gural.

The news had stripped Yeeran of her spirit. She felt raw, untethered to life. Her father hadn't always made the right choices, but he had always tried to provide for them, even if it meant thievery. In turn, she too had taken up arms to fight for the Waning Army in order to send money back home. With Lettle on her way to the city to work herself, she felt she lacked purpose.

Salawa made a sympathetic sound in her throat. She didn't hesitate to comfort a stranger as she embraced Yeeran with strong arms, forcing Yeeran to let go of the flip knife in her pocket – and the awful thoughts that had taken root there.

The leaflets Salawa had been holding fell to the ground, and Yeeran could just make out some of the wording of the political manifesto.

An end to poverty. An end to the war. Food and peace are what we fight for.

The slogan was a little rudimental, and over the years Salawa refined her campaign. But in that moment, it was exactly what Yeeran needed to hear.

Here was something to fight for.

Salawa earned Yeeran's loyalty then. Love came later.

Not even Lettle knew how close she had been to letting her grief consume her that day. And now, when Yeeran looked at Salawa she saw all the ways in which the chieftain had saved her.

But she could not save her today.

'No. I won't do it,' Salawa said. She knotted her fists in her velvet dress. The fabric fell to the floor by her feet in a pool of blue. The hem was embroidered with silver waning moons. Yeeran watched the moons shimmer as Salawa trembled.

'What other option is there? I killed over three hundred of my regiment.'

'You made a mistake.'

'A big one.'

Salawa locked eyes with Yeeran and nodded sadly.

'You can't let your feelings for me cast a cloud over what is just and right. The law is the law,' Yeeran said through tense lips. Lips that wanted to press down on Salawa's and beg for her life.

But her pride was more valuable to her in death than love was. Her pride was her legacy.

'The law is the law,' Salawa whispered. Something flickered behind her expression. Something hard and unyielding. She walked away and perched back on her throne. From there she could look down at Yeeran.

There were two people within Salawa, the chieftain and her lover. One hard, one soft. It was in that moment that Yeeran saw her lover disappear.

'I heard you refused to take a drum-bearer,' Salawa said.

Yeeran released a short breath.

'Yes.'

Salawa's features went carefully blank.

'Why?'

Yeeran didn't respond for a time. The chieftain knew that Yeeran didn't agree with her policy on child soldiers, it had been a bitter argument that had lasted weeks.

She wondered whether Salawa ripped open this scar between them to harden her resolve over what had to be done.

No, Yeeran would not let them part in bitterness.

'Salawa, did you read my statement about Crescent tribe? About the new magic they seemed to be using?' The question was meant to lead Salawa away from the topic, but Yeeran could see she had peeled back the scab of the old wound and was letting her anger flow forth.

'We will look into it.' Salawa's hand absently ran over the fringe of braids that fell across her forehead. 'The drum-bearer . . . she left the army and has run away with the gold coin you gave her.'

Yeeran had always known Salawa had spies in her ranks, though she had never admitted it.

She clenched her fists to stop them from quivering.

'The girl was malnourished. You're not feeding the children enough.'

Yeeran regretted her words as soon as she said them. Salawa had been fighting for children like Hana – like Lettle – since the day she sat on the throne.

But is it enough? She shook the intrusive thought free, but it was too late. Salawa had seen it written across her face. Something akin to a sneer settled onto her features.

'That is *precisely* why we need to gain more land on the Bleeding Field. We need those fraedia mines to feed the troops.'

Salawa had always said her purpose in the war had been two-fold: to liberate those oppressed by rulers like the Crescent tribe's Two-Bladed Tyrant, and to bring an end to poverty.

It was why she had Yeeran's allegiance so totally.

'But now I'm down another soldier,' Salawa continued.

Yeeran didn't voice what she wanted to say, that the girl wouldn't have made a difference in battle except as another body to feed the vultures.

Instead, she said, 'I'm sorry.' Though she wasn't sorry at all.

Salawa made a sound in her throat that wasn't quite a laugh.

'War plays by no rules. There are only fighters and failures,' she said.

The silence that followed spoke the unspoken: *Today, you have proved you are a failure.*

Yeeran dipped her head with the heaviness of her guilt.

Salawa let out a long sigh.

'You've helped many people over the years it seems. There are crowds at the gates of my residence calling your name, begging for me to spare your life. Even a group of diviners have chained themselves together in an attempt to plea for your freedom.'

Lettle. Yeeran choked back a sob.

'My crime warrants execution,' Yeeran whispered. She had accepted her fate and now she just hoped that they'd let her see Lettle one more time before she was killed.

Salawa tapped her lacquered nails across the ivory throne. 'But I cannot afford an uprising. You are more popular with the civilians than I ever knew – I have to wonder, how many gold coins have you given out over the years?'

Hundreds. Thousands. Every bit of money that didn't go to Lettle went to the hungry or the homeless.

Salawa's eyelids fluttered and the hardness of the chieftain melted away, and the softness of Yeeran's lover appeared once more.

'Come here.'

Yeeran went to her, kneeling by her feet below the throne. The magic from the obeah horn prickled her skin, its magic a similar sensation to being in Salawa's presence. Her love for Salawa was potent, all-encompassing.

Salawa slipped from the throne and knelt beside Yeeran until their foreheads were pressed together. Yeeran breathed in the scent of her, lavender, and the heavy tang of metal, committing it to memory before she was taken from this world.

'Know this,' Salawa said. 'You are the fire of my heart, and the beat of my drum. I am yours under moonlight. Until the rhythm sings no more.'

Then she kissed her, long and slow. Yeeran pulled them both to their feet so her hands could roam across the shape of Salawa's body as she took the kiss deeper.

Salawa broke away before Yeeran was done with her. But Yeeran could never be done with her.

The chieftain turned and rang a small bell that was laid on a cushion next to her bare feet.

'Salawa—'

But her lover was gone once more. The look she gave Yeeran was all chieftain. She knew then she would never see the face of her lover again.

The chieftain's advisers filed back in, the general leading the charge of smug smiles. Yeeran had long been envied by those in the upper ranks for her relationship with Salawa.

'I have made my decision.' The chieftain did not look at Yeeran as she spoke. It curdled her stomach with the feeling of dread. 'Yeeran Teila is hereby dismissed from the army for insubordination. Furthermore, she must atone for the souls she lost on the field. She is sentenced to exile. Nevermore may she step foot in the Elven Lands. A scroll will be sent to every tribe.'

Yeeran's knees cracked against the marble floor. *Exile.*

Who was she without an army, without a tribe?

It was a sentence worse than death.

CHAPTER FIVE

Lettle

'Sister, friend, ally, neighbour. Free Colonel Yeeran Teila. Sister, friend, ally, neighbour. Free Colonel Yeeran Teila!' Lettle lent her voice to the crowd.

The protest against Yeeran's arrest had started before Lettle arrived. Her sister was well liked among the community. Over the years she'd been generous with her wealth and influence, supporting those who needed it.

But as the crowd grew in numbers, so too did the soldiers. As they tried to disperse the protesters Lettle knew she had to do more to get the chieftain's attention. So, she chained herself to the palace walls.

And I'm not moving until they release my sister.

Lettle hadn't expected the rest of the diviners in Gural to follow suit. There were twenty of them all told. Shaman Namana had been the first to join her. She clipped her cuffs to Lettle's chain without question. Lettle was glad of it. As Shaman, Namana was the leader of the Gural diviners and had been training Lettle to become her replacement one day. Her quiet strength helped Lettle keep her nerve in the face of the unthinkable – Yeeran being executed.

Lettle rattled her chains against the gates to add more noise to the cacophony. The manacles chafed away the top layer of her skin. But she didn't notice her hands get slick with blood.

After all, Lettle was used to constant pain. Her left arm was knotted with aches where the wasting pox had atrophied part of the muscles there. Though the mobility in her shoulder was limited, she wrenched the manacles against the railings as much as she could.

I will not let them take her.

Soldiers began to cajole the protesters on the outskirts of the group, their drums slung in front of their chests ready to release drumfire should the protest turn violent.

Lettle's chant spread through the crowd, gaining volume as more people fought for Yeeran's freedom.

'Sister, friend, ally, neighbour. Free Colonel Yeeran Teila. Sister, friend, ally, neighbour. Free Colonel Yeeran Teila!'

To Lettle's right a man began to scream in earnest with the same amount of gusto as her. She would have ignored him if she hadn't noticed his captain's uniform. The blue stood out like an old bruise.

'Who are you?' Lettle asked with narrowed eyes.

The man turned to her, his soft lips parted mid-sentence. He stood at least a foot taller than her and had a sharp jaw finely dusted with stubble. His nose was a little crooked from past combat, and he looked down it at her with eyes that were glassy with emotion.

'She is my colonel.'

If he thought that was answer enough, it was not.

'So, your loyalty lies with your colonel and not your chieftain?'

'I was with her . . . when we retreated . . . it wasn't her fault. I pushed her to explore the eastern bank. But the general wouldn't listen to me.'

Lettle recognised the sound of guilt in his voice. If what he said was true, then he was as much to blame for Yeeran's predicament as her.

Seek your glory to the east.

She shook the prophecy from her mind with a scowl and turned away from the captain.

'Pull on the gates, maybe we can get into the courtyard,' Lettle shouted down the line to the group of diviners.

'Pull harder.' Lettle's voice began to grow hoarse. But the gate wasn't moving. It had been constructed to keep people like her on the outside.

The palace was set back at a distance, so even squinting Lettle couldn't see the shadows of the people through the windows. The building was tiled in pale blue hexagons, creating the illusion of a shimmering mirage. Palm trees grew in abundance on either side of the entrance and a fountain burst into the air spraying droplets onto the faces of the protesters. But even the mist couldn't cool Lettle's raging heart. The palace was a tumour of opulence growing up from the centre of Gural, and it made Lettle sick to look at it.

War was a profitable business.

'Lettle, look.' Namana tried to point to the stables on the edge of the palace, but her hands were steadfast in the shackle next to Lettle's. Instead, she shrugged her greying locs over one shoulder in the direction of the approaching carriage.

The coach was the type used to transport prisoners. Two camels pulled it along, their heavy gait revealing the weight of their load. The carriage was all metal, sealed with bars of iron that hid the prisoner within.

But Lettle knew who it was.

The diviners were yanked forward as the gate opened to let the carriage past. Lettle untucked the small key she had stored in her cheek and pushed it towards her teeth with her tongue. If threatened, she planned to swallow the key. She slotted it into the cuffs' keyhole, releasing her hands.

It all happened in a few breaths, but the man next to her, the captain, began to push through the opening ahead. Lettle tried to elbow him out of the way, but he shrugged her off. The force of it sent her backwards and she tripped and fell hard on her hip. As she picked herself up from the ground with a growl, she saw him reach the carriage before the soldiers could stop him.

Lettle saw a hint of curly hair, and a hand reaching forward.

She saw his mouth move as he spoke to Yeeran.

Lettle began to run. Soldiers lunged for her as she dashed past. She was close now, she could almost hear Yeeran's breathy reply.

Then there was the unmistakable lurch of drumfire in the air. Lettle turned towards the feel of it, and there was the chieftain, her gilded drum strung across one shoulder standing in the equally ostentatious doorway of her home.

It's impossible to see drumfire, but what Lettle did see was the captain fall to the ground.

How Lettle *hated* Salawa. She was the figurehead of the power structure that placed decorated soldiers above the common elf. In Salawa, Lettle found everything she loathed: the upper classes, authority, and violence. But her relationship with Yeeran had Lettle biting her tongue raw over the years.

Salawa's eyes connected with Lettle's, and she gave her a small sad smile. Lettle was glad to see that her cheeks were wet from tears.

The chieftain drew back her hand and played another light beat on her drum.

Lettle didn't have time to glower at her before the second shot of drumfire moved through the air.

Then there was only darkness.

The first thing Lettle was aware of was an aroma so pungent, it woke her from her slumber.

'Why does it smell like a spice rack in here?' she murmured with dry lips. She cracked open an eyelid to the bright light of a gas lamp swinging above her.

Lettle was in the infirmary. The scent that had woken her was coming from the jars of herbal remedies that lined the wooden walls. The quiet murmuring of the other patients on the ward was broken by the soft lilt of a song.

'Efriam Duke had coins aplenty, copper, silver, gold, he had many. No one could tell him how to spend his wealth, then one day he came down with ill health.' The tune was coming from Lettle's left. 'All he had was his money and pride, no medicine or healers, and so he did die.'

Lettle turned in her bed and caught sight of the singer.

'Hello, Imna.'

The man grinned back in response, his head lolling to the side.

Imna was one of the oldest Gural diviners. He had first introduced Lettle to the art of reading the Fates. That was before disease had robbed him of his abilities. Now his memories were lost in the corridors of his mind. As he looked at Lettle, it was clear he was wandering those hallways now, only half-present.

'I knew you once, did I not?'

Lettle tried to give him a kindly smile.

'Yes, Imna, you did.'

He nodded and turned to the notebook that lay open on his lap. Every diviner kept a record of all their prophecies, but it had been a long time since Imna's had seen fresh ink. The pages were as mottled and wrinkled as his skin.

Three years ago, he spoke of a prophecy that foretold the second coming of the fae. It was then that the diviners knew that his illness was progressing – the fae only lived in faerytales now.

Imna's eyes kept shifting to a spot behind Lettle as if he was perceiving another layer of the world. His hands balled a page in his journal and his gaze stuttered to a stop, locking with hers.

'What is your name? I'll find you in the words.'

'Lettle Teila.'

For a second there was a flicker of recognition in his expression before it disappeared again. Lettle felt her eyes burn and her throat bob. It had been a long time since she had visited him, and she regretted it.

What was she doing in the infirmary anyway?

The last thing she remembered was . . .

Yeeran.

Lettle lurched forward. The memory hit her with the same force as the chieftain's bullet.

'What happened to Yeeran?' Her hand went instinctively to her necklace. When Father had stopped hunting and turned to thievery, nameday presents became a thing of the past. Upon seeing Lettle's crestfallen face on her next nameday, Yeeran had started a new tradition. Every year they would go to the forest near their home and select a seed pod from the woodland floor as a gift. One day Yeeran presented Lettle with a chain she had scavenged. They had cleaned off the specks of blood together and threaded the little beads onto it.

Over the years Lettle's fingers had worried the chain smooth.

'Yeeran? Who is she?' Imna asked with earnestness.

Lettle made a frustrated sound as she pulled off the covers from her ward bed. She swung her feet down onto the cold tiled floor.

'Yeeran's gone. She was exiled.'

Lettle located the speaker in the bed across the room.

She tilted her head, trying to place the man's face. He was entirely unremarkable, except for a slightly crooked nose. The skin above his short beard was a shade darker than hers, and glossy from the humidity of the room. His soft eyes were at odds with the sharpness of his wide frame, which filled the width of the headboard of the small bed.

'*You*,' she said with a finger poised like a weapon. 'You tripped me up, you got in my way.'

He flinched at the onslaught of her anger, but she wasn't done.

'I didn't get to say goodbye to her because of you.' Her voice cracked at the end, but under the moon's mercy she *would not cry in front of him*.

'I'm sorry.' He said it so simply, with so much sincerity that it made Lettle loathe him more.

She turned away from him, her silk dress billowing around her.

'Where are my shoes?'

A healer appeared from the far end of the room and held out a tincture to Lettle.

Lettle could smell the crushed snowmallow flower in the mixture. It smelled of her nightmares.

Cold skin, clammy in death, open eyes devoid of life.

Lettle pressed her eyes shut from the memory of her father's corpse.

'I'm fine, I don't need it,' she said, recoiling from the smell. The healer grunted before shuffling off. There were always people who needed healing in a country torn apart by war.

Lettle spotted her shoes under the bed and lunged for them.

From across the room, the captain lifted himself out of the bed with the lightness of someone with more muscle than bone. As he walked over to her, his torso filled her eyeline.

'Where are you going?' the captain asked.

She didn't answer him.

'Lettle, where are you going?' he pressed.

She finished buttoning up the leather of her boots – buttons were easier for her than laces as her left hand had less dexterity. She turned to the man.

'Am I under arrest? Is this an interrogation?'

He shook his head but didn't move out of her way as she tried to pass him.

Lettle scoffed. 'Not used to being ignored, are you? Well, I'm not one of your soldiers you can order around.'

He shifted away from her then, his eyes downcast.

'I'm going after Yeeran, you'll need to use drumfire like the chieftain if you mean to stop me.'

He frowned, his mouth gaping in confusion.

'The chieftain,' Lettle said. 'She's the one who shot us both. She didn't want us talking to Yeeran.'

Understanding slackened his features. Understanding, followed by a flickering fury – cold coals reignited. He curled his fists by his sides, and Lettle heard the knuckles there pop.

'I'm coming with you.'

Lettle laughed.

'No, you're not.' She shouldered past his looming form and marched her way through the infirmary.

There was the slapping of feet on tiles behind her, and she turned to face him, but it wasn't the captain, it was Imna on unsteady feet. He reached out a hand to Lettle's and pressed a crumpled piece of paper in her hand.

'I found your words. I found you,' Imna said.

Lettle uncurled the torn piece of paper in her hand. It was from Imna's prophecy journal, and at the top was Lettle's name dated a few years prior. As she read, Imna spoke the words aloud in the hushed tones of the clandestine, *'The one born of a storm's mist shall be your beloved. But when the waning moon turns, you will grant them their death.'*

Imna's eyes were clear, present, and full of concern. Despite that, Lettle felt the corners of her lips rise into a smirk.

Love? Who has time for love? Certainly not her.

'They wouldn't be the first person I've killed.' She meant it to sound sarcastic, maybe a little dry, but the words were wooden – a door hiding the depth of grief beyond.

Imna cocked his head and watched Lettle's performance.

'Lettle, a prophecy denied is a prophecy left to fester. It will come true either way, but by refusing to acknowledge it you allow for the rotten roots of doubts to grow.'

The clarity of Imna's words chilled her, turning Lettle's skin to the pebbled texture of crocodile leather. But the spell of his lucidity was short-lived as his expression grew distant, his lips widening into a smile before he lurched away singing.

'Efriam Duke had coins aplenty, copper, silver, gold, he had many . . .'

'See you soon, Imna.'

His song echoed in Lettle's mind for a long while after she left, but she drowned it out with one thought:

I'm coming for you, Yeeran.

CHAPTER SIX

Yeeran

Yeeran was thrown out of the carriage into the wet mud.

'Good luck.' The words were said with a snarl and a globule of spittle. The soldier had lost a friend in the retreat, so was less than enthused to see Yeeran get off lightly. They threw a heavy pack at her before closing the carriage door.

'Trust me, this is the worst punishment Salawa could have given me,' she muttered to the retreating carriage.

They didn't let her see Lettle. Instead, they took her straight to the administrators, who stripped her of her title and slashed a knife through her ears, marking her with the scar of dismissal.

She touched her ears gingerly, each now twice pointed. The shame hurt more than the wound.

Once she had been cut, she was escorted to a barred carriage and led through the streets of Gural to her exile. Yeeran had heard the chants of the protesters as the coach reached the gates of the chieftain's palace. She'd searched the crowd for Lettle, but she couldn't see her in the chaos that ensued. But one face caught her eye.

'Colonel, where are they taking you?' Captain Rayan pushed through the masses. His army-calloused hands gripped the bars of her jail.

'No,' he whispered as he took in her slashed ears.

'I've been sentenced to exile,' Yeeran confirmed grimly.

'They can't—'

A guard grabbed Rayan by the arm and began pulling him backwards.

'Stand down,' Rayan shouted, indicating his captain's epaulettes.

The guard dipped her head in submission and let go of Rayan. Still, Yeeran knew their time was limited.

'Rayan,' she said urgently. 'Look after Lettle, promise me, you'll look after her.'

Rayan thumped his hand against his chest with the salute reserved for a general of the army. It told Yeeran all she needed to know.

It was then that she felt it – a twang of magic in the air. So subtle, only those attuned to the soft vibrations of drumfire would hear it. The shot struck Rayan on the side of his head. The beat was soft enough to knock him out without penetrating the skin.

Yeeran looked towards the direction the drumfire had come from, but the assailant was out of sight.

Then the carriage was moving again, the crowd dispersing with the use of weapons. Soon, the city of Gural was hidden in the dust cloud behind the carriage.

Now she was miles away from home, but she took comfort in knowing Lettle would be safe with Rayan looking out for her.

Yeeran bent to pick up the pack that the soldiers had left her. She began to rifle through it. They had provided her with a water canister and some dried meat. Enough for a day or two. There was a change of clothes, and underneath all that was something large and hollow.

She smiled and withdrew the mahogany drum, Salawa's last parting gift.

'You are the fire of my heart, and the beat of my drum,' she whispered the vow to the forest. 'I am yours, Chieftain Salawa, under moonlight. Until the rhythm sings no more.'

Yeeran looked around her. The carriage had travelled for over four hours, only pausing to pass through the Crescent district and out to the edges of the Elven Lands. She was now standing in the canopy of a thick forest, less humid than the rainforests she was used to on the edges of the Bleeding Field. Though neither was the ground dry.

Ferns sprouted from the knotted roots of eucalyptus trees whose swaying branches scented the air.

She knelt down and picked the purple fruit from a wispseed shrub. It grew across the borders of the dirt pathway that snaked through the centre of the woodland.

As she chewed on the bitter berry she listened to the sounds of the animals and suddenly felt uneasy. Something felt wrong. Different.

There is no sound of drumfire.

For the first time in her life, Yeeran couldn't hear the echoes of the Forever War. The constant rhythm that had given her purpose had been stripped away.

Yeeran looked to the sky.

East.

She began to laugh. The laugh started small, then grew into big guffaws startling birds from trees. She wasn't sure when her laughter turned to sobs. It was only when she noticed the length of the shadows that she realised day had turned to night.

Yeeran dried her tears and stood.

'I will survive this; I will find my army again.' She tried to say the words with conviction, but they felt hollow in this empty forest.

There was a sound beside her.

Not so empty.

It was time to make a fire.

Yeeran built a makeshift shelter out of the wetter branches and used the drier ones as kindling. She had often accompanied her father on his hunting expeditions when she was younger, at least until Lettle once squealed in the middle of a clearing, scaring away the obeah they had been tracking for almost a fortnight. After that, he left the girls behind in the village when he went out to hunt. Still, he had made sure to teach his daughters the basics of survival.

Yeeran was glad of it, as her father's lessons were the only way she'd be able to survive out here.

But where to next?

If she kept travelling east the land would soon become hostile. The Wasted Marshes was a dangerous territory where both plants and creatures were poisonous. Those who ventured there rarely returned.

But neither could Yeeran go home.

Exile was irrefutable. Once condemned, an elf was never allowed to set foot in the Elven Lands again upon pain of death.

Yeeran had only heard of one case of an elf's exile being revoked, and it was a story that had been bloated with exaggeration over time. It was said that the elf had presented the chieftain with a gift of fraedia crystal so large that the chieftain had to reinstate their citizenship.

Great, all I need to do is find a wagonload of fraedia.

Helplessness pulled at her throat and though she tried to swallow the sob, it shook her shoulders until she let out an anguished cry. Hot tears fell down her face once more.

She pressed the meat of her palms to her eyes.

'I will get through this.'

With a ragged breath she let her hands fall back to her sides.

There was a shifting of shadows on the edge of the firelight and two orbs of light.

Eyes.

Big blue eyes.

Yeeran stopped breathing.

There in front of her was the largest obeah elder she had ever seen. At least eight foot long from horn to tail, its black fur was glossy like it was cloaked in the night's sky. Its head, so similar to a leopard's, and yet infinitely more ethereal, cocked to the left. The two horns atop its head glimmered white, with smaller branches weaving from it like a filigree crown. Its ruff was as thick as a lion's mane, proudly adorning its chest like an extravagant collar. The obeah's tail swished to the left and right, full like a wolf's but in the same obsidian black as its fur.

And those eyes, unblinking, intelligent. It was in those eyes that Yeeran saw her future, and the path to her freedom.

This was a prize worthy of a chieftain.

CHAPTER SEVEN

Lettle

Yeeran's carriage tracks led Lettle out towards the forests on the edge of Gural. She'd been walking for hours before she realised she was being followed. The woodland was nearly empty of wildlife due to overhunting. Spindle trees thrust up from cracks in the cobbled border of the road. Like their namesake they were tall and thin with dark green branches that quivered in the breeze. By their roots sprouted bushes of sweet cactus which Lettle dipped behind to hide, careful not to prick herself on the thorns.

Now, I wait.

Whoever was following her wasn't used to tracking a target in a forest. Lettle had her father to thank for her skills – though Yeeran had always been the better hunter, except for the one time Yeeran had scared off an obeah her father was tracking by making Lettle laugh. Still, Lettle's talents were good enough that she could catch the odd obeah. She was unlikely to find any this close to the city though.

A few elves had tried to raise obeah in captivity over the centuries but, no matter their conditions, the creatures all died swiftly. The magical beasts needed to live in the deep wild.

Thud, thud, thud. Her stalker's footsteps startled a few birds from their slumber.

The moonlight framed the man on the path in front of her. He walked with a tense and regimented gait. When he reached where she'd dipped behind the bushes, he paused.

It was the captain she'd left in the infirmary.

'Moon's mercy, why won't this guy leave me alone,' she muttered under her breath.

He frowned, then slowly turned in a circle. His eyebrows were stitched together as he looked for the direction she had gone in.

Lettle swung her bow off her shoulder and nocked an arrow.

Yeeran had altered the weapon for Lettle so that she could draw it back with the nock between her teeth, allowing her to use the bow one-handed. Though her left arm had some strength, it couldn't stay steady enough to aim true when using a standard bow.

With the nock gripped tightly between her front incisors she pushed the bow away from her until the string was taut and vibrating under the tab she bit down on. Then she aimed and let go.

'Argh.' He jumped backwards as the arrow missed him by a hair.

'The next one strikes your eye,' Lettle shouted.

The captain turned with wide eyes towards Lettle's voice. She stood up from behind the cactus bushes.

'Go back, now.'

'I'm coming with you,' the captain said.

'No, you're not.'

'I can help you find Yeeran.'

'I'll be fine without your help,' she said.

'I'll just keep following you.'

Lettle pulled out an arrow from her quiver.

'And I'll just keep shooting you.'

Then the captain did something unexpected. He shrugged.

'Shoot me then. I have nothing and no one to go back to.'

'You're a fool, you'll be reprimanded, maybe even exiled yourself if you try to return. Especially if you return with her.'

He nodded slowly as if the weight of this decision was only just occurring to him.

'But . . . it was my fault that she was exiled.'

His shoulders dipped almost imperceptibly. Guilt was a heavy weight.

I would know, she thought bitterly.

He continued a bit quieter, 'We can't leave her out there. Exiled and alone.'

Lettle examined him more thoroughly. His drum was slung over one shoulder, helpful for hunting, his travelling bag over the other. Full of what she hoped was food. She had left in such a rush that all she had packed was her prophecy journal, some spare clothes, a down sleeping bag, and finally her hunting bow.

Her larder had been empty, and she didn't have time to purchase food. She'd planned to forage for what she needed from the forest.

So when she spotted the captain's camping stove her decision was made.

'Can you cook?' she asked him.

He nodded.

'I brought some herbs and spices with me too,' he said.

Lettle dropped the bow.

'You can stay. But you're making every meal.'

She hated cooking more than anything.

Lettle and the captain didn't speak again until the pink rays of dawn lit the sky. It was only then that she realised she didn't even know his name. But neither could she be bothered to ask for it. Yeeran knew about Lettle's disdain for the war and so rarely introduced her to her comrades. Frankly, Lettle was grateful for it; soldiers were the worst kind of people. They were all self-serving nationalists, hungry for power and violence. Except Yeeran, of course. Her sister was simply disillusioned about what the war could achieve.

The captain trudged on a few paces behind her, the cadence of his footsteps dragging a little more than they had done an hour ago. She looked back at him. Bags sagged under his eyes where tiredness had robbed his skin of vibrancy. His sharp chin dipped down to his chest, his brown eyes dulled from exhaustion. Lettle wondered if the drumfire had given him a concussion and then chastised herself for caring. He was the one who wanted to come with her. She wouldn't let him slow her down.

But no matter what, they needed food and rest. They were still half a day's walk from the Crescent district, which they'd have to pass through in order to leave the Elven Lands. Lettle hoped that they'd have no trouble there. The residual laws left over from Chieftain Akomido's rule in Crescent were more oppressive than any other tribe. History now labelled Akomido as the Two-Bladed Tyrant, infamous for executing a hundred citizens who had been merely attempting to broker a peace treaty with him.

There could be no peace after that.

Though he disappeared ten years ago, the district had suffered from the penalties imposed by the other three tribes. Brutal sanctions and plummeting trade left the country destabilised. Lettle hadn't been there for years, not since her father had taken them hunting in the woodland on the other side of Crescent's border.

That's where they will have left Yeeran.

That was at least two days' walk away, but it had been a short carriage ride for Yeeran. With that realisation, Lettle felt her bones grow weary.

All camels were reserved for the army's use alone. Lettle had considered stealing one but had changed her mind in case she was caught. Though it was unlikely she actually would – she was a very capable thief – it still wasn't worth the risk.

'We should stop and rest for a short while,' she said.

The captain nodded but Lettle saw the relief in his bleary eyes.

Definitely concussion, she thought.

'We'll reach the Crescent border by sunset and can spend the night there,' she continued.

The captain stiffened beside her.

'Is that wise? Staying in Crescent?'

Lettle didn't answer for a moment. She was used to seeing a soldier's hatred translate from the battlefield to everyday life and it galled her. The Forever War was a fight for power for those *with* power. Citizens had little say in politics.

'What do you think the difference is, between us and them?' Lettle asked him.

'They followed a tyrant, killed countless in his name?'

Lettle parted her pursed lips. 'And have you not killed countless?'

The captain dragged his feet in the dirt and shrugged.

'That's different. They were soldiers who chose this life.'

Choice. A boon so few had in this war.

But she didn't argue with him, like Yeeran it seemed fighting was his one purpose. It was not Lettle's. Though her hopes of one day becoming the shaman of the diviners were all but dashed. She couldn't return to Gural without Yeeran. And Yeeran was exiled.

There was no going back.

I'll smuggle her home if I have to, she thought fiercely, refusing to give up the dream she had fostered for so long.

The captain stopped by an overturned tree, but Lettle waved him away.

'It'll be safer to rest in the forest.'

'Surely the road has fewer wild beasts?'

Lettle snorted. He sounded like someone who had never stepped foot outside of the Bleeding Field. Maybe he hadn't.

'Wolves and obeah won't hurt you unless threatened, and even then, your death will be quick. It's the skin traders you need to be worried about.'

'Skin traders? I thought they were just stories to scare kids.'

Lettle's laugh was brittle.

'Skin traders definitely scare kids. I was eight when I watched a group of them skin an elf.'

It had been Yeeran who had found her crying under a witch hazel bush after the horrors she had seen. She'd suffered from nightmares for years, and again it was Yeeran who had soothed her back to sleep each time.

The captain inhaled sharply as Lettle stepped towards him. She ran her gaze over him slowly.

'They'd especially like skin like yours – dark enough to look like an obeah elder. There are people who will trade for it without real-ising it's not obeah leather.'

He shuddered before nodding once.

'Lead the way.'

Lettle led them through to a small clearing out of sight of the road. She dropped her pack in the centre.

The captain sank to the ground beside it. The pallor of his skin had turned a slight ochre.

'I feel sick,' he murmured.

Lettle knelt on the ground next to him and pressed a hand to his clammy forehead. His temperature wasn't up, but he had started to shiver.

'I think you have a concussion. Does your head hurt?'

He nodded, his face tight with pain.

'Stay here, don't move. I'll get you something to help.'

She didn't need to go far. Snowmallow was a weed that grew in abundance in the Elven Lands. Its white flowers were a painkiller, and its stems could be used to brew a strong anaesthetic. Lettle hesitated before picking the petals.

She swallowed, trying to disperse the acid that was burning up her throat.

Stomach bloated with gas, eyes red from burst blood vessels—

'No!' she shouted at her memories of her father, sending a flock of birds to flight.

She steeled her nerve and plucked the small flowers in a rush. Their sickly-sweet scent filled her nostrils. They smelled of death.

'Here, place this petal under your tongue,' she said upon returning to the captain. Her hands shook as she passed him the flower.

'These extras are in case you need them later, but don't take too many. It can be lethal.'

He nodded, then reached for her with his other hand.

'How do you know all this?'

'My father was ill, for a time. I learned what I could of healing . . . to help him.'

He squeezed her forearm and looked into her eyes.

'Thank you, Lettle.'

His warm hand lingered on her forearm for longer than it needed to. She was about to comment on that fact when he raised his hand to something in the distance.

'A faery ring.'

'What?'

'Look.'

He waved around them with a small smile on his face. A circlet of blue and white mushrooms surrounded the clearing.

'They say wherever you find a faery ring, a fae has died,' the captain continued, his voice a little surer as the drug began to ease his pain. 'Me and my mother used to sit in them and tell faerytales under the moonlight.' There was still the faint smile of childhood memories around his lips. 'My favourite was the story of the Wandering Human. Do you know it?'

Lettle nodded, though she didn't tell him that it was her favourite faerytale too. It told the story of the last human left alive by the mercy of the fae, to wander the world alone. Until their death.

'I used to love reading, but I don't have space for books in the barracks,' Lettle said.

She smiled, remembering how annoyed Yeeran had been when Lettle kept bringing home more books.

Now all she wished for was to see Yeeran frown once more.

'What's that?' the captain asked.

'Huh?'

He pointed to her necklace. She hadn't realised she was holding it.

'We didn't have a lot of money growing up. On my nameday Yeeran and I would go to the forest and select one of the fallen seed pods and thread it onto here.'

Her finger ran across one of the larger beads; a dried spindle tree nut.

'It doesn't have many tokens on there. You must be younger than I thought.' He was trying to be funny, but the joke had only reminded Lettle of the fact Yeeran had left her for the war when Lettle was nine years old.

The memory curdled her stomach.

'I'm going to see if I can find any game,' she said gruffly.

A flicker of confusion crossed the captain's gaze from Lettle's abrupt change of mood but he nodded.

'Be careful,' he said.

She rolled her eyes and went on her way.

Lettle didn't go far. Just far enough away that the captain's snoring couldn't be heard. The snowmallow flower had sedative properties and she couldn't blame him for succumbing to its effects.

Still, she couldn't wait to find Yeeran so her sister could order him back to Gural.

There was a rustle ahead of her and she dipped low. She drew her bow carefully, her jaw clenching as she held the nock between her teeth.

She saw the glint of dark fur in the weak dawn light. It looked like a hare, but she couldn't be sure.

Squawk-caw, squawk-caw.

Lettle heard the hunting call of the nighthawk at the same time as the prey did. She had to shoot now, or risk losing breakfast.

Thwum.

The arrow shot through the air and buried itself into flesh. There was a small sigh as the life left the body of the creature.

Lettle jumped up and ran towards the prey. The sooner they ate a good meal, the better they'd be. She wondered if Yeeran had been given a weapon to hunt with.

Yeeran will be fine, she told herself. *She has to be.*

Lettle parted the shrub where the prey had been hiding and gasped.

It wasn't a hare. It was an obeah cub.

She lifted its lifeless form out from under the bush and down in front of her.

It was small, perhaps only a year or so old. Its fur a light brown, before the darkness that came with age. Its horns were two small knots on the wideness of its forehead, the size of her fingernail. Its features were shaped like a kitten's, but its tail had the breadth of a fox's.

Lettle didn't mourn the beast, only the magic it could have harboured if it had been fully grown. Obeah were creatures born to be harvested. They were the source of all magic, and so were reaped like corn for the sustenance of civilisation.

She removed the short dagger she always had in her boot. It was lovingly sharpened for frequent use.

Divination was best practised under the light of the moon when the Fates were at their brightest. But Lettle couldn't pass up a chance at a reading as fresh as this.

'Hail, shining one that grants me light. Hail, shining one that guides the night,' Lettle murmured as she made a slow and careful incision in the underbelly of the obeah cub up towards its sternum.

The arrow had punctured the beast's lungs and ruptured the heart. It was a quick kill, soaking the ground with blood.

Lettle cut through the diaphragm with nimble fingers, releasing the upper cavity of the cub's organs. Then she sliced through the windpipe and placed her dagger to the side.

'Hail, Bosome, give me wisdom with this sacrifice. Hail, God on high. Grant your knowledge with this here prize.' Lettle reached into the warm flesh pulling free the intestines. She tipped her head back, her braids pooling around her kneeling form as she looked up at the faded sliver of the moon.

'Tell me of the fate of my sister.'

Though Lettle prayed for news of her sister, she knew the moon god might not listen. They were fickle with the future and shared only what they wished to be known.

Lettle drew in a deep breath and prepared herself for the reading.

Unlike drumfire that required intention to draw on magic, divination called for the exact opposite. Instead of focusing the mind, divination magic was achieved by detaching from one's mind – by becoming heedless.

Becoming heedless was like second nature to Lettle now. For the first few months of training, she'd only felt glimpses of what it meant to truly be isolated from the world and her mind.

When in this state, Lettle could see the shimmers of magic among the entrails of the obeah. Like pearls of moonlight, they shone in patterns over the intestines sparkling in a language only diviners could read.

Though divination wasn't a language, not really. It was more a feeling, a knowing from deep within your bones. It was an art form.

The smaller intestine blossomed with three pearls of magic whose trails shone like shooting stars over the bloated organ. Their direction was east, but because of the way the intestine was twisted – hiding its bulk – Lettle knew that the magic wasn't describing orientation, rather time. This prophecy would come about under a waxing moon.

The double-chambered stomach was bloated, with a broken chain of magic swirling around the centre. This indicated a binding, or a partnership, soon to be wrecked. She looked to the liver and then the heart, systematically drawing from it a sense of what the magic told of the future.

The lungs were next. Though they'd been punctured by the arrow, the magic bubbled and burst around the wound making it easy to read. The two people who were the subject of this prophecy were going to die by poison.

Lettle continued through the reading, interpreting every blood clot and engorged organ. When she was satisfied that she had learned all she could she withdrew from her heedless state and returned to the present. It took a moment for her body to settle back into her skin. The brightness of the morning sun was harsh against her eyes.

Once she reclaimed her thoughts, she withdrew her prophecy journal. She wrote down the words of the Fates, the action giving the foretelling meaning.

Under a waxing moon that no one can see, when the sun flares and twilight reigns. A burdened partnership will die when poison passes their lips. One gilded, one pearl.

'Oh.' She let out a sound of disappointment. Though it was a powerful telling – it was rare to foretell a person's death, let alone two people – it gave her no indication of who the two murdered people would be. So, she found it hard to care that their lives would be soon cut short. But such was the nature of divination.

Disappointment turned her stomach sour and her gaze slipped to the page from Imna that she had slotted into the journal:

The one born of a storm's mist shall be your beloved. But when the waning moon turns, you will grant them their death.

Neither prophecy was helpful. Neither told her of Yeeran's fate.

Without a backward glance she left the obeah cub to feed the forest. When she was ten paces away, she heard the call of the nighthawk up above, claiming the prize as its own.

Squawk-caw, squawk-caw.

She marched all the way back to their camp to find the captain singing over the cooking stove.

His voice was a deep baritone with an almost crystal-clear pitch, as smooth and sweet as honey. He kept time with the stirring of the pot.

'You're feeling better,' she remarked.

He jumped at the sound of her voice, but when his eyes met hers, they softened with a wide smile.

'Well, you have been gone for over an hour.'

Lettle looked to the sky. He was right, the sun had risen during her time reading the obeah's entrails. All that effort for a useless prophecy.

Thankfully he didn't make a comment about the lack of game for their meal.

'Food's ready,' he said.

'Thank you, *Captain*,' she said, sinking as much mockery into his title as possible. Her irritation was sparked by his good spirits. She folded herself next to the camp stove and helped herself to the potatoes.

She had to swallow her gasp as she tasted the food. Somehow, he'd turned the vegetable into a creamy, buttery mash. Happily savouring it, she missed what he said.

'What?' she asked with her mouth full.

'I said my name is Rayan.'

Rayan . . . she turned the word over on her tongue. The way the 'y' was drawn out gave the name a sense of melody. It suited him.

Then his voice dropped lower than a whisper. 'I'm not a captain. Not any more.'

She felt a small pang of sympathy towards him. Rayan was sacrificing everything to be here.

For the first time Lettle wondered if it might be more than just guilt driving his actions. Perhaps it was love.

She felt a flash of jealousy at the thought. Despite Lettle's own beauty, Yeeran drew loyalists and lovers like fish to bait. Lettle had always been harder to love than her sister.

She shook her head in annoyance.

Let him pine for Yeeran. If he helps me find her, that's all that matters.

He started humming, a haunting tune that sent a shiver down her spine. His foot tapped to the beat, the rhythm pounding like the drumfire on the Bleeding Field.

But there was no battlefield of tribes here. Instead, their enemy was time. And somewhere ahead of them Yeeran was moving further and further away from the trail.

The reminder turned the food to ash, and she stood.

'It's time to go.'

CHAPTER EIGHT

Yeeran

Yeeran had been tracking the obeah for two days. The wind was blowing in from the east, ruffling the leaves of the eucalyptus trees and lifting her scent in the direction of the creature. She'd tried to mask herself by covering her skin in loganberry juice but twice the obeah had still spotted her and dashed in the other direction. Yeeran was sure it looked like it was grinning as it did so.

Now she was covered in sticky red syrup that attracted flies, and her water canister was empty so she couldn't even wash it off.

But the obeah was still close, and the evening rains would fill up her water canister soon enough.

'There are three skills that every hunter must master.' The vibrato of her father's voice rumbled up from the memories of her past.

'One: know the terrain. Navigating the forests of the Elven Lands is paramount. Knowing where the watering holes and the best feeding spots are will improve your rate of success.'

So Yeeran had set about learning the rules of this new land as she went through it. She'd learned that it often rained just before sunset, washing away any signs of the obeah's tracks, but also that the mud the rains brought was perfect for preserving the obeah's large paw prints.

'Two: a hunter must know bushcraft. How to read the markings of footprints in the ground when an obeah is fleeing and when it is grazing. Without bushcraft, a hunter has no hope of finding prey.'

After years of being taught by her father, Yeeran's bushcraft skills were nearly as good as her battlefield skills. She lowered herself into a crouch as she spotted a scuff on the moss of a fallen log. The marking was subtle, but Yeeran knew that it was left by the flight of the obeah. Coupled with the tuft of hide left on a bramble, it showed her the direction she needed to go in.

She noticed scat on the ground and bent down to examine it.

Obeah were known herbivores, their faeces predominantly fibre and mucus. She prodded the scat with a stick. It was soft and long in shape, suggesting the creature had eaten stoned fruit such as plums or peaches. She stood and looked around, trying to locate the fruit trees where it may be grazing.

Then she saw it. Less than fifty feet away the obeah stood in the dappled light of the forest canopy. This wasn't the first time she'd come face to face with the beast that day. The sight of it still tore the breath from her throat.

The obeah raised its head, the curve of its neck adorned with thick black fur speckled through with the grey of old age. Its horns brushed the leaves of the tree above, sending a shower of autumn leaves through the forest. It scuffed the ground with its giant paws, each one ending in claws the size of Yeeran's fingers.

She imagined the talons strung through a necklace adorning Salawa's neck as she kissed her collarbone. She imagined the feel of the magic soaring through her palms as she struck the drum made of the obeah's skin.

She imagined its last breath as the song of her own freedom.

'Three: the greatest skill a hunter can have is marksmanship. Knowing when and where to strike is part instinct, part talent. We always aim for the jugular or the heart. Maximum chance of fatality without damaging the core asset – the obeah skin.'

Yeeran inhaled and lifted her hand up to her drum. She drew her focus towards the drumskin while taking aim at the obeah. The beast was quartering away, its wide eyes fixed on the distance ahead. Due to the obeah's position, she would need to strike behind the animal's left shoulder, a third of the way up from its stomach. This would give her the best success of piercing the heart, lungs, or a major artery, penetrating the skin in two places distanced diagonally apart.

The beast is big enough to make two drumskins out of, if not three, she thought as she narrowed her eyes on her prey.

With a swift rattle of her fingers, she harnessed the magic of the drumbeat, shooting the force towards the obeah's heart with intention.

The small sound she had made from the drum wasn't enough to alert the creature to her presence, yet it still sensed her just before the shot flew. In the milliseconds before impact the obeah turned and locked eyes with Yeeran. The bright blue of its gaze held more intelligence than any other animal she'd ever known, and right now it didn't look surprised.

The obeah had known she was there.

With a snort it charged off into the bush.

'Fuck,' she cursed and threw her drum over her shoulder to give chase.

The obeah had seen Yeeran, so she didn't step lightly. Silence wouldn't help her now. All she needed to do was keep the beast in her sights.

But after two hours of following the creature, fatigue was settling in her bones. Her water canister still hung empty from her waist. The world had grown fuzzy at the edges, her head pounded, and she couldn't remember the last time she'd had to urinate.

Yeeran was ready to give up. The thought coincided with a bout of dizziness, and she stumbled.

She used a hand to steady herself against the bark of a birch tree. Her breathing was laboured, her lips swollen and cracked. She let her chin fall to her chest.

'Though geography, bushcraft and marksmanship are the three skills mastered by successful hunters, I believe there is a fourth skill that makes the most elite hunters far superior: mental perseverance.' Once again, Yeeran's father spoke from her memories. But this time, her ten-year-old self spoke back.

'What does that mean, Father?'

'It means that even the fittest, cleverest, sharpshooting hunter can still be thwarted by the clever wiles of an animal. It requires stamina of the mind over stamina of the body.'

She nodded, bringing herself back to the present.

'Stamina of the mind,' she said to the birch tree.

With a grunt she pushed herself back to standing and set off after the obeah's trail. The delay had given the creature a chance to lengthen the distance between them. And if she lost sight of the obeah, she lost sight of her freedom.

Yeeran set off at a trot using breathing techniques she was taught in the army to maintain a steady rhythm. But about twenty paces in she stumbled again, her vision going dark.

She needed water.

With shaking fingers, she pulled out her drum and fired three shots into the birch tree next to her. Her aim was a little off, but she managed to penetrate the bark to the greener matter within. With a final round of drumfire, the hole was deep enough to collect sap.

She pressed her cracked lips against the bark and sucked.

At first, she just breathed in the debris, but a second or so later she could taste the sugary nectar of sap.

But it wasn't enough.

She fell to her knees and shut her eyes.

A faint buzzing invaded her cloudy thoughts. It was only when the swarm of midges were on her that she realised the sound wasn't just in her mind.

She swatted them away with feeble hands.

Why were there so many of them?

She cracked open an eyelid and scowled with bleary eyes. Ahead of her the vegetation grew shorter and lusher than the other areas of the forest.

'Where there are insects, there is likely water nearby.'

She crawled towards where she heard her father's voice, a part of her knowing that it was a hallucination caused by the dehydration.

'Father, I'm coming, I'm listening.'

The ground under her hands grew colder and denser. She stopped and parted the fronds of a fern. What she saw made her want to weep.

It was a lagoon, lit bright blue by the sky, hidden among the trees of the forest.

And there in the centre of it was the obeah.

They locked eyes. Yeeran was too weak to aim true, though her hand tightened on her drum with a strength she didn't know she still had.

The obeah dipped its head as if to welcome her.

Am I dreaming?

She blinked and rubbed her eyes. When she looked up the obeah was gone, the only evidence that it was ever there was a ripple in the water.

Yeeran let out a breath and crawled into the pool, careful to leave her drum on the side.

The pool was fed by a waterfall above that tinkled over moss-covered rocks and into the water below. The moss filtered out debris, leaving the crystal-clear waters for Yeeran to submerge herself in and drink her fill.

She forgot all about the obeah and her exile for a few short moments of ecstasy as the water ran down her throat. When she was full, she floated on the surface of the lagoon, letting the water soothe her cracked skin and aching muscles. With weary hands she started to remove her clothes – they too had benefited from the cleansing water – and left them on a rock to dry.

Sweet green raspberries grew by the edge of the pool, and she ate until she felt the sugar buzzing through her veins. It gave her more energy than she'd had in days.

That night Yeeran camped by the water's edge. Thankful that the obeah's trail had led her there.

Tomorrow she was back on the hunt.

CHAPTER NINE

Lettle

Rayan and Lettle's footsteps took on a weary rhythm. Their rest had been short, like Lettle's temper. Exhaustion had drained her of the ability to make pleasant conversation. Rayan had begun to walk a few paces behind her after she berated him for three full minutes for stepping on her toe.

The forests in Waning district began to thin the further away they got from Gural. As the sun set, they heard the tell-tale signs of civilisation ahead of them: camel hooves on cobbled lanes, a flour mill turning, and, as always, the steady beat of warfare from the Bleeding Field in the distance.

As the border came into view, Lettle walked on with surer steps. The blisters on her feet had long burst and she could feel her heart-beat in the throbbing of the wounds. She ignored it.

It took them over two hours to be processed at the border to the Crescent district and when they were finally given permission to pass through the territory it was late into the night.

'I've never known a border to be this strict,' Lettle muttered. She was clutching the travelling pass to her chest as if it were a shield against the clusters of soldiers who watched them pass with ill-concealed hatred.

They had been granted twenty-four hours to pass through Sharr, the capital of Crescent. Though borders between the districts had existed since the Forever War began, they had always remained open to allow for essential trade and travel. But after twenty-four hours their welcome was over. Lettle hated how the war bled into all aspects of life.

'The Two-Bladed Tyrant strengthened the border in the last few years of his reign,' Rayan said under his breath.

The whites of his eyes flashed in the dark as his gaze moved systematically from one soldier to another, assessing the greatest threat. His posture had changed subtly too, he seemed taller, the lines of his face harsher.

He wields his jawline like a weapon, Lettle thought. She was so focused on the shape of it that it took her a moment to realise he had asked her a question.

'Hmm?'

'When was the last time you passed through Crescent?' he repeated.

'It was a while ago; I was a kid. My father, he was a hunter . . .' she screwed up her nose as she tried to think back. 'Oh . . . it's been twenty years.'

'That was early on in Chieftain Akomido's dictatorship, before his true nature was known by the world. Much has changed since then.' He said the Two-Bladed Tyrant's name with a bitter hatred.

Though his reign had been short, his impact had been mighty.

The streets grew quieter as they moved away from the border, but soldiers still prowled on every street corner.

Unlike Waning, Crescent had a stricter policy on alcohol and there were no taverns teeming with tired soldiers singing war songs. Nor were there any late-night sellers of shisha scenting the air. It left the city seeming hollow, the joy scooped out of it like the yolk from an egg, leaving only the blandness of stately white-brick homes.

Lettle looked up at Rayan from under her eyelashes as she walked beside him through the city's heart. There was something magnetic in the way his profile tugged at her gaze, and it frustrated her. His gaze was flint thin as he kept vigilant. She noticed the centre of his eyes were slightly golden, like the crystals in honey left to set.

'When were you last here?' she asked, and he turned his syrupy eyes to hers.

'I . . . I was born here.'

Lettle's lips parted in shock. Defecting from the district you were born in was rare. So rare that Lettle had never met someone who had done it.

Rayan was watching her, waiting for her response, his expression guarded. But Lettle had never let the prejudices of the war seep into her opinions.

She let a bored expression spread over her face.

'So?'

The smile he gave her in return was so radiant she had to look away.

'Shall we try and find somewhere to stay the night? I'd like to leave early, but we should get a few hours of rest in at least,' she said.

Rayan turned to her.

'Lettle.'

His breath fogged in the cold night air, and she felt herself leaning in, ever so slightly, into the cloud of his scent. Bergamot and sage: the forest come alive.

He reached a hand up towards her cheek. But the hand passed over her shoulder as he pointed to something in the distance.

'I think that's an inn.'

Lettle let out a long breath between her teeth and it came out as a hiss.

She turned on her heel and marched towards the inn. It was small, a one-storey cottage with a squat ugly door.

'Two rooms, please,' she asked the elf at the desk inside. She placed down their immunity documentation.

The woman was less than half awake, her unfocused eyes blood-shot with fatigue. She ran her gaze over the travel passes and sniffed.

'We've only the one, the others are booked.' Though she didn't look concerned in the least.

'Booked by who?' Rayan said, stepping into the gaslight.

She turned her weary eyes to him.

'Never you mind.'

'It's fine,' Lettle cut through. 'One room it is.'

The innkeeper showed them to a small room in the back of the cottage that may once have been the servants' quarters. The bed took up the majority of the floor space.

'The fire's out, it'll take you but a sneeze to fix it up. There's only one bed but be glad for clean sheets.'

She handed Lettle the key.

'We'll be leaving at sunrise,' Lettle said.

'Good,' the innkeeper replied. 'Leave the keys on the counter when you go. I won't be getting up to see you out.'

She sauntered off the way she came, leaving Rayan and Lettle to the silence of their breathing.

Rayan let out a heavy sigh.

'Well, she was a delight,' he said.

'You can't really blame her, the way Crescent citizens have been treated since the tyrant's rule would make me hate travellers too.'

Rayan's expression darkened, but he didn't reply for some time. He moved to light the fire.

'Akomido was voted in as chieftain with an overwhelming majority. I remember his campaigns on the streets when I was a boy. His motto was "To rule with honour is to rule without mercy."'

He struck a match against the kindling and the fireplace crackled to life casting one side of his face in flickering shadows.

'The first thing he did was clear the jails of prisoners of war. But he didn't release them, no, that would have been a mercy.'

His eyelids shuttered closed, reliving memories Lettle couldn't see.

'First, he cut off their ears, sending the torn flesh to their respective tribes. Then he hanged them.'

Lettle swallowed. Rayan turned towards her, his eyes as bright and as fierce as the firelight.

'He didn't have to cut their ears off first. But he wanted them to suffer. And do you know what the worst thing is? The citizens voted him in again.'

'It's a good job he disappeared ten years ago, because you look ready to murder him.' Lettle was trying to lighten the mood, but her tone came out annoyed and Rayan looked away.

She busied herself with getting ready for bed and stripped down to her underclothes.

'I'm putting these pillows across the middle of the bed, OK? Stick to your side.'

Rayan's laughter rumbled to a stop as he realised she was in her underwear.

She cocked her hip at him. 'What? I didn't think I'd be travelling with anyone else, so I have no nightclothes. And I'm not sleeping in leggings. Too hot.'

Lettle knew she had an enviable figure. She wore her weight around her hips, which accentuated the dimple of her waist. Years of malnutrition had once robbed her of her fullness. It was only when she moved to Gural that her curves were able to blossom.

Rayan made a strangled sound in the back of his throat and turned away.

'I'm going to go for a walk.'

Lettle frowned. 'Do you think it's safe to split up—'

He left before she had finished her sentence.

Lettle watched the space he had occupied for some time. Her thoughts clouded, her anger brewing.

Rayan didn't come back for two hours. Lettle tried to stay awake to spite him.

She found an old faerytale book covered in dust lining a shelf to the side of the bed. It was the story of the Wandering Human, the one Rayan had spoken of earlier that day. The spine made a satisfying crack as she opened it. She began to read.

With teeth of knives and eyes of fire, the fae killed every human, for humans were the most magical of beings. When the fae drained their life force they became imbued with their power. Until only one human remained. Afa he was called. The last of them. Damned to wander the land alone. He travelled across seas, across continents, gaining knowledge wherever he went . . .

The bed shifted beneath her, and she woke with a start.

'Rayan?'

'Yes.' His voice was hoarse.

He pulled the covers over him, careful not to disturb the pillow fort that separated her leg from his. The dim light of the fire's dying embers cast him in a soft golden glow.

He really is quite beautiful, her thoughts sluggish with sleep.

'You came back.'

He let out a sigh that held a smile in it.

'I did.'

Lettle yawned and nestled into her pillow.

'Goodnight, Rayan. May Bosome light your dreams.'

She heard him laugh quietly.

'It's been a long time since I've heard the god's name.'

Lettle's eyes narrowed to slits. She hadn't told Rayan she was a diviner, but the prayer had given her away. She rolled over onto her stiffened arm; though uncomfortable to lie on, it was better than seeing the shadows of mockery on Rayan's face. Lettle wasn't in the mood to have to justify her profession, not again, not with him.

The faerytale had fallen open to the last page on the floor beside her bed and she could just make out the last lines.

The knowledge enhanced Afa's power, and when they returned to the Fae Lands, he cursed the fae for what they had done, banishing them to Mosima, a land entombed in time.

Rayan spoke into the silence. 'My mother was a diviner.'

Lettle sat up and turned back to Rayan, resting heavily on her right elbow.

The fire had now died out completely, instead the only light to fill the room was the sliver of the moon through a gap in the heavy curtains. It bathed Rayan in a beam of its light and when he looked towards her, the gold of his eyes sparkled.

'I was raised in Crescent during the tyrant's rule. My mother was a diviner in a time when the truth wasn't sought, nor given credibility. Though diviners aren't often hired in Waning, they were actively persecuted in Crescent.'

It was rare that Lettle recognised when it was time to be quiet and listen, but she knew right now was one of those times. Something had compelled Rayan to speak and speak he did.

'Her name was Reema, and she made the best roast lamb in the whole of the Elven Lands.' He chuckled, and somehow it sounded like a rain shower. Bright and tinkling. '"The secret ingredient," she'd say, "is three times more butter and salt than you think, and when you think that's enough double it."'

Lettle found herself smiling too, until she saw the joy drop from Rayan's face.

Rayan continued, 'One day she was arrested for reading prophecies. The chieftain heard of it and brought her forward for entertainment during one of his feasts.' His mouth twisted with hatred. The expression looked alien on his face.

'He asked her for a reading.' Rayan swallowed. 'Akomido brought in a newly slaughtered obeah. And though she knew the risks, she read for him.'

Rayan looked away, though not before Lettle saw the shimmer of tears in his eyes.

'I don't know what the reading was, all I know is what one of the servants told me afterwards. The chieftain flew into a fit of rage and ran her through with his daggers. One on either side of her gut.'

Lettle wanted to reach for him, but she had no words of kindness. This world was a brutal one and they both knew it.

'That was twenty-three years ago. I was nine. And that day I vowed I would kill Akomido on the battlefield.'

Lettle would have laughed at the proclamation if she hadn't heard the resolute truth in Rayan's voice. It was a promise he was going to keep.

'It was why I crossed the border and joined the Waning Army. I wanted to fight against the people who had killed my mother. I wanted to fight under a ruler I believed in.'

He didn't speak again for a long time and Lettle thought that was the end of it. So, she rolled back over.

When he spoke again, she had nearly drifted off, and the words were blurred by sleep.

'My yearning for vengeance drew me to the eastern bank that day. I knew the Crescent Army would be there. And since Akomido has been missing for so long I . . . I couldn't pass up the opportunity for a little more revenge.'

She couldn't let him take all the blame. It was hers too.

'It wasn't just your fault,' she said drowsily. 'I had done a reading for Yeeran that morning. I told her to find glory to the east. We're tied together now, you and I.'

'Tied together,' he repeated, and she could hear the sound of a smile in his voice. 'Sleep now, Lettle.'

She hated doing what people told her, and she was going to retort as much, but then she felt the tug of her dreams and was gone.

Lettle woke in a sour mood. She had dreamed of Rayan's mother, but when she leaned over the body it had been Yeeran. The panic of helplessness lay just under the surface of her mind.

They breakfasted on the road after stopping at a bakery in Crescent. Lettle had tried to buy a warm, fresh loaf but when Rayan had paid with Waning currency the loaf was swapped with two stale knobs of bread. She was sure one had a bite mark in it, but Lettle wasn't fussy. Childhood poverty had bred that out of her.

Leaving Crescent was much less trouble than entering it. Mainly because there was nothing worthwhile outside of the Elven Lands.

The forest grew dense a day's walk out from Sharr. Yeeran's tracks were long gone, distorted by the many footprints that covered the dirt path. Though they were yet to meet another person.

'Isn't this road a little more well-travelled than you'd expect?' Rayan asked.

Lettle had been thinking the same thing, but she worried if she spoke she would breathe fire, such was her mood. So, she ignored him instead.

At sunset Lettle caught a pheasant which she prepared by the edge of the road. Rayan set up the stove and was frying wild garlic in preparation for the meat. And yes, he was also singing.

That morning she'd even caught him crooning a lullaby to a butterfly when he thought she wasn't listening.

Lettle plucked out the last of the pheasant's feathers with short, sharp pulls as his voice travelled across the camp:

> *Bless our god, with words alone,*
> *Sing them loud of purest tone,*
> *Blessed are we in moonlight shine,*
> *Living as the moon's divine.*

Lettle couldn't take it any more.

'Shut *up*.' She sprang up from her crouched stance, the pheasant's neck swinging from her clenched fist.

Rayan turned to her with a raised eyebrow.

'And now you talk to me? After a whole day of silence?'

'Silence?' she hissed. 'All I want is silence, but you won't let me have it.'

Rayan's second eyebrow shot up, though his gaze was still frustratingly calm.

'I'm not sure what I have done to cause you to hate me so?'

'Everywhere I look you're there, *singing*.'

Rayan shrugged his broad shoulders.

'I'll stop then.'

'Ah . . . no . . . but . . . well . . .' Lettle's anger spluttered to a stop.

Rayan stood, and though she still radiated hatred he braved the distance between them.

Bergamot and sage. That maddening smell.

When he was close enough for her to feel his breath on her cheek, he said gently, 'Is that ready to be cooked?'

Lettle sucked her teeth and thrust the carcass against his chest.

'Don't burn it this time.'

He didn't contradict her that he hadn't burned any of the meals thus far. He returned to the stove and began to diligently fry the pheasant, a slight frown between his brows.

It wasn't until after they had eaten that Lettle spoke again.

'I . . . I've started to worry that we might not find Yeeran.'

And if we do, will she still be alive?

Rayan nodded as if he could hear the rest of her thoughts.

'Remember, your sister is one of the most decorated colonels the army has ever had. There is nothing, not skin traders, not rabid beasts, that could cut her down. Not without a fight.'

Lettle sniffed and she realised she was crying.

Rayan moved to her side and laid a hand on her forearm.

'She'll be all right.'

There was a crack of thunder above them, and the sky too began to weep.

'Here, I brought a tarp.' He pulled out the waxed leather from his pack and drew it over them. Lettle hesitated for just a moment before pressing herself against his torso under the cover of the tarp.

He wrapped his arm around her, pulling her nearer.

'Is this OK?'

Lettle nodded. She couldn't speak. The air felt thinner closer to him, like she couldn't breathe.

They listened to the rain for a time, but even after it slowed, they lingered under their shelter.

'Sorry for today,' Lettle said heavily.

'It's OK. You were just worried,' he said, his voice deep and simmering.

She could feel his breath on her cheek. He was watching her, the flecks of honey in his eyes twinkling.

'The rain's stopped,' she said.

'Yes.'

But he didn't lower the tarp.

Then she heard it. The distinctive sound of wet shoes in mud.

'There's someone here,' she whispered.

Rayan's arms tightened around her shoulders as if he could hide them from whoever's shadow was stretching across the clearing.

But it was too late, they'd been spotted.

CHAPTER TEN

Yeeran

Yeeran wasn't alone. She had seen signs of other hunters in the forest. There were six of them at least, moving as a group after the obeah.

I have to get to the beast first, she thought, running with renewed energy.

Today was the day the hunt would end.

She wondered how Lettle was faring and if Rayan had kept his promise to her.

I'll see you soon, sister. Once I bring this prize back to the chieftain, I'll come home.

Yeeran didn't linger on whether Salawa would accept this gift. If she lingered, then she may have begun to question if the offering would be enough to secure her freedom. And she couldn't think that way.

No, this was the only path ahead of her. A path lined with the lifeblood of the obeah.

The evening rain was here, leaving only a residue of the obeah's path in the mud. She was sure the beast was running in circles, as she'd seen that eucalyptus tree before. When Yeeran bent down to examine the tracks she noticed two more sets of footprints she hadn't seen before.

Her heart began to pound in her chest.

The other hunters were close. Too close.

She thought about camping for the night until she saw two globes of light flash in the darkness.

The obeah was once again in her sights.

'. . . the rain's stopped.' The murmur of voices came from her left.

Yeeran dropped into a crouch, her drum poised ready ahead of her. The obeah had fled, and she cursed the speaker for scaring it off.

Then another voice spoke. 'There's someone here.'

The familiarity of the speaker drew her to them like a magnet.

No, it couldn't be.

Violet eyes locked with hers.

'Lettle?'

Yeeran stood there, slack-jawed.

Was she dehydrated and hallucinating again?

She clutched her head and shook the image of her sister from her mind. But when she opened her eyes again, Lettle was still there, a foot from her. So close she could see the mist of her breath.

The air was knocked out of her lungs as Lettle threw herself at Yeeran and wrapped her arms tightly around her in one leap.

'How dare you . . . how dare you leave me?' Lettle's anger was blunted with relief.

Yeeran found herself going limp in her embrace.

'Are you really here?'

Lettle's laugh was muffled by Yeeran's shoulder.

'Moon's mercy, yes, you fool.'

In the middle of the forest, here was her sister, safe and whole. Yeeran rested her chin on the top of Lettle's cornrows and inhaled her familiar scent.

'Now we've found you, we can go home,' Lettle said.

'Yes, you could at least have left an address.' The voice came from over Lettle's shoulder.

Yeeran let go of her sister and turned to Rayan.

'You, too?'

He gave her a lopsided smile before thumping his chest in salute. 'Colonel.'

'What are you both doing here?'

Lettle cocked her head at Yeeran.

'I told you, to bring you home.'

'That's not how exile works.'

Lettle lifted her chin.

'Well, I've decided you're not exiled.'

Yeeran smiled and shook her head.

'If only it were that simple.' She reached out and squeezed Lettle's hand.

Yeeran looked between the two of them and felt lighter than she had in days. Despite the circumstances, she was glad to see them.

'We should move out of this clearing. I spotted at least six sets of hunter's tracks, and we don't know what type of hunters they are.'

They moved upwind from the hunters' trail until they were too tired to walk any further and set up camp. All three of them had suffered over the last few days and Lettle was eager to fill Yeeran in on all the pain she had undergone in trying to find her.

'. . . then we stayed the night in Crescent in this inn that was definitely *not* full, but the innkeeper wouldn't give us more than one room. And then this bakery only sold us stale bread . . .'

Yeeran was smiling faintly.

'What?' Lettle asked, unsure whether she should be offended.

'Nothing, it's just good to hear the sound of your voice.'

Though it had been less than a week, Yeeran had thought she might never hear it again.

Lettle gave her a small smile in return.

Yeeran was warming herself by the fire, the first she had lit since hunting the obeah.

They had caught and roasted a rabbit for dinner and were now sipping raspberry leaf tea that Lettle had foraged. Rayan had fallen asleep soon after the drinks had brewed.

'At least he isn't snoring this time,' Lettle said once she noticed that he hadn't touched his cup.

'You should join him.'

'Join him?' Lettle's voice squeaked to an unusually high octave.

'Yes . . . aren't you tired?'

'Oh.' Lettle rubbed the tip of her nose with the flesh of her palm. 'Yes, I am deathly tired.'

'I'll take first watch. You sleep. You've got a big day tomorrow.'

Lettle's brow furrowed.

'Do I?'

'Yes, you're going back to the Waning district, and I'm going to continue hunting the obeah.' Yeeran had told them of the creature she'd been stalking. It had lit Lettle's eyes with hope.

'No, I'm not.'

'You can't stay out here in exile with me. What if I never find the obeah again? The tracks will have gone after all this rain. I'll have to start afresh.' Yeeran couldn't help the frustration that ebbed out in her voice. 'You have your whole life back in Gural. You need to return to it.'

'Not without you.'

Yeeran saw the set of Lettle's jaw and knew there was nothing she could do to win this battle right now. Sometimes the easiest way to deal with Lettle was pretending she had won.

'We'll talk tomorrow.'

Lettle paused as if she wanted to say something more, but then the frown was gone, and she smiled.

'Goodnight, sister. May Bosome light your dreams.'

Lettle padded over to her sleeping bag.

'Goodnight, little sister.'

Yeeran woke Rayan just before dawn.

'What happened to the raspberry tea?' he said, wiping sleep from his eyes.

'That was half a night ago.'

'I fell asleep.' He said the words with such abject misery that Yeeran would have laughed if it wouldn't have woken Lettle.

'You did. Can you take watch for the next hour or so? I just need a few hours' sleep.'

'Yes, Colonel.'

Yeeran winced. 'Just Yeeran, please.'

He nodded but didn't correct himself. He looked like he was working up to saying something.

Yeeran was desperately tired, but she waited patiently for him to speak.

'It was my fault,' he said with an exhale. 'I encouraged you to explore the eastern bank. I'm so sorry.'

Rayan's expression was tortured, and it saddened Yeeran to think he'd carried the guilt all this way.

She laid a hand on his wrist.

'It was no one's fault but my own. Do you deny that I was the highest-ranking officer on that field?'

'You were.'

'And do you agree that I was capable of making my own decisions *as* the highest-ranking officer on that field?'

'. . . Yes.'

'By taking a share of the blame you are denying both those facts. Now, I don't believe that's something you'd like to do?'

'No.'

'Right. So, it's settled then. No blame lies at your feet.'

Rayan's head dipped with part sadness and part relief.

'Thank you, Colonel.'

'It is I who owes you thanks. You looked after Lettle above and beyond what I thought that duty would entail at the time. But I should have known my sister would come after me. I know she isn't the easiest and I imagine she gave you a hard time for accompanying her. But I'm glad she had you to watch her back.'

Rayan was looking at Lettle with a small smile on his lips.

'She didn't need me. Not really.'

Yeeran settled down into the sleeping bag Rayan had vacated. For a moment she thought she saw Lettle's eyes open, but when she looked again, her face was relaxed in the peacefulness of sleep. Yeeran joined her shortly after.

There was someone watching her. Yeeran could feel it. She wondered if the obeah was back. She let her eyelids flutter open softly, trying to catch a glimpse of the spy.

'Finally. I thought you were never going to wake.'

Lettle was sitting across from her.

Yeeran groaned and rolled over.

'I've been waiting for hours,' Lettle said.

'What time is it?'

'Noon.'

Yeeran sat bolt upright.

'You let me sleep until noon?' she shouted. A flock of small green birds scattered from the canopy above them.

'See, told you we should have woken her sooner,' Lettle said to Rayan. He sat behind her stirring a pot of stew over the fire. The smell was divine, and it drew Yeeran out of the sleeping bag.

'Lunch?' he said to her with an apologetic smile.

'Lunch,' she grunted.

It was only after she had devoured the meal – a delicate combination of forest mushrooms and tarragon (who knew Rayan could cook?) – relieved herself, and then washed her face in a nearby stream, that she was able to string together her next sentence.

'It's time for you two to go back to Gural.'

Neither Rayan nor Lettle responded. In fact, they were pointedly looking away from her.

'Hello? Are you listening?'

'Oh, we're listening,' Lettle said, her voice curiously neutral. 'We just disagree.'

Yeeran leaned back onto her elbows and crossed her ankles. She appraised the two of them with a cocked eyebrow.

'I see, you two have been chatting.'

'We're not going back without you,' Lettle responded.

Yeeran picked at her nails.

'Yes, I think you are.'

'We're going to help you track the obeah.'

Yeeran laughed, she couldn't help it. She wasn't a cruel person, and she regretted it once she saw the hurt on Lettle's face.

'I'm sorry, sister, but I don't need help.'

Fury burst across Lettle's face.

'You always do this, act like I don't have any skills of worth. Well, I managed to find you.'

'I didn't need finding.'

'I'm twenty-eight years old, Yeeran. The last words you said before leaving the Elven Lands was to order one of your minions to look after me. As if I'm a *child.*'

She was sure acting like one. But Yeeran knew that wasn't the way to defuse the situation.

'You heard that last night.'

'Do you deny it's what you said?' Lettle was breathing heavily.

'No, and I'd do it again. I'm your older sister, I just want to—'

'Moon's mercy! You spend half your time acting like I'm the younger sister you used to know, not the person I am today. I haven't been that child since the moment you left me for the war.'

'Left you for the *war?*' Yeeran could feel herself rise from the ground, as if pulled by the surge of her anger. 'I joined the Waning Army to make something of myself—' Yeeran stopped before she said something she regretted.

'Go on. Say it,' Lettle hissed through her teeth.

'Unlike you.'

Lettle stormed off towards the stream leaving Yeeran and her anger alone.

'Fuck.' Yeeran kicked the ground with her foot.

'Well, I haven't seen you that angry before.'

Yeeran jumped. She'd forgotten that Rayan was there. He sat on his haunches at the edge of the camp.

'Sorry. Lettle, she just . . . you know?'

He nodded.

'How old was she when you joined the Waning Army?'

'Nine.'

'She didn't want to go to Gural with you?'

Yeeran shook her head. 'She stayed with Father. I sent them money.'

'Where is he now?'

'Father?'

Rayan nodded.

'Dead.'

'Must have been hard for her. With his illness.'

Yeeran frowned. Her father had died from a heart attack.

'What illness?'

'Oh, I thought Lettle said . . .' Rayan's jaw worked but no sound came out. He looked away.

Yeeran lifted her chin and watched him, waiting for him to collect himself and explain. But he didn't speak again.

'You understand you two can't stay here, right?'

Rayan didn't answer at first.

Then he said in a drained voice, 'They'll dismiss me if I go back.'

'No, they won't.' Yeeran was adamant. 'You'll tell them that I threatened you, that I held you hostage. They won't dismiss you. They can't.'

Rayan was shaking his head.

'It's too late.'

'It's not too late. You'll blame me, then you'll be promoted to colonel. You're the obvious choice.' She started pacing back and forth.

'Yeeran.'

'No, don't give me that. I can't have you losing your job. The army needs you. You're the only one I trust to help win this war.'

'*Yeeran.*'

'No—'

'Look.' Rayan's voice had dropped to a whisper.

Yeeran turned to him and frowned.

'What?'

His hand shook as he pointed. Yeeran followed the shaking path of his finger.

There, standing in the flecked sunlight of the forest, was the obeah.

Yeeran slowly reached for her drum. The strap brushed her fingers. She extended a little more, wincing as her back cricked.

'Don't make any sudden movements,' Yeeran said to Rayan as she brought the drum to her waist. She pulled her mind into focus and steeled her intention. Then she inhaled, knowing this was the moment.

The obeah tilted its head at her, its eyes boring into hers without judgement. The wisps of fur around its feline mouth were white with age.

Why isn't it running from me?

She pushed the thought from her mind. It didn't matter why. Now was the time for the kill.

As Yeeran breathed out she splayed her hands against the drum, splitting her fingers into two groups: the index and middle, and the little and ring finger. She then rotated her wrist in quick succession, rattling the groups on either side. This had the effect of creating two fast drumbeats while the wrist muffled some of the resonance. The bullets were less powerful, but more precise to aim.

The obeah turned its azure gaze towards Rayan. It raised its feline head and tilted its horns to the left, watching him sidelong. Its jaws parted in a distinctly human gesture before its neck snapped backwards from the impact of Yeeran's drumfire.

The beast fell to the ground.

'Sun sins, that is the biggest obeah I've ever seen,' Rayan said.

Yeeran ran towards it to confirm the kill. The shot was clean, its lifeblood nourishing the ground as death inched closer.

She ran her hands over the obeah's warm fur. The texture was a little wirier than the fur she had worn in her uniform, and she wondered how old this creature was. Its body was ripples of corded muscle, and the tail that had seemed almost delicate in the distance had curled around its legs with the strength of another limb.

'It was almost like it was waiting for you,' Rayan murmured.

Yeeran nodded. 'Like it was waiting to die.'

She felt a wave of sadness that the hunt was over. The adrenaline of it could no longer sustain her. But at least she could go home now with her prize.

'Farewell, friend,' she whispered.

As the breath left the obeah for the last time, there was a scream in the distance, too deep to be Lettle.

Yeeran leapt up.

'Did you hear that?'

Rayan was watching the obeah, his mouth slightly parted. At Yeeran's question he jumped and turned to her. 'I didn't hear anything. Was it Lettle? Is she OK?'

'It wasn't Lettle.'

The concern left Rayan's features.

'Help me skin the beast so we can begin the journey back. The other hunters must be nearby, and I don't want them claiming my prize.'

Rayan squirmed a little.

'Skin it?'

'Yes, how else do you propose we travel home?'

'I've never skinned anything before.'

'You don't have to do anything, just help me lift it up, I need to turn it onto its side.'

Rayan followed Yeeran's instructions as she prepared the obeah for skinning. He had to turn his head away as she brought out her knife.

'Put down the dagger,' a voice said from behind. Their accent was lilting, the R rolled like the purr of a cat. It was unlike anything Yeeran had ever heard.

She jumped up and held out her knife ready to attack. A woman dressed in a cloak of spun gold was standing in the centre of their camp.

'This is my kill, step aside, hunter,' Yeeran said fiercely. She would rather die than give up the obeah.

The newcomer's laugh was brittle, tinged with pain.

'You have no idea of what you speak. This beast is not yours. It never was.'

Yeeran saw the hint of a sharp nose and wan cheeks wet with tears. She held no weapon out towards them, nor seemed strongly built enough to take Yeeran bare-handed.

'I will hurt you, stay back.'

But still the woman walked forward.

'Drop the dagger, elf.'

Yeeran saw a movement out of the corner of her eye and realised that Rayan had lunged forward towards her drum. He sent out a couple of beats towards the figure dressed in gold.

The woman held out her hand. The fingers were long with gold paint covering them from knuckle to nail. A spark appeared in the centre of her palm. The drumfire dissipated uselessly into the air.

It was magic that Yeeran had never seen before. But she didn't have time to ponder, instead she charged forward with the dagger held high. If drumfire wasn't going to do it, she'd have to resort to more basic measures.

As she thrust forward, her aim seemed to waver, the dagger glancing off the woman as if an invisible barrier surrounded her. Yeeran fell to the ground, winded.

'I said, drop the dagger,' she repeated coolly.

Yeeran picked herself up and dived again, only to fall as she was deflected away.

'Would you stop that?' the woman said.

'No.' Yeeran skipped to the side and lunged from behind, to fail once more.

'Are you done?'

Yeeran was breathing heavily. She looked at Rayan, who shook his head. The drumfire he'd been shooting hadn't landed once.

'Who are you?' Yeeran asked.

The woman whistled low through her teeth. Shadows moved out of the forest.

Yeeran's gasp clogged in her throat.

Five obeah at least as large as the one she'd killed appeared. On their backs were five other cloaked figures, *riding* the creatures as if they were steeds.

The woman lowered her hood.

Her hair was streaked blonde, like fallen sunlight. Her eyes were a vibrant brown, so striking it was hard to look away. Her skin was burnished bronze and lightly freckled.

And when her full lips parted, they revealed sharpened canines Yeeran had only read about in stories.

'No, no, no,' Yeeran murmured.

'Oh, yes,' the woman said. 'And you, *elf*, are under arrest for the murder of the prince of Mosima.'

The woman was fae.

CHAPTER ELEVEN

Lettle

Lettle had waited long enough. Yeeran wasn't coming after her. She threw a rock into the stream and watched it sink with a heavy heart.

She had known that Yeeran didn't approve of her career in divination; she thought everyone should be conscripted into the war effort. But Lettle had seen the power of divination at a young age, and ever since that first prophecy, she knew it was the only path for her.

She'd been sixteen when her father had died. Bereft from loss and remorse, she had found solace in an abandoned temple on the outskirts of her village. When she and Yeeran had been children they had often played in the ruins of the building. Perhaps it was those happy times that drew her there that night. Or perhaps it was the touch of her god.

'Bosome feels your pain, child.' The diviner's words floated out of her memories like wisps of smoke.

'Who are you?' At sixteen Lettle was small for her age. Though Yeeran sent home money, she earned a mere foot soldier's salary and so Lettle remained scrawny. A violent wind blew through the remnants of the temple, plucking the tears from her eyes.

'I am a patron of this temple. One of the few who still pray to Bosome.'

'Bosome?' Lettle's education had been limited, and her knowledge of history and the gods was lacking.

The diviner stepped into the light and Lettle met Imna for the first time. His hair was thicker and longer than it was now, the blond strands falling to the back of his knees.

'Bosome, our creator, our god.' He tipped his head upwards to the sky.

'Gods aren't real.'

The shaman cocked his head at Lettle, causing his hair to ripple in turn.

'That is what people say of the humans and the fae. But we know they existed from our histories. Just because you cannot see something, doesn't mean it is not real.'

Lettle thought of her grief then, how it had poured over her like molten iron, burning her skin, the fumes choking and robbing her of air. Then it had solidified, weighing her down with every step, clinging to every movement.

But no one could see it.

She nodded to the shaman.

'I understand.'

'I see you, child. Bosome sees you. It was our god's gift of prophecy that led me here today.'

Lettle narrowed her eyes, her gaze flickering to the exit. Imna laughed lightly, like the trickle of a stream.

'I am not here to hurt you, child. But I am here to give you a message, a message from your future. *You will wield magic unmatched, speak prophecies unspoken. You will be the leader we seek, and the leader we are due.*'

Lettle shivered, feeling the ghostly fingers of prophecy for the first time.

'The Fates spoke to me of you,' Imna continued, 'and in turn I must do my duty to guide your will. You must come with me to Gural, study well, for divining is your calling. And it calls to you now.'

Lettle had been lost until that moment. She was all but estranged from Yeeran, but here was her opportunity to make something of herself.

It had been foretold.

She threw an even bigger rock into the stream and watched the eddies of its descent.

And now I am here.

So far away from the Gural diviners and her future as a shaman.

A guttural scream erupted from the bush, making her jump. It was so full of anguish and grief that tears pricked the corners of her eyes.

'Rayan . . .' she thought. Her heart was thunder in her chest.

She sprang up and began to run back the way she had come through the forest. In her haste she tripped over a raised root and fell, cutting her knee.

It was then that she heard an unfamiliar voice ahead.

'. . . And you, *elf*, are under arrest for the murder of the prince of Mosima.'

Lettle crept forward and parted the branches to see through to the camp beyond.

'No . . . no . . . this doesn't make sense . . . you can't be here . . . you don't exist,' Yeeran said to a figure dressed in gold. Rayan stood a few paces behind her, and behind him was the body of an obeah. The biggest obeah Lettle had ever seen. The euphoria that Lettle felt in seeing Yeeran's freedom laid bare was gone the moment she locked eyes with Rayan.

He had seen Lettle. And he was scared. Lettle sucked in a breath, knowing better than to alert the newcomer to her presence.

What was going on?

She tried to angle herself forward to see the woman's face more clearly. They must be skin traders for Yeeran's shoulders to betray so much fear.

As Lettle moved, she noticed something shift in the shadows of the trees.

Lettle had to clamp her mouth shut to stop the scream that started there. Surrounding the golden woman were five people *riding* obeah.

Each one of them wore a boiled leather shoulder plate with a setting sun branded black in the middle. The rest of their uniforms were scraps of silk strung together with thin strips of chainmail. There was more skin than armour, and the skin that Lettle could see was varying shades of black, brown, and white. If it wasn't for the obeah, Lettle would have assumed they were elves dressing up for a pageant.

'You elves are foolish folk, have you forgotten all truths of this world?' The woman's tone was cool and melodic. It grated on Lettle.

'I don't understand,' Yeeran said.

Neither did Lettle, until she saw the woman's teeth. Sharp canines made for ripping human throats.

Fae.

A wave of nausea came over Lettle and she pressed her lips together.

'You don't need to understand.' The fae turned to the soldiers behind her and spoke in a language Lettle had never heard before. It had the cadence of a carriage over cobbled stones, staccato and heavy.

Another of the fae jumped down from the back of an obeah in response to their leader's request. She had short tight curls dyed silver like the bark of a birch tree. Her thick eyebrows were threaded with gold jewellery. She stalked towards Rayan with swaying hips and a sly smile spreading across her face.

There was a flash of light and Rayan's hands were drawn together as if tied up. He looked down at his wrists in horror.

Why wasn't he fighting back?

The muscle in his jaw was working again, and Lettle saw him make a subtle shake of his head. She understood. *Keep hidden.*

There was a small breath behind her and Lettle turned. This time she couldn't stop the yelp that escaped her lips.

An obeah towered over her, its yellow eyes curious as it watched her. The horns that grew from its head spiralled upwards like two coiled springs and for the first time Lettle was able to see how different each obeah's horn formation was. The beast snorted, breathing in her scent as if she was something foul.

'Get gone,' Lettle hissed, trying to make it scatter before the fae noticed her.

The obeah trotted backwards on its large paws as she flailed her arms in its face. Its black tail flicked side to side like a large cat making its annoyance known.

It growled, showing its incisors. Lettle had to remind herself that obeah were herbivores, otherwise she would have been fearful for her life.

Lettle growled back in response.

'Get going, I said.'

The obeah huffed at her before padding out into the clearing.

'Amnan, there you are,' the fae in the gold said. She reached out towards the obeah as it approached her. She scratched its head fondly.

'Oh, indeed?' the woman said, before looking towards the bush where Lettle was hiding. 'Berro?' The fae whose magic – for magic was what it must be – had just finished tying up Yeeran, stood to attention.

'Yes, Commander Furi?'

'Amnan's found another in the bush over there. He says they smell like this one's kin.' The leader, Furi, spoke in elvish as if to taunt her.

Lettle tried to get up and run, but it was too late. Berro's hand clamped around her wrist, and she was pulled roughly to the side.

'Get off me.'

But Berro was efficient and managed to tie her hands together quickly despite Lettle trying to bite her. Lettle looked down at her hands but couldn't see anything holding them together.

'What magic is this?' she whispered in horror.

Lettle looked to Yeeran, whose face was crestfallen after Lettle's capture. All fight had left her.

'Gag her,' Furi said.

Lettle felt pure dread unfurl its long fingers up her throat and force out a ragged scream.

When the strip of leather wrapped around her mouth, Lettle felt her necklace catch on the fae's hands. She watched all the beads tumble to the ground, followed by the thin chain around her neck.

Her eyes burned with unshed tears, and she was pulled into the centre of the camp. Rayan looked panic-stricken as Lettle was marched to stand next to him.

Furi barked out orders in her strange language and the fae sprang into movement. One soldier, with eyes a deep blue like the open ocean, set about clearing the camp and stashing the elves' packs. Another doused the obeah's body in oil and set it alight.

Lettle watched Yeeran's face grow wet from silent crying as her freedom burned to ash.

Furi spoke over the beast solemnly, and though Lettle didn't understand the words, she recognised the cadence of a prayer. Her shoulders shook with tears but when the fire had faded and Furi looked back at the elves, her face was brittle with hatred.

'Three prisoners will never make up for the loss today. But three prisoners we will take. Let's move out.'

Lettle felt Rayan's eyes on her back, but she couldn't turn around. She was concentrating on putting one foot in front of the other. Her muscles shook with the effort as she picked her way through the uneven terrain.

The group had been marching for five hours without respite. The magic around Lettle's wrists burned, but when she looked down at her skin it was unblemished. It irritated her, though not as much as the gag around her mouth.

They were deep in the Wasted Marshes now and the landscape had more rocks than trees. Where the ground cracked, swamps seeped out of the earth laden with poisonous insects and snakes. It was a harsh land, where few had ventured, and those who did, didn't survive.

Lettle stumbled, the invisible rope of magic pulling taut as she yanked the connection between her and the fae who led her, the one their leader had named Berro.

A stream of insults was flung Lettle's way as she lay dazed, blinking up into the unyielding sunlight.

Pain blossomed across her left arm where her damaged muscles longed to be stretched. The stones beneath her back were soothing, and she decided she might just stay here.

'Lettle, are you all right?'

She could hear a tussle as Rayan tried to get closer, but the fae guarding him held him back.

'She needs water, we all do. Can we not take a break?' That was Yeeran's voice, urgent, pleading.

There was a shout from somewhere further up the route. Then Lettle heard the soft cadence of an obeah's paws running across stone. It grew louder until the obeah came into view.

Lettle could see its whiskers first, thin strips of silver protruding from a wide face, whose beauty hid their sharpened teeth within. Just like the leader who scowled at Lettle from the obeah's back.

'Get up,' Furi said in her sing-song voice.

Lettle couldn't have replied if she wanted to. Instead, she bit down on the leather gag and attempted to snarl.

'We need rest. And perhaps you will grant me an audience, give me a chance to explain this misunderstanding.' Yeeran was attempting to be diplomatic and Lettle wanted to laugh. She wanted to parley with the fae? If every story had an ounce of truth, then they were monsters, human-eating monsters.

She felt her shoulders begin to shudder with the beginnings of a giggle. It drew the leader's gaze back to Lettle's.

'Lettle, it's all right. Don't worry,' Rayan said softly. He must think she was weeping. She felt a flash of fondness for the man. It was quickly followed by annoyance.

These fae will not break me so easily.

Lettle pulled herself to standing then turned to Furi, her chin lifted high. Though the obeah's horns were only a few inches from her face, she refused to cower from the sight of their pointed tips.

Furi smirked at Lettle's glower before barking out an order in fae.

A few minutes later the march was brought to a standstill and water was handed to the three prisoners.

Berro removed Lettle's gag and passed her a handful of dried fruit.

'What, no human? Isn't that what you fae eat?'

Berro looked startled by Lettle's first words before tipping back her head and roaring out a laugh.

'Hosta, did you hear that?' Berro called the youngest of their guards over and recounted what Lettle had said. Then they began to chuckle too.

Lettle's annoyance grew as she waited for their laughter to stop. Eventually Berro wiped a tear from her eye and walked away, but every now and again she'd look back at Lettle and start chortling again.

It was then that Lettle realised the magic restraints around her wrists had been released.

She turned to Yeeran and Rayan, who had both just reached the same conclusion.

'Have they let us go free?' Lettle whispered.

A frown creased Yeeran's brow as she assessed the surrounding area.

'No, it doesn't make sense. There are guards stationed in a circle around us, but they don't seem concerned.'

Rayan looked around, his eyes lingering on Berro in the distance. The woman was removing her shoulder plate revealing a thin translucent undergarment beneath.

Lettle narrowed her eyes.

'At least we now know nothing's different under there.'

Rayan jerked his gaze away.

'What do you think, Colonel? Should we try to run?'

Yeeran looked perturbed.

'Six people I can handle, but this new magic they have?'

Lettle's hand went to her neck, and she felt the bitter loss of her nameday necklace. She cleared her throat to stop it from bobbing, then spoke. 'The obeah, I've been watching them, I think they're somehow linked. We need to head towards terrain that they'll find difficult, or it won't just be six fae, we'll have to fight their obeah too,' Lettle said.

Yeeran nodded sharply, the plan decided it seemed.

'Yes, quickly now, eat your fruit and drink your water. This might be our only chance.'

The food felt like sand on her tongue, and though the water was a sweet relief, it wasn't enough.

'See that crag in the distance?' Yeeran pointed to a rock formation that grew out of the swampland a few leagues ahead. 'If we get split up, meet there.'

Rayan's gaze had crystallised to golden sapphires, the muscles around his neck coiled with tension. His fists, clenched by his thighs, carved contours up his forearms. Though his beard had thickened over the last few days, it did nothing to soften the jagged edge of his jaw. Set with determination, it vanquished all of the warmth that Lettle had come to know. This was not the man who sang while he cooked – here was a soldier, poised to fight for his life.

Feeling her eyes on him, he turned to her.

'Give me your hand.' It was a command that in any other circumstance Lettle would have baulked at, but here, with panic threatening to surge up from her stomach, she reached out to him.

As their fingers latticed together, he squeezed her hand.

Yeeran nodded to them both, a signal to begin their flight.

That was all the warning Lettle was given before Rayan launched forward into a run, pulling her with him.

There was a jarring second when the world tilted and Lettle's vision burst with black spots as her whole body struck something solid.

It took a moment for Lettle to realise she had fallen. She blinked away the starbursts from her sight and sat up. Yeeran had already recovered and was crouching a few feet away, her hands pressed against an invisible barrier.

'Fae magic,' Lettle whispered.

'No, it can't be.' Rayan sprang to her side, his hands pressed to the sky above.

Lettle watched him circle their small camp, ascertaining the width and breadth of the boundary. Yeeran followed him in the opposite direction before she turned to Lettle to voice her chilling conclusion.

'We're trapped.'

CHAPTER TWELVE

Yeeran

'What's the plan, Colonel?' Rayan said under his breath. They were on the march again after the fae had left them in the invisible cage all night. No matter how hard the elves had thrown themselves against the boundary, the magic the fae used had remained steadfast, and all they had gained were bruises and a poor night's sleep.

The path the fae now led them on wound through the rocks and swampland. Rayan had slowed his pace incrementally over the morning until he was almost level with Yeeran. The fae didn't seem to notice, or if they did, they let the elves talk quietly between themselves.

Because they know we can't escape. Yeeran quashed the intrusive thought.

Lettle walked on ahead, though from the way her head was angled, Yeeran knew she was listening to Rayan and Yeeran's conversation.

'I . . . I'm not sure. We're outnumbered, and outmatched. They have the geographical advantage in this place, we have no means of further support or diplomatic immunity . . . we didn't even know fae existed until yesterday. We have no idea where they're taking us.'

Yeeran felt tendrils of helplessness tighten across her chest. Rayan and Lettle expected her to have the answers, but she was coming up empty.

'Mosima,' Lettle said softly.

'What?'

'We're going to Mosima. It's the land where the last human banished the fae.'

Yeeran snorted. It drew the attention of one of their guards, Hosta, who looked their way. They scowled when they caught Yeeran's gaze on them. She dipped her head until she felt their eyes divert.

'That's just a faerytale, Lettle.'

Lettle turned her head, her expression stony.

'Look around, Yeeran. This isn't a faerytale.'

Yeeran let her gaze slip to the leader of the group. She was walking up an incline towards the noon-day sun, the rays burnishing her hair golden like the dress she wore. Her lithe figure cast a shadow on the procession that followed. She was the head of the snake, with fangs to match.

Yeeran let out a heavy sigh.

'What do you know of Mosima?'

Lettle didn't speak for a minute, and in that time, she managed to stumble twice. Grace was not a quality Lettle possessed. Neither was balance.

Rayan reached out as if to help her, forgetting his own bound hands.

'I don't need your help,' Yeeran heard Lettle mutter, her dark skin flushed.

The path narrowed, jagged rocks pressing up from the earth on either side of them. Yeeran strained to hear her sister speak.

'The fae were banished to Mosima for crimes against the humans. Cursed to a realm no one could enter, nor could they escape.'

'Well, they got out somehow,' Yeeran grunted. 'How is it they roam this close to the Elven Lands without Crescent knowing, without *any of us knowing*?'

Yeeran's questioning was cut short as the procession came to a standstill. She tried to peer over Rayan's shoulder to see what was happening.

'Why have we stopped?'

'I don't know,' Rayan replied. 'Lettle? Can you see anything up ahead?'

'The leader has disappeared down a cave . . . oh no . . . I think we're going in there.'

The group started moving again and soon Yeeran was at the mouth of the cavern. Darkness consumed them ten steps in, but the fae walked on with sure steps.

The tunnel, because that was what it appeared to be, smelled of moss and river water. Yeeran ran her fingers across it. The walls were thick with moss.

How can moss grow without sunlight? She was dragged from her thoughts a moment later as she saw a warm hue of light up ahead.

'Sunlight,' Lettle confirmed unnecessarily.

The glow grew brighter the closer they got until it blinded them. It took a minute for Yeeran to make out the curves of Furi's body in the light. She stood at the end of the tunnel, her eyebrows knotted in concentration, her hands splayed outwards. Berro ushered the prisoners past her and onto a platform at the top of a set of steps.

Yeeran's skin itched, and her stomach lurched forward as she passed the golden woman. The smell of moss and river water disappeared, and the quality of the air seemed fresher, colder. It was as if she had crossed an invisible barrier into a new world.

'Welcome to Mosima,' Berro said from the top of her obeah. As she moved out of the way the three elves saw their new prison for the first time.

Lettle let out a soft 'oh' beside Yeeran. It encapsulated all Yeeran felt.

They had thought the light was sunlight, but they were still underground. Red stone marked the edges of a great dome, so vast Yeeran could only just see the far end of it. The light shone from a globe in the centre that brightened the world like the sun.

'It's fraedia,' Lettle breathed.

And she was right. It was a huge deposit of fraedia crystal growing from the top of the dome's roof. Enough of the gemstone to feed the entirety of the Waning district for the rest of their lives. Enough to end the Forever War.

This was information that Salawa needed to know.

Yeeran let her gaze roam over the city below. Plants teemed from stone buildings and across walkways. Vines lined roads and twirled up trees that shaded gardens. Fae children ran through fields of sugarcane and swam in a river that wound through the centre. Bees and songbirds flew in the sky, making their way to hives and nests in the walls of the great cavern. There was no breeze, but the air smelled sweet like honeysuckle and mead.

'This is a utopia,' Yeeran said, trying to voice her awe.

She cast her gaze out further and noticed a patch of agricultural land that seemed darker than the rest, the ground black, the plants there withered and decaying.

'You see that?' Yeeran whispered to Lettle.

'Yeah, looks like the ground's been poisoned.'

There was a sigh and Furi slumped in the corner of Yeeran's vision. Her obeah was there to lend his strength. She leaned heavily on the beast and Yeeran wondered again at the significance of their connection.

The leader's eyes locked on Yeeran's with a weary malice. The fraedia lit her like a flame, shining across her brassy skin, while casting her profile in shadow.

Yeeran didn't think she'd seen anything more beautiful.

Then she spoke. 'Enjoy the view. It's the last you'll ever see.'

With that, Furi turned her obeah away and walked with him down the steps into the centre of Mosima.

The fae led them down the shallow staircase carved into the rock face towards the belly of the city.

When they reached the bottom Yeeran saw that Lettle was shaking from the effort. Rayan's bound hands were supporting her lower back.

'That was a lot of steps,' Lettle said weakly.

'Yes, it's been a long day. We all need rest.' Yeeran shot a dark look towards Furi. She sensed Yeeran's gaze and walked over with a swagger that reminded Yeeran of the young soldiers in the Waning Army's training yard. Those who had the arrogance and skill for battle, but not the experience.

'Berro,' Furi barked, then pointed to Rayan and Lettle. 'Take those two to our *guest quarters*.'

The way she said 'guest quarters' did not sound welcoming.

'You can't separate us.' Lettle pressed herself to Yeeran's side like an anchor.

'Where I go, she goes,' Yeeran confirmed.

Furi looked at her and sneered.

Then Yeeran saw a spark and the next thing she knew she was being pulled to the ground with the strength of a whip of nine tails. She hissed as the magic bit into the back of her knees.

Lettle and Rayan were being dragged away by Berro and the rest of the fae soldiers. Though they both buckled against the restraints, there was no stopping the magic of the fae.

Lettle and Yeeran locked eyes and though no magic passed between them Yeeran could feel Lettle's thoughts as if they were her own.

I will find you again.

Yeeran was still kneeling in the dirt, Furi's magic woven around her legs. She looked up as Furi came to stand above her, blocking out the fraedia light.

'Now it's just you and me.'

Her words sounded like a promise of pain to come.

Furi kept her close as she walked, and Yeeran found herself wondering if she could fight her way out of the situation. But being this near to her, Yeeran could see the strength of the muscles that twined their way around her biceps and forearm. The fae's posture was taut, battle-ready, and though she wore no weapon, she wielded her pride like the threads of her magic, ready to ensnare you with the strength of her disdain.

The streets on the edge of the city were empty, the red-brick houses vacant and abandoned, unlike the bustling city Yeeran had seen from above.

They walked through the tree-lined roads until they stopped at a building with metal railings on the windows, though most of the glass had been smashed.

As Yeeran stepped through the broken door frame she coughed and brought a bound hand to her mouth to mask the scent of mould and damp. The prison was in even more disrepair on the inside. Yeeran could see four cells with roofs caved in, and another without bars.

They don't have visitors often, if ever. The thought swirled in her mind. *Maybe that is how they kept hidden all this time.*

One of the guards had reached the prison before Yeeran and Furi. They saluted their leader by fanning a hand and pressing it against their forehead.

'The second cell is ready, Commander. What do you want me to do with their packs?'

'Leave them here, Hosta. I want to show them to the queens.'

Hosta dipped their head, and when they straightened, their eyes landed on Yeeran, their stare full of loathing. The irises were a deep blue, like two bruises made all the more striking by the contrast with their black skin.

'It would be my pleasure to attend you at the trial, Commander.'

'Thank you, Hosta.' Furi looked more distrustful than thankful. 'But it will be a closed court. For now, return to the barracks.'

Hosta saluted again before leaving. They couldn't have been older than seventeen.

Once Hosta left, Yeeran was tugged forward by a strand of Furi's magic until she was behind the metal bars of one of the few cells still standing.

The inside of the prison was lit by a hanging fraedia crystal. The gemstone glowed yellow during the light of the day, just like the sun. It was why the substance was so valuable. To have this much hanging in a decrepit old building meant they had a lot of fraedia in reserve.

So much that it isn't even precious . . . it is common, the thought bewildered her.

Furi locked the door of the cell and turned to leave. The magic around Yeeran's wrists released.

'Wait. I have a proposal,' Yeeran called.

Furi didn't turn around, but she paused.

'Please, just give me two minutes of your time.' Yeeran wasn't sure where she was going with this, but she knew she needed to keep Furi here, because Furi clearly had power in this land.

Furi's shoulders tensed, and her voice came out low and deadly. 'What gives you the right to think you have any voice here?'

'Well . . . I'm a colonel of the Waning district, I have significant influence in—' The lie choked her throat.

Furi turned, her lip curling upwards.

'I ask you again, what value do you bring?'

Yeeran ground her teeth. It was rare someone other than Lettle could stoke the flames of Yeeran's anger so quickly.

'If you would let me *speak.*'

Furi interrupted once more, but this time with a light laugh that seemed more hurtful than the scorn of her words.

Yeeran clamped her lips shut.

Furi waved a limp hand in her direction.

'Speak then, for I have things to do.'

'Free Rayan and Lettle. Let them return to the Elven Lands and spread the word that obeah are not to be killed. I understand that they are steeds to you, or perhaps more than that, a deity of some sort?'

The fae's nose wrinkled ever so delicately. Yeeran continued, 'They were not involved in harvesting the beast that day. I alone killed the animal, I alone hunted it.'

Furi still wore her sardonic smile.

'Who are the others to you?'

'The younger one is my sister. The other is my captain.'

Furi tilted her head to the side. It reminded Yeeran of a cat. Or maybe an obeah.

'Captain?'

'He helps me lead my soldiers in war.'

'Ah, I see. We don't have captains, just commanders. Like me.'

Yeeran filed away this piece of information for Salawa. The more intelligence she could gather on their warfare, the greater the Waning Army's advantage for when they came for the fraedia crystal.

Because come for it we must.

They wouldn't have to mine a lot of it, just a quarter of what the fae had hanging from the sky would do.

Furi moved away from Yeeran towards the shadows of the prison to retrieve something. 'We had no idea fae existed any more,' Yeeran called. 'You have not been seen in centuries.'

'A millennium,' Furi said from the far corner of the room.

There was a soft inhale of breath as Furi brought into the fraedia light the object she was looking for. It was Yeeran's drum.

Furi was careful not to touch the drumskin as she laid it down on the ground next to the bars of the cell door. Her lips were drawn back showing the sharpness of her canines.

'This . . . abomination . . . is what you kill us for?'

Yeeran didn't comprehend.

Furi circled the drum as if ready to pounce.

'It is what we hunt obeah for, yes . . . to create weapons to aid us in the Forever War.'

Furi hissed, 'I care not for the trivialities of your war.'

You asked. Though Yeeran wanted to voice the thought, she bit her tongue. It wouldn't help get Lettle and Rayan out of here.

'If you let Rayan and Lettle free, I'll confess willingly. You said there is to be a trial? Well, let me make it easy for you.'

But Furi was no longer listening. Her eyes were focused on the black drumskin. She reached a shaking hand towards it. As her fingers brushed the surface she grimaced before clutching her hand back against her chest.

'Needless murder, for this. A magic-wielding weapon, so primitive and crass—'

'I think you'll find drumfire is the most effective use of obeah skin. Though, the Crescent tribe might disagree, as they prefer to fletch their arrows . . .' Yeeran trailed off, realising Furi was not listening. The fae was quivering, from heel to head. The soft light highlighted her gentle beauty; she looked vulnerable, haunted, her full lips slightly parted.

Yeeran had the strange urge to comfort her and shifted forward.

Furi whipped around, a spark igniting from her hand as an invisible wire wrapped around Yeeran's throat, pulling her up against the bars of the cell until her lips were pressed painfully against the cool metal.

Furi hadn't been scared, no, she'd been shaking in anger.

The thread of magic tightened and tightened around Yeeran's neck.

'You make demands of me?'

And tightened and tightened.

'You, who have killed my kin?'

And tightened and tightened.

Furi stepped forward, close enough for Yeeran to feel the breath on her cheek. Just the iron beams separating their lips.

'I cannot wait to see you condemned for the murder of a prince of the fae.' Tears overflowed out of Furi's amber eyes and onto her cheeks. She turned away.

The magic loosened around Yeeran's throat, and she gasped for air.

'I don't understand,' she choked out. 'I killed an obeah, not a prince.'

Furi looked ready to throttle her again, but Yeeran needed to know the truth.

'The obeah are bound to us, you fool. In killing one you kill the other.'

Realisation hit Yeeran's skin like a cold shower. Her eyes widened as she looked at her drum in shocked realisation.

'For every drumskin . . .' Yeeran murmured, but she couldn't finish the sentence.

Furi's eyes were ablaze, their golden warmth more like fire than anything else.

'You will be executed, and your sister can watch. Just like I had to watch you murdering my brother.'

Furi strode out of the prison leaving Yeeran with her thoughts.

All the obeah murdered over the years. All the fae killed.

Yeeran stumbled backwards from the door until the back of her legs touched the straw pallet in the corner. A trough of grey water and a metal chamber pot made up the contents of the rest of her prison.

She dropped her head into her hands, but before panic could consume her there was a noise from the cell opposite hers. A shadow shifted on the edge of the fraedia light.

Then it spoke. 'Welcome to the last days of your life.'

CHAPTER THIRTEEN

Lettle

L ettle was not going to leave Yeeran in the hands of Furi.

She got two bites into Berro's forearm before she was gagged again. She was then dragged the rest of the way to their new destination by two of the three guards that had accompanied them. Rayan had stopped struggling soon after leaving Yeeran.

They were led to a small cottage that overlooked a river.

Berro released her gag once they were inside. Lettle yelped at the spasm of pain in her left arm as the magic chains also fell away.

'Such small teeth,' Berro said, inspecting the bite marks.

Lettle hissed and lunged at her, but Rayan held her back.

'You'll just get hurt.'

She turned her ire on him.

'We left Yeeran alone with their leader!'

Rayan didn't engage with her wrath. Instead he turned to Berro. 'What is to happen to the colonel? To Yeeran?'

Berro's gaze travelled up and down Rayan's body for a beat longer than was polite.

'It's a shame it wasn't you who bit me . . .'

Lettle broke free of Rayan's grasp, but the door closed before she could get to Berro and wring her neck.

Lettle tried the handle, but despite the ominous sound of a lock clicking she didn't give up. She yanked on it with all her strength.

Nothing happened.

A second later it opened to the frowning face of a guard.

'Stop that.'

Lettle pressed her nose into the crack of the door.

'Let me out of here.'

The guard didn't even bother to respond. He shut the door with a bang.

'It's probably sealed with magic, Lettle.' Rayan said her name quietly, as if to soothe her.

It didn't help and she balled her hands into fists until she felt her nails dig painfully into her skin. She breathed heavily through her nose and turned to Rayan.

He was lying down on the only bed in the room, his hands tucked behind his head, his eyes slitted as he watched her.

'How can you be relaxing when Yeeran is out there . . . with that woman?'

Rayan pushed himself onto his elbows and moved over on the bed.

'I'm not relaxing, I'm thinking. Come and join me.'

Lettle pressed her lips into a tight line.

Thinking was too still for her. She needed to move, needed to try to get back to her sister.

Lettle went to the wicker cupboard in the corner. She began to rummage in it, pulling out anything and everything she could find. There were dresses in bright mangoes and luscious creams. Some studded with gems and others lined with linen. They all had the slightly musty smell of having been worn before, but Lettle barely noticed that. She checked through pockets and linings with practised hands, trying to find anything in them that could aid her in escape. And when she'd exhausted that avenue to no avail, she pressed her hands into the seams of the wood panels at the back. But they didn't budge.

'Move,' she commanded Rayan.

'What is it?'

'Move, I want to check the bed.'

'Can I help—'

Lettle shrugged him away and lifted the mattress with strength driven by fury. The bed itself was smooth polished wood, and the mattress was stuffed with down and not springs.

She stripped the sheets, hoping, praying, there was something hidden under the covers. It was only when she came up empty-handed, tangled among the woven cotton, that she realised she was crying.

Rayan was beside her in a moment.

He wrapped his arms around her shoulders, pulling her close. His calloused hands rubbed up and down her forearms leaving the skin there tingling.

When the sobs ceased, she looked up at him, red-eyed and miserable. The intensity of his gaze made the breath hitch in her throat. She had to fight the instinct to stop breathing.

Rayan noticed too, and the hands that had been rubbing her forearms paused. His lips parted and he uttered a single word.

'Lettle . . .'

There was a rap on the door and the two of them sprang apart, the moment gone.

A fae they hadn't met before entered the room. He was tall with braids that hung to the back of his knees. His proud nose was studded with a gold ring, his eyes lidded with gold powder. The smile he gave Lettle as he walked in was mischievous and more than a little alluring. His stubble was so precise, there was not one hair out of place. As Lettle followed the flow of braids and jewellery she noticed that one of his legs was entirely encased in gold and silver with a hinge where his knee would have been.

There were many people with disabilities in the Elven Lands – war stole limbs and fractured minds – but this was the first time Lettle had seen any replacement leg quite as beautiful as this one. It swirled around the top of his thigh like metal lace, ending with a matching leather boot.

In one hand the fae held a cane that he used to support his steps. In the other he held a cotton bag.

'What happened here?' His voice was just as Lettle expected it to be, syrup with a little spice. He quirked an eyebrow at the sheets and mattress in disarray.

Lettle put a hand on her hip, unabashed by the intruder.

'Who are you and what do you want?'

The fae laughed, seemingly amused rather than annoyed by Lettle's directness.

'I'm Golan, and I'm here to make you ready for an audience with the queens.'

'We look fine as we are,' Rayan said. He was watching the space between Lettle and Golan warily.

There was a tap as Golan stamped his cane on the ground with a snort.

'You look like you've been dragged through the sewers several times and, forgive me, my lady, but you look even worse.'

Lettle snarled, 'I don't give a shit. Where is my sister?'

Golan's shoulders tensed almost imperceptibly. He knew something.

'I'm afraid I've no idea. I'm here to sort you two out. And first things first, you need a bath.'

'There's no bath here,' Lettle growled.

Golan's chuckle was deep and throaty.

'Oh, you really are elves, aren't you?' He walked forward across the bedroom and stopped in front of a flagstone with a bubble carved into it. Lettle hadn't noticed it before now.

Golan pressed his cane down on one side of it and there was a click. He bent down and lifted the flagstone to the side, revealing a set of marble steps.

'Come on, then.' Golan beckoned to them.

They were both too intrigued to disobey, so Lettle followed Golan down the stairs, Rayan a pace behind her.

Steam curled its way up from a glittering pool built into the rich red earth of Mosima. Clusters of a dark green plant grew around the water, blooming with a purple flower.

'Water peonies,' Golan said, noticing where Lettle was looking.

Glittering lights covered the cavern ceiling, shining like the night sky and casting the room in a warm light.

'And those are gleam anemones. They are bioluminescent. They light up the entire network of hot springs throughout Mosima.' He pointed to the narrow tunnel leading out of the pool that went on to feed other bathhouses.

Lettle swallowed and Golan gave her a genuine smile.

'I'll leave you two here for a little while. The water peonies' leaves will lather if you rub them between your hands.'

He began to leave, then added, 'Please do wash well. I don't like working on a dirty canvas.'

Lettle didn't let the silence brew. Instead, she pulled off all her clothes without a glance at Rayan. She walked past him towards the stone steps that lowered into the pool. The water was warmer than she expected, and she couldn't help the groan that slipped out of her as she immersed herself in the shallows.

For a second every concern fled her mind. She wasn't a prisoner in a faerytale land. Her sister wasn't entrapped with a dangerous leader of the fae. Lettle was just there, in the luminous pool, present in the moment.

She dipped her head down and under. When she emerged, she tilted her chin to the ceiling, the gleam anemones lighting the droplets on her skin silver. Her chest parted the water as she lay backwards, baring her navel to the ceiling.

Lettle was unashamed. She had always been comfortable in her body. There was a splash as Rayan joined her in the pool.

The hot spring wasn't overly large, and Lettle knew that if she just stretched a little more, she'd collide with Rayan's . . . parts.

This is not the time to be distracted, she chastised herself. They needed a plan to get out of Mosima.

Lettle cleared her throat.

'Do you think we can fit through the tunnel? To the other bath-houses?'

Rayan swam over to where the water flowed and inspected it.

'No, I don't think anything bigger than an eel would fit through there.'

'Oh.'

Yet another idea dashed.

'Do you think they filter the water?' Rayan muttered. 'Or are we swimming in the entirety of Mosima's filth?'

'It smells clean, it looks clean.'

She tried to stand up and slipped, not realising the pool grew deeper further in. Not being quite the height of the average fae and elf, she couldn't stay above the surface without treading water.

Rayan reached out to steady her and grazed her breasts as he grabbed her forearm. Both of them ignored it.

She stretched out her left arm as far as she could and began massaging it from top to bottom. The warmth of the water eased the pain in the atrophied muscles.

Rayan's eyes glittered as he watched.

'The wasting pox,' she answered his unasked question.

'That's not what I was thinking,' he said. There was a heat in his eyes that kindled a warmth in her core.

Lettle moved to the pool's edge and plucked a few leaves from a water peony. She rubbed her hands together, lathering the sap. It worked quite effectively.

Neither of them spoke again as they cleaned. When Rayan was done, he rose from the water and went to grab the towel Golan had left for them.

Lettle's eyes lingered on his hip bone, refusing to stray.

She dipped her head under the water in an attempt to extinguish the growing flames between them.

When she surfaced, he was gone, only wet footprints on the stairs remained.

Golan dressed Lettle in a fine silk dress with sleeves that fell to the ground. It was gossamer, like the rest of the fae attire she'd seen, but with a thicker woven pattern across the bust and below the waist that swirled in shades of maroon. She ran her hand over the embellishment.

'Each weaver gives meaning to the pattern of their clothing. This one is called "to have courage when given none".'

Lettle looked up sharply to see if Golan was being condescending, but his gaze was open and warm. He had chosen this pattern to give her strength, not to mock her. She found herself liking him. It annoyed her.

Golan inspected her cornrows.

'Your hair needs rebraiding, but we don't have time for that,' he tutted as he began to twist her hair into a bun.

'Usually my sister does it.' Lettle was defensive. 'But you've taken her away.'

'So I hear.' Golan's plump lips snapped shut. No matter how much Lettle tried to goad him, he didn't offer up anything on Yeeran.

This close to him she could see that his beard had been drawn on in fine ink. He saw her looking.

'Not all men can grow beards like him.' Golan lifted his eyebrows in the direction of Rayan. 'I prefer to draw mine on than drink the tincture that aids in its growth.'

'Melury root?' she named one of the herbs that increased hormone levels in the Elven Lands.

'Yes, do you have some botany skills?'

'A little.'

They have some of the same plants as us, Lettle mused. *And like the Elven Lands, Mosima celebrates gender of choice. I wonder what other similarities we share.*

'Anyway, I find melury root a little bothersome on the guts. But I think this looks better anyway.' He smiled, tilting his face left and right.

Lettle nodded. It *did* look good, and she found herself wondering how the style would suit Rayan. She turned to him. Rayan's face was screwed up in thought.

'Why do you have two queens?' Rayan asked. He had been slowly probing Golan for details about Mosima.

'Our god was born a bat with two heads: when the sun shines one face lights the earth, and when darkness reigns, the other face looks down on the world. So, when Mosima was created, we were tied to the dual reign of the Jani dynasty. The two sisters Queen Vyce and Queen Chall currently sit on the thrones.'

Rayan leaned forward on his chair. He wore linen trousers and an open silk shirt that showed the curves of his stomach muscles.

She jerked, causing Golan to smudge some of her make-up.

'Stay *still*,' he scolded.

Rayan continued, 'But who's in charge?'

'Both of them. They reign in tandem. If one dies then the next chosen are put on the throne.'

Lettle snorted, imagining what it would be like to share a throne with Yeeran. They'd bicker incessantly.

'Close your eyes,' Golan commanded Lettle. She barely had time to do as she was bidden before a brush was swept across her eyelids.

When Golan was done, he held her at arm's length.

'There,' he said with a triumphant smile. 'I knew that lilac shimmer would bring out the violet of your eyes. Doesn't she look wonderful?'

Lettle looked to Rayan and his expression grew tender.

'She does,' he said quietly. Then his gaze slipped away from hers and he turned to Golan with more questions.

'So, how are the next monarchs chosen? And what happens if there isn't a sibling?'

'They're chosen from the wider Jani dynasty.' Golan indicated for Rayan to stand, and he looped a thin maroon belt around his waist. 'There, that's what was missing. Now you look like a matching pair.'

Lettle bristled.

'I'm not sure why we need to be dressed up in such finery just to see the queens. Aren't we prisoners?' Rayan grumbled.

Golan's expression turned clouded, and he spoke a simple truth.

Perhaps the first truth he had given them. 'Power. You are elves dressed as fae. Humbled, cowed.' He looked away, his lip quivering.

Lettle felt dread coil around the pain in her left arm and branch across her ribs to her heart.

The door to the cottage swung open and Berro stood in the fraedia light next to her obeah.

'Time to go.'

Golan grinned, the ghost of his last words gone. 'Just in time.'

'Where's Yeeran?' Lettle rounded on Berro.

'She doesn't say much else, does she, Lightless?' Berro said to Golan.

Golan shook his head with a sad smile.

'Lightless? I thought your name was Golan?'

Berro laughed, not cruelly.

'Lightless isn't his name, it's his *condition*.'

Golan winced.

'It means I'm not faebound. I never bonded to an obeah.'

'Like elves – all of you are Lightless,' Berro said with pity. Then she spotted Rayan. 'Shined up nice.'

She winked at him and Lettle ground her teeth.

Golan gave them an apologetic look as they were ushered out of the door.

Berro led them through throngs of fae weaving between tree-lined streets. It would be so easy to slip away. The two guards at their back could be distracted, the crowds a perfect getaway. Even Berro's obeah was facing forward, away from the elves. She was about to say that to Rayan when Berro snapped something in fae to the guards and Lettle felt the grip of magic bind her wrists once more. The fae gave her a cheeky grin.

'Don't even think about it,' Berro said, reverting to elvish.

Fae began to notice them after that, parting as the prisoners and the guards moved towards the peaked turrets in the distance.

Lettle ignored the whispers and the glances at her. The light from the fraedia was warm on her cheeks. Despite their dire circumstances she felt fresher than she had in days.

Rayan was lingering in Berro's shadow, and it irked her.

'What did Golan mean, about being faebound?' he asked her.

Berro was looking at him with a small smirk on her lips. Lettle could see she was debating whether to answer.

'The obeah,' she eventually said. 'Anytime between the age of twelve and thirty we become faebound. Our lives are intertwined with that of our obeah. We can share thoughts.'

Berro patted her obeah's side.

'Sanq here wants you to know she can break your spine with her horns if you try and flee.'

Rayan's brow furrowed. 'But surely being bound to an obeah is a bad thing? It makes you more vulnerable in battle.'

Lettle rolled her eyes. Of course, his thoughts always went back to combat. But she inched closer, trying to hear the rest of the conversation.

'No, being faebound gives us power. Once tied to an obeah, we can use magic.'

Lettle was tugged forward by a magic thread.

'No one likes an eavesdropper,' Berro said to her.

Lettle's nostrils flared, but she offered no retort. Rayan was getting helpful information and she didn't want to risk ending the conversation.

Berro's hand twirled through the thicker black fur of her obeah's ruff.

'And with fae magic, comes the fae language.'

'What?' This interested Lettle and she ended her vow of silence. Despite not going to school, she had found her inner scholar during her training in divination.

'Yes, the fae language comes to us fully formed once bound to an obeah. Some of the Lightless have managed to teach themselves how to speak fae, but it's a very difficult language, and some of the sounds don't come naturally unless you are bonded.'

'Language separates those bound to an obeah and those not?'
Lettle's mind was reeling about the ramifications of a society
constrained so. 'How does it affect education? News circulation?
Legislation?'

Berro gave her a sour look and Rayan let out a heavy sigh.

'Enough. This way,' Berro said, leading them towards a square
that was filled with people. The audience was facing a stone dais in
front of two wooden doors circled with rose vines.

Lettle had once tried to cultivate roses in their small patch of dirt
in the village. The only thing that had grown successfully were
dandelions. She'd been proud of them until Yeeran had told her the
flowers were just weeds.

'Where is Yeeran? Will she be here?' she asked.

'She will.' Berro sounded distracted, bored almost.

'Lettle . . .' Rayan's voice was urgent.

Then she heard the whispers.

'Execution . . . Execution . . . Execution . . .'

Why did she feel so sick all of a sudden?

Perhaps it was because the truth was trying to come out.

'Where is Yeeran?' Lettle asked again urgently.

Berro's grin was full of satisfaction. 'You'll be able to see your
sister soon enough. It's her execution after all.'

Lettle screamed.

CHAPTER FOURTEEN

Yeeran

Yeeran's cellmate shifted into the light.

The first thing she noticed was his flattened canines, gleaming like stars in a night sky face. The man was an elf. His green eyes crinkled as he smiled at Yeeran, his expression open and kindly. She thought he was around sixty years old, perhaps a little older.

'So, you killed the prince of Mosima?' he said.

'That's what they say,' Yeeran said, barely containing the anguish from her tone.

She rubbed her eyes and sat down on the straw pallet.

'What did you do to be imprisoned?'

The man was silent for a minute, then he spoke, his voice grave.

'I found them.'

'What?'

'I came across a scouting camp in the Wasted Marshes. At first, I thought they were nomadic elves. There had been rumours in Crescent for some time that there were elves free of the constraints of the Forever War in the east.'

He's Crescent tribe. Yeeran let out a low hiss between her teeth. The man continued as if he hadn't heard.

'When I realised they weren't elves, I followed them back to Mosima. They captured me and sentenced me to this prison. That was ten years ago.'

'*Ten* years?'

'Thereabouts. I try to keep track by marking the wall, but I'm sure I've missed some days.'

Yeeran stood and began to pace.

'But there must be a way out of here. The foundations of the prison don't seem too solid—'

The man let out a soft laugh.

'I've tried it all.' His voice was devoid of emotion.

And devoid of the fight, she thought to herself. *But I cannot give up. To give up is to commit Lettle to her fate. To give up is to die.*

There was a crunch and Yeeran jumped. She thought at first the man was eating bugs.

'Pistachios,' he confirmed. 'The food that grows here is better than anything I've ever had.'

'I wouldn't know, they've only fed me dried fruit and water.'

He grunted.

'I suppose, why waste food on someone they're going to execute. Here.'

He rolled over a handful of nuts through the prison bars.

Yeeran, overwhelmed by his kindness, felt her eyes begin to heat.

'Thank you . . .'

'Komi, my name's Komi.'

'Yeeran.'

They crunched their nuts in silence for a little while and Yeeran had to admit, they did taste very good. But Yeeran wasn't ready for this to be her last meal. She inspected the bars of her prison.

'Why is it that they use iron here, but not the magic they used to ensnare us on the road?' she asked.

'Aha, they used a threaded cage?'

'Sure, if that's what it's called.'

'Made of magic, invisible to the eye, but impossible to cross?'

Yeeran nodded.

'Sounds like it.'

'That takes a considerable amount of magic to sustain. You need to not only weave the magic without gaps, but you must maintain the flow. Did they change guard often?'

'Every two or three hours.'

'Yes, yes. They will have been transferring the flow of magic, so no one got too exhausted.'

'And the only way to use fae magic is by being bound to an obeah?'

'Yes,' Komi said simply. 'Once faebound, they can speak the fae language, use magic, and in turn, the obeah's fur goes from brown to black.'

Obeah elders are just beasts that are bonded to a fae . . . Salawa needs this information.

'What about the fraedia? It's the largest deposit I've ever seen,' she asked.

Komi nodded. 'Yes. They call it "the fray". They believe that their god granted them a slice of the sun as a gift to allow Mosima to prosper. Little do they know the riches that shine above them.'

'Indeed.'

'So it was the commander who found you? Over the body of the prince?' Komi asked.

Yeeran shook the image of the obeah's lifeblood from her mind; she wasn't ready to face the guilt there.

'Why is she called commander, and not princess? If she is the sister of the prince I killed?'

'Furi is a princess, but her title of commander supersedes it. Though when she becomes queen, that role will eclipse all others. And now, Furi *will* be queen as there are only two children of the Jani dynasty left to inherit the throne.'

Yeeran paced the length of her cell, her thoughts heavy.

'Did Furi say that you arrived with your sister?' Komi asked.

Yeeran closed her eyes and let out a slow breath. 'Yes.'

'I'm sorry.'

'So am I.'

She wondered what Lettle was doing and if she was safe.

'Is she older or younger?'

'Six years younger . . . though I forget that means she's twenty-eight. We were apart for a few years, and she stayed with my father – I called him father, but really, he was only hers. Still, he was the one who raised me.'

'Yes, most elves have lost parents on the battlefield.'

Yeeran nodded. She'd lost two. She shook the decades-long grief from her mind.

'How is it that the fae have survived for so long without anyone knowing?'

Komi shrugged.

'All I know is what I have pieced together from Hosta, the guard who was here earlier.'

Yeeran scowled, remembering the bloodthirsty look in their eyes. They wanted Yeeran to suffer.

Komi laughed and waved a hand in her direction.

'Oh, Hosta is not that bad. A little excitable maybe, but they're young and so have to prove themselves twice as hard in the eyes of the faeguard.'

'So, the faeguard is the name of their army?'

Komi's grin grew.

'Were you a captain or a colonel?'

'Colonel. You?'

He didn't answer, instead he just shook his head sadly, his long locs swaying.

'It all seems so long ago,' he whispered, quiet enough that Yeeran knew he was speaking to himself.

Am I feeling sorry for one of the Crescent tribe?

Yeeran splayed her fingers across her temples and moved away from the bars of the cell. If he didn't want to talk, she wouldn't push him. Isolation could be detrimental to a person's mind. She'd interviewed enough prisoners of war to know.

'I'm not the same person I was back then,' Komi said, his voice calling Yeeran back.

Then a wicked grin spread across his cheeks, lifting his heavy beard. 'How many of my tribe did you kill?'

'Not enough,' Yeeran answered honestly.

He laughed, and though dry, it seemed to transform him.

'Yes, I suppose not. Either way, we're on the same side now.'

'That we are.'

Yeeran tapped the iron bars with her boot.

'Our faerytales made real. I'm surprised they haven't eaten you.'

Again, Komi laughed, and it lightened the bleakness of Yeeran's situation.

'The trickster fae, wicked fae, who killed all the last humans on earth? They may be wicked sometimes, but no more wicked than us.'

Yeeran sighed, 'I suppose the stories weren't just stories but histories. As here we are in Mosima.'

'Here we are in Mosima.'

They each returned to their thoughts.

Yeeran didn't realise she had fallen asleep until there was a loud bang by her head that startled her awake.

At first Yeeran thought she'd carried her dreams to her waking mind, as the person in front of her couldn't be real. Hair that fell in waves to her navel, streaked with sunlight. Eyes like a cat lined with white make-up that accentuated her feline features. Her lips were glossed in a deep brown that brought out the amber in the centre of her irises. The dress she wore was simple but exuded quality. It was butter yellow lined with gold chains and sleeves that billowed outwards. The waist of the dress was cinched in by the chest plate that she wore, the rising sun of the faeguard blazing in the centre.

Yeeran savoured her desire before she realised who it was, and her lust turned bitter.

'Furi,' Yeeran growled.

'Get up, it's time to meet the queens.' Then she smiled so cruelly Yeeran flinched. 'It's time for your sentencing.'

*   *   *

Yeeran was led through the streets flanked by four fae riding their obeah. Furi took the lead. Even though she walked, she seemed taller than those who rode. Yeeran stoked the coals of her frustration and projected it at her back.

Furi turned, as if sensing Yeeran's hatred. She smirked, her glossy lips parting.

If Yeeran's hands were free she would have let loose a punch just to wipe the smile off her face.

No, anger solves nothing. Yeeran schooled her features back to neutral. Furi's smile slipped, and she glanced away. It seemed to gall her to see Yeeran unaffected by her mockery.

Yeeran drew her attention away from Furi and back to her surroundings. If she managed to get out of here alive, she wanted to be able to give a full report to the chieftain.

I'll come back to you, my love, with something more precious than an obeah – the truth.

The fae's red-brick houses seemed to be made out of the same stone as the walls of the cavern. The homes were spacious, with arched windows that looked out onto the paved streets. Yeeran caught a few faces pressed to the glass as she was marched past. And the faces looked no different to the elves in Gural. All shapes and sizes, colours, and genders, some with long hair, some with short. It was only when they drew back their lips that there was anything different.

Canines made to rip out throats. That's what she'd always been taught. But as a young girl ran out into the street chasing an obeah cub and laughing, Yeeran found she could no longer give credence to the faerytales.

The walk was a long one, and Yeeran wondered if parading her before the gathering crowds was part of Furi's attempt to humiliate her. But Yeeran didn't mind, she'd already undergone the worst humiliation possible. The slits through her ears had begun to heal over, making the cutting permanent.

Maybe I can stitch them back together when I go home.

The thought was a futile one, but Yeeran still clung to the shred of hope it gave her.

She was led over a wooden bridge that crossed the turquoise river Yeeran had seen from the top of the cavern. It teemed with fish that a few fae were catching and releasing on the riverbank below. They stopped and watched Yeeran as she passed.

Yeeran looked away from them and towards the arable land being cultivated on the rolling hills in the distance. She could just see the shadows of the blackened fields she'd first seen from the boundary. The plants looked decimated, the ground burned.

'What happened over there?' she asked, but no one was listening.

Once they crossed the river the homes grew grander in scale, blotting out the barren fields. One of the buildings was taller than the rest with three red-brick turrets that thrust into the sky. The glass in the windows was stained in an array of sunbeams that cast patterns on the ground around it. Stone steps led to two wooden doors that were the size of Yeeran's entire house.

This building had to be the palace.

Sure enough, Yeeran was pulled through the doors and into a courtyard teeming with life.

Acacia trees sprouted up from fertile soil. Flowers gathered in the knots of marula bark and birds sang sweet music from the leafy boughs.

The procession weaved through the foliage along a white-tiled path.

There was a rustle in the bushes to Yeeran's right and a young obeah sprang out, making Yeeran jump.

Of course, Furi laughed to see it.

They passed a pond with bloated frogs sunning themselves on blooming lily pads. A salamander made their way across the path ahead and all the fae paused to let them cross. If Mosima was utopia, then this forest was the heart of the paradise.

'This is the Royal Woodland,' Furi said to Yeeran. 'Where you'll learn of your fate.'

Yeeran detected glee in her captor's voice at the prospect.

Slowly the trees began to thin out, revealing a clearing surrounded by blue and white mushrooms. In the centre of the faery ring was the largest baobab tree Yeeran had ever seen. She craned her neck to try and see the top of its branches, but it disappeared into the ceiling of the cavern. Its presence was oppressive, filling her vision with its ashy bark. Carved into its girth were two thrones covered in vines where the queens sat patiently. Cursive script was scoured into the bark behind them, but Yeeran couldn't read it.

Furi bowed low and gave a formal greeting in fae before adding for Yeeran's benefit, 'You are now at the mercy of Queen Chall and Queen Vyce.'

A gold basin filled with flickering white coals simmered on the dais in front of the thrones. Yeeran stepped into the sphere of its warmth as she came face to face with the family of the fae she had killed. Queen Chall had hair the colour of blood, cropped close to her oval face. She wore a crimson diaphanous fabric that accentuated the curves of her body. Her skin was a lighter brown than Yeeran's, her cheeks flushed red. Her obeah rested its head in her lap, its horns adorned with silver pendants that tinkled as the creature turned to look at Yeeran.

Queen Vyce was reedier, with a greyer complexion, perhaps older too. She wore a stiffer fabric cut low over her modest chest, her neck laid heavy with gold. Her hair was dark with soft highlights of sunlight that made Yeeran certain this was Furi's mother. Vyce's obeah lounged in the branches above her. It was bigger than her sibling's and it growled as Yeeran approached.

Both queens wore crowns that replicated the sun, though Vyce's was gemmed with yellow sapphires and Chall's peppered with pearls.

Yeeran was tugged by the magic thread around her wrists. But instead of forward, she was pulled downwards. Her knees gave way and she fell into the dirt.

There was the patter of laughter from the congregation.

'Furi, that was unnecessary,' Queen Vyce said.

'I think it was *very* necessary, Mother.' Furi went over to sit by the base of her mother's throne. She rested on her elbows and crossed her ankles, revealing the length of her legs through the slip of her dress.

Yeeran spat out the earth from her mouth and sat upwards, scrounging together the last of her dignity. Something caught her eye in the treeline. It moved like a sentient shadow, its silver gaze locked on hers. When the obeah saw her watching, it slipped away.

She wondered which fae was bound to it. The animals seemed to live freely among the fae.

Yeeran swallowed her pang of guilt.

There was a cough, and another person entered the woodland. The newcomer appeared riding his obeah and slipped from its back with grace. He had the same proud point to his features that Furi did. But instead of the leather chest plate that indicated Furi's commander status, this fae wore a gold circlet on his brow.

'So, you are the fae who killed my cousin?' he said, watching Yeeran with interest. He must have been older than Furi by perhaps a decade. His hair was tinged with the same red flame as Queen Chall's.

'Nerad.' Chall's voice was soft and harmonious. She held out a hand to her son and he walked over to her, kissing it before sitting by the foot of her throne.

The four royals cut a remarkable sight in the dappled light.

'Yes, I am the person who killed your cousin,' Yeeran spoke up in response to Nerad. 'Though I did not know that was the consequence of killing the obeah.'

Furi's mother hissed, and her composure cracked. Here was a mother grieving. Tears sprang to her eyes and the vines that twisted around the armrests of the throne grew in knots. When Yeeran blinked, they had stopped. She wasn't sure if she'd imagined it.

The queen's words came fast and thick.

'Consequence indeed. *You* shall face consequences.'

The trees surrounding the clearing seemed to shiver. Like the queen's anger affected them too.

Maybe it did.

Vyce continued, 'All you elves do is murder and murder and murder.'

Yeeran bowed her head. After all, it was true. Yeeran had made a profession of murder, though she couldn't say in that moment she regretted it.

'You have nothing to say for yourself?' the queen pressed.

Yeeran raised her eyes. Furi looked triumphant, sitting by her mother's bejewelled feet. She muttered darkly in fae to her family, and though Yeeran didn't understand it, she could tell the tone of an insult.

'It was not my intention to murder your son,' Yeeran said with sincerity. 'I had no idea obeah were bound to the fae. I have killed many people in my life, but this is the only bloodshed I had no intention of carrying out.'

'See? They don't see obeah as people,' Furi muttered.

Queen Chall spoke to Furi in fae and Furi smarted. Nerad laughed then smothered it after a glare from his cousin.

Yeeran had no time to revel in the clear chastisement, because Chall's next words, though spoken sweetly, sealed her fate.

'Whether you meant to or not is beyond and beside the point. You said it yourself, there are consequences for your actions. And it is because of those actions that you are sentenced to death. Furi, have the faeguard send word that there will be an execution, and call forth the citizens of Mosima. Let us settle this and begin to heal.'

Yeeran was yanked to her feet.

'My sister, what about my sister?' Yeeran choked out.

But the queens were already vacating their thrones. Neither of them looked back, so it was Furi who answered.

'Don't worry, she and that man of hers won't be killed. Not for your crime. Though she will watch you die, just as I promised.'

'What will you do with them?'

Furi shrugged as she pulled Yeeran along.

'They will live as prisoners. Never leaving Mosima until they die.'

Yeeran thought of Komi, the elf left to rot in his cell for ten years, and how all hope had ebbed from his mind.

Then Furi smiled and it turned Yeeran's heart to ice. 'At least she won't be dead, though I can't promise I'll make it pleasant for her.'

Yeeran felt all strength drain out of her. She would be abandoning Lettle to misery, and there was nothing she could do about it.

The execution was to be carried out in the square in front of the doors of the Royal Woodland. Yeeran had been left chained to a tree as she watched the crowds gather. Furi wasn't far, though there were also two other guards flanking Yeeran.

She watched the fae and obeah congregate. There must have been thousands, tens of thousands, in this cavern. The atmosphere was that of a festival. Music erupted in small pockets as people brandished fiddles and drums, obeah pranced and weaved through throngs of revellers, and drink was passed from hand to hand as people grew merry.

Her execution was entertainment for them.

Or, perhaps, retribution of the sweetest kind.

After all, how many fae had died at the hands of elves? More than Yeeran could count. Obeah skin fuelled the Forever War. It was the source of all magic. How could they have not known this before?

Yeeran saw the crowd part and a hush grow as two people were led through the centre.

Lettle and Rayan. They were dressed in the same silks as the other fae. Lettle's braids had been woven on the top of her head and clipped with a sun emblem of brass. Yeeran could see their hands were unnaturally twisted – bound by magic – though their little fingers were intertwined together by their sides.

At least they have each other, Yeeran thought.

Salawa came to her mind then. Beautiful, fierce Salawa, who had loved her so painfully. She felt wretched at the thought of never seeing her again.

There was a snuffle beside her and Yeeran turned to see the same obeah from the palace courtyard. She wasn't sure how she knew, but she was certain it was the same one. It cocked its head at her, its eyes flashing silver.

Yeeran smiled at the creature, hoping not to scare it away. It stepped forward into the light a little more and Yeeran saw that its fur wasn't fully black, it was a ruddy brown. Unbound then.

The two guards on either side of Yeeran acknowledged the beast with a nod.

The obeah ignored them, its eyes fixated on Yeeran's.

There was a scream up ahead and Yeeran recognised it as Lettle's. She must have realised what was about to happen.

Sure enough, Lettle was being held down by three guards as she bucked against her restraints. Rayan was beside her, trying to calm her, but nothing seemed to be working.

Oh, sister, how I'll miss you.

A tear fell down Yeeran's face.

Furi appeared just at that moment. Her lips curled upwards at Yeeran's raw emotion.

Yeeran raised her chin, not afraid to show her love for her sister.

But when Furi spoke her voice was softer than Yeeran had got used to hearing, 'The queens are on their way. Time to go.'

Yeeran nodded and let herself be led towards her death.

Shortly afterwards the great doors to the Royal Woodland opened, and the queens arrived on their obeah. From this vantage point Yeeran could see how much larger their beasts were than the other creatures in the crowd. Their horns were huge, spanning four or five feet.

They approached the clearing where Yeeran stood facing the crowd. It was only then that Yeeran realised there was no rope to hang from. No executioner to cut off her head. In fact, she had no idea how she was going to die.

The queens dismounted, leaving their companions flanking Yeeran.

Then a whistle pierced the air, a warning sign for the crowd that the main event was about to happen. Silence gathered like the tension of a taut string.

Yeeran searched the crowd for Lettle once more and found her bound and gagged by the front. She was shaking, sobbing silent tears. The fight had gone out of her, all that was left was grief.

I wanted to die on a battlefield, but I suppose dying among the fae is worthy of a tale too.

'You are sentenced to death for the murder of a prince of Mosima,' the prince's mother said, for in this moment she was mother not queen. She spoke in elvish, not in fae, so that those unbound could also understand the gravity of Yeeran's crimes.

Her words were all the warning Yeeran got before sparks erupted on either side of her. Invisible threads began to choke her.

'As is our way, when we choose to take light from the world, we must all partake in the duty of punishment.'

Yeeran didn't understand at first. But then she saw flickers of light from across the crowd and Yeeran felt the audience weave their magic around her throat, adding more pressure.

All of the fae were sharing the guilt of her murder.

The ritual was both horrifying and fascinating. Yeeran didn't have time to wonder further. Her vision was going black.

She looked at Lettle one last time. As she swung her gaze round, she saw it again. The obeah with the pearl eyes. It stood at the front of the crowd watching her.

A jolt of fire burned against her brain and Yeeran shuddered. Then a warmth started in her stomach and spread outwards. She tried to look down to see if she'd been shot with drumfire, but her vision was still blurred and blotchy.

Then there was a light, so bright that Yeeran thought she must have died. But would she still feel pain? She wasn't sure.

The magic around her neck disappeared and she fell forward

onto the ground. It was only then that she realised the light was her. Her skin shone a bright gold.

Something hummed in her mind, and it took her a while to recognise it for what it was.

Hello, I'm Pila, the voice said. The sound of it conjured the feeling of drinking cold water on a hot day; a relief, a sustenance.

But it couldn't be . . . could it? Yeeran gasped for air, trying so desperately to clutch onto reality as she looked the obeah in the eyes.

You are not dreaming, and you are not dead.

The obeah was speaking . . . in her mind.

I've been waiting for you for a long time.

'I might not be dead or dreaming. But I sure have gone mad,' Yeeran mumbled before passing out in a heap on the floor.

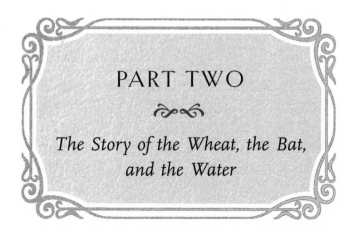

PART TWO

The Story of the Wheat, the Bat, and the Water

There dwelt in the world, fae, humans, and elves. Born from the parts of the gods, Asase, Ewia, and Bosome. The gods had granted their children free will, laying cause for conflict. Wars were won and lost, and the gods grieved and fought among themselves.

'You have made the fae too powerful. They are killing all my humans,' Asase complained on the breeze.

And so, the god Asase granted the humans the magic of the earth, teaching them the language of trees and earth and rocks.

'You have taken all the power from the fae, they are being killed by your humans,' Ewia complained with the setting sun.

And so, the god Ewia, seeing the fae attacked so, granted them a boon: magic spun of sunlight to pull and push, to whip and ensnare. And the fae used their new strength to wage wars once more.

'Bosome, what say you? We have granted our children magic to win the battles they fight. How will you gift your elves?'

The god Bosome was silent for some time except for the rushing of water that followed them wherever they went.

'I will grant them the gift of prophecy, so they can grow in wisdom, the greatest of strengths.'

And so, Bosome taught the elves how to read the silver magic of the Fates, learning the truth of prophecy. It was with this power that they saw their future and avoided the destiny that lay in wait.

For soon the fae and humans would live upon the earth no more.

CHAPTER FIFTEEN

Yeeran

Yeeran woke and cracked open an eyelid.

She was lying on a bed in the centre of a small room that smelled vinegary and sterile. The walls were painted a soft yellow, with white tiles on the ceiling and floor. She was tightly tucked into cotton sheets and for a second she thought she was bound again. But when she moved her hands, she realised they were free.

As her eyes adjusted to the bright light from the window, she spotted two people standing in the doorway in front of her.

The queens hadn't realised she was awake yet.

'Vyce, there is no precedent,' she heard Chall saying.

'Exactly, so we can banish her and be done with this mess,' Vyce responded.

The words, she could understand them, almost feel them, in her mind. But they weren't speaking in elvish.

'You wish to free an elf who possesses the power of fae?'

'An elf *faebound*.' There was a heavy sigh from Vyce. 'That is not a truth we can tell.'

No, they were speaking fae, she was sure of it. And yet Yeeran could *understand* them.

Vyce continued, 'Nerad has already started circulating the story that she was caught in the binding of another guard behind her. But that tale won't hold long.'

'Not for those who saw it happen with their own eyes. Our reign is blighted already.' Chall's soft voice nearly lulled Yeeran back to sleep.

'What do you suggest we do with her?'

Who was this 'her' they were speaking of?

You. They're speaking of you.

The words rang in her mind as if someone had spoken them. Yeeran looked around the room, desperately searching for the source of the voice.

I'm outside, below your window. Though we are bound they have not granted me access to you.

Yeeran inhaled, catching her breath.

Who are you? What is this magic? She projected at the voice. If the person could implant their thoughts in Yeeran's mind, then maybe she could use it to talk to Lettle.

Lettle.

The last she'd seen of her had been at the square before . . .

Am I dead?

No, my name is Pila. We are bound, you and I.

The obeah. The bright light. She gasped as the memory flooded her mind. The sound drew the queens' attention.

Vyce rounded on her, her heels clicking on the tiles as she marched over to Yeeran's bedside.

'What are you?'

Yeeran didn't understand the question.

'My name is Yeeran Teila of the Waning tribe.'

'Were you born fae?' Vyce pressed her face closer. And Yeeran found herself noticing all the ways in which the queen was duller compared to her daughter, Furi. Where Furi was sharp, Vyce was blunt, where Furi was feline, Vyce was equine.

'Vyce, the doctor said she wasn't born fae. They checked her teeth, there was no evidence of filing.'

Yeeran sat up further in the bed and stole a look down the corridor outside her room. She could make out the shadows of other beds in a ward across from hers. So she was in a hospital of some kind.

'What happened to me?'

I told you, the voice in her head said. *We became bound.*

Yeeran flicked her head, trying to shake the voice from her mind.

'You are faebound.' Another person answered, but this time it was said from the doorway.

Furi stood there. Her jaw set, her eyes alight. She looked achingly beautiful and Yeeran found herself missing Salawa fiercely.

'Who are your parents?'

'Teila and Samson of the Waning tribe, both dead,' Yeeran said it matter-of-factly.

'And your family tree, what do you know of its roots?'

'My family has been part of the Waning tribe for generations.' It was a point of pride. She pressed a hand to her chest.

Furi shook her head. 'Somehow you have become bonded to an obeah.'

'What does that even mean?' Yeeran asked.

Queen Vyce straightened and left Yeeran's bedside.

'We need to convene the cabinet,' she said, walking out of the door.

'I've sent Meri already. She's alerted the others,' Chall said as she fell into step beside her sister.

Meri must be her obeah.

Yes, the voice that called itself Pila said.

'Stop that,' Yeeran said.

Furi's brassy gaze snapped to her.

I will not. Pila bristled. It felt like cactus spikes in Yeeran's mind. She rubbed her brow, wondering if she'd gone insane.

Furi stalked to her bed and tilted her head as she surveyed her. Her hair ran down one side of her shoulder, like a golden waterfall pooling in her collarbone.

'Your beast speaks to you?' Furi's eyes went wide, like she had doubted the truth despite seeing the binding with her own eyes.

Yeeran nodded, setting her jaw against the fear.

'So, the connection is truly there.'

'What does it mean?'

What Yeeran had mistaken for wonder in Furi's gaze turned hotter, more scalding. Her lips drew back as she let out a snarl.

'It means you're an abomination.'

With that, Furi marched out, leaving Yeeran alone.

You're not alone, Pila said.

Yeeran grabbed her pillow and screamed into it. It was the kind of dramatics that Lettle used to indulge in when they were kids, and Yeeran had to admit it was quite satisfying to let out her frustration into the duck down.

She screamed until she had no breath left. Until tears ran down her face. But Pila didn't speak again.

'Are you still there?' Yeeran said to the empty room.

There was no reply, but Yeeran could feel Pila's presence in her mind still. Like a part of her was running in an open field, exhilarated and free.

But Yeeran herself didn't feel free, because she had realised she'd never be truly alone again.

An hour later a guard came to escort Yeeran back to the palace. The guard didn't speak to her as she was led through the hospital, but neither were Yeeran's hands bound. She could have run if she wanted to, and as the fresh air hit her face, she almost did. But then she felt her insides go taut as something, no, someone, slunk out of the shadows.

Hello, Pila said in her mind.

Yeeran froze. The obeah was just as magnificent as the first time she had seen it. Her two horns each branched three times, curling outwards like the fronds of a fern. Her eyes were a cloudy silver like pieces of the moon. The fur on her back that had been ruddy just that morning was now a deep black.

Yeeran watched Pila as she strode forward on paws the span of her hand. It was like looking into a river of her own reflection, but the image looking back at Yeeran wasn't her. It was discon-certing and her mind itched. She felt a wave of dizziness and she fell to the ground knees first.

Pila galloped over and pressed her cold nose against Yeeran's, shocking her out of her daze.

Yeeran's breath stumbled over and over itself; she didn't know if she was breathing out or in. Pila's eyes bore into her own. And Yeeran felt herself crying.

Perhaps it wasn't such a bad thing to never be alone again.

No, indeed, I think not, Pila said, and Yeeran felt, rather than saw, her smile.

'How did this happen?' Yeeran said, reaching a tentative hand upwards towards Pila's fur. The obeah let out a low purr as Yeeran scratched the underside of her chin like she'd seen Furi do with Amnan once.

I know not. All I know is I have been searching for a long time. And then I found you.

'We need to get going,' the guard said. He looked horrified, swinging his gaze between Yeeran and Pila.

'Can she come with me?' Yeeran asked the guard. Now that Yeeran had met Pila, she couldn't imagine leaving her again.

He nodded.

Pila moved into step next to Yeeran, her head coming up to Yeeran's shoulder. She wasn't as big as some of the obeah Yeeran had seen, certainly not as large as the one she had killed. Ichor burned down her throat as Yeeran truly understood the horror of what she had done. To kill an obeah was to kill someone's soul.

Yes, Pila whispered in her mind.

Yeeran felt a knot of guilt grow in the pit of her stomach.

You did not know. But now you do. Pila's words were simple but spoken with understanding.

Yeeran nodded though she didn't reply.

The walk to the palace was a short one and Yeeran watched the fraedia crystal above them – the fray as the fae called it – dim with the oncoming sunset.

Soon Yeeran found herself back in the Royal Woodland where she'd been condemned less than five hours ago. But this time Yeeran was infinitely different.

Pila said in her mind, *We both are.*

The queens were on their thrones in the bark of the baobab tree. The large branches above them swayed as an obeah pranced down from the bough and came to rest by the throne of Queen Chall. Nerad leaned against the tree, his ankles crossed. He smiled faintly at Yeeran as she entered. Furi, on the other hand, was looking pointedly away from her, arms crossed, lips pursed.

The guard who had escorted Yeeran was dismissed. Whatever was being discussed here was for the Jani dynasty's ears only.

There was an expectant silence. Yeeran did not bow or acknowledge the royals. They'd put her through enough.

A spark erupted from Furi's hand and the next second Yeeran was pulled to the ground.

'Would you stop that,' Yeeran spat out, her cheek pressed against the dirt.

Pila growled in Furi's direction.

The thread of magic released and Yeeran stood back up. She shot a scathing look Furi's way.

Queen Vyce's lips quirked upwards. The woman shared Furi's hatred of her. She flicked her hair backwards over her shoulder, drawing Yeeran's line of sight to the cursive script scoured into the bark above the thrones. She started as she realised it was now readable.

'Cursed to endure, cursed to survive. All shall perish lest all three thrive,' she read aloud.

'Afa's curse, as prophesied by your ancestors,' Queen Chall said. 'No matter how many times we try to sand it away, the words remain, and so too does the curse.'

'Afa?'

Vyce snorted, but Chall said more kindly, 'Afa, the last of the humans. The reason we are made prisoners underground.'

The name seemed to chime a bell in her memory. But Lettle

was the one who'd always been more deeply versed in faerytales than she.

'Lest all three thrive?' Yeeran muttered to herself. The prophecy must mean elves, humans, and fae. 'You're cursed to live here until all races live in harmony?'

'Sun spirit, you elves are idiots. There are no humans left, so cursed we remain,' Vyce said, and Yeeran threw her a dark look.

She really does hate me.

You killed her son, Pila said. Her words held no judgement. She was simply stating a fact.

Yes, I did. Yeeran projected back at her, and Pila's long tail twitched.

Not so loud, she said.

Sorry.

Better.

'Are you even listening?'

Yeeran jerked upright, realising she'd missed what Queen Chall had said.

'No,' Yeeran responded simply. She'd learned in her time with Salawa that honesty was the most unnerving of weapons against those in power.

Furi smiled at her response and then frowned, annoyed with herself.

Queen Chall blinked slowly, her serene face impassive, almost bored. Vyce on the other hand jutted out her jaw, wearing her anger plainly.

'I think we should execute her anyway,' Vyce muttered.

Chall turned to her sharply. 'You know we cannot, we would be condemning an obeah, one of our own, to death. She may have murdered the prince, but her obeah was innocent in this crime.'

'We do not separate obeah and fae in this way in our court system. She is not fae. Murder is murder.'

'But her obeah was not bonded to her when she committed the crime.'

They speak of the death of Hudan, Pila said to Yeeran.

Hudan?

My brethren you killed.

Yeeran winced, though there was no blame in Pila's sentiment, only a sadness that tasted bitter in her mind. At least Pila had said 'killed' and not 'murdered'.

'I did not murder the prince,' Yeeran said, spurred on by Pila's words.

'What exactly did you do, then?' Vyce said, almost rising from her chair. The branches on the nearest acacia tree seemed to contort and twist with the queen's anger. Chall laid a hand on her forearm to calm her.

Yeeran dipped her head. 'I concede that my actions resulted in his death, but I did not murder him. Murder suggests intent. I had no intention of murdering the prince. My ignorance was deadly, I attest to that, but there was no murder. There was a death of which I am the cause.' Yeeran looked at Furi, imploring her to see the remorse that had become her daily burden. It was not a light load.

Furi broke the stare first.

'When I killed the obeah, my only thought was to use the beast like a hunter uses prey.'

'To make a cursed object.' Furi's fists shook by her side.

'Yes, to make a drum, which I intended to give to my chieftain.'

Vyce snorted in mockery of Salawa's title. It held no authority here.

You are the fire of my heart, and the beat of my drum. I am yours under moonlight. Until the rhythm sings no more.

The memory of Salawa's parting words gave Yeeran strength. She needed to survive this to get back to her.

'The fact remains,' Yeeran said, her voice surer, louder. 'There was no intent. A sentence of murder surpasses the crime. I took something from you, but I didn't know I was taking it when I killed Hudan.'

There was a hiss from Vyce. Chall shook her head, a red curl falling out of its pristine plait – the only indication of her discomfort.

'We do not speak the names of the dead in case we raise them from their infinite slumber,' Nerad spoke and ran his hands over his short hair. He gave her a genuine smile revealing two pear-shaped rubies set into the tips of his fangs.

Why didn't you tell me? Yeeran said to Pila.

I know not of fae custom. Before you I was a beast searching, now I am Pila.

Wait, what?

'You wish to have the charge of murder dropped?' Queen Chall pressed.

Yeeran frowned in Pila's direction before answering Chall.

'I suggest a different sentence. One of thievery. I took from you something, despite not knowing what I was doing. But I agree, I must pay the price.'

It was the biggest gamble of Yeeran's life. She wasn't sure what the sentence would be. The Waning tribe took thievery lightly and often just reprimanded thieves with a whipping. The Crescent tribe, on the other hand, took the thief's little finger.

Yeeran looked at her hands. She didn't want to lose her little finger. But it was the price she'd pay if she could go back to Salawa.

The queens took counsel with each other. Furi paced around the baobab tree, her chin lifted. She watched Yeeran with half-lidded eyes. Amnan, her obeah, hung from a tree branch above. Furi saw Yeeran watching her and raised her top lip to release her canines. Instead of looking threatening she looked alluring.

Yeeran felt an unwelcome stirring of desire and broke eye contact, looking down to where Pila lay curled up by her feet.

Despite being the size of a stag, Pila had the dexterity of a mountain lion. She rested her left horn on Yeeran's waist and looked up at Furi with her silver eyes.

She hates you, Pila said, looking at Furi.

Yes, I don't much like her either.

Amnan appeared by Furi's side again. It looked like they were conversing as Furi nodded.

Can you talk to her obeah, like you talk to me? Yeeran asked Pila.

Pila frowned in Yeeran's mind, and it felt like a knot being tightened.

I can . . . communicate with Amnan, beast to beast. It is less . . . clear . . . than with you. With you I can talk freely.

How does that work?

Pila tried to convey the feeling over their mind link. An amalgamation of images, growling and snarling, along with a range of powerful smells burst across Yeeran's thoughts. It gave her a throbbing headache.

What was that?

How we talk.

Don't do that again.

All right, she said simply.

Both queens had broken apart from their counsel. They sat back in their thrones, both looking faintly unhappy. Yeeran wasn't sure which way the coin toss had fallen. Was she about to lose a hand, a finger, her freedom? Her life?

'We understand the logic in what you have suggested,' Vyce said through tight lips. 'Given your condition—'

'Pila, my obeah's name is Pila.'

Vyce met Yeeran's eyes levelly. 'Given your binding to *Pila*, we are unable to carry out an execution. Fae life is precious, and the law preserving life is tantamount to our customs.'

Yet you were so willing to execute an elf not that long ago, Yeeran thought.

Pila huffed out of her nose.

'Though you are *not* fae, you are bound to one of us,' Vyce clarified. 'This presents a conundrum. We cannot execute you without murdering your obeah, and yet you are not protected by our laws.' Vyce clamped her mouth shut and settled back in her throne as if she were done.

Chall stepped in.

'What you have suggested is reasonable. An offence of thievery may not fit the crime, but it does allow us to seek punishment without jeopardising an innocent.'

That's me, Pila said happily.

Yeeran patted her on her head with the flat of her palm.

'We will announce that you have fae bloodline, so as not to cause disruption among the citizens. Your sister, as we have gathered, has a different father, so this tale sits well among your past.'

How had they found that out? Had Lettle mentioned it to someone? Had Yeeran?

Chall continued, 'Being part-fae will grant you some clemency. Your sentence itself will be in line with the gravest offences for theft: five years of servitude to the faeguard.'

Five years of loyalty to another army? That feels like a lifetime.

At least it's a life. We'll be fine, you and I, Pila said.

Though their bond was only hours old, Yeeran took comfort in it. They had each other now.

'In addition, you will never be allowed to leave Mosima. You are tied to us and us to you.'

No, Yeeran had to leave. She had to get back to Salawa and her people and her war. Without Salawa, without the Forever War, she had no purpose.

She'd find a way out. She had to.

'What of Lettle and Rayan?'

Furi snorted and answered before her aunt could.

'They are safe. Though that is tenuous. They too are imprisoned within Mosima, never to leave. They'll be outsiders, worse than the Lightless. They won't be happy. But neither will they be dead.'

Furi was twisting her words cruelly, grinding the facts in like a hot poker in an open wound. Yeeran wanted to smack the smirk off her face.

She felt a burst of anger unleash around her. The air shifted and Furi was struck, her head snapping backwards. A breath later the queens had Yeeran bound in magic, her arms twisted crookedly behind her.

Did I just do magic? Without a drum?

Yes, Pila said in her mind.

Another thread of magic wrapped around her neck and Yeeran twisted her head to see Furi stalking towards her with a fine red mark up her cheek.

Yeeran wasn't sorry.

When Furi was a step away, Nerad spoke up.

'I think it was an accident, cousin, she doesn't yet know how to wield her power.'

Furi bent down, her nostrils flaring, her hair quivering with anger.

'Daughter,' Vyce said. A warning call.

The thread around Yeeran's throat released and she took in a ragged breath.

'I won't do it. I won't pretend I have fae lineage. I'll tell them all you're lying.'

Vyce's lips curled just like Furi's. 'I do not bargain with murderers.'

'I'm not a murderer. We established that,' Yeeran said.

Chall interrupted before Vyce could speak.

'What is it you want?'

'My sister and Rayan, I want them to be free to leave.'

'We cannot let them free. It is impossible, non-negotiable.'

'Then give them their freedom within Mosima. Give them everything they need to live *happily*.'

While I figure out how to escape, she thought.

Before Chall nodded, Yeeran remembered one other request. The kind soldier who had been living in prison for the last ten years.

'And free Komi, too. Give him the same provisions as Lettle and Rayan.'

'Komi?' Chall said, looking to Furi.

'The elf in our care.'

Chall nodded, remembering.

'We can house them all in the palace as honoured guests. But there is nothing we can do about the prejudice against elves that runs in our land. Your people have been slaughtering obeah for centuries. They are hated, nay, loathed.'

Furi nodded deeply at that.

'As long as I will have access to them,' Yeeran said.

Vyce sniffed before looking to her sister.

'She needs to be trained. We cannot have her drawing magic every time her anger surges.'

Chall nodded. 'Covertly, though. We cannot let it be known that she is not truly fae and we know not how her skills will develop.'

'Furi,' Vyce wielded her daughter's name like a whip. 'You will train her.'

'What?' Both Furi and Yeeran said at the same time.

Vyce ignored them both and continued, 'And, Nerad, you can teach her the fae customs, so she does not cause any disruption, particularly towards the cabinet ministers. There are those who will use this opportunity to leverage any dissent in their favour. You will both train her for three months.'

Nerad nodded, he looked a lot less annoyed than Furi did.

'Mother—'

Vyce cut her off. 'Once three months have passed, Yeeran O'Pila will be initiated into the faeguard.'

Though Yeeran liked that sound of her new name entwined with Pila's, she didn't have time to savour it. Furi's frown had turned into a wide grin and trepidation raised the hair on Yeeran's arms.

This was the real retribution.

'What is the initiation?' she asked.

Vyce licked her lips before answering.

'In years gone by, we tied fae to the Tree of Souls for twelve days.' Vyce patted the baobab. 'The fray, as a gift of our sun god, gave the fae sustenance aplenty. Now we have discovered those of the Jani dynasty are able to open the boundary, we hold the initiation above ground, under the gruelling heat of the sun.' Vyce inspected her nails. 'The initiate is left with no food or water – only the rays of our two-faced god to sustain them. You see, fae are born of the sun and can survive under its heat far longer than the average elf. Only the weakest fail this test. In fact, we haven't had any failures for some time, right, Furi?'

'The last was four years ago. We're due one soon.' Furi relished the words.

Yeeran understood what 'failure' really meant. They knew Yeeran wasn't fae, so they also knew she'd die without provisions. It was a death sentence after all. But this way they'd avoid breaking their own rules about preserving fae life.

Yeeran cleared her throat.

'I want to stay with Lettle and Rayan, in their chambers during my training months. I want to spend time with them before . . . initiation.'

Chall said, 'That's acceptable.'

They all waited, expectant. This may be a prolonged execution, but Yeeran saw it as an opportunity. In three months, they'd take her topside.

That was when she'd escape.

'If you agree to my terms, I agree to yours.'

There was no contract, no handshakes. The queens nodded once and slipped away through a door in the palace walls. Nerad followed with a sheepish grin.

Furi lingered, her gaze felt like flint sparking across Yeeran's skin.

'You know the best thing about the initiation? Family members and close friends are encouraged to watch.' Amnan was circling Furi, a predator ready to lunge. He growled low in his throat at Pila, whose pointed ears turned flat against her skull.

'A promise is a promise, and I told you your sister would watch you die.'

Yeeran had to still the twitch of her lips as Furi stalked away. Once her and Amnan's shadow disappeared, she let the smile bloom.

Furi had let slip a bit of information that had given Yeeran hope: both Rayan and Lettle would be taken topside too.

It would be a perfect storm for escape.

Yeeran and Pila were alone for less than a breath before Berro was there.

'I'm to take you to your sister before guiding you both to your new rooms.'

Pila stretched her front paws forward before rippling upwards to standing, revelling in Yeeran's feeling of relief.

We're not going to die today? she said.

No, we're not going to die today.

Yeeran didn't linger on when their death would be. For today, that was enough.

CHAPTER SIXTEEN

Lettle

Lettle looked down on the ground expecting to see footsteps in the stone where she had worn it away. But the flagstones were smooth and unblemished. She hadn't stopped pacing since Berro brought them back to the cottage.

She walked to the door and banged on it again. The guards had stopped answering it an hour ago.

'Lettle, there's no use. You're only hurting yourself,' Rayan said.

He was right. The edges of her hands were bruised from striking the wood. But if she didn't stop, if she didn't at least try, then the tears would begin to fall.

'Do you think they carried out the execution after she fainted?' she asked.

Rayan was sitting on the bed, his arms crossed behind his head. The only indication that he was stressed was a tightness in his shoulders.

'I don't know. But I know you hurting yourself won't help.'

Lettle banged on the door once more for good measure.

This time, it swung open.

There on the doorstep was Yeeran.

Lettle flew into her arms.

'They told me you were going to die. That you were going to be executed,' Lettle sobbed onto her sister's shoulder. In a moment of panic, she broke apart the embrace and held Yeeran at arm's length.

'It is you, right? They haven't got some type of magic that turned a fae into you?'

She looked like Yeeran, if a little tired around the eyes. The proud jaw, the faint aroma of cedar, the crooked eyebrow that rose in mockery at Lettle's words.

'It's you, all right,' Lettle clutched her once more.

As she looked over Yeeran's shoulder she saw an obeah standing in her shadow. It was watching Lettle intently.

'Yeeran . . . there's an obeah behind you that looks like it's going to kill me.'

Yeeran swivelled round, searching for the threat, her eyes skimming over the beast Lettle had spotted before realising that's who she meant.

'Oh, that's Pila,' Yeeran said with a sigh of relief.

'Pila? You know its name?'

'You'd better come with me. We've got new rooms in the palace.'

Lettle put her hand on her hip.

'What are you talking about?'

'Just come. We're to return to the Royal Woodland with these friends of mine.'

Lettle hadn't even noticed that the guard had doubled in size.

Berro's ashen hair flopped to the side as she cocked her head at Lettle.

'Hello, elf.'

Yeeran gripped Lettle's elbow.

'Let's go, I'll tell you all when we get there.' There was an edge to Yeeran's tone. A warning.

'All right.'

Lettle turned to call Rayan but as she spun, she collided with his chest. It was like walking into a brick wall.

'Are your muscles made of stone?' she seethed, though she couldn't help appraising his form.

His lips quirked upwards before he turned to Yeeran.

'Glad to see you're alive, Colonel.'

'Thank you,' Yeeran said, standing straighter. 'But we'd better get moving, my freedom is fickle and brief.'

Lettle took Yeeran's warning to heart and didn't ask any questions on their walk to the palace. Her tongue was red and raw from biting down on it, her lips itchy with the urge to know more.

As they walked through the Royal Woodland the shadows of the trees lengthened and reached for Lettle's ankles. She didn't like this forest. Everything seemed to be watching her. The mossy smell was oppressive and cloying, it filled her mouth with the taste of dirt and her mind with the memory of digging her father's grave.

'Argh.' A bird swooped low towards her, its feathers raw pink like a gash in the sky.

Yeeran spun, and the obeah next to her turned with her.

'It was just a bird,' Lettle said.

Yeeran nodded, the concern in her eyes dimming. Yeeran's hand absently twirled in the obeah's horns and Lettle frowned, confused by the intimate action.

Who was this creature to her sister?

'This way,' Berro said, stretching a graceful hand towards a clearing.

Lettle's gaze was dragged away from the beast towards the opening in the foliage ahead of her.

'Moon's mercy, that is the biggest tree I've ever seen,' Lettle said, spotting the baobab tree.

Rayan nodded, his eyes rounded in awe. She smiled at his softened features, the hard lines of vengeance blunted by his wonder.

'It must be sixty feet wide, maybe bigger. You could build a house in its trunk. Maybe *two* houses,' he breathed.

Lettle laughed and he turned his twinkling eyes to her.

'It'd be a tight fit, but I think we could do it.'

'I prefer my own house, thank you. Back *home* with my diviners' sect.'

The reminder of how far away they were from the Waning district sobered him, and she chastised herself for causing the smile to ebb from his face.

'How long have you been with them?' he asked.

'Over a decade. Yeeran is my sister, but my sect . . . they're a type of family.'

He nodded. 'It's how I feel about my regiment.' He winced. 'They're really the only family I have left.'

'I'm sorry,' she murmured, her hand reaching towards his before she could stop it. She snatched it away without him noticing.

'What's it like, having a sister? I never had any siblings.'

Lettle looked to Yeeran ahead of them and barked out a laugh.

'It's terrible!' This drew a small smile from Rayan, but it wasn't enough. 'But it's also like . . .' she searched for a metaphor he'd understand, 'it's like wearing a shield. It's heavy to carry, but it protects the most precious parts of you. I love Yeeran more than anything.'

Rayan looked at her sidelong.

'I can't say the same about my comrades in the army . . . but my mother. Yes, I loved her more than anything.'

'I didn't know my mother. She died on the battlefield after I was born.'

Rayan nodded.

'Yeeran told me.'

Lettle rubbed her hand across her brow.

'Though I still felt her presence in Gural. I miss it now.'

He reached out to the space between them where Lettle's hand had been a moment ago.

'We'll go home again, Lettle.'

She looked down at where his fingers lingered, her thoughts troubled.

'How do you know?'

She could feel his eyes on hers, though she didn't look up, she couldn't.

'Because I'll make sure of it.'

Lettle snorted at his arrogance, but she had to admit his words had made her feel better. Safer.

'This way,' Berro called. She had guided them around the width of the baobab tree and towards a glass staircase that led into the building beyond. The panes of glass were floating.

'To not block any of the fray's light for the Tree of Souls,' Berro explained.

'Tree of souls? Fray?' Lettle asked.

Berro pointed to the baobab tree, 'The Tree of Souls,' then pointed to the ceiling at the fraedia crystal, 'the fray.'

If Berro thought that was explanation enough, she had not come face to face with Lettle's curiosity before, but Berro cut her off before she could speak.

'Up you go.'

Lettle's mouth hung agape.

'You mean for us to walk up there?'

Berro gave her a frank look.

'It's perfectly safe. The panes of glass are held up by the magic of the Jani dynasty. The only way they will fall is if the queens die.' She gave a sardonic smile. 'And that won't happen for a long time while I'm part of the faeguard.'

Yeeran skipped ahead with the obeah, Pila. Her shoes chimed on the glass as she rose in height. Lettle scowled to hide her fear. Rayan was next, but instead of continuing up he turned and extended his hand to Lettle.

'It's stable, you'll be safe,' he said. Lettle wanted to grasp it, wanted to feel secure in his hands, but the smirks from the guards stung her pride.

She shouldered him away and marched up the steps, her head held high.

'That one has the makings of a queen if ever I saw it,' one of the guards said.

Lettle took it as a compliment.

She let out a sigh of relief as her feet touched the flagstones in the building above.

Yeeran had stopped at the top of the staircase where a stone archway opened out into a long corridor. Her gaze was frozen in place on a sculpture that had been carved into the wall. It was of a man riding an obeah. He held out a gold sabre, a large ruby encrusted in the hilt. Two yellow diamonds filled the marble of his eyes, which glinted at Lettle in the fray-light.

'Creepy,' Lettle said. 'Who is he?'

The plaque along the bottom had been scoured out, removing any reference to the name of the person.

'That is the prince your sister murdered,' Berro said simply.

Lettle met Yeeran's eyes. They were red and shimmering. It was the first time her sister had seen the person behind the obeah she had killed.

She reached for Yeeran's hand and squeezed it.

Berro beckoned them on.

The corridor overlooked the woodland below, it made Lettle feel queasy looking down on the tops of the trees. About ten yards away from the central staircase they stopped. Berro handed Yeeran a key.

'I'm not sure how you did it, but here are your new living quarters.'

Yeeran gave Berro a tight smile.

'There's a hatch in the windows for your obeah,' Berro continued. 'It leads to another set of stairs directly into the central courtyard where your beast can graze. Food will be sent to your chambers. It's been decided that access to the dining hall will be prohibited for your safety. Though you are not prisoners, I encourage you to stay within these four walls unless escorted by a fae. Not all of my kind are as *forgiving* of your crimes.'

The jibe seemed to strike Yeeran between the eyes, and she took a step back. Lettle found herself rounding on Berro with her teeth bared. Rayan held her right arm firmly.

'Leave it,' he said in her ear.

Berro gave Lettle a pitying look, like she was a ladybug that had just crawled under her shoe.

Lettle hissed at her.

'Keep a rein on that one, Rayan,' Berro said. The way she said Rayan's name, full of warmth and possibility, made Lettle want to rip out her throat.

Berro smirked and made a signal to the faeguard. They turned and left.

Lettle shrugged Rayan off her arm and strode into their new rooms.

The hallway opened out into a living room with four green velvet sofas arranged around a bay window. The window looked down on an inner courtyard in the centre of the palace where an orchard of fruit trees grew. Lettle could see a small herd of obeah grazing in the oncoming twilight.

To the right of the window was a dining table. It was made of rich mahogany, marbled with knots of age. A cluster of fraedia crystals lay in the centre of the room in a copper basin.

Yeeran knelt next to it.

'So much fraedia . . .' she whispered.

'Our travelling packs!' Lettle rushed to her bag and checked through it until she found her prophecy journal. She pressed it to her beating heart, feeling the warmth of home emanating from its pages.

Were these the last prophecies she'd ever make?

The truth of it turned the weight of the notebook to stone. No longer could she kill an obeah to talk to the Fates. To do so would be to kill one of the fae. She felt a part of her identity strip away as she placed the journal back in her pack.

'They took my drum,' Yeeran said weakly.

Lettle continued down a small corridor. It led to four bedrooms, each with a plumbed toilet. Lettle staked her claim on the one closest to the living room which had the largest bed.

Rayan located the flagstone that uncovered the stairs to the bath-house, which was down far more steps than the cottage they had been in.

As they explored, Pila followed Yeeran around. Lettle gave the obeah a wide berth. It seemed at home here, as if the palace had been built to accommodate the width of obeah horns and the height of their torsos. The doorways were larger, the rooms bigger.

It made Lettle feel smaller than she already did.

Only once they had circled the entire place did they collapse onto the velvet sofas.

Lettle rounded on Yeeran.

'All right, what in the name of the three gods is going on?'

CHAPTER SEVENTEEN

Lettle

'You're faebound?' Lettle asked.

'Yes.' Yeeran nodded. The obeah was sitting by her feet. Lettle felt an unexpected stab of envy.

'And that . . . creature . . . can talk inside your head?'

'Yes.'

'And you can do fae magic too, now?'

'So it seems.'

Rayan was sitting silently, his legs crossed, watching the scene unfold. It was only when the silence swelled that he filled it with a question of his own.

'They are going to announce you have fae ancestry?'

Yeeran nodded.

'Is it possible that it's true?'

Lettle answered the question for him. 'We've both traced our ancestors before. We're Waning tribe through bone and skin.'

Yeeran shrugged and looked away. 'Who knows any more. Perhaps someone on my father's family tree was actually fae. The queens said something about filing down teeth as if it were a possibility. Without that distinction, would we know who was fae?'

Rayan shifted, uncrossing and recrossing his legs with a slight frown. Lettle saw his jaw move as he ran his tongue over his own canines, considering the possibility.

Lettle shook her head.

'That doesn't make sense though. The fae have been restricted to Mosima. Golan said the first time they were able to leave was only thirty years go. It would mean your fae ancestors were from before the curse. That was a thousand years ago. Surely the bloodline would have been diluted since then?'

Yeeran had no answer to that, and the silence grew again. It was only when she gave a soft nod that Lettle realised she was talking to her obeah.

Lettle bristled and stood.

'What are we going to do? Just stay here, trapped, forever?'

'No.' Yeeran's voice was firm, and it blunted Lettle's surge of panic.

'We're getting out of here,' she continued.

'How?'

Something flickered across Yeeran's gaze. Lettle wasn't sure what, but she didn't like it.

'In three months, they're letting us all out topside.'

'Why?'

Yeeran's eyes shifted again.

'It's part of the training I have to go through, an initiation that friends and family are invited to. That'll be our chance to leave.'

'What does the initiation entail? And how are we going to get away?'

'I'm not sure how we're going to do it yet. That's the part we need to work on.'

Lettle noticed Yeeran didn't answer her question about initiation. She was about to ask again but Rayan interrupted her.

'We have three months to figure it out. You need to learn all you can about wielding your power. Lettle and I can explore Mosima. Perhaps we won't even need to wait until initiation.'

Yeeran nodded.

'We'll meet every night and share details.'

Lettle stood and went to retrieve her prophecy journal. She opened it and saw the foretelling she'd made on the road.

Under a waxing moon that no one can see, when the sun flares and twilight reigns. A burdened partnership will die when poison passes their lips. One gilded, one pearl.

She sighed.

My last ever prophecy.

She laid the journal down in front of Yeeran. 'Since I won't need this anymore, we might as well use it to make notes, jot down anything of importance.'

Yeeran gave Lettle a sympathetic look before nodding. 'Yes, maybe I can trade the notebook to Salawa for my freedom. The truth is better than any obeah skin.'

Rayan looked from Lettle to Yeeran and said with the same confidence he'd had earlier, 'We'll go home again.'

The three of them basked in the little hope they had.

Pila stood, hearing something the others didn't. A few seconds later there was a knock at the door.

It opened before anyone could answer it.

An older-looking man stood in the doorway of their new rooms. His face was split by a beaming smile that revealed his flattened canines.

Yeeran rose and greeted him by pounding her chest in salute. As he saluted her back, Lettle noticed how they both appeared to be cut from the same cloth – or perhaps uniform. Both straight-backed, arms corded with muscles and an aura of leadership that Lettle found distasteful. Rayan wasn't like that though, not until he was given a drum. Then something shifted in him, and he became the battle-worn weapon of his comrades.

That Lettle didn't find distasteful . . . not at all.

'Who are you?' Lettle's words cut through her errant thoughts.

'Lettle, this is Komi. He was in the cell opposite mine. His release was part of the deal I made.'

Lettle peered at the man. His curling moustache was a style that had been popular a decade past. So much so that those who couldn't grow beards would buy the style ready-made and glue the moustache on. Lettle had been one of those to partake in the fashion, but she'd had so little money that she'd tried to use tree gum instead of fish glue. The result had been a brutal waxing that took off a layer of her skin. Yeeran had laughed about it for weeks.

'What did you do to be captured?' Rayan asked, his voice laden with distrust.

'I found the fae in the Wasted Marshes, and when I followed them to the cavern that led to Mosima they captured me and have not let me go home since.'

Yeeran pulled Komi into the centre of the room.

'What tribe are you from?' Rayan's eyes flashed with distrust.

Komi laughed, his long locs swaying by his chest and when Rayan didn't smile back he sobered before saying, 'Crescent.'

Lettle watched Rayan's nostrils flare.

Yeeran waved a hand in his direction. 'It doesn't matter, Rayan. He's an elf. He's one of us.'

Komi whistled low and began to wander the room with a soft expression of awe on his face. There was something behind his eyes that suggested he wasn't fully present. Isolation had stolen some parts of him, Lettle was sure.

She turned and stole a glance Rayan's way. His knuckles were white on the velvet armrest.

'Your feud with the Two-Bladed Tyrant has no purpose here. It is time to let go of the fight,' she said quietly, hoping to soothe him, knowing any reminder of the Crescent tribe rekindled the fire of vengeance.

His eyes flashed.

'We've still the fae to contend with,' his voice rumbled out deep and quiet. 'And I will cut them all down if it means you'll be free.'

You, not we. She felt her stomach swirl.

There was a sound at the door and a servant arrived with a tray of food.

Lettle surveyed the dishes as they passed.

'They're all . . . *vegetarian.*'

The servant looked at Lettle with disdain.

'We do not eat others.'

'I'm not talking about others. I'm talking about rabbits, deer, beef. I wouldn't even turn down a roast squirrel right now.'

The servant shook their head.

'We don't eat others.'

'Leave it, Lettle. It's quite good,' Yeeran said, coaxing Lettle to the table where the elves had congregated.

They took their seats around the wooden dining table, which had four chairs just for the purpose.

'These rooms . . . they're ours?' Komi spoke with his mouth full. 'I honestly can't believe it.'

'I can count the florets on the cauliflower in your mouth,' Lettle said, grimacing.

Komi opened his mouth wider and wagged his pink tongue, peppered with chewed food. Lettle laughed despite herself, perhaps because it was such a childish response from someone with such an august appearance.

Rayan chuckled too, and soon Yeeran joined in. It felt so normal to laugh and to revel in each other's company. No matter what tomorrow brought. For now, under this roof in the chambers they called their own, they were free.

If only just a little bit.

Lettle had a restless sleep despite how soft the bed sheets were. She kept waking with a start and wondering where she was. At three in the morning, she gave up and went to the living room.

As she walked into the firelight, she was startled by the brightness of two eyes staring back at her.

'Three gods, you gave me a heart attack.'

The obeah tilted its head, its horns grazing the velvet sofa.

Lettle lingered in the doorway, uncomfortable with being in the room with the obeah on her own. What if it attacked her?

No, this beast is now bound to Yeeran. If the fae had it right, then the obeah is part of her now. And Yeeran would never harm me.

Lettle shifted from foot to foot.

The darkness gathered in corners where the firelight didn't stretch. There was no moon in Mosima, just the darkness of the fae god's other face.

'I couldn't sleep,' she explained to the creature.

It felt foolish talking to an animal. Especially an animal whose countless brethren she had sliced open and read from their entrails. She felt herself grow morose.

'I will never be able to do divination again, will I?'

Lettle felt the grief of that loss keenly. Now she knew the truth of who the obeah were, she could never kill one again. They were no longer prey, but people in her eyes.

Pila snorted, her nostrils flaring as she stood.

Lettle took a step back, but Pila was quicker. Before Lettle could gasp, the obeah was there, her snout of a height with Lettle's nose.

Pila smelled faintly of peaches and grass and the distinctive aroma of animal hide. Her horns stretched far above Lettle's head and as she surveyed them, she realised they were slightly iridescent, like the inside of a seashell.

After the initial shock, Lettle knew she wasn't in danger. The obeah merely wanted to get a closer look. And look she did, with eyes the colour of moonlight and lashes as thick and long as a camel's.

Lettle reached a hand out to stroke her, like she'd seen Yeeran do, but Pila skipped backwards, her claws clacking on the stone floor.

'I'm sorry,' Lettle said, wondering about the etiquette.

Pila's eyes blinked slowly as if to say, *It's all right. Everything will be all right.*

'Thank you.'

Pila nodded and settled back down.

Lettle moved to the velvet sofa opposite and sank into it, her bones weary. She massaged her left arm, the shortened muscles there stinging from exhaustion. The last few days had taken their toll on her. She so rarely took painkillers. Pain was a constant, reliable friend that Lettle welcomed. It dulled the truth of her nightmares.

Pila's own eyes were drowsy as she watched Lettle from across the room. Her eyes blinked slower, then slower.

Then closed.

Lettle jerked awake. She couldn't remember falling asleep. The fray shone in from the bay windows, lighting the empty living room with its gold glow. Pila wasn't anywhere to be seen and Lettle wondered if she'd left through the hatch designed for her to access the courtyard below.

Knock. Knock. Knock.

The sound that woke her finally registered.

Lettle dragged herself to the door and opened it.

A servant with large, hooded eyes handed over a tray of food to break their fast.

Komi marched into the room as if the aroma of breakfast had summoned him.

'Is no one else awake?'

Lettle rubbed the sleep from her eyes.

'No, and neither am I.'

Komi took the tray from her and put it down on the dining table with a clatter. He clinked some of the mugs together for good measure too.

'What's the noise?' Yeeran appeared with Pila by her side.

Komi winked at Lettle.

'Your breakfast awaits.'

Lettle took her seat at the table and reached for the bread and butter on the tray. As she lifted a plate, she saw a piece of parchment.

'They've sent up a letter.' It was sealed with gold wax with an emblem of the sun in the centre.

Lettle opened it only to find it was scrawled in a text she didn't understand. Komi looked over her shoulder.

'It's in fae.'

'Oh,' Lettle said, and placed it back down.

'Sleep OK?' Yeeran asked Lettle. Her sentences would be two words long until she had some coffee. Lettle poured her a mug and Yeeran accepted gratefully before sinking into a seat opposite her.

'Not terrible.' Lettle wondered how much Pila had told her of their late night meeting.

When Yeeran didn't press for more details, Lettle knew Pila had told her all. It unnerved Lettle that Yeeran's presence had grown to encapsulate another. It had just been the two of them for so long.

Yeeran reached for the open letter and frowned.

'I can read it,' Yeeran said.

'You can?' Lettle said.

'Ever since I bonded with Pila, I can read and speak fae like it is my mother tongue.'

Lettle bristled.

'But it's not.'

Yeeran set down her mug of coffee. 'I know that, Lettle.' She ran a hand over her face. 'The twilight dynasty—'

'Twilight?' Lettle asked, the word catching on something in her memory.

'Oh, sorry, Jani dynasty, it means twilight in fae.'

Lettle frowned but couldn't recollect why it was important.

'The Jani dynasty invite us all to a binding banquet this evening to celebrate . . . Pila and I.'

Yeeran's head thudded onto the table in dismay.

Rayan came in yawning.

'I had the best sleep,' he announced. He looked to Yeeran. 'What's up with her?'

'She's just found out there's a party to celebrate her binding.'

Yeeran groaned into the table, her voice muffled as she said, 'I'm not going.'

There was another knock on the door, louder than knuckles on wood.

When Lettle opened it, she knew who she'd find.

'Golan.' She smiled, welcoming him into the room.

He entered, his cane tapping against the flagstones with a satisfying clang.

'I've only got six hours to make you all ready for the binding banquet, so no time for chatter.'

Golan strode towards Yeeran first.

'You're the one with fae blood?' he asked.

Yeeran nodded though her expression remained faintly queasy.

It turned out that they were all expected to attend in full traditional fae dress. Golan laid out the garments he'd brought. All of which were as diaphanous and as translucent as the next.

'I like this.' Lettle plucked at a glittery wine-red top that would at least reach her midriff. The sleeves draped to the ground in ruffles that she thought were quite charming. The pattern running through the centre of the garment was geometric.

Golan's eyes twinkled with delight. 'I thought that would look wonderful on you too, with this deep purple cape.'

'What does the weave mean?' she asked, remembering that he had said each pattern was named by the tailor.

'Aha.' He smiled, pleased she'd remembered. 'This one is called "to grow in tolerance, to wither in wilfulness".'

'What does that mean?'

'The tailor is a friend of mine and I asked them the same thing. They said it's about having an open mind as well as an open heart.'

It was an unsatisfactory answer for Lettle. Still, the pattern was beautiful, and she'd wear it proudly.

'And for the woman of the night,' Golan continued. 'This gold silk suit. The sleeves are perhaps a bit long and I don't have time to hem them up. You'll have to be careful when you dance.'

Yeeran snorted. 'I won't be dancing, don't worry.'

Golan looked offended. 'You must dance. It's the best part of a binding banquet.'

'Well, we don't even know what a binding banquet is, so how would we know that?' Yeeran cut in. Colour was rising in her cheeks.

Lettle could see she was struggling, unused to finding herself in a situation beyond her control.

Golan said, 'Binding banquets are thrown by the newly faebound, though admittedly very few are ever hosted by the palace. I imagine this is intertwined with more politics than show.' Golan raised an immaculate eyebrow at Yeeran, but she gave him nothing back.

'There's dancing, what else?'

'Food, drink, all things joyful.'

'Fun,' Yeeran said the word like a death sentence.

Lettle laughed. She loved dancing. There weren't many opportunities in Gural, but during the harvest and the first snow festival Lettle was always the last to leave the dance floor.

She fingered the fabric of the dress.

'The last time I wore a dress this colour was for my graduation ceremony. Do you remember, Yeeran?'

It was a barbed comment. Yeeran had missed it: an unexpected assault from Crescent had meant she was needed on the Bleeding Field and her approved time off had been rescinded.

'I remember,' she said with troubled eyes.

It had been one of the many times Lettle had been abandoned by her sister.

'Graduation?' Golan asked.

'Yes, I was a student of divination.' Wistfulness seeped into her voice.

Komi interrupted their conversation by strutting into the room wearing the long tunic Golan had given him. It was made of finely woven blue cotton, with a bright red waistband.

'Isn't this wonderful?' He twirled, his hair fanning around him. 'I look like I'm fae.'

After ten years in prison Komi could have been bitter, but instead he found delight in everything. Lettle was glad he was now part of their little group.

'You look perfect, I just need to do your make-up. Where's the other one?' Golan said. 'Come out, pretty boy.'

There was a sigh, a swallow and then footsteps.

Rayan was wearing a long cloak of spun silver silk that fell to the floor. The collar was high and pointed, and it brushed his ears. He wore nothing but his muscles underneath, and a loose pair of shorts in the same matching fabric.

Lettle's mouth dropped open. She shut it hastily.

There was a cough, then a cackle and Lettle swung her gaze to Yeeran, who held two hands over her mouth to suppress her laugh.

'You look ridiculous,' she chuckled.

Rayan flushed.

Komi went over and clapped him on the back.

'Don't listen to her, she has no taste. I think you look brilliant.'

'I agree,' Golan added.

'So do I,' Lettle said quietly.

Rayan's gaze narrowed in on hers. His lips stretched outwards into a smile. She glanced away quickly.

'What does the weave mean on this?' he asked Golan once Lettle had broken eye contact.

'Well . . . yours means "lusts of the night".'

Lettle choked on her saliva.

Everyone in the room looked at her. Rayan's expression was mischievous as if he knew exactly what she'd been thinking.

That the garment is aptly named.

She scooped up the burgundy top.

'I'm going to go and try this on.'

She ran from the room keeping her eyes averted from Rayan's. Though she felt his gaze burning on her back.

CHAPTER EIGHTEEN

Lettle

G olan had said getting ready was going to take six hours, and it did. He rebraided Lettle's hair and Komi's locs growth then scented their scalps with mint oil. He shaved the sides of Yeeran and Rayan's heads, both of them preferring to maintain their soldier's cuts. He then applied intricate make-up to all their faces.

For Lettle he had opted for white vines across her forehead and cheekbones, whereas Yeeran wanted a more subtle gold streak that ran from ear to ear across her face. Their hands were scrubbed raw then dipped in gold paint up to their knuckles.

When Golan was done, they looked wonderful.

The binding banquet was held in the Royal Woodland. Golan led the way, though it was simple enough to retrace their steps down the glass staircase.

'*Man saeakum hurack allaylah?*' Yeeran said.

Lettle looked at her in confusion. Only Golan seemed to have understood.

Yeeran must have realised she had spoken in fae and gave the elves an apologetic smile.

'Sorry, I'm still not used to speaking two languages.'

'To answer your question,' Golan replied in elvish. 'There will be lots of people at the banquet but most importantly for you will be the cabinet – namely the fae who run Mosima. They'll be the five senior members of the faeguard, the chancellor of the treasury, the minister of agriculture and so on. Bureaucrats and such. Do you have those in the Elven Lands?'

'We do.' Yeeran's lips pressed together and Lettle wondered if she was thinking of Salawa.

Lettle felt her nose crinkle in a snarl as she thought of the chieftain. Yeeran had once said she and Lettle were similar. Lettle had never been so offended.

'What are you scowling about?' Rayan said, his voice low and breathy.

'Oh, nothing.'

They entered the woodland to find the entire forest strung up with gas lamps. But as they grew nearer, Lettle realised they weren't gas lamps but little lizards with wings and glowing bulbous heads.

'I have never seen anything like it . . .'

'The star gliders? The queens will have drawn them in. The Jani dynasty's magic is bound to this land,' Golan said.

'What does that mean?'

'It means they're in control. Of everything.' Golan's smile was rigid as he guided them into the centre of the party where fae were dressed in glorious sheaths of silk and fine cloth. 'They have a connection to the very heart of Mosima, animals, plants, earth – they are all soul bound to the Jani dynasty.'

'But, *what does that mean?*' Lettle repeated. She was getting frustrated she couldn't grasp all there was to know.

'Look at the flowers that bloom by their feet, you see how Vyce's are thistles and Chall's are roses? That tells me Vyce is particularly prickly today. The land has reacted to her mood. It takes a lot of restraint for it to have only sprouted that one plant, early on in her reign fields of thistles grew in the Royal Woodland.'

Lettle watched Vyce's foot absently tap the top of the thistle blossom by the edge of her throne. Queen Chall's smile next to her was lit by a circlet of star gliders that gathered in her crown.

'Fascinating.'

Lettle's attention was drawn to a band playing beside a copse of trees, the music a beautiful haunting melody that lifted at odd intervals. A fire burned in a gilded bowl on a dais in front of the thrones. It glowed warmly on the limbs of those dancing nearby as their obeah weaved through the throngs of people. A mountain of food was laid across oak tables around the edge. Birds swooped in and out of the clearing, and a family of tortoises sauntered by.

'This is incredible,' Rayan said, and Lettle agreed. The woodland, which had been eerie and full of shifting shadows before, was now set alight by the festivities.

As they entered the clearing, the music stopped.

Queen Vyce, who Yeeran had said was the taller of the two, and Furi's mother, stood in the centre.

'We welcome Yeeran O'Pila to Mosima as a descendant returning home. May our god's faces shine upon your brow.'

'And shine upon yours,' the congregation muttered.

Yeeran shifted from foot to foot, her bejewelled sandals padding down the dirt. Lettle reached for her and hooked her arm around hers, drawing her closer to lend her strength.

Her sister gave her a grateful smile.

The music started again and soon the fae turned back to their conversations as if the elves weren't even there.

Furi appeared by Yeeran's side. She looked stunning in a pale blue gown, with two slits up to her thighs.

'Lightless,' Furi acknowledged Golan with a stiff nod.

Golan bowed low in response.

'I am to introduce you to the cabinet,' Furi said to Yeeran. 'Come.'

She reached out a hand to Yeeran and she grasped it with a grimace.

'And smile, you want these people to like you,' Lettle heard Furi mutter as they walked away. 'They are your long-lost family, after all.'

Pila slipped out from between two trees and fell into step beside Yeeran and Furi. Yeeran didn't even look back at Lettle as she left.

Yeeran O'Pila. They've even changed her name.

Rayan drifted off towards a thicket of trees murmuring about 'something he wanted to look at', and Golan was quickly whisked away by two young men and onto the dance floor.

'Just you and me,' Lettle said to Komi.

'Is that cheese? I haven't had cheese in years!' Komi wandered off towards the food platters.

Lettle smiled and turned her gaze back to the dance floor. Golan was moving to the music, his head thrown back, his hips swaying, the cane in his hand both support and twirling baton. She found herself being pulled into the centre of the clearing, the music lulling her to dance.

But as soon as she entered, the crowd parted, moving away from her as if diseased.

One spat at her feet.

'Your sister may be fae, but you are not. Don't taint our dance floor with the blood of our ancestors on your soles.' She recognised the face of the person. It was one of the guards who had escorted them into Mosima. Hosta they were called.

A hand came to rest on her lower back, and from the way their touch lingered, she knew it was Rayan.

'What's going on here?' he said. He towered over Hosta by half a foot.

Hosta's blue eyes narrowed.

'You should be killed for what you have done to our kind.'

Rayan pulled Lettle back and tried to block her from Hosta's line of sight. She didn't have a chance to protest before Rayan spread out a placating hand towards the fae.

'We are not here to cause you harm.' He sounded level, almost soothing.

'Harm? You speak to us of *harm*?'

There was a flash of metal and Lettle cried, 'They've got a dagger, Rayan, watch out.'

'Oh, Hosta, put that away.' Golan had found them, and he turned to chastise the young soldier. 'They're guests of the Jani dynasty, do you mean to defile this night by shedding blood?'

Hosta screwed up their pinched face.

'I do not take orders from one of the Lightless.'

'Right. Well, by all means, stab our new friends.' Golan spread his arms theatrically, waiting for Hosta to take the bait.

There was a second where it looked like they might.

'Golan . . .' Lettle said.

Then Hosta twirled on their heel, their silk cloak whipping at Rayan's calves.

'You both all right?' Golan asked.

'Fine,' Lettle said through clenched teeth. All she had wanted to do was dance; it seemed that too was dangerous here.

'Maybe stick to the edges of the woodland just for tonight,' Golan said. A young man dressed head to heel in gemstones came to drag him back to the dance floor.

Rayan and Lettle moved towards the shadows of the trees.

She could feel the heat of him by her side.

'I'm sorry, I shouldn't have left you,' he said.

'I could have handled it.'

To Rayan's credit he didn't contradict her.

She twirled one of her plaits in her hands.

'Where did you go just now?'

Rayan looked away from Lettle's imploring gaze, the colour in his cheeks had risen slightly. It did nothing to assuage her curiosity.

'Well?'

He slipped a hand into his pocket and withdrew a small red stone. No, not a stone, a seed pod.

'I saw that you lost your necklace when we were captured and I thought . . . maybe . . . I don't know. I just saw this, and it made me think of all those seeds you had. I know it's not your nameday but maybe you can start a new collection?' He held out the little red bead to her and she wrapped her hand around it.

The seed was warm from Rayan's touch.

'Rayan . . .' His name came out like a wisp of mist, and she tried again. 'Rayan, thank you.'

She put the bead into her pocket.

'Do you want to dance?' he asked suddenly.

'They won't let us onto the dance floor.'

'We can dance here.' There was a warmth in his eyes that Lettle didn't ever want to extinguish.

'Yes, we could.'

He led her into a smaller area surrounded by acacia trees but within hearing distance of the music.

'Do you know the waning skip?' he asked.

The dance was part jig, part waltz. Of course she knew it. As soon as she could walk, she learned the steps by watching the village mothers dance during full moons.

Instead of answering, she led Rayan into the movement.

A delighted smile split his face and he stepped to the left as she stepped to the right. She tapped her feet twice and he reciprocated. They clasped hands in the centre then broke apart and twirled, only to meet in the centre again.

They danced until they were breathless and laughing. And when the song ended, Lettle flung her arms around his neck.

'Thank you. I missed this. I missed *dancing*.'

He gently moved her away from his shoulder until their noses were touching. She felt his breath on her lips. Bergamot and sage.

Her throat tightened. It was hard to breathe.

'Lettle,' he rasped.

She ran her fingers from the tips of his ears down to his jawline and he shuddered. She laughed lightly at the power of her touch.

Her fingers brushed a slightly raised bit of skin on the underside of his jaw. She leaned closer, letting her breath warm his throat.

The birthmark was a beautiful swirling pattern of dark skin that embellished the edge of his beard. She was surprised she hadn't noticed it before.

'My mother said it was a mark of the sky.' Rayan's voice rumbled out deep and quiet.

Lettle smiled, it did look like clouds.

'The night she bore me, a thick fog hung over Crescent. She always said I was fathered by the storm's mist. Though frankly, I think that was a way of not telling me who my true father was.'

He barked out a bitter laugh, but Lettle didn't hear it, her thoughts were drowning out all other sound.

The one born of a storm's mist shall be your beloved. But when the waning moon turns, you will grant them their death.

'Imna's prophecy . . .' she whispered to herself. 'No. It can't be.'

Her heart was hammering against her chest.

'Lettle, what is it?'

'You . . . you're . . .' She didn't know how to voice her panic.

He reached for her, cupping her cheek. She felt herself craving more than his hand on her.

But if she leaned forward, just a little, it would be the start of the end of his life.

She pushed herself away from him.

'I . . . I'm sorry,' he said softly.

But what did he have to be sorry for?

Together they had woven the first few stitches of a tapestry that depicted a future Lettle had never before considered. And now the threads had to be shorn away. She knew better than anyone to fight a prophecy. But fight it she would. She must.

To love him is to kill him.

'No, you and I, we cannot, Rayan. We cannot be together.'

The heat she had so desperately wanted to keep burning was gone in Rayan's eyes. For a second he looked hurt, but then it was smoothed over by pride to something more impassive and that broke Lettle's heart even more.

'I am truly sorry. I thought you felt the same way,' he said roughly, like shattered stone.

'It is no matter, we cannot be. That is all there is to it.'

With that, Lettle turned and ran, before he saw the tears in her eyes.

Lettle fled from the binding banquet towards the staircase that led to their new rooms. Her hand squeezed the red seed in her pocket, and with it she felt her heart constrict tighter and tighter.

She held her breath to stop the flow of tears that threatened to fall. As she stepped onto the glass staircase, she saw a shadow stretch to her right. She paused.

So quickly I forget that I'm in a hostile land. Perhaps Hosta has returned to finish what was begun.

Lettle tensed to run, the stairs less frightening than the shadows.

'I won't hurt you.' Lettle turned to face the source of the sound. The voice was deep and gravelly. It didn't match the man's thin face; where his voice was rich and thick, his body was fleshless and lean. The clothes he wore clung to the empty spaces where Lettle's curves would have swollen. He had aged more than the other fae she had seen, indicated by the silver strands in his braids. The lines across his face were faint, but it was in the etching of them that he had garnered wisdom and experience.

When he spoke Lettle could see the length of his canines.

'I'm Seer Sahar.'

Lettle looked at him down the length of her nose.

'Seer? What do you see?'

The fae laughed but didn't answer. There was something about this man that Lettle felt drawn to and all fear shed away.

'Why aren't you on the dance floor with the other fae?' she asked him.

Sahar smiled but it looked more like a smirk.

'I do not mingle with those who deny the Fates.'

Lettle felt her heart begin to pound with exhilaration.

'The Fates?' she whispered. Did the man know divination?

'Come and see me tomorrow morning, I will have painkillers for that arm of yours.'

Lettle wasn't sure how he knew; the sleeves of her dress covered most of her physical differences. She raised her chin.

'I don't take snowmallow flower.' The drug was the smell of her nightmares.

'That's why I harvested owen tree sap this morning instead.'

'Oh? Where can I find you?'

'Follow the main street leading out from the palace. Cross the second bridge and you'll find my apothecary on the right. It has a purple sign hanging above the door.'

Lettle nodded, committing the instructions to memory.

He bid her goodnight before retreating the way he had come.

Lettle lingered on the stairs, her mind brimming with possibility.

If she could do divination again, maybe she could learn more about Imna's prophecy?

The hope was a weak one – once told, no prophecy could be thwarted – but still it was hope. She clutched on to it like the bead in her pocket as she ascended the stairs.

When she reached the top, she looked down on the party below.

There was Rayan, a crooked smile hanging from his mouth as he spoke to another fae. The sight of the fae's ashen hair was enough to confirm it was Berro.

Rayan laughed, his head tilting back to the sky. For a second Lettle thought he would see her there, framed by the stone archway of the cloisters. But then his chin dipped back down, and he looked at Berro.

She felt her gut twist with disappointment. Hot tears fell down her cheeks as she turned and ran to her chambers.

CHAPTER NINETEEN

Yeeran

Yeeran couldn't recollect any of the names of the people she'd been introduced to. Her head was buzzing from the peach wine she was drinking, and her lips ached from smiling.

She had seen Lettle storm off and felt jealous that her sister had managed to slip away. Rayan stood on the edge of the dance floor talking to Berro, and Yeeran wondered if that was the reason. Komi on the other hand was standing by the food, where he'd been all night.

He smells different, Pila said in Yeeran's mind.

Who? Komi?

No.

An image sent by Pila flashed behind Yeeran's eyes. It was of Rayan from Pila's perspective in soft sepia hues.

What do you mean? Yeeran pressed.

'. . . and Ostrum here is in charge of the postal service within Mosima.' Furi gestured to a young man who sat astride his obeah.

Yeeran was brought back into the moment by the tightening of Furi's hand around her wrist.

'Nice to meet you,' Yeeran said reflexively. The phrase was rinsed of feeling from overuse.

Ostrum nodded and Furi whisked Yeeran on.

I'm tired, Pila complained in her mind as she trotted by Yeeran's side to the next group of people.

Go and take a nap then – at least you can go to sleep. I can't. I have to stay here and get paraded about.

Oh, I think I will go to sleep then. Goodbye. Pila loped away, and Yeeran felt herself giving her first genuine smile of the night. She was still getting used to the new voice in her mind. At the same time, it felt like meeting a childhood friend again after many years. An odd childhood friend, one who was neither elf nor beast but something in between.

'You need to at least look interested,' Furi hissed.

'I am.'

'You'll be pleased to know that's the most important ones. Particularly Ostrum, he'll spin the tale of tonight like a worm spinning silk and seal the story that you're fae.'

Yeeran nodded, a yawn cracking her jaw.

Furi seethed.

'Stop that.'

'I can't help it, I'm tired.'

'The night is nearly over.'

Thank the three gods. There was an acknowledgement of relief along the thread of her connection with Pila.

Furi grasped Yeeran's elbow and pushed her through the crowd towards the Tree of Souls.

The music stopped and a small bell was rung. Everyone turned to look at the queens.

'My mother and aunt will now bless you as faebound,' Furi murmured.

Furi's words were little warning as both Vyce and Chall sent shards of magic to wind around Yeeran's waist.

Yeeran started to resist but Furi hissed, 'Stand straight, you idiot.'

Vyce took a step towards her. Yeeran noticed her shoes were the colour of blood. Chall was only a step behind.

'As bestowed by the god Ewia, we submit to the highest glory,' both queens said in tandem. 'Yeeran O'Pila, we welcome you. Faebound forever more.'

The magic disappeared and the blessing was over.

'Can I go to bed now?' Yeeran said out of the corner of her mouth to Furi.

'Not quite. You must end the formal festivities by setting the sun.'

'What? I'm not a god.'

Furi released her fangs from her top lip. 'The metaphorical sun. You must douse the basin of fire with the chalice. It is the symbolic ending of every celebration.' She pointed to the gilded bowl of embers in front of the throne that had shone gaily on those swaying nearby.

'Then,' she continued, 'those who wish to choose a lover are given the guise of darkness in which to proclaim their chosen. Some may lie among the trees, though others may choose more civilised surroundings in their beds.'

Yeeran stumbled.

'Am I to choose a l-lover?' she stuttered, avoiding Furi's eyes.

They were warmer than Salawa's and reminded Yeeran of a setting sun.

'No, and I wouldn't recommend it. We have a busy day of training tomorrow and you're likely unaccustomed to the . . . stamina . . . of the fae.' Furi's grin was wicked, but it held no malice. For a change.

Yeeran felt a touch disappointed, but she wasn't sure why.

'Let's douse the basin of fire so I may go to bed then.'

It was a simple procedure. A ceremonial chalice was brought forward. For a frightening moment Yeeran had thought the liquid inside was blood. That was until she sipped it and recognised the sweet tartness of pomegranate juice. Then she poured it liberally over the fire. As soon as the smoke rose, she heard shrieks.

At first Yeeran thought someone was being attacked and she shifted into a defensive stance. Then the shrieks became moans of desire and Yeeran felt foolish.

She turned to talk to Furi, but the commander had vanished. No doubt she had gone to seek her own pleasure.

Yeeran made her way through the cloisters towards her room. Two figures moved up ahead and she found herself tensing her hand as if to beat a drum.

But her drum was gone forever.

She swallowed her sorrow.

Fraedia crystal no longer lit the hallway, given the time of night. Instead, torches burned bright, setting the profiles of the two people aglow, their heads bowed together as they murmured.

'Komi,' Yeeran greeted the older elf.

He turned a lazy smile to Yeeran.

'I drank too much mead,' he slurred. The other person held him propped up by his arm. As the fae turned towards Yeeran he smiled, showing his ruby-encrusted canines. His brown eyes, so like Furi's, simmered like hot coffee.

'I found him wandering down the wrong corridor,' Nerad said with an apologetic smile.

'He did. He did.' Komi was rocking back and forth on his heels as he nodded.

Nerad grimaced.

'You really should be careful with the mead here, it's stronger stuff than you're used to.'

'They had cheese, Yeeran, can you believe it? I've lived on a diet of lentils for so long.' Komi reached for Yeeran, and Nerad transferred custody of the elf.

'You can't begrudge him his first taste of freedom,' Yeeran said. 'You have kept him locked up for ten years.'

Nerad ran a hand along his clean-shaven jaw; his hands glittered with the same gold paint that most of the fae wore.

'He might be free from the jail, but he's still in a cage,' Nerad said quietly. 'We all are.'

Then the fae prince walked away, his gait slow and forlorn. Yeeran frowned at his retreating form.

Komi's head lolled to the right.

'He's sad.'

'Yes, he is,' Yeeran said. 'Come on, time for bed.'

Pila was waiting for Yeeran in the living room once she had deposited a snoring Komi on his bed.

Sleep well? Yeeran asked.

Yes, I think I may graze some more in the courtyard.

Be careful, there are still a lot of fae around.

Pila tilted her head in a way that Yeeran was coming to realise meant confusion.

I have no fear of fae. I am fae.

The reality of it shocked Yeeran to the core. Though they were bound, they would never be the same, Pila and her.

Pila reached out a paw and laid it softly on Yeeran's foot.

That is not what I meant. We are the same, you and I, because together we make one. We share a soul now. Fae or not.

Yeeran nodded, though her mood had sunk further.

Go and graze. Furi wants us to meet her in the courtyard at dawn for training.

Pila huffed out her nose.

I don't want to train with Amnan. He's rude, and empty-headed.

I don't want to train with Furi either. But such is the deal we struck.

Until we find a way to escape.

Indeed.

Pila rose and made her way to the obeah hatch in the window. It was wider than a normal door but instead of sliding sideways it opened from the bottom up, so when Pila pressed her nose against it, it lifted.

I will bring you back a plum, Pila said.

Thank you.

Yeeran smiled as she watched Pila leave.

She wanted to ask her to watch out for Furi, but there was no reason Yeeran could muster for such a request.

Yeeran shook her head, the simmering rage she felt towards the woman growing hot as she filled her mind once more.

Why did it matter if Furi had found a lover in the night?

Because she gets to experience pleasure while I have only my memories of Salawa to keep me company.

The thought dragged Yeeran to bed, where she dreamed of kissing fire and sleeping under the stars in Salawa's arms.

Pila was waiting in the Royal Woodland at dawn, having spent the night gorging on fruit. She rolled to the side when she saw Yeeran, exposing the underside of her chin for a scratch. The whiskers around her mouth were stained with fruit juice.

I'm glad you ate well. We'll have a busy day training. I can't imagine it's going to be pleasant.

Pila snuffled her hand.

You're strong already. Why do you have to train?

To learn to control my magic.

Yeeran tucked the front of her shirt into her shorts where the fabric had pulled free. She didn't expect Furi to implement uniform drills like the Waning Army had, but habits were hard to shift.

She had dressed in the simplest clothes she could find in the wardrobe she'd been given, though the sleeves had floated longer than she'd liked. So she'd hacked them off at the armpit with the bread knife from breakfast. The shirt was now a tight-fitted vest that gave her far better range of movement in her arms. The shorts she suspected were meant to be undergarments, but either way they were light and loose enough to train in.

She stood in the courtyard waiting. The fray shone down on the forest, the dew drops on the trees shining like diamonds in the morning light. There were still groups of fae lying with each other in the shadows of trees, moans of passion and grunts of release still permeating the air.

Yeeran averted her gaze from them, feeling the heat of her embarrassment in her cheeks. She hadn't been there long when a naked woman strode out of the trees towards her.

'You're on time at least,' Furi said.

The glimpses she'd got earlier of Furi's naked form underneath the sheer fabric of her dress hadn't prepared Yeeran for the sight of the woman standing in front of her. Heart-shaped bruises peppered her neck and the black lipstick she had been wearing had long smeared. In the morning light Yeeran could also see the faint cut on her cheek where Yeeran's wild magic had struck. These details didn't mar her perfection, though.

Yeeran couldn't choke out anything but a nod.

'This way,' Furi said, turning on her heel.

She led Yeeran through a side gate on the edges of the courtyard. They passed two couples, a threesome and perhaps a fivesome? Though Yeeran didn't count all the limbs. It was hard enough averting her eyes from Furi's behind.

The gate led through a stone tunnel that smelled of moss and salt. Pila stood close to Yeeran, her ears flat. After thirty paces they emerged onto a sandy bank.

There was the unmistakable sound of crashing waves and as Yeeran reached the peak of the hill she had to blink twice before she believed what she was seeing.

Waves lapped onto black sand littered with shells and rocks. Young seagulls sat bobbing on top of sea foam and strings of seaweed danced beneath clear water.

Yeeran was speechless.

'Welcome to Conch Shore,' Furi said with little fanfare.

'But . . . how?' The sea stretched to the cavern walls in the distance.

Furi frowned. 'Did you doubt the extent of Afa's power?'

'Afa?'

'The last human.'

'Oh.' It was hard to turn fiction into history. Humans had long lived in her mind as characters from faerytales. But then again so had fae.

'We believe the sea is fed in from an estuary south of Mosima.'

An estuary . . . perhaps that could be an escape route.

Perhaps, Pila mused.

'There's no way out,' Furi said, as if reading Yeeran's mind. 'The boundary is sealed all the way around Mosima. Trust me, fae have been trying for years. The only gap we know of is the one you entered and that can only be opened by one of the Jani dynasty. You're trapped here.'

Yeeran nodded, tucking all that information away to parse later.

Pila pranced towards the shore, chasing the young seagulls, her jaw snapping up sea froth and air as they evaded her.

'We'll train here for the next three months.'

'Here?' Yeeran said doubtfully. There was nothing but a beach and an old shack by the shore.

'Yes, here. Unless you'd prefer training in front of the other faeguard. Those of your ability are about ten or twelve years old, though I'm sure they'd pose a good challenge for you.'

Yeeran didn't give Furi the satisfaction of a scowl.

'Here is suitable. But perhaps you could put on some clothes.'

Furi looked down as if she'd only just realised she was naked.

'You elves are such prudes.'

'And you fae are so crass,' Yeeran responded.

Furi's gold eyes snapped to hers before she turned and stalked towards the old shed.

A few minutes later she emerged in cotton slacks and a leather vest.

'You can dismiss your obeah.'

'I thought we're to train my magic.'

'You do not need your obeah nearby for that. Besides, we are training you to act like fae. Your obeah already knows how to be an obeah.'

Furi didn't speak to Pila directly, and Yeeran wondered if that was part of obeah etiquette that she didn't know about.

Are you all right by yourself? Yeeran asked Pila.

Her response was like ocean spray, sudden and salty.

I have been fine these past twenty years, so I think so.

Yeeran laughed.

Go and explore, ask the other obeah about the boundary, but don't let it be known that we're trying to escape.

My past self has pressed their paws into every grain of dirt. Though, those memories are cloudy to me now. I will do as you say.

Pila ran off into the distance. Through the thread of their binding, no matter how far Pila went, Yeeran could still feel the thunder of her paws on the ground.

During her conversation with Pila, Furi had been moving up and down the beach, her bare feet leaving footprints along the sand. She pointed to a tree in the distance.

'Run to that tree and back again.'

Yeeran let out a breath to stop the growl that started in her throat. She set off at a jog. It was like being a first officer all over again, proving her worth and fitness to those who judged and—

Something smacked her across the face and Yeeran stumbled.

There was a surge of concern from Pila and Yeeran wondered if the obeah felt some semblance of Yeeran's pain.

I'm OK, Yeeran assured her.

Yeeran looked left and right and saw nothing. But when she took another tentative step forward something swept under her feet causing her to fall to her knees.

When she looked back her suspicions were confirmed. Sparks were igniting from Furi's hand as she whipped magic towards her.

'Fire-wielding bastard,' Yeeran grumbled.

She took off at a faster pace, but no matter how quickly she moved she underwent the stinging onslaught of Furi's magic. Red welts sprang up on her forearms and her neck. Her grazed knees bled down to her ankles.

When she returned to Furi, she didn't give her the satisfaction of showing her how much pain she had caused, nor did she acknowledge the smug smile on her face.

'Again,' Furi said.

Yeeran ran to and from the tree four times that morning. She did not complain, nor let out a sound of protest. Though her jaw was sore from clenching, she knew that silence was her best weapon against Furi's cruel actions.

Lunch interrupted her fifth run, brought by a servant on a tray. They laid it down with wide eyes in the sand before running away again.

Yeeran knew she was a sorry sight.

'Eat,' Furi commanded.

But before she did, Yeeran went to the sea to cleanse her wounds.

She hissed through her teeth at the stinging of the open cuts. The seawater was cold and biting. After a few painful breaths, the pain eased, and she was able to wash the blood away. Yeeran removed her sodden vest and inspected the deepest gashes on her torso. Though she wasn't as trained in healing as Lettle, she had seen enough battle wounds to know the one across her chest needed stitching.

She didn't put her vest back on, instead she strode back to Furi in just her undergarment, the white cotton now soaked in her blood.

'I need stitches.'

Furi laughed, her sun-gold hair trailing backwards as she tipped her head to the sky. No one in that moment could believe this woman was capable of the violence of the last few hours. Until she spoke. 'Elves really are weak.'

She sauntered slowly to the wooden shed. There was the sound of rummaging. Yeeran had started to feel dizzy, so she followed her to spur her along.

The shed was full of an assortment of things. It was part children's play box and part weapons cabinet. Books and chess pieces littered the floor, and daggers and axes lined the walls. Furi knelt in the centre, holding out a needle and thread. Yeeran ignored her because something had caught her eye.

The sabre was hanging above its scabbard on a wall, bare of other objects. It was pure hammered gold, with a ruby-encrusted hilt. A weapon fit for a chieftain, or perhaps a prince.

Yeeran reached out to touch it, but before her fingers could brush the metal Furi was there, her eyes ablaze, her nostrils flared.

'You dare touch his weapon? You who killed him?' She held up a dagger of her own and pressed it against Yeeran's cheek.

There was a sharp pain as she cut into Yeeran's skin. This was a wound she wanted others to see.

'I didn't know it was his,' Yeeran said tightly, careful not to split her skin further.

Furi dropped the blade, but it wasn't the dagger that had cut the deepest. The raw grief that distilled in Furi's gaze was more painful than any knife. Tears gathered in her eyes, turning them glass-like, droplets shattering as they fell.

'I didn't *know*,' Yeeran repeated.

They were so close that they shared the same breath, so close that Yeeran could reach over and wipe away the pain that ran down her cheeks in rivulets. Yeeran raised a hand.

Furi lurched away, startled. Gone was the grief. In its place was its twisted cousin: hatred. She left the shed in a few strides. Yeeran followed her but it was too late. Her obeah had appeared, and in one motion she pulled herself up and over onto Amnan's back.

Yeeran watched them ascend the sandy bank and disappear down the tunnel towards the palace.

She stood there for a long time, looking down the empty beach as blood poured down her face and chest.

She would have stood there for longer if Pila hadn't said, *Do you think we could ride like that one day?*

Yeeran smiled.

One day.

CHAPTER TWENTY

Yeeran

Yeeran remained on the beach after Furi left and stitched herself up with the needle and thread. Thankfully the wound that Furi had carved along her cheek with the dagger was shallow enough that she didn't have to stitch that too. By the end she was sweating, and her head was throbbing. But at least she wasn't bleeding anymore.

She ate the food that the servant had brought. Boiled yam with a fermented rice dish that was both tangy and sweet. Yeeran found that not only had she ceased to miss eating meat, the thought of it now churned her stomach. She wondered if it was the connection with Pila that had quelled her appetite for meat.

She remained on the beach for some time listening to the gentle lapping of the waves, her head tilted towards the fray.

Enough fraedia to stop the war.

With that much of the crystal, no child would ever again have to scrounge off the spoils of war or suffer the smell of putrid flesh as they searched pockets.

There was a sound behind her and Yeeran turned, expecting to see Furi. But instead, it was her cousin Nerad. She groaned inwardly.

It must be time for my next lesson.

Yeeran wasn't sure she could take much more torture.

'Hello,' he said. He was smaller than Furi in height, but just as beautiful. His lips were full and red, and his eyes soft and welcoming. They crinkled at the corners as he spoke. 'Furi said I'd find you here.'

Yeeran wasn't sure how to respond, so she simply said, 'Here I am.'

'Looks like my cousin gave you a good beating.'

Yeeran looked at him sharply, but his expression was devoid of mockery.

'Yes, she did.'

He sat down next to her and leaned back on his elbows, looking up at the fray. She followed his gaze.

'In the Elven Lands, fraedia crystal is the most valuable commodity,' Yeeran said.

Nerad didn't look surprised. 'How can something from nature be a commodity? Do you tax your rivers for running? Do you pay the trees for their leaves in autumn or charge the sky for its rain?'

Yeeran barked out a laugh and then realised Nerad wasn't joking. He gave her a bashful smile and added, 'We don't value things in the same way.'

'What do you mean? Do you have no currency?'

'We do not.'

'But how are people paid?'

How do the starving beg for food? she thought but could not bring herself to say.

'Instead of paying people for their work, our penal codes favour labour. Most of the servants in the palace are there because they have been sentenced to a term of service as punishment. In terms of craftmanship, there are those who specialise in different skills who trade their work for things they need. When it comes to food, we share everything of the earth equally—'

'Equally? No one goes hungry?'

'Equally,' he said with a grin. Two dimples grew on his cheeks, and his eyes, more hazel now, glinted with an openness she'd not seen in any of his family. The rubies on his canines glittered.

Yeeran couldn't imagine a world in which the Elven Lands oper-
ated without a currency.

'What of the queens? How is it they have power if wealth is shared
so equally?'

'The Jani dynasty's power is of the land, not of the people.'

'Huh?'

Nerad stood.

'If I'm to teach you fae customs, then I must start at the beginning. This way.' Nerad started off down the beach, his heels bouncing
as he whistled tunelessly.

He is so different to Furi in every way.

But he is still your captor, Pila reminded her. The thought was like
a snowflake down her back.

'Where are we going?' Yeeran asked.

They walked back the way she had come, through the tunnel
towards the Royal Woodland.

'You'll know when we get there.'

'Sun sins, nothing is simple here.'

His brows knitted together. 'First things first, don't say "sun sins",
you'll end up with an axe between your eyes.'

'I thought the fae didn't kill other fae.'

Nerad raised an eyebrow. 'What gave you that impression?'

'The queens said it was the law: no fae life can be taken.'

'And laws are never broken in your land?' Nerad said, genuinely
interested.

'Well . . . yes . . . but . . .'

Nerad waited, but Yeeran had stuttered to a stop. He went on,
'Anyway, no one will *actually* kill you for saying "sun sins". But the
expression is derogatory, it's rooted in bigotry towards the fae by
suggesting our creation in the sun's light was a sin.'

Yeeran's eyes widened.

'Oh, you didn't realise?' he said.

She shook her head. 'No . . . I guess I had never thought about
the words' origins.'

'No one ever does.' The grin he gave her lessened some of the tension that had brewed between them. 'I happen to have an interest in etymology.'

Yeeran's thoughts were troubled. How much had elves contributed to the vilification of fae throughout history?

The Royal Woodland was now quiet, except for the scuttling of salamanders and the occasional obeah crossing their path.

Nerad began to circle the baobab tree. The gold basin on the dais in front of the thrones flickered with warm coals.

'Isn't it a bit dangerous to have fire this close to all this kindling?' Yeeran waved a hand towards the tree.

Nerad let out a short laugh.

'Don't worry, the Tree of Souls cannot burn. It cannot be damaged or cut down. Not while the Jani dynasty live. The basin of fire is a symbolic reminder of the sun god, Ewia, who shines on us still.'

There is so much I don't know about this land, this culture, Yeeran said to Pila.

Though the obeah wasn't with her, she felt the comfort of Pila's wet nose against her leg as she said, *So, we'll learn together.*

This close to the Tree of Souls, Yeeran could see that the thrones weren't carved into the bark but had grown with the tree. Vines circled the arches of the thrones' backs and Afa's curse was scrawled above them.

'The tree is over a thousand years old?'

'Yes,' Nerad said heavily. 'Come this way.'

He rounded the trunk where a metal ladder hung from one of the taller branches. He began to scale the rungs.

'Why are we going up there?' Yeeran asked.

'I promised to take you to the beginning, and the beginning you shall have. The Tree of Souls isn't just sacred to the Jani dynasty. No,' he paused, looking down at her, 'it *is* the Jani dynasty.'

Yeeran frowned and began to follow him. The bloated trunk of the baobab tapered the higher she climbed. The branches that had seemed spindly from the ground were as thick as her thighs and knotted with age. As the foliage got thicker she noticed that the green leaves were skeletal, like feathers, delicate and fragile. She reached out to pluck one.

'Don't,' Nerad warned her. 'Each leaf is a soul of my ancestors.'

'What?' Yeeran's hand dropped to her side.

Nerad sighed, and continued walking. He stopped when they reached a flattened branch that served as a platform about thirty feet from the ground.

'A thousand years ago, the fae were cursed and sent to live in this world by Afa, the last of the humans.'

'Why did Afa curse your people?'

Nerad's jaw worked silently before he spoke.

'We don't know. All we know is he used the power of the earth to place us here.'

'You mean you didn't kill all the humans?'

'No more than you have killed all the fae,' he said, his words cutting her to the quick. His frustration ebbed away as quickly as it had come. 'Sorry. Our histories are not complete . . . and it irks me some.'

Yeeran nodded, accepting his apology.

'When Afa cursed us, he bound the rulers of the fae to this tree.'

'Why?'

'The Tree of Souls is the lifeblood of Mosima. Though it is tied to the magic of the boundary that keeps us captive, its roots also fertilise the land, and its leaves purify the air.' Nerad rested a hand on the shiny bark. 'And so too is the Jani dynasty tied to the land.'

'What does that mean?'

'It means that we must always have two monarchs from my family on the thrones . . .' He looked at her, and Yeeran could see in his eyes that he was debating whether or not to share the next piece of information with her. He pressed his lips together, turned his face back to the tree and said, '. . . or Mosima will fall.'

This was a critical piece of intelligence, a failsafe if their escape didn't work. All they'd need to do was kill . . . all of the Jani dynasty.

Kill Furi. Could Yeeran really murder someone outside of war?

Mosima is a type of battlefield, and Furi is just another enemy. The thought rang hollow, perhaps lacking true conviction. Yeeran shook Furi from her mind and looked up at the bough above them, the leaves glittering in the fray-light.

'When a new pair of monarchs reign two new branches grow.' Nerad pointed to the limbs of the tree. 'The branches are bound to the monarchs who rule. The monarchs cannot abdicate. Only the death of either ruler can end the pair's reign.'

'They're bound to the tree? Like fae are bound to the obeah?'

Nerad frowned, considering. 'Yes . . . a bit like that.'

'How long do fae live?'

'A hundred and fifty years, give or take. So most reigning pairs are on the throne for under a hundred years.'

Yeeran tipped her head back and surveyed the heavy-set branches. Each one sprouted smaller offshoots filling the bough of the tree, but it was clear that the thickest ones, grown in symmetry on either side, represented the monarchs' reign.

'But what if the rulers have no siblings, or there are more siblings than places on the throne?'

'Aha, good question. Our population is a small one, and over the years the Jani dynasty bloodline has . . . mingled with commoners. There have been two occasions that the Tree of Souls has chosen a monarch from a family outside the royal bloodline. Though this happens only when the sitting monarchs produce no children.'

Yeeran looked at the Tree of Souls with new eyes. Each leaf, each dew-drop, was a symbol of the dynasty – it was the heartbeat of the monarchy.

'The tree doesn't always choose siblings, then?'

'Not always, sometimes it is cousins. The only law is that the pair must start and end their reign together.'

'And you and Furi are the only children of Chall and Vyce?'

'Now we are.' He didn't say it cruelly, but still Yeeran looked away.

The view from the baobab tree was vast. From its vantage, Yeeran could take in the expanse of Mosima for leagues around.

It is so green, so vibrant and full of life. She imagined seeing the Elven Lands this way, lit by a great shard of fraedia.

As her gaze travelled, Yeeran noticed the blackened fields in the distance. She'd seen them before from the boundary line.

'What is that?'

Nerad knew what she was pointing at without looking. 'The blight.' His nostrils flared, and he indicated that they should descend from the tree.

Yeeran didn't move and instead waited for an explanation. When he at last spoke, his words were laden with a weary sadness. 'I have made it my life's work to study the blight, but still, I have no real answer for you. It started around thirty years ago, about the time my cousin found a way out of the boundary.' Yeeran heard the smile in his voice. 'That was a happy day. Each fae was let out above ground in batches, to feel the true sun on their face. Not this cheap imitation.' He waved a hand towards the sky at the fraedia.

Yeeran felt a spark of annoyance. In the Elven Lands, fraedia was not cheap.

'Why didn't you all just leave? There and then?'

'Because,' he said heavily, 'Mosima cannot survive without the Jani dynasty. Every time one of the Jani dynasty leaves the boundary, the trees begin to shed leaves, fish start to die, or the sea slowly becomes acidic. It is why all scouting missions are brief. To leave is to sacrifice it all.'

'Oh.'

He took a deep breath and began descending the tree. Yeeran followed, listening.

'When the blight began, we thought at first it was due to the fact my cousin had broken the boundary. For years we banned any further expeditions topside. But even after that the blight kept getting worse. Now it stretches across three fields of arable land.'

They had reached lower ground again. Nerad was out of breath from the effort, and Yeeran realised he was not the soldier his cousin was.

'This way, one last place before the end of the lesson,' he said.

The fray had dimmed to a soft orange, outlining everything in a golden halo.

Nerad set off deeper into the Royal Woodland, leading her further away from the palace. The trees soon began to thin, revealing rows of white pebbles piled up in mounds.

The precise design had Yeeran wondering about their purpose. She was about to ask Nerad, but then it struck her.

The mounds were graves.

Nerad knelt by one of the closest ones. The white stones were brighter than the others, the earth upon which they pressed was freshly churned.

It must have been the prince's grave.

So this was to be her torture for the afternoon.

'I was with him, at the end,' Nerad said. 'He looked like he was smiling when he died. His soul left him with his last breath. It was peaceful, though I suspect the way you killed his obeah was not as bloodless.'

Yeeran wanted to run, wanted to leave, wanted to be anywhere but here. Instead, she found herself falling, her knees striking the ground with the heaviness of her guilt.

'I didn't mean to. I didn't mean to,' Yeeran said over and over.

'And yet you did.' Nerad wasn't speaking harshly, like Furi had. She tilted her face up to his. It wasn't streaked with tears like she expected. It didn't show much emotion at all.

'Why did you bring me here?'

'Because you need to know. Not all of us grieve his loss.'

Yeeran inhaled sharply at his words, so afraid to speak, to presume, that she let Nerad fill the silence instead.

'There are those of us that are glad he is now nameless rubble, no longer destined for the throne.'

Nerad turned watery eyes to hers. 'He was the eldest of the three of us, at nearly sixty years of age.'

This didn't surprise Yeeran: she remembered the obeah's whiskers had been white. Yeeran nodded, prompting him to continue.

'Before Furi was born, it was just the two of us: him and I. There are no marriages in our lands, no duties for our parents. Couplings can be as brief as a spring rain, or as long as the fray's beam. Babies are born and handed to those who desire to raise them. But not the Jani dynasty. We have no way to extricate ourselves from our mothers.' His lips twisted with a depth of bitterness that was in contrast to his gentle friendliness of a few minutes prior. 'So he raised me, my cousin. Twenty years my senior, he became a father to me. But once he learned to open the boundary everything changed. Our disagreements became chasms.'

His lips pressed together until the edges of them turned pale brown and bloodless. It was clear that he was finished talking about his cousin. He stood and brushed the soil off his cotton trousers.

Looking at him, Yeeran could see the conflicting emotions roiling beneath the surface.

There was the feeling of hot stones under her skin as Pila stretched along warm flagstones in the courtyard some distance away.

Love and hate are oil and water, separate but similar, and sometimes they swirl together, making it difficult to tell one from the other. Pila's observation startled Yeeran with its complexity and wisdom.

Pila sensed Yeeran's surprise, and her next words felt like biting down on a chilli seed. *I too have a mind and thoughts of my own.*

Yeeran tried to contain her laugh from Nerad as Pila rounded off the conversation with, *I'm off to chase grasshoppers.*

You do that. I'll see you soon.

Nerad cleared his throat, drawing Yeeran's attention back to him.

'Leave your guilt here.' Nerad's voice was surer. 'His death was not your fault, no matter how much Furi wishes to leave the burden at your feet.'

Yeeran nodded.

Nerad's gaze had taken on a faraway quality.

'If you do not mind, I think I will retire for the rest of the evening. Can you make your way back?'

'Yes, I think so.'

Nerad said nothing further as he walked away. His torso was slightly hunched as if he nursed an invisible pain in his abdomen.

Yeeran stood looking down at the grave. Murder was not a new crime to her, but she'd never killed anyone outside of the battlefield.

'May your passing be like the light of the moon, banishing all of darkness, all of doom. May your soul rest among the starlight and your heart shine bright.'

A tear fell down her cheek as she mourned the man she'd never known. Despite what Nerad had said, her actions had still caused his death.

Yeeran stood there, among the bones of the dead. Until hunger tugged at her senses, and she made her way back to the palace.

She had much to share with her sister.

CHAPTER TWENTY-ONE

Lettle

Lettle couldn't stop thinking about the binding banquet. About the kiss that almost was.

That night, though her eyes grew heavy and her bones weary, sleep did not find her. At two in the morning there was a sound in the living room. She thought at first it was Pila, but the footsteps were heavy, unlike the graceful footfalls of the obeah. Lettle crept to her door and opened it a crack.

A shadow moved in the dim glow of the firelight. Lettle's hand shook as she held open the door. She stopped breathing and listened.

There was a grunt of pain as the silhouette bumped into the velvet sofa.

'Rayan?'

Lettle stepped out of the doorway and moved towards him.

'Sorry, did I wake you? I stubbed my toe.'

Sweat beaded Rayan's brow and he was a little breathless. A stupid smile hung about his lips.

'Where've you been?'

'I-I went for a walk.'

'A walk? Where?'

'I . . . to . . . around . . . the woodland.'

The muscle in his jaw twitched, revealing the lie. She knew exactly

where he'd been, and who he'd been with. She made a sound of
disgust and turned away.

'Lettle, I really was, Lettle . . .'

She closed her bedroom door and leaned her back against it. She
heard Rayan's footsteps pause outside her door. She could feel the
blood pounding in her ears and for the first time she wasn't sure
what scared her more – that one day she would come to love this
man, or that one day she would kill him.

When he moved away, she let out a gasp that grew into a sob.

She didn't try to sleep after that. Instead, to distract herself from
the thought of Rayan's sweat-slick face, she thought about Seer Sahar.
The fae had known Lettle didn't take snowmallow flower and he
had mentioned the Fates. Hope surged and bubbled in her mind
like a hot spring.

If she could get back her powers of divination, maybe she could
glean some of their future here. Maybe she could even find out more
about how Rayan would die.

No, how I will murder *him.*

She winced and turned over in the bed. The sheets had tangled
around her legs, and she shrugged them off in frustration. The light
from the fray began to grow brighter as dawn beckoned. She missed
the light of the moon.

A thought struck her like a spark against her brow, leaving the
skin there hot and prickling. She sat up in bed.

'Under a waxing moon that no one can see,' she murmured the
words of her last prophecy to herself. 'When the sun flares and
twilight reigns . . . '

Twilight . . . Yeeran had said that Jani meant *twilight* in fae.

'A burdened partnership will die when poison passes their lips.
One gilded, one pearl.'

Her last prophecy would come true in Mosima. Two of the fae
were going to die. Now she had three people's deaths on her mind.

She dragged herself out of bed and pulled on a pair of cotton
trousers and a shirt that was far too translucent. But finding some-

thing less transparent was difficult, until she discovered a thick hooded shawl in the back of the cupboard. It was chequered in red and green, the knit large and chunky. It was clearly a winter accessory, but Lettle didn't care. It covered her chest quite nicely. She pulled it around her now, for comfort rather than warmth.

She marched out of their apartment, a line of determination etched across her forehead.

The apothecary wasn't far. Seer Sahar had said to look out for a purple sign hanging above the door. Lettle's feet pounded across the tiled street. In her haste to leave, she'd forgotten to wear shoes, though that requirement – much like underwear – seemed to lapse in Mosima.

Those who recognised her moved out of the way and bared their teeth at her. Those who didn't were soon told, so that they too could throw hostile looks her way. She watched one fae's hand wrap around the hilt of their dagger while another watched her with morbid fascination.

She hissed in his direction, 'Shut that mouth before I shut it for you.'

He jumped back, startled. Then, delighted, he said, 'It's true! She has no fangs!' He proceeded to clap his hands as if watching a play.

Lettle saw the purple of the apothecary sign and ducked into the shop before she did something she regretted.

The familiar scent of herbs and spices reminded her of her father's final days, when his illness hung in the air like the cloying scent of snowmallow flower. She closed her eyes and tried to vanquish the memories from her mind. She breathed in slowly, smoothing the sharp edges of the past.

'Can I help you, *elf*?'

So brief was her respite. All sense of calm fled as the world 'elf' was thrown at her like an insult.

Lettle opened her eyes to slits and saw Seer Sahar standing five paces away, surrounded by bottles and jars of remedies.

'You mentioned the Fates yester—' she began to say.

Sahar stepped forward with sure and even steps and interrupted Lettle by grasping her stiffened arm and cradling it with surprisingly soft hands. He clicked his tongue behind his teeth.

'Mm-hmm, yes. A teaspoon of sap from the owen tree will ease your pain.'

Lettle snatched her arm back, and though it hurt, the gesture had the desired effect of annoying the seer.

'It's impossible to understand my ailment by just looking at it.'

Lettle had never been one to mince words. She wore her ignorance as proudly as her intelligence.

The seer's laugh started from his belly and worked its way up.

'Oh, I know more about you than you could ever imagine, Lettle.'

Lettle grimaced. He'd been keeping his ear to the palace ground.

'Do you have any of this owen tree sap then?' she asked.

'I do, I told you yesterday. I've had it ready since you arrived,' Sahar said. 'It's that jar.'

A spark flared from Sahar's hand, but Lettle could see no jar.

'Where is it?'

'I'm showing you.'

'Huh?'

The seer huffed through his nose.

'Do you not know how to use your inner eyes?'

Lettle was getting annoyed by this fae's cryptic nattering. She was about to tell him so when she had a thought.

What if I became heedless? Being heedless was what enabled Lettle to parse the Fates during prophecy. And so, with practised precision, she let her mind go blank.

When she opened her eyes again and looked around, she almost stumbled. Sahar's hands hummed with a single strand of golden magic which shimmered towards a jar on the second shelf.

No, this can't be.

Divination showed Lettle pearls of magic that she could read, but she had never thought that becoming heedless would allow her to see fae magic too. She followed her hunch and walked outside.

Threads of gold wove in and out of the street, flung from the hands of fae. One woman was using it to push back an overlying tree branches in her path, another was using it to pull along a cart full of vegetables.

The whole of Mosima glowed like a crackling fire.

Lettle clapped a hand to her mouth and slipped out of her meditative state. She strode back into the apothecary where Sahar was calmly measuring out what must have been owen tree sap into a jar.

'How is it possible?' she asked.

'How is what possible, *elf*?'

Lettle bristled.

'The magic.'

'The god Ewia granted the fae the magic of sunlight. Once a fae bonds with an obeah, they come into their power. That is the way of things.'

Lettle couldn't believe it, that all this time the elves could have *seen* the magic at work if they had just become heedless.

'Is that how you read the Fates? Through your magic?' she asked.

Sahar looked up sharply. '*Your* magic, do you not mean? Where Ewia granted the fae magic to whip and ensnare, Bosome gave the elves the ability to read the Fates.'

Lettle nodded deeply. It was rare that she spoke to someone who believed in the gods.

'Bosome blessed us.' She looked skywards. 'In the Elven Lands we practise it by reading entrails.'

Sahar clicked his tongue again and shook his head, the braids in his hair shaking. 'Reading entrails. A needless task.'

Lettle stepped forward. 'So it's true, it's possible to read the Fates without killing an obeah?'

Sahar laughed again. 'If it was not, how did I know I'd need to harvest owen tree sap when you arrived in Mosima?'

Lettle reached for the countertop and pressed her hand into the grain of the wood.

'Teach me.' It was meant to be a request, but it came out as a desperate plea.

Sahar looked deep into Lettle's eyes. Then he chuckled once.

'My connection to the Fates is strong.' Lettle's voice was closer to a whine than she would have liked. 'My last prophecy, it's going to come true, here . . .' Then she repeated the words she had foretold, '*One gilded, one pearl* – does that mean anything to you?'

Sahar's brown eyes had narrowed but he didn't answer.

'Teach me, please,' she begged again.

If she could talk to the Fates, then maybe she could save Rayan's life.

And let herself love him.

Sahar let out a slow breath, then turned and stepped out into a back room.

'Hello?' Lettle called after a few minutes had passed.

Lettle felt the hope that had bubbled and popped in her just a few seconds earlier fizz and dry out.

When Sahar didn't come back, Lettle picked up the jar of owen tree sap and left with a growl.

On her walk back to the palace Lettle shifted her sight again and became heedless. Though it was a hard state to maintain, the experience left her reeling.

She kept to the edges of the streets, letting the brightness of the magic guide her. Everything in the world had a spark of magic in its core, she'd known that, seen it first-hand when training for divination. Yet somehow here, under the light of the fray, everything glowed brighter.

'Watch out!' someone called. She turned as a faeguard riding an obeah cantered past. Together their glow was almost blinding, a swirling mixture of syrup and bronze, like liquid gold pooled into two forms.

Lettle found herself running to keep up with them, to keep the warmth of that light in her sights. They crossed a bridge teeming with specks of glowing fish. The distance between the faeguard and

Lettle stretched but still she ran, marvelling at the flare of magic
the pair created.

Further down the road, houses were sparser and the trees lining
the road grew in number. The flame of the pair's magic flickered
in the distance, where the road opened out to a field and disappeared
over a hill.

Here the grass was well worn and packed tight. It reminded Lettle
of the Bleeding Field.

She held a hand to her beating heart, her breath coming fast and
short. She let the magic sight slip from her gaze. The strain of
maintaining the heedless state had caused a slight headache to bloom
in her temples. She was used to being heedless during a reading,
not consistently.

Once her breathing and heartbeat had calmed, she wiped the
sweat from her brow and crested the hill.

She could hear the distinctive sound of clattering armour and
swords, and for a moment she was dragged back to the battlefield
when she was a child – her pockets laden with stolen goods, her
hands sticky with blood from prising out golden teeth.

She shook the memory free and looked down the hill at the
training grounds below.

There were around five hundred of the faeguard dressed in full
warfare uniform as they conducted training drills, clashing and
ducking and kicking.

*Why do they need so many of them? There are no wars waged in
Mosima . . . so why did they need armour?*

At least Lettle knew where to steal weapons from when they
found an escape route.

Lettle watched the soldiers for some time. Then, out of curiosity
she became heedless again. Sure enough, the soldiers were wielding
magic along with their swords. The magical threads were beautifully
hypnotic and hummed with energy. The soldiers spun in formation,
pulling their opponents' legs out from under them or whipping their
arms backwards.

Lettle dropped the veil of magic sight. The throbbing of her arm was now coupled with a full-blown headache, and she reached for the jar Sahar had given her. She dipped her little finger into the sap and placed a drop of it on her tongue. It was thick and sweet.

The easing of the pain in her muscles was instantaneous and Lettle had to admit that Sahar was right about the medicine.

Lettle let her gaze wander over the faeguard for a little longer. It occurred to her that Yeeran might be down below, training with Furi. But she couldn't see her.

She was about to go when she noticed someone she recognised.

To the edge of the clearing in a section separated by a high brick wall, Lettle saw Rayan with a woman. The white-blonde hair was unmistakably Berro's. The wall meant the majority of the faeguard couldn't see them, but from Lettle's vantage point she could watch their actions very clearly.

Berro's dark skin rippled with muscles as she lunged forward, her magic slipping around Rayan's waist, a blade in her other hand as she pulled him towards her. Lettle cried out, but she was too far away to warn him. It turned out he didn't need the warning, as he twisted out of her arms, dropping to the ground before swiping his feet under hers. Lettle was about to run to him, to help him in any way she knew possible, but then she saw something peculiar.

Berro was laughing.

Rayan offered her a hand up and she clapped him on the back before they dropped into defensive stances again.

They were training together.

Lettle felt sick. This was her own fault. She had pushed him away and into another woman's arms.

Lettle's nails dug into her own stiffened bicep, numb now from the owen tree sap. She let out a ragged sigh before leaving.

She couldn't watch anymore.

As Lettle walked through the city, colourful birds swooped low and settled in the branches of myrtle trees that lined the roads. Wildflowers grew in clusters among their roots in blues and yellows. Mosima was beautiful, Lettle couldn't deny it. But it wasn't *home*.

She felt a pang of helplessness. She'd been content with her life in Gural. Now she was a prisoner – in paradise – but a prisoner, nonetheless.

I will get home again, Rayan promised me. Though the thought was tinged with the bitterness of what might have been, she took comfort in his words.

Now that she was armed with the ability to see fae magic, she wanted to inspect the boundary. It was easy enough to make her way there – she simply walked to the cavern's wall. She was so determined to reach her destination that she didn't notice one of the fae following her ten paces behind.

The city grew less populated as she neared the boundary. She wondered how many of the empty homes belonged to fae who had died because an elf had killed an obeah.

How many fae did Father kill? How many did I?

Lettle steeled her will. She refused to feel guilty for committing a crime she'd had no knowledge of. And unlike Yeeran, Lettle had killed outside of a battlefield before.

The smell of snowmallow flower rose from her memories once more, but she pushed it away and quickened her pace.

She reached the cavern walls breathless and sweaty. The stone was rust-coloured, powdery, and rough. Lettle felt anticipation prickle her armpits as she became heedless.

The boundary glowed so bright it took her a moment to understand what she was seeing. The walls weren't bound with the golden threads of fae magic like she'd thought. The magic looked different to that of the fae. She stepped forward, trying to make sense of it.

Instead of gold the magic glowed a deep brass, and as she got closer, she realised the bronze threads were shaped in a language she couldn't understand.

Was this human magic?

If the fae had it right, Afa, the last of the humans, had banished them here.

Lettle was pulled from her thoughts by a sound behind her.

An obeah stood in the shade of a tree. It cocked its head at her, and she noticed it had a broken horn. It blinked its green eyes once, twice.

'Can I help you?' Lettle said.

It snorted, drawing its teeth back, its black fur rippling as the muscles in its hindquarters tensed. Lettle prepared herself for a quick death. If the obeah lunged, there was nothing she could do.

'Bosome protect me, this is not how I die.' She hissed at it and tried to make herself look bigger.

There was a movement on the path behind her and Lettle noticed the glint of steel and the flash of blue eyes.

Hosta.

Lettle felt panic burn up her throat. If this obeah was bound to Hosta, then this was indeed where she was going to die.

But then the obeah wheeled around, facing the fae.

Wait, was the obeah *protecting* her?

Hosta twirled their dagger in their hand and gave Lettle a wave. With the obeah between Lettle and them, there wasn't much more Hosta could do than threaten her.

But nevertheless, the threat hit home.

Lettle swallowed and waited. Hosta raised an eyebrow as if to say, 'I'll get you eventually,' before turning on their heel and leaving back down the path.

When Lettle's breath settled, the obeah turned its green eyes to her once more, before loping off in the direction it had come from.

Lettle held a hand to her beating heart, closed her eyes and let out a sigh. 'I need to get out of this place,' she said to herself.

Then she heard another voice. 'Lettle!'

Her heart nearly stopped until she saw who it was.

'Golan? Komi?'

'We've been looking for you everywhere,' Komi said in exasperation. He ran a hand through his moustache, twirling the points with an excitable expression. He wore his freedom like a vibrant cloak, colourful and full of life.

'Are you all right?' Golan noticed Lettle was still holding her hand to her heart.

'I just saw Hosta . . .'

Golan looked around with a worried expression.

'What did they do to you?'

'Nothing, they just followed me here and threatened me with a knife.'

'What?' Komi's permanent grin clouded over.

'It's OK, an obeah came to my rescue.'

'*What?*' It was Golan's turn to exclaim. 'Whose obeah?'

Lettle shrugged. 'Not sure.'

Golan looked troubled. 'You shouldn't leave the palace on your own. I don't think Hosta would actually hurt you, but the threat should not be taken lightly.'

Lettle nodded and ran a tired hand over her brow.

'What were you doing out here anyway?'

'Golan is supposed to be taking us on a tour. I think he drew the short feather and is stuck with us,' Komi said.

'I am not *stuck* with you, but yes, I'm to give you a tour of Mosima, but it seems, Lettle, you've done it yourself.'

Lettle didn't want to spend the next hour touring farmland. She looked at the boundary, her mind swirling with questions.

'Is there somewhere I can learn more about Mosima? A library maybe?' she asked. Then added when she saw his frown, 'If it's to be my new home, I want to learn all I can.'

Golan nodded slowly. 'I understand. I know exactly where to take you.'

'Where?'

'The Book Orchard,' Golan said.

Komi clasped his hands together. 'Are there apples there too?'

Lettle let out a rare laugh.

'Let's go.'

CHAPTER TWENTY-TWO

Lettle

Golan set off west along the cavern wall with Komi and Lettle flanking him. 'You'll always know you're going west because the fray is slightly off centre, you see?' Golan said.

Lettle had the absurd thought that he might be taking them topside. She voiced her thought and he laughed.

'Unfortunately not. I am not one of the Jani dynasty and therefore I cannot part the magic of the boundary to let you out.'

'That's a shame,' Komi said before getting distracted by a blue bird he'd never seen before. Lettle wondered how much of Komi's mind had fractured during his isolation.

She turned to Golan. 'How do the Jani dynasty do it? Break the boundary?'

'The prince, he discovered a remnant of the human magic, I think. It's not exactly something they care to talk about, especially to someone like me.'

'Someone like you?'

'Lightless.'

Lettle shook her head. The politics in Mosima seemed as senseless as those of the Elven Lands.

'Even if I did know how,' he added, 'you have to be one of the Jani dynasty, their blood is tied to the land.'

Lettle saw a flash of brown fur and watched as an obeah made their way towards the boundary and slipped through a crack in the stone.

'Why is it that obeah can travel beyond the boundary and fae cannot?'

Golan shrugged. 'Some think it is because the obeah were innocent in the wars between human and fae. Others think it was an act of mercy, letting the creatures free so they can live in their rightful habitat, should they choose.'

'Or maybe not mercy.' Komi had reappeared. Lettle hadn't realised he was listening. His next words were forlorn and distant. 'It is a cruel torture to let half of your soul soar, while the other is caged down here. Mercy is, after all, the antithesis of power.'

Lettle wasn't sure if she gave credence to that statement; she thought that the most merciful of leaders were those who were the most powerful. She turned back to Golan. 'It cannot be all that bad,' Lettle said. 'Mosima is wonderful. Except the fae, of course.'

Golan laughed at that.

'Yes, I agree. My kind have been confined to this cavern for too long and like the red stones that cage us, we have become brittle. But Mosima without the fae is no Mosima at all. So, we endure.'

They had arrived at a tunnel carved into the rock face.

'Golan?'

Had she been too quick to trust him? Was he luring Komi and her to their deaths?

'It's not much further,' he said. Four words had never sounded more ominous.

There was no light in the tunnel, and eventually the darkness blotted out the fray.

Lettle stumbled and caught her arm against the side of the tunnel. The pain there flared, and she hissed.

'Are you all right?' Komi asked.

'Yes, it's just so damn dark down here.'

'Aren't you using your magesight?' Komi said.

'What?'

'Magesight, it's what they call it, when you see the magic.'

Of course, Komi knew about magesight. He'd been a prisoner in Mosima for over ten years. He must have picked up a lot about the fae during his time here.

She reminded herself to question Komi later.

With a sigh Lettle softened her sight and became heedless. What she saw made her gasp.

The words of magic she had seen from the cavern's walls wove like dancing eels across the tunnel's surface. The magic banished the darkness with its shimmering light. She winced, her headache blossoming once more, but her curiosity was more potent than the pain.

Her gaze followed the stream of magic to a domed room, the ceiling latticed with more bronze threads. The boundary had stretched into the tunnel, the words of human magic contoured along the shape of the room.

'The Book Orchard was created when my ancestors dug a tunnel in an attempt at escape from Mosima,' Golan said up ahead. 'But the more my ancestors dug, the further the boundary moved into the tunnel to encompass it. Now, though, it is a library – a perfect place of sanctuary.'

Lettle brought her gaze downwards. Stacks and stacks of books rippled outwards in a spiral. The shelves themselves let out a faint spark of magic and as she took a step forward, she realised they were made out of the twisted branches of a tree.

'For a hundred years, the trees have been growing here, nourished by the rich soil and our magic. Then my great-grandfather began to train them to twist and flatten their branches into shelves. And here we are.'

'This is incredible,' she breathed.

'There is another, more well-stocked library in the university north-east of here. But I didn't think you'd enjoy the crowds there,' he said to Lettle.

Or the threats to my life.

'I thought this might be more to your liking.'

Lettle turned and hugged Golan, pulling him close. He let out a squawk before relaxing into her body.

She dropped her magesight and gasped as the darkness filled her senses once more.

Golan withdrew some fraedia crystal and handed a shard to her and Komi.

'Here,' he said. 'I find it hard to maintain magesight sometimes, too.'

'Is it because you are not bound to an obeah? That you find magesight hard?' Lettle asked.

The fraedia light cast the creases of his frown in shadow.

'Yes. I have not and will not come into my full power. I am unable to wield magic like other fae my age.' It was as if the words left a bitter taste in his mouth.

'Will you find your obeah soon?'

He shook his head firmly.

'I no longer harbour hope. There are many like me, and it is rare past forty to find your soul partner.'

'Why do you think an obeah didn't bond with you?' Lettle knew she was pressing a bit too hard into a wound. But she had told Yeeran she would collect information, and this may lead to something important.

Or maybe since seeing Yeeran with Pila, she had been wondering if she might get an obeah of her own.

'My obeah may have been killed by elves before they could find me.' His words had bite and Lettle knew she had gone too far.

'I'm sorry, it must be very painful for you.'

'Yes, I'm outcast, like you.' He grinned and Lettle could tell all was forgiven. 'Would you like to explore some more?'

'Yes.' Lettle ran her greedy eyes across the rows of books. 'I would like that very much.'

Lettle quickly learned that the majority of the tomes were written in fae.

'I can't read any of this,' she groaned.

Golan gave her an apologetic shrug and scuffed his cane across the floor.

'Sorry, I didn't think . . .'

Lettle was sitting at a raised oak table that grew in the centre of the room.

Komi sat next to her studying a map that he'd found.

'That's Lorhan,' Golan said, pointing to a landmass on the map. 'The capital city of the old Fae Lands, before the curse.'

The shape of the map looked vaguely familiar, but the words were so alien that she glanced away lest her headache get worse.

She pulled out a stack of books and ran her fingers over the raised ink on the pages. The paper was feather light, almost translucent. Fae used the same alphabet as elvish but the letter forms were archaic, the words nonsensical to her monolingual mind. She was fascinated by the swirling language.

'Can you speak fae even though you're not faebound?'

'Yes,' he said heavily. 'A lot of my clients are faebound, and they find it easier if their stylist speaks to them in fae.'

'Why is it that fae isn't the language that is taught in schools? Why do you speak elvish?'

Golan laughed and tapped his cane on the ground.

'Elvish? We do not call it that, it is simply the universal tongue.' He chuckled again, shaking his head. 'The language of fae is not taught because it is difficult to master. Some Lightless will never learn it.'

It sounded like a challenge. And if the answers to escaping Mosima were here in the library, she would find them.

'That is why even those faebound switch between the two languages so seamlessly,' Golan continued.

'Will you teach me fae?' Lettle asked.

'I don't think I would be the best teacher . . . plus I'm very busy most days and my work takes me all over Mosima.'

Lettle deflated. If Sahar wouldn't take her in, and Golan wouldn't either, then what would she do with her time until Yeeran's initiation?

'It would be different if you were my apprentice, and I was teaching you about style and make-up. Which I must say is something you do need me to guide you in. That shawl is for winter and should never be worn with that style of patterned shirt.'

Lettle ignored the insult. She'd had an idea.

'Why don't I become your apprentice then? You can teach me how to speak fae while you teach me how to do "style".'

Komi laughed.

'You? His apprentice?'

Lettle shot him a glare.

'Shut up.'

Golan shook his head.

Lettle anticipated the refusal and said, 'You wouldn't have to tell anyone I'm an elf. I can hide my teeth, rename myself – whatever you want. Please, I need to do something.'

'Well, I intend to sample every single tavern in Mosima, and after that I'm going to do the bakeries,' Komi announced. Lettle ignored him.

'Yeeran's off training and even Rayan has found something to occupy his time. I tried to get Seer Sahar to teach me, but he turned me away.'

Golan jerked upright. 'You went to see Sahar?'

'Yes, what of it?'

'He's dangerous, Lettle.'

Lettle rolled her eyes. 'Divination isn't dangerous. People just fear what they don't know.'

'Divination?' Komi asked. His eyes narrowed. 'Divination is a fool's game.' His words reminded her that he was once Crescent tribe where diviners were actively persecuted.

'Oh, not you too,' she groaned.

'Seer Sahar was once an adviser to the queens,' Golan pressed. 'But his ways of magic were condemned. Banned from the court.'

'Good,' Komi said, in a voice that was unlike his usual cheerful tone.

Lettle gave him an irritated look and turned back to Golan. 'Why though? What made them ban him?'

Golan clenched his teeth together. 'Lettle, please remember, I do the queens' hair. That is all.'

Lettle looked away. She had upset him again.

'Like a dark cloud over the sky, rain will come whether you want it to or not. But if you know that there is drought coming in a day or so, you can put out a bucket. Divination gives us that bucket.'

Golan shuddered. 'Let us speak no more of it. I am glad he turned you down.'

Golan's prejudice was root deep, impacted by the way the fae treated the seer. The royals had a lot to account for.

She turned her gaze back to the library. If there was knowledge to be found about Mosima, and about divination, she might find it here.

'Teach me,' Lettle pleaded.

'All right, all right.' Golan held up his free hand. 'I admit defeat, you can be my apprentice.'

'Aha!' Komi clapped Lettle on the back.

'But please,' Golan said. 'Don't wear that shawl tomorrow – my clients will never book me again.'

Lettle twirled, the shawl spinning outwards. '*I* think it's quite fetching.'

'Fetching for a fire. Now come on. I need to get you both back to the palace before my next appointment.'

Golan left Lettle and Komi at the door to their rooms.

'And I'll see you tomorrow? At dawn?' she pressed.

'Yes,' he sighed, but his heart wasn't in it. 'I'll see you tomorrow, here, at dawn. Don't pick out your own outfit. I'll have something sent up.' He followed the chastisement with a wicked grin.

Golan waved them both away and walked down the length of the corridor, his cane clicking beside him. She watched him go, his steady gait taking him down a different hallway opposite the glass staircase. Lettle realised his next appointment must be with the queens.

She turned and stepped into their apartment.

The room was warm, filled with the smell of red wine and buttered potatoes. Food had already been brought in and Yeeran and Rayan were sitting around the table eating. They looked up as Komi and Lettle came in.

Komi joined them at the table. 'What a day we've had. First, Golan showed me to the best taverns, then we went past the market hall through to the school district. Then to the boundary where we eventually caught up with Lettle.' Komi sat down, took a breath and continued, 'We spent the afternoon in the Book Orchard, which is a library. That was probably the most boring bit, but Lettle liked it.'

'Sounds like quite a day. I was worried.' Yeeran's brow was furrowed.

Rayan snorted, easing the tension that the coldness in Yeeran's voice had brought.

'Worried is an understatement. She threatened one of the faeguard until news was brought that the queens had asked Golan to entertain you both.' Rayan's soft eyes sharpened as they ran over Lettle's face. It was the first time they had spoken since she had found him in the living room the night before.

'It seems the fae don't want us unsupervised. I had another run-in with Hosta,' Lettle said.

'What?' Yeeran said, blade sharp.

The gaze Rayan gave her was one of concern. 'You shouldn't travel alone, Lettle. It's clear there are fae who want us hurt.'

'It was fine. I won't do it again.' Lettle's tone ended the topic. She turned to Rayan. 'How was *your* day?'

His nostrils flared. 'I was at the training grounds.'

'I hope you had a nice time with Berro.'

Rayan's fork clattered against his plate as he dropped it. He met Lettle's challenging stare but didn't say anything.

Yeeran filled the lull in conversation. 'Rayan was just telling me about the weapons storage there, and the way the fae train. It's almost as if they're preparing for war.'

She pointed to the open journal, and Lettle looked it over. It was filled with notes on the fae's military structure.

'War?' Komi laughed. 'Who are they going to fight? Themselves?'

The silence felt strained.

Lettle reached for Yeeran's full wine glass instead of pouring her own and took three large gulps.

Yeeran watched her. 'I could have poured you one.'

Lettle placed down the empty glass and wiped her lips. 'Too slow.'

It was then that she saw the gash running down Yeeran's face. She reached for it and Yeeran flinched away.

'What happened?'

'Furi happened.'

'Training not going well?'

'No.'

Lettle grabbed the buttered potatoes, the wine already simmering in her veins as Yeeran told her how her day had gone.

'Moon's mercy, I want to boil and skin that woman . . .' Lettle said with her mouth full as Yeeran explained how Furi had used magic against her.

'So I'm guessing she didn't tell you about magesight,' Lettle continued.

'What?'

'Their magic isn't invisible. You just have to let your eyes see it. It's the same technique we use in divination to read entrails.'

'What do you mean?' Yeeran said.

'You need to become heedless.'

Yeeran's nostrils flared.

'You mean, the whole time there was a way to see her magic . . . and dodge it?'

Lettle nodded, still filling her mouth with food. 'We can practise after dinner. I want to hear about the Tree of Souls.'

Yeeran shared all she had learned of the fae, of the dual rulers and the Jani dynasty.

'So all we have to do is kill them all then?' Lettle said.

'But that would result in the entirety of Mosima being destroyed,' Rayan said.

'We would be free though,' Komi said.

'No, it's good knowledge to have, but we can't ever wield it,' Yeeran said.

Lettle wasn't so sure about that.

Once they had finished dinner and Lettle had made them all laugh by saying she was going to become Golan's apprentice, they settled on the sofas in the living room.

'Do you remember when those big yellow coats were in fashion, and you tried to make your own out of a hessian sack? It looked hideous but you still wore it for days,' Yeeran teased.

'I'm not doing it to learn about fashion, I'm doing it to learn how to speak fae,' Lettle replied hotly.

They had laughed some more, made merry by the wine, until Lettle felt herself being tugged along and soon her giggle joined the others.

It was then that Yeeran's obeah made an entrance. She was a looming presence, the last light of the fray illuminating her iridescent horns. The alcohol had blurred the edges of the room and heightened Lettle's fear of Pila. As her silver eyes locked with Lettle's she felt a shiver of apprehension. The obeah's lips drew back and Lettle screamed as she saw the blood dripping from them.

'Hush, Lettle, it's just strawberry juice.' Yeeran had risen to greet her beast. There was silence as they communicated with each other.

Rayan sat opposite Lettle. He'd been careful to ensure they were as far away as possible though she could still feel his eyes on hers. His brown eyes glittered like pebbles under water, and she found herself leaning in, yearning to swim in their shallows.

She had tipped too far forward and felt the wine pull her to the ground. Rayan reached forward to stabilise her. He held his arm out until she was steady.

'Get off,' she said, pushing his arm away. Knowing full well without his support she would have fallen. But the other option was to thank him, and if she'd thanked him, he would have given her a smile that was all warm rain and sunshine. And she would have started to fall another way.

One day I will murder you. The thought came unbidden, bringing with it sobriety and a deep sorrow. She looked away from him.

Pila let out a huff as she collapsed on the floor by Yeeran's feet, her head resting on her large paws. Yeeran scratched between her horns absently.

'Tell me then, how do I become heedless?'

'Magesight, they call it magesight,' Komi said.

'You can do it?' Yeeran asked, incredulous.

Komi nodded. 'Hosta taught me a couple of years ago, it busied me for a few months.'

'Why didn't you tell us?' Lettle cut in.

'I've become so used to seeing it, it didn't occur to me.' Komi rubbed his brow. In that moment Komi wore every year of his life. The ghost of loneliness haunted the wells of his eyes.

Lettle was an impatient teacher, and Rayan's detachment towards her had put her in a bad mood.

'Becoming heedless is not like drumfire. You do not harness intention, so you will need to remove all that regimented teaching from your mind.'

Lettle's students nodded.

'You must instead let yourself meld with the consciousness of all things around you. Drop all boundaries between sight, smell, taste, hearing, and touch. It is within all five that you'll find another sense, another way of experiencing the world. Only then can you become heedless.'

There was silence as Rayan and Yeeran frowned at something in the distance. Lettle thought back to one of the earliest exercises in her training. She let her voice drop to a low lull.

'Close your eyes and press your toes firmly into the ground. Start first with your breath. Feel the air as it moves inside and out. Then follow its journey a little further, from the tip of your heels and to the world around you. Let go of your sense of self and become that breath, you have no purpose other than to simply be. You are no longer a person, but a vessel of life.'

'It's not working,' Yeeran complained after a moment of silence. Lettle shrugged.

'No, I can't imagine it will work this quickly. It's not an easy feat. It takes some people days, some people months—'

'I see it . . .' Rayan breathed. His lips hung open, his eyes wide and dilated.

Lettle smiled seeing the wonder on his face. The grin that spread over his lips only increased his allure. She dug her nails into her palm. The biting pain brought her back to the moment.

Yeeran turned to Rayan. 'How did you do it?'

'It comes naturally to some,' Lettle said. Though she could see that wasn't comforting to Yeeran.

'I just did as Lettle said. Yeeran, Pila, you both shine so bright.' Rayan jerked upright. 'Oh, it's gone.'

'You have to practise, every day. It'll always be a bit of a strain, but it will become easier and easier.'

They kept trying for another hour, Lettle suggesting different exercises for Yeeran to try. Komi grew bored a few minutes in and excused himself for bed with a cheery wave. Rayan proclaimed he had a headache not long after. He was able to see in mage-sight for around a minute by the end, but Yeeran wasn't able to see at all.

'Yeeran, we should go to sleep,' Lettle eventually said.

'I need to be able to see it.'

'You will, in the morning. Try again then.'

Yeeran shook her head firmly. Lettle recognised the sharpness of it. There was nothing Lettle could say to change her mind. Yeeran did not allow herself to fail. Ever.

'All right, but don't stay up too late practising.'

Lettle picked up the journal where they were keeping their notes on Mosima. She wanted to fill it in with everything she'd learned so far. Including her thoughts on divination.

Yeeran didn't look up as Lettle turned to leave. Instead Pila did. Her grey eyes blinked slowly once, saying goodnight for the both of them.

It left Lettle feeling hollow.

As she closed the door to her bedroom, she saw something glint on her bed.

She knelt softly on her covers and reached for it.

The chain was a little rough, the links looped together from excess chainmail. But it was clear what it was. A smile blossomed over her lips.

Rayan had made her a necklace to replace the one that was lost.

She withdrew the bead that she'd kept in her pocket and threaded it onto the chain with a bit of force. She looped it over her head, and it rested between her breasts close to her heart.

A prophecy denied is a prophecy left to fester. Imna's words came to her with clarity.

No, she could not succumb to Rayan, not without sentencing him. No matter how much she desperately wanted to.

CHAPTER TWENTY-THREE

Yeeran

Furi did not turn up for training the next day, or the one after it. Yeeran was glad because she was able to spend her time learning to perfect her magesight.

Becoming heedless came slowly to her, much to her frustration, but after the third day she could sustain it for a stretch of five minutes. She was using it now as she looked across the expanse of Mosima's arable land, watching the magic pulse and coil as fae used it to harvest crops.

I wish Salawa could see this. She felt her breath hitch in her throat. *Oh, how I miss her.*

Yeeran's lessons with Nerad had been invaluable, each new piece of information a step closer to exonerating her exile. Today he was showing her the agricultural heart of the land.

Pila and Xosa, Nerad's obeah, had come to join them on the walk. Their lithe bodies pranced between the wheat, billowing up pollen and butterflies, and Yeeran smiled as she watched the spark of their magic swirl among the life in Mosima.

'I'm sorry Furi didn't turn up again,' Nerad said.

The sound of Furi's name snapped Yeeran out of magesight like the twang of a rubber band against her skin. Yeeran hissed a breath between her teeth. 'I can't say I'm not glad of it.'

'I'll have a word with her. She must train you.'

'Must she?' Yeeran muttered. 'Is there any point when the end goal is for me to die in initiation?'

Nerad winced. 'You might not die . . .' he said weakly.

'But what's the point?'

Nerad scuffed the ground with the point of his shoe.

'Though the queens' reign is irrefutable they still must fight for respect among the cabinet. There was no way to execute you, and there was no way to let you free. So this sentence bridges the two sides – those who wanted you free, and those who wanted you dead.'

Yeeran shook her head.

'Why would anyone have wanted me to be free after I killed the prince?'

Nerad looked at her frankly. 'I wanted you free. What you did was a mistake.'

'But if you let me free, I'd be able to tell the world about Mosima.'

'Maybe it's time the world knows we exist.' He pressed his lips together, making it clear that this was an argument he'd had many times with the queens. 'Fae were not made to hide beneath the ground.'

Yeeran felt a prickle of apprehension. Sometimes she forgot that Nerad too was a prince. A fae prince.

Nerad smiled, all trace of pride gone. 'I know Furi can be a little irritable—'

Like a forest cat with ringworm.

Yeeran snorted at Pila's interjection.

'But she is fair,' Nerad continued. 'And without a doubt the best person to train you in Mosima. And the only one who *can* train you. For the Jani dynasty alone know you are not truly fae.'

'Furi's training is more like torture—'

It was as if by saying her name Yeeran had summoned her. There in the field ahead of them, shoulder to shoulder with the other fae chopping down mangoes, was Furi. Her mind reeled seeing the commander carry out such a domestic task.

Nerad chuckled. 'Because of the blight, our resources are more limited than they have been in the past. It requires more field hands.

Furi volunteers here most days. When she isn't training new soldiers in the faeguard, that is.'

Furi's forehead glittered with a sheen of sweat as she hacked at the stems of the fruit tree. She laughed as a bunch of mangoes dropped, landing on the head of another fieldworker.

It was like watching a different woman altogether.

'Furi's helping to harvest the land.' Yeeran thought that by voicing the facts it'd make it seem less ridiculous.

Why does it surprise you so? Should not a leader help to provide?

Yeeran thought on Pila's words. *In my lands leaders provide by harvesting fraedia crystal.*

Do you eat fraedia? The obeah's thoughts were said innocently with true intention.

Before Yeeran could respond Nerad spoke again. 'She is more than the person you have seen. Furi is selfless to a fault, and when something needs to be done, she will volunteer herself before anyone else. There is nothing she would not do for Mosima.' There was true affection in Nerad's tone.

Yeeran could not stop watching Furi work. Not a wrinkle of scorn furrowed her face.

'Come on, this way.' Nerad tugged on her forearm.

Yeeran reluctantly followed.

The further they walked the shorter the wheat became and the greyer its leaves. Soon the ground gave way to cracked earth and the decayed mulch of old plant matter.

The darkness surrounded them for leagues.

'This is the blight,' Nerad said.

The dark lands. Pila confirmed in Yeeran's mind. *Where the magic dies.*

'It's been thirty years since the crops began failing. At first we thought it was just a bad season, despite the magic that sustains us, the environment mimics topside. But then we lost half a field, a whole field, two more. And now this.' Nerad waved his hand across the blackened earth.

Yeeran dropped to a crouch and ran her hands over the ground. The soil was chalky, almost like ash.

'How long until it covers the entirety of Mosima?'

Nerad lowered himself to the ground beside her, his shoulders drooping. 'It's accelerating. I estimate we have ten years, no more.'

Ten years was not long at all. It almost meant that, no matter what, she would be free in a decade. That, though, still felt too long.

Yeeran brushed her hands across her trousers and something green caught her eye. She wondered why her mind had even bothered to register it until she remembered that nothing was meant to grow in the blight.

'Nerad . . . eh . . . can you see that, or have I been practising magesight for too long and I'm hallucinating?'

Nerad leaned forward. Where she had touched the earth, a small green shoot had appeared. His eyes widened.

'It's not possible.'

His hands scrubbed at the ground beside it. More shoots were revealed next to the first.

Nerad's eyes widened in shock. 'I need to go back to the palace. This news – this news is important.'

'Go, go. I'll make my own way back.'

Nerad nodded and ran off, leaving Yeeran alone.

Alone, and not far from the boundary.

Pila, do you want to go for a run?

Pila pranced towards her, increasing speed until she was running at full pelt. Yeeran crouched, waiting to spring. When Pila drew parallel, she dipped her horn in Yeeran's direction.

Yeeran grasped it and swung herself onto Pila's back like she had seen Furi do with Amnan. Wheat whipped past them and Yeeran let out a battle cry.

Being a prisoner had never felt so freeing.

The boundary was exactly how Lettle had described it. When Yeeran looked at it through her magesight, she saw a magical barrier covered in a scripture that wasn't fae or elvish. Yeeran had tried to summon her magic, like she'd managed to do that one time in the Royal Woodland, but it didn't work. Not that it would have helped. It was human magic, and Yeeran didn't have access to that.

She made her way back through the fields and lingered where she had last seen Furi, but the woman was gone.

Nerad said she's often training new faeguard. Shall I take us to the barracks? Pila said.

Yeeran wanted to say no, that she didn't want to see Furi, but that would have been lying.

I know when you lie. Pila's laugh was like the sprinkling of rain on a hot day.

Take us then.

The fray's light was weakening for the day, bringing on the shadows of sunset. So when they arrived at the barracks, most of the faeguard had gone, their training over.

The few soldiers who were there didn't look up as Yeeran rode past. She approached one of them.

'Where is Furi – your commander?'

The soldier scowled, and for a minute Yeeran thought he wouldn't answer but then Pila scuffed at the ground near his feet, and he spat out, 'She's in the inner courtyard, training. Go left around the next bend.'

Here was someone who clearly thought Yeeran should not be free.

But how can I blame them? When elves have slaughtered so many of the obeah?

That was before you knew, Pila said firmly. *Go, find your teacher, I will join my brethren in the amphitheatre where they train.*

The amphitheatre?

Pila cocked her head and Yeeran knew if she could smile, it would have been bloodless.

Listen for the clashing of horns.

She slipped from Pila's back and the obeah loped away.

Yeeran found herself following the young soldier's directions, her feet moving before her mind could catch up.

She could smell Furi, sweat and spice with a touch of earthiness from the mango orchard. And as Yeeran rounded the corner she saw her too.

Furi spun and twirled through the air, wielding a spear. Her golden hair flew free behind her. She wore a leather harness that covered her vital organs, and a pair of leather shorts that left the curves of her muscled legs free as she kicked through the air. She was slick with sweat, her expression one of fierce determination.

'Did you see how I turned my wrist outwards to take advantage of the weight of the weapon?'

At first Yeeran thought Furi was talking to her, but then a shadow moved to her right.

'Yes, Commander.' The boy was no older than seven.

'You don't need to call me commander, Cane. You're not part of the faeguard.'

The little boy, Cane, puffed out his chest.

'But I will be one day.'

Furi crouched on the ground and grasped his shoulders.

'Do not wish past the years.'

Cane's shoulders dipped, and she tweaked his nose to pull a smile from him.

'Come on, I should get you back to your mother.'

'Oh no, please, can I stay a little longer?'

'You've been here two hours. It's time to go home.' Furi was trying to sound stern, but a grin quirked her lips.

Yeeran found herself smiling at the tender moment.

Cane pouted. 'Show me one more time.'

Furi let out a small laugh before swinging the spear round again. Yeeran crept closer to get a better view of the demonstration. It was then that she saw the sparks emanating from Furi's hand as she twirled the spear.

Yeeran slipped into magesight, and her gasp caught in her throat.

Furi's magic filled the courtyard with the brightness of the sun. Her magic threads whipped around her in a hypnotic deathly dance as she moved. The magic wasn't just a tool, it was a part of her, as in tune with her steps as any limb.

When Furi saw Yeeran, she faltered, her magic dropping from her grasp.

'What are you doing here?' Gone was the affable tone she'd used with Cane. Here was the commander in all her glory.

Yeeran couldn't speak to the sunlit wraith, so she let go of her magesight, blinking away the light of Furi's glow.

'You . . . you stopped coming to training.'

'I know.' Furi turned to Cane. 'Go home, Cane. Tell your mother I'm sorry I didn't come for dinner, I'll make it up to them another time.'

This time Cane didn't protest and slipped out like a minnow in a stream.

The silence dragged on.

Yeeran felt foolish. She wasn't sure why she was here. The woman hated her, didn't want to be around her, and Yeeran wasn't sure she didn't hate her a little too.

'I was told you're the best trainer in Mosima,' Yeeran finally said.

'I am.'

'Then, I'd like you to train me to use my magic.'

'No,' Furi said with finality.

'Why not? Is it because you fear that an *elf* could wield fae magic?'

Furi was on her throat in a moment. Her nails were long, and they scored into Yeeran's neck.

'It is because you killed my brother.' The heat of her anger was intoxicating.

'Then train me, is that not part of my punishment? To serve in the faeguard?' Yeeran whispered. Their lips were so close together. She felt herself yearning for Salawa. For the heat of her love, and the fierceness of her loving.

Yeeran's mouth parted, and Furi's gaze was drawn to it.

Furi released her grasp on her neck and ran a finger down Yeeran's cheek. Then she slicked her tongue over her fangs and said, 'I hope that wound hurt as it healed.'

Yeeran pushed her away. Furi was *not* Salawa. She could never be. Where her lover was ruthless, Furi was cruel. And where Salawa was soft, the fae was sharp.

But Furi isn't always like that, she found herself thinking. *Just with me.*

'I didn't ask for any of this either, you know,' Yeeran said.

Furi's eyes flashed.

'Pain is a funny thing.' She touched her own cheek. The faintest mark remained where Yeeran's wild magic had struck her. 'There is the physical. Then there are the scars that others don't see.'

Furi's gaze turned downwards, her eyes shimmering. Her hand fell from her cheek, limp and lifeless. Her expression was vulnerable and gentle. Yeeran stepped towards her.

But when Furi lifted her head again her face was hard and unyielding.

'The only comfort I have is that your sister will know this same pain soon enough.'

Yeeran's anger was lit by a spark, and Furi dodged backwards, Yeeran's wild magic lashing outwards. With that realisation, Yeeran's anger left her as quickly as it came.

She slipped into magesight, to see what it looked like, but only the echo of the magic remained, mere sparkles on the breeze.

When Yeeran dropped her concentration and looked around again, Furi was gone.

Yeeran spent the rest of the day watching the obeah train in the amphitheatre. The thunder of their horns as they struck each other thrummed through the room. It felt like the pounding of her heart which, for some reason, had not stopped racing since seeing Furi.

CHAPTER TWENTY-FOUR

Yeeran

Furi still didn't turn up for training the next day.

Yeeran rested her forehead on Pila's hide, the waves of Conch Shore crashing behind her.

The only difference between us and them is the ability to use fae magic. If I hope to be able to fight my way out of initiation, I'm going to need to know how to wield it.

Yes, Pila agreed. *It will also be a good show of force for when we return to the Elven Lands.*

Yeeran imagined what Salawa's face would look like when she watched Yeeran return astride Pila. She could see the tears rolling down her beautiful skin like pearls.

Is it just her beauty you love? Pila asked. The question wasn't barbed, more curious.

No, Salawa is the greatest chieftain Waning has ever had. She will bring an end to poverty and liberate all of the Elven Lands.

Pila grunted and nudged Yeeran with her cold nose.

Liberation? Yet she condemned you for a simple mistake.

Pila's line of questioning was unsettling to Yeeran. Perhaps because talking to Pila was like talking to another part of her. The concerns her obeah had were simply the resurfacing of her own thoughts that she'd kept buried in the depths of her mind. She ran a hand into Pila's mane before pulling herself onto her back.

'If Furi won't come to us, let us go to Furi.'

Pila cantered towards the glade of mango trees where they'd seen Furi yesterday.

Yeeran slid from Pila's back.

I'm too early, no one's here yet.

Pila sniffed. *Up there.*

Yeeran looked up towards the bough of a tree and between the pointed fronds of the leaves, a face appeared, freckled and brown from constant exposure to the fray.

'You're early,' they grunted, before dropping down to the ground beside Yeeran.

'Huh?'

'I guess the rest of your cohort are arriving later? I hope they have the muscles you do. When Commander Furi offered up more of the faeguard to help, I jumped at the chance.'

The farmer handed Yeeran a woven basket and continued chattering on.

'Every inch of fertile farmland has been sown. Which was all well and good when the queens made the order to sustain food demand . . . but no one thinks these things through when it comes to harvest.' They shook their head, their shaggy hair spinning outwards. 'You hear the blight is ending? Word on the bee's wing says the fields are fertile once more.'

Yeeran nodded.

'Probably why the rest of your friends are late this morning, the taverns were teeming last night with the news.'

Again, Yeeran nodded. She was too scared to open her mouth this close to the fae in case they saw her flattened canines.

The farmer continued, 'I'm fine with the blight ending and all, but it'll be a while before we get production back on track. Anyway, less talking, more working I think.'

Yeeran worried the edge of the basket in her hands. If she corrected the farmer about their mistake, then she'd have to deal with the bitter hatred as they realised who in fact she was. Or she could pretend to be one of the farmhands sent and wait until Furi turned up.

I like mangoes, Pila chimed in unhelpfully.

'What are you standing around for? Start picking. A lot of the pickers are Lightless, but your obeah is welcome to carry the produce to the crates out back,' the farmer said.

Do you want to help too? Yeeran asked her.

If it means that more people get food, then yes. Pila understood what the pang of unending hunger felt like from the echoes of Yeeran's memories.

Thank you, Pila.

It was over an hour before more farmhands arrived, and by that time both Yeeran and Pila were soaked with sweat and tree sap. They had cleared four trees and moved on to a fifth when a cold voice said, 'What are you doing?'

Yeeran looked down from the bough of the tree to see Furi. Her eyes were narrowed and full of anger.

'I'm picking mangoes.'

'I can see that, but why are you here?'

'If you won't train me, I can at least be of help. The land needs harvesting and I have time. Watch out.' Yeeran dropped a bunch and Pila dashed forward to catch it in her horns. Furi skipped out of the way with a scowl before spinning on her heel and marching away.

That morning Yeeran felt the warmth of Furi's gaze on her in quiet moments when she passed her in the field or up in the branches of a tree looking down. Whenever she turned to smile at her, Furi's eyes would skitter away.

But not before Yeeran noticed that the anger of her expression had cooled from burned sugar to warm caramel, hot and sweet.

I'll make a friend of you yet, Furi. Then the secrets of your magic will be mine to wield in my escape.

Furi turned up to training the next day.

When she started the drills and Yeeran was able to dodge all of her magic, she didn't smile or look pleased but simply said, 'You finally figured out magesight then.'

After a few more hours of training, Furi packed up and headed towards the fields to help harvest. When Yeeran fell into step beside her, she wheeled on Yeeran. 'Training is over today.'

Yeeran shrugged.

'I know that, but I thought I'd keep helping.'

'Why? This is not your land to harvest.'

Yeeran gave Furi a shrewd look. 'Yes, you've made that clear, but still, I would like to lend a hand. Particularly if it brings food to more people even if they are not *my* people.'

She'd enjoyed the fieldwork more than she'd realised. It felt good having a purpose in the production of food in Mosima. It wasn't quite the same as her role in the Forever War, but it eased her feeling of helplessness.

Furi's lips drew into a thin line. She opened her mouth to say more, but then closed it again, dismissing her unspoken thoughts.

As she strode off ahead, Yeeran followed in the wake of sand that the pounding of Furi's feet drew up.

It was like following a tempest. Wild and stormy.

Their routine continued like that for two more weeks. They'd meet on the beach and Furi would train Yeeran in drills that were physical and reactive. Then Yeeran would help harvest fruit under the watchful gaze of Furi, and Nerad's training would follow shortly after.

It was a gruelling time and Yeeran was no closer to learning how to use fae magic.

She has yet to teach me how to truly harness my power.

Pila yawned and rolled onto her side, the fray lighting her horns silver. Her lips shone with mango juice. *I am getting fatter though.*

Yeeran scratched her chin and the great beast purred.

'Get up,' Furi barked.

Though the fae had softened to her, she was still not friendly.

Yeeran did not move. 'No.'

Furi's eyes narrowed. '*What?*'

'Not until you teach me how to use my magic. It's been weeks.'

Furi didn't speak. Her sharp features pinched together as if she were battling some inner argument.

'Furi?'

The fae closed her eyes slowly, and when she opened them again, they were focused, clearer. She lowered herself to the ground next to Yeeran and let out a heavy breath.

'These exercises have been designed to draw out your power. Usually when I'm training soldiers, they have instinctively learned to grasp it. You . . . do not seem to be able to do that.'

Her disappointment was as bitter as bile. Yeeran swallowed. 'What does it feel like? Drawing on that power?'

Furi frowned. 'It's a bit like using magesight. It requires you to be unfocused, while also present. You must split your mind in order to wield it successfully. It is hard to envision, so that is why I hoped to elicit the power from you intuitively first.'

Yeeran had wondered what the trick was. She had tried to call forth the strands of magic many times, but it seemed that simply summoning it was not the answer.

Furi continued, 'Once you can understand both concepts, that of the unfocused magesight and the concentration required to exert it, you should be able to release the spool of your magic.'

She searched in the sand and withdrew a shell.

'Enter magesight and then try to focus your energy on pulling this shell towards you.'

Yeeran tried for an hour, but just like magesight had at first, it eluded her. No matter how hard Yeeran tried, she couldn't find the threads of her magic.

'Why isn't it working?'

Furi's eyes shuttered closed and she let out a short sigh. 'Perhaps because you are an elf, and our god knows you are not worthy.'

Yeeran was used to her insults now, and she let them wash over her, perhaps because they had less bite than they once had. Time had softened some of Furi's sharpness.

'There must be something more to it.'

'Or you're not trying hard enough.' Furi's face twisted with frustration.

'Yes, I am,' Yeeran replied calmly.

The shell sat on the ground between them. Furi bent to pick it up. 'You're either not trying hard enough, or you can't do magic at all.'

Furi's nostrils flared and Yeeran could tell that she was seeing Yeeran's failure as her own.

Yeeran bridged the gap between them and placed a hand on Furi's shoulder.

Hit her, Pila said in her mind.

Yeeran had to fight to keep her expression neutral as she said, 'Let's take a break.'

She pushes and pushes you, Yeeran.

I know, but I don't think it's me she's actually angry at any more.

'You don't need a break,' Furi retorted.

'I might not, but the shell does.'

Yeeran brandished the conch she had pilfered from Furi when she hadn't noticed. Furi's eyes widened like a child seeing a trick for the first time.

'What magic is this?'

Yeeran laughed, delighted by the awe in Furi's face.

'When I touched your shoulder I deflected your attention, it's a simple trick.'

'Teach me.' It was a demand.

The next half an hour was spent teaching Furi the basics of pickpocketing. But she didn't have the gentleness to carry it out successfully. She grew bored of trying soon after.

'Is this a game you play in the Elven Lands?'

'No.' Yeeran lowered herself to the sand heavily. 'It was a necessity. Lettle and I . . . after our father stopped . . . working . . . we had to find other means to survive. Thievery was just one of the ways we didn't starve to death.'

Furi looked down at Yeeran, her expression inscrutable.

'Your father, he is dead?'

'Yes,' Yeeran said.

'Good.'

There was a brief silence.

'Did you know your father?' Yeeran asked.

Furi's smile was uncharacteristically shy.

'Yes, he was consort for a time.'

'Consort?'

'The formal title given to those who choose to partner with a monarch.'

Yeeran nodded.

'But how was he consort for "a time"?'

'Mother and he argued. He left the court.'

Yeeran laid a hand on Furi's.

'That must have been difficult for you.'

Furi looked down at Yeeran's hand resting on hers. 'It was hard,' she admitted. 'But he couldn't go far, that's the thing with being captive down here.'

'But you're not captive, not really. You're Jani, you can leave at any time.'

Furi glanced at Yeeran, and she wondered if she'd gone too far. So rarely did Furi open up to her.

Then she spoke so softly Yeeran had to strain to listen. 'And where would I go, Yeeran?'

She said her name like a song. It stirred something in Yeeran that she thought belonged to Salawa.

That does belong to Salawa.

But three gods, Furi was beautiful.

This close Yeeran could count the freckles that ran across her nose and cheekbones. She could smell the spice of her perfume, the sticky mango juice that had dried on her lower lip.

Oh, to lick it off.

Furi pulled her hand away from Yeeran's and stood. It broke the spell of the moment.

She offered Yeeran a hand up. 'I can't make our training session for a little while. I'm going away.'

'Away?'

Furi didn't answer. *She must be going topside.*

'I'll be back in time for the flare festivities. A couple of weeks, no more. Keep working on your magic in the meantime.' She began to make her way back to the palace.

'What are the flare festivities?'

'Ask Nerad,' Furi called back. She was smiling as she did so, and that smile lit up her face with a tenderness Yeeran was beginning to glimpse more and more.

She watched Furi's hips swaying with a slight swagger as she walked away, until she disappeared from sight.

Yeeran tipped her head to the fray. Her mind had grown foggy from straining to use her magic. Not because of Furi, certainly not.

The fraedia crystal glowed bright white as it reached midday. Yeeran had secretly been stashing any fraedia lamps she had come across. She'd bestow them on the people who needed them most when she returned home.

Home. It felt so far away. So out of reach.

Perhaps getting closer to Furi was not a bad idea. It wouldn't be infidelity if it was a matter of survival. And Salawa would not be waiting for her, she knew that. From the beginning Salawa made it clear she sated her passions with whoever she wanted. Though in recent years that had only been Yeeran.

Her heart began to thump in her chest.

This could work, Yeeran had been speaking to herself, but Pila replied.

You look for ways to gain power over feelings that make you powerless.

Yeeran was struck by the sincerity of Pila's wisdom.

What are you? Yeeran said back, laughing.

Pila replied in her unique way of smells and sounds and feeling. It was the aroma of fresh earth and the sound of rainfall and the feeling you get from the wind on your face after a long day inside.

'Why do you look like you've just been given the best news?'

Nerad sat down in the sand next to her, pulling her from her conversation with Pila. 'Did you manage to do magic?'

That soured Yeeran's mood. 'No.'

'Oh well, you'll get there.' He handed her a sandwich. 'Or maybe you won't.'

She grimaced.

Nerad shrugged. 'You *are* the first elf to ever have access to fae power.'

'I know that.' Yeeran tore through the sandwich with frustration. To have something so close, within her grasp but not being able to master it, was maddening to her.

'What's the flare festivities?' she asked, changing the subject.

'The Flare Feast is a traditional festival that started when we arrived in Mosima. Once a year the sun shines on the top of the Tree of Souls.'

'What? How?'

He pointed to the cavern ceiling.

'You see that small slash in the ceiling? Through that.'

Yeeran had explored every inch of the boundary but had never thought that the roof of the cavern could be their escape route.

'You can't get out there,' he said, seeing her thoughts churning on her face. 'We tried. Twice. Once about five hundred years ago, and again one hundred years after that. The curse runs across the gap, just like the tunnel you entered through. Without someone from the Jani dynasty, you can't leave.'

Hope sank like a pebble in her stomach.

'So, this Flare Feast, you celebrate a bit of sun touching the baobab tree?'

Nerad gave her a stern look.

'You take for granted the years you've had in the sun. It is a precious and sacred thing to fae. You may have forgotten your god, but we have not. Ewia granted us this life and we will celebrate it when we can.'

Seldom did Nerad make her feel an outsider, but when he did it was always as surprising and cutting as an eagle's talon.

'This year is particularly important, as we are celebrating the end of the blight.'

'Have all the fields become fertile again?'

'Yes, I've tested the acidity of all the soil. The blight has completely disappeared as abruptly as it came.' He didn't sound as happy as Yeeran thought he should.

'Isn't that a good thing?' she asked tentatively.

A range of emotions crossed his features, and he didn't speak for a while until he settled on, 'Of course it is. I just hate not knowing how or why we were plagued by it in the first place.'

The rest of the lesson that day was overshadowed by Nerad's irritable mood. Today his teachings were about fae poetry. His tutelage ranged from cutlery etiquette to Mosima geography, from anthropology to philosophy. This approach suited Yeeran, because if Nerad became too interested in his own lectures – which happened often, his tangents self-indulgent and long – her mind could wander, jotting down notable things for the journal that night. Sometimes Pila and Xosa joined them, running and playing in the fields around them.

Today there was only one thing on her mind.

Furi.

A week after Furi left, Yeeran began to feel helpless.

'There's no need to mope, Yeeran,' Komi said. 'All you need to do is fill your days with the pleasures of Mosima . . . for trust me, they are plenty.'

He was sitting in a pool of fray-light with a glass of mead in his hand, a grin on his face.

'Komi, it's ten o'clock in the morning.'

He swirled his drink and sighed. 'So? I had a busy day yesterday.'

She laughed because he really did mean it.

'I spent half the day in a tavern learning all the best drinking songs. I put them in the journal,' Komi said.

Yeeran rubbed her brow in exasperation, though she still smiled.

Komi had spent the last few weeks living his life, and she could not begrudge him that.

He stood and walked over to where Yeeran sat, treading on a sleeping Pila's tail as he did so.

The obeah awoke with a hiss, baring her fangs at him.

Komi dropped into a defensive stance, his muscles pulling taut. His eyes drew to slits and his hands balled up ready to fight.

Yeeran raised her eyebrows. 'Good to know some things you don't forget from being a soldier.'

He let out a breath and gave her a bashful smile.

'Yes, there's a lot I will never forget.' There was something dark behind his eyes, but she didn't want to draw it out.

Are you OK, Pila?

Yes, she grumbled. *He stood on my tail.*

I saw.

He didn't say sorry.

I think he's a bit drunk.

Pila grunted in Komi's direction. *That's no excuse.*

The obeah hadn't warmed to Komi as much as the others, and no matter how many times Yeeran asked her to explain why, she could never describe it better than sending Yeeran an image of a vine growing up a tree.

It did not help.

'Why don't you join me in the fields today? I've been helping with the harvest,' Yeeran said.

Komi tipped his head left and right, considering. 'Do I get to eat the fruit I pick?'

'Some of it.'

'All right.'

Pila opted to stay in their rooms. So Yeeran and Komi walked towards the fields on their own.

Yeeran looked up to the fray, the cluster of crystals shining a deep orange. 'To think, the Forever War rages on and there's enough fraedia reserve here to end it all.'

Komi hummed deeply before replying, 'The Forever War was never about fraedia.'

Yeeran frowned. 'What is it about?'

'Power, domination, greed.'

Yeeran thought of Salawa; she couldn't deny she had some of those traits. But still she shook her head. 'No, I do not think that's the case with our chieftain. She has always wanted to bring prosperity to her people.'

'You were Waning, were you not?' Komi asked.

'I *am* Waning,' Yeeran corrected him, and his smile crinkled the corners of his eyes.

'Remind me of your chieftain's slogan that got her elected?'

'*Forgotten never, avenged forever*,' Yeeran replied, unsure what he was getting at.

Komi shook his head and spoke. 'I think the whole slogan was: *There will be no peace until we have liberated all those under a tyrant's rule. Forgotten never, avenged forever.*'

'Yes. She was responding to the massacres wrought by the Chieftain of Crescent. Your chieftain.'

She tried to muffle the accusation, but it was hard to shed the preconceptions that had so long fuelled her actions.

Komi bobbed his head. 'But none of that is about the fraedia reserves? Is it?'

Yeeran settled into her thoughts. He painted Salawa as a vengeful politician with a lust for power.

Is she not? Pila said from afar.

No, she is more than that, she is kind and cares deeply for people.

She can be both one and the other.

I suppose.

They had reached the less populated part of Mosima, where the unused housing backed onto the agricultural land. To the left were the steps leading out of Mosima, ahead was the Book Orchard.

'Is that Lettle up ahead?' Komi asked. 'Why is she running?'

Yeeran felt a prickle of fear.

'I'm sure we're about to find out.'

CHAPTER TWENTY-FIVE

Lettle

'Are you really going to spend another hour on his *eyebrows?*' Lettle hissed under her veil to Golan.

He looked at her sidelong before muttering quietly, 'Yes, this is the job, Lettle.'

Golan's client lay back on a chaise longue, a glass of wine hanging limply from manicured fingernails as Golan painstakingly drew individual hairs onto their brow. It was one of the most boring appointments they'd had that day.

It had been over a month since Lettle had become Golan's apprentice. The appointments had mainly been hair braiding and Golan had let her pitch in, but it seemed this week was all eyebrows and lip lining. The work was monotonous to Lettle, but in between the client-facing moments Golan was teaching her to speak fae.

'Did you say something?' The client sat up, his eyes opening blearily.

'No, I did not,' Golan replied in fae, and for the first time Lettle understood it.

'Continue then, Lightless. I do not have time for delays today.' That, Lettle wished she hadn't understood. Every time a fae called Golan 'Lightless' he flinched, the wound freshly salted with every reference.

'Will you pass me the black tattoo ink, Prisa? Please be careful, it is poisonous if ingested,' Golan said to Lettle in fae. They had decided that giving Lettle a new name was prudent, along with a veil to cover her small canines. It wouldn't be good for either of them if Golan's clientele knew she was an elf.

'Pardon?' It was one of the first words she had learned. She hadn't fully grasped what he had said. Despite Lettle's predilection for learning, the fae language was unruly to master. There were some sounds she would simply never be able to utter without being faebound, as they didn't come naturally without the connection to an obeah.

Golan repeated the question, pointing to the ink, making clear the description for 'poison' so Lettle could learn it. She nodded and handed it over.

'Your assistant is simple, is she not?' the client said. Lettle jumped at the interruption, she had thought the man had fallen asleep.

'She is, sir, quite simple.'

Lettle simmered quietly, the fine veil lifting with her hot breath.

'Makes sense why she's apprenticed with you.' The insult was unnecessary. Despite only catching half of it, Lettle still understood the malice in his words.

Golan said nothing and bent back down to work. Lettle wanted to comfort him, but she didn't know how, so she stood there like the simpleton she was meant to be, silently reciting all the words and letters she had learned over the last few weeks.

When they were done it was just after lunchtime. The fray was warm on their cheeks, the breeze small but welcoming.

'. . . and you have to tattoo that same pattern every two weeks?'

'Yes, the squid ink we use to draw the hairs doesn't last very long,' Golan replied in elvish and fae in turn.

'That was squid ink?'

Golan laughed at her distaste.

'Yes, the clammer squid is found in the bay. It is deathly poisonous when consumed, that's why we can't leave the ink on long.'

They turned a corner down a street of large villas when Lettle heard the rustle of something in the tree beside them. So far Hosta had not realised that Golan's new apprentice was Lettle. That or they had given up taunting her. Still, she remained vigilant when she was out of the palace.

Lettle scanned the bough of the tree where she'd heard the sound. She expected it to be a young obeah, as they often prowled the canopy, but instead something small and furry dropped to the ground beside them and Lettle screeched.

'It's just a haba, Lettle.'

'A what?'

'A haba.' Golan grunted as he bent down towards it, his cane turning outwards.

The creature's two eyes filled most of its head. The fur on its back was striped white and orange. Its features were somewhere between a bear and monkey, but it was the size of a possum. In its black paws it held a scroll which Golan grabbed.

'It *carries* messages?'

Golan straightened and read the note. When he didn't immediately read it out Lettle asked, 'Is it your gentleman sweetheart? Summoning you to his rooms?'

Golan gave Lettle a tight smile. He had refused to admit the name of his paramour, despite Lettle pressing him for details. At first, he had denied the caller was a lover until Lettle had snatched one of the messages before he could hide it. It had been written in fae, but she'd been able to understand enough.

'He wants you to do *what* to him?' she'd asked after reading it.

Golan hadn't even blushed. 'Learn more fae and you can find out.'

After that Lettle came to spot the patterns of their secret meetings. Occasionally Golan would arrive at appointments with swollen lips or wearing the same clothes from the night before.

'No, only the queens can summon the creatures of Mosima to do their bidding,' Golan muttered. 'If you see a haba with a scroll, it has only come from one place.'

His eyes ran over the words once more, before he added a few sentences to the paper with a pen and handed it back to the creature.

The haba turned and ran back the way it had come.

Golan rubbed his eyes with his free hand and smudged some of the charcoal that lined them. It made him look even more attractive.

'The queens would like me to go to them.'

'Can I come?' Lettle asked.

'I don't think that would be a good idea.'

'But how will they know it's me. Remember, I'm Prisa.'

'If you think the queens haven't been watching your every move then you are foolish, Lettle.'

She bristled.

'I'm sorry,' Golan said. 'I should not have snapped like that. I'm tired, it's been a long day, and I've just found out it's going to be even longer. There's this traditional fae festival happening in a couple of days. The queens want me to start prepping them.'

'All right,' she replied, still a bit annoyed by his tone.

'Keep practising your fae,' he said.

'I will, I think I'll go and study at the Book Orchard.'

She waved him away and set off west. She was so distracted churning over phrases in fae that she didn't see the obeah slip out of the foliage ahead of her. Lettle screamed as she brushed against its rump.

It cocked its head at her, and she noticed the broken horn. This was an obeah she'd seen before.

'What do you want? Go away.' She shooed it with her hand.

It blinked slowly, its eyes apple green.

'Go on, I have things to do.'

It dipped its large feline head before galloping off again. Lettle scowled at it until it disappeared off in the distance.

'Stupid obeah, appearing around every corner,' she muttered to herself. Then yelped as a person shifted on the path ahead of her. She connected with solid muscle.

'Lettle.' There was only one person who said her name like that. Like a plea. Like a promise.

'Moon's mercy, Rayan. Are you trying to kill me?'

He gave her a small smile that turned her insides into syrup. 'Sorry, I was on a run, and I saw you up ahead.'

Sweat trickled down his temples, the vest he was wearing clinging to the contours of his torso. The scent of him, bergamot and sage, made even headier by his perspiration.

Though they'd grown more distant in the last few weeks – a distance Lettle had wanted – they had fallen into a hesitant friend-ship. It wasn't like before, but it was better than falling in love with him. Now, being near him and the possibility of what could have been sparking between them, stung her more than she liked.

It hurts me more than it hurts him, she thought bitterly. Every night since that first time, he'd been slipping out under the cover of darkness. The first few occasions she had waited up for him, watching the smile he wore through the crack of her bedroom door when he returned. She hadn't been the one to put that smile there.

That hurt most of all.

'Aren't you meant to be with Golan?' he asked.

'Aren't you meant to be with Berro?' she countered with more spite.

He didn't seem to notice as he shrugged and said, 'She's gone on a scouting mission with Furi.'

'What are they scouting?'

He looked unsettled.

'They wouldn't tell me. The more I learn about the fae military, the more I feel like there's something amiss.'

'Hmm.' Lettle continued walking towards the Book Orchard and Rayan fell into step beside her.

'I have, however, managed to stash away enough armour and weapons if we need to fight our way through the boundary.'

'It doesn't work like that,' she muttered.

'I know. But it's good to have a backup. I can't just sit around and do nothing. Have you managed to find anything useful in the library?'

Lettle shook her head.

'It's slow going. I'm better at reading fae than speaking it, but it's difficult. I'm going there now.'

'Can I come with you?'

She looked at him sidelong, considering.

'If you want.'

'It is incredible,' Rayan breathed into the silence.

'Yes, it is.'

The Book Orchard was brought to life with the gleam of the fraedia crystal. Rayan's face took on a childish glow.

'This way.' Lettle beckoned Rayan towards the table in the centre. She moved a stack of books off a chair to make room for him.

'You've read all these?' he asked, indicating the hundreds of books strewn across the table.

Lettle laughed.

'No, I translate the first few pages and if it doesn't seem like it'll give me much information about the boundary or divination, I move on.'

Rayan picked up the book closest and flicked through it.

'You've found nothing?'

'Less than nothing. The history books are lacking, and those that do mention the curse have conflicting accounts.'

He shifted through some more books.

'Why is there a map of the Bleeding Field here?'

Lettle looked at where he was pointing. The scroll had been left where Komi had first found it.

'It's not, it's a map of the Fae Lands. You see that bit in the middle, that's the capital, Lorhan.'

Rayan shook his head. 'No, that's the Dying Hill, and you see that there, that's the eastern bank. This section down here would be Gural.' He pointed out the landmarks to her, but she wasn't all that interested. She had more important things to do.

'Maybe the Fae Lands used to be there. It has been a thousand years.'

Rayan looked a little unsettled.

Lettle turned back to her books, wincing as she twisted her arm painfully.

'Are you still taking the owen tree sap?' he asked, seeing her pain.

'I've nearly run out.' She began to massage the muscles at the top of her shoulder with her free hand.

Rayan stepped into her shadow.

'May I?'

His hand hovered above her shoulder, his expression simmering hot beneath the surface.

She didn't speak. Couldn't.

So, she nodded.

Then his hands moved across the knotted muscles of her back and shoulder. The pressure firm but soothing.

She let out a groan and she heard his lips draw back in a smile. Suddenly she found herself yearning for more than this brief touch. She stood up, stretching the distance between them.

'That's enough.' Her throat was raspy, her cheeks flushed.

His eyes met hers and she caught the echoes of rejection in them. It twisted her guts.

If he asked me to love him now, I'm not sure I have the will to say no.

'Lettle.'

'Yes,' she answered, perhaps a little too quickly.

'There's something I need to tell you.'

Her heartbeat was like the wings of a hummingbird.

He closed his eyes, winced, then opened them again.

Her hands went to the necklace between her breasts, and she withdrew the chain, clasping the bead in the centre of her fist. Rayan's eyes were drawn to it and his lips parted.

'You're wearing it.'

He looked surprised.

'Yes, I haven't taken it off.'

'I . . . I didn't know,' he said softly.

She looked away, unable to keep contact with the heat in his gaze. It burned her too much.

You and I, Rayan. We cannot yield to this thing between us. It will only end in death.

'What was it you had to tell me?' she said as lightly as she could, though her heart was twisting, convulsing in on itself until it tore itself to shreds.

Rayan looked crestfallen, before smoothing his expression into something more neutral.

'There was something I learned in the training grounds. The fae, they have come to respect me, a little, I think. So sometimes they talk to me.'

'And?'

'The initiation into the faeguard is brutal. They tie a fae to a tree above ground for twelve days. The fae have a stronger constitution in the sunlight than elves . . . Yeeran isn't expected to survive it.'

Lettle felt the blood rush from her face. If she hadn't been sitting down, she would have fallen.

'What?' she said between her teeth.

'The initiation is in six weeks,' he said patiently. 'It's a way of executing her without giving the order.'

Lettle stood, knocking down a pile of books.

'No.' She refused this truth. She could refuse it like she had refused Rayan.

'Lettle,' he shouted after her, but she was already running.

Lettle spotted Komi and Yeeran on the street ahead of her and was grateful that she wasn't going to have to nurse her wrath all the way to the palace.

'What's happened?' Yeeran's hands twitched and Lettle wondered if she were reaching for an invisible drum.

But no drum, make-believe or otherwise, would protect her from Lettle's fury.

'You didn't tell me,' Lettle spat.

'Tell you what?' Yeeran replied.

Rayan jogged up to join them. A star glider followed in his wake. The little flying lizards came out in droves in the Royal Woodland, and this was the first time Lettle had seen one fluttering so far from the queens. Their bulbous heads shone gold like the luminescence of a firefly.

'I told her about the initiation,' Rayan said heavily.

Yeeran looked pained as she shook her head.

'Don't deny it. I know that you'll likely *die*.' The word 'die' ventured up into another octave.

Komi looked between them.

'I'm going to need some filling in this sandwich, please.'

Rayan turned to him.

'The initiation, Yeeran's not expected to survive it.'

Yeeran scrubbed her hands over her eyes. 'I might.'

Lettle scoffed. 'We have six weeks, Yeeran. Six weeks until your initiation.'

'Yes, but I'll have the ability to use magic by then,' Yeeran said.

'And if you don't?' Lettle demanded.

Yeeran's nostrils flared. 'Then the three of you will need to escape without me.'

There was a cacophony as both Komi and Lettle shouted their concerns. Lettle didn't hear Rayan until he raised his voice.

'Be quiet. There's something not right here,' he said urgently.

Lettle became aware of how silent the streets were. They were on the outskirts of Mosima proper, to the left was arable land, but there was no one close enough to hear them if they screamed.

She felt her hands prickle as they started to sweat.

Yeeran's eyes darted around them, realising the same thing that Lettle had.

They were alone.

'Lettle, get behind me,' Rayan urged. Lettle didn't have time to complain before Rayan's hands gently eased her towards him.

'Komi, flank Lettle's left,' Yeeran commanded.

For a second, Komi looked like he was going to refuse. Lettle wondered what rank he'd held in the Crescent Army to feel like he could refute Yeeran's order.

Then he nodded, and all the joy from the person she'd come to know fled his features. In its place stood a hardened soldier.

The fae came out of the abandoned buildings. Five to the left, six to the right.

Yeeran let out a breath.

'We can take them—'

Then came the obeah, one for each of them, slinking out of the fields towards them.

Lettle recognised Hosta as they withdrew a blade from a sheath at their waist. They looked at Lettle and smiled.

'We were hoping to catch just the mouse of the group, but here we have the whole nest. Serendipitous indeed.'

The fae circled closer, sparks flashing from their hands, daggers glinting at their belts.

'How far away is Pila?' Rayan whispered to Yeeran.

'She's coming, but she is just one obeah.'

There was a hiss from the fae, and they looked beyond the elves to someone further down the street.

Lettle stole a look backwards to see the green-eyed obeah she'd seen before. It dipped its broken horn at her when it saw her looking. Its black fur rippled in the dim light. Twice now it had come to her rescue.

'Dammit, they've surrounded us,' Yeeran murmured.

'No, the one behind us, it's on our side,' Lettle said.

But they still wouldn't be enough.

Hosta's blue eyes twinkled. They knew it.

'It's time to claim our revenge for those we've lost to the brutalities of the elves' action. It's time for them to be *hunted*.'

The fae surged forward. Lettle felt a coil of magic grasp her ankles as she was pulled away from Rayan along the ground.

'Rayan!'

He reached for her but had to lunge out of the way as an obeah charged at him.

Lettle saw blood. She wasn't sure if it was her own.

Komi was grappling with two fae, his expression bloodthirsty, almost euphoric. But Lettle had no time to linger on him.

Hosta was above her, brandishing a dagger.

'Hello, little mouse. It's time to die.'

CHAPTER TWENTY-SIX

Yeeran

'. . . It's time to die.'

Yeeran heard Hosta's words and saw red. She barrelled towards where they stood over Lettle.

Yeeran felt the sharpness of Hosta's blade as it bit into her side. But the pain only fuelled her.

She brought her fists down on Hosta's face, one after the other, turning their bruise-coloured eyes into real bruises. Hosta's blade was still buried in her abdomen.

I'm here, Yeeran. Pila thundered into the skirmish. Yeeran saw through the obeah's eyes for a second, and all she saw was pandemonium.

Hosta had gone limp beneath her fists.

One down, but they were not winning this fight.

There was a clatter as an obeah with a broken horn stood over Lettle, locking horns with one of the attackers' beasts.

Yeeran staggered towards Pila, but the obeah was fending off the magic of two fae who were pinning her down.

'No, no, this is not where we die. This is not where we die.'

But blood was pouring out of her side, and she found herself falling to her knees.

'Yeeran,' Lettle screamed.

I'm sorry, little sister. I tried.

Hold on, Yeeran, help is coming, Pila urged.

Blood loss brought on a haze, and Yeeran felt herself slip into magesight.

She gasped.

A ball of light was coming, a molten swirl of bronze and gold as a fae on an obeah hurtled towards her. Tendrils of magic spiralled outwards and Yeeran flinched as they came her way.

But they didn't strike. Instead, the magic struck the nearest assailant.

This fae was helping them.

Bursts of sunshine filled the street as more and more fae arrived. Yeeran smiled as the brightest of them came towards her.

'You must be the god Ewia,' Yeeran said to the light wraith.

There was a harsh laugh, then gentle hands eased Yeeran up.

'Where are you taking her?' Lettle sounded teary.

Why is she so sad? We were saved.

Because you are bleeding out, Yeeran. Pila's voice sounded far away.

Am I?

'I'm going to take her to a healer I know nearby. I have to go now.'

There was a scuffle, then Rayan said, 'Let her go, Lettle. She needs to be seen by a doctor before the dagger is removed.'

She was lifted and placed onto Pila's back.

'Yeeran, listen to me. I need you to hold on. OK?'

Yeeran's eyes slitted open and she reached for the sunlight that spoke to her.

'Not to me, to your obeah.'

Hold on, Yeeran, Pila shouted in her mind.

It felt an age before Yeeran could tighten her hands in Pila's mane.

'Follow me.' The words were barked out.

Then Pila was running, and Yeeran felt the breeze on her face. She smiled into the oncoming darkness that blurred the edges of her vision.

Until it consumed her completely.

* * *

'Hello. I know you're awake.' The voice sounded young.

Pila?

I'm outside, you are safe. So is Lettle.

Yeeran felt a wave of relief. She cracked open an eyelid to find Cane, the boy she had once seen Furi train, standing over her. He wrung his hands in front of a grubby stained shirt.

'Well, I wasn't awake. Until now.' Her throat was dry and hoarse.

'Oh.'

She was in a small bed in a room not much wider than the width of it. Rudimental drawings lined the walls.

'You're in my bedroom. Mother told me I had to give you my bed. "Temporarily".'

He saw Yeeran looking at the pictures and pointed to one of the largest ones. It was of a warrior wielding yellow paint for magic.

'That's Commander Furi.'

Furi – of course, the sunlit wraith was Furi.

Yeeran tried to sit up to get a closer look and winced.

'Mother gave you twelve stitches.'

'Thank you to your mother.'

There were footsteps and Furi appeared in the doorway. She wore her leather chest plate over a black sheer tunic. Her unusually dishevelled hair fell across her face, which was pinched with worry.

'Cane, did you wake her?'

He gave Furi a bashful smile.

'No, she was awake already.'

Yeeran nodded.

'I was.'

He gave Yeeran a wicked grin.

'Cane, will you go and fetch your mother from the apothecary? Tell Jay their patient is awake.'

'If I have to.'

'You do.'

He dragged his feet as he left.

Now alone, the silence hummed between them, vibrating with unspoken words.

'Thank—'

'I—'

They both stumbled into the conversation, then smiled as they cut off the other.

'Sorry, I was just trying to say thank you. For saving us. Hosta and their crew would have killed us all.'

Furi's grin fled from her face.

'You're lucky I returned a week early. If I hadn't seen you from the boundary.' She closed her eyes; when she opened them, they were full of anger. 'What were you doing all on your own out there? You know people want you dead.'

People like you, Yeeran thought. Then she wondered if that was still true.

'I was going to the fields, to harvest.'

Furi's gaze softened to something almost affectionate. But the expression was fleeting.

'It was foolish. Now you are wounded, which will delay your training even more.'

Of course, Yeeran thought bitterly. *She doesn't care about me. All she cares for is obeying her mother's orders.*

'So what?' Yeeran said quietly. 'The purpose of the training is to kill me in the end anyway.'

'That's not true—'

Yeeran laughed.

'And so I'm expected to survive the initiation?'

Furi's mouth snapped shut and she breathed heavily through her nose.

'Well?' Yeeran prompted.

'You were not supposed to die today.'

Then she left, though her words remained, echoing in Yeeran's mind.

* * *

Yeeran wasn't on her own for long. Cane erupted back into the room shortly after, his mother in tow.

His mother didn't look like Yeeran expected them to. Dark eyes laced with thick lashes sat in a delicately boned face. Their hair shone a glossy black, like the fur of an obeah, and it fell in straight sheets by their immaculate eyebrows. Lipstick glossed full lips which parted in a smile as they saw Yeeran awake.

'Hello, I'm Jamal, but call me Jay.' Even their voice was exquisite, like the trill of a bird in spring.

Yeeran realised she was staring. 'Are you all right? You're not seeing spots in your vision, are you?' Jay asked.

'Sorry, no. I'm . . . I'm fine.'

Jay knelt down next to the bed, their skirts filling the rest of the space in the room.

'Mother, can I have my bed back now?' Cane whined.

Jay tutted at him. 'No, you'll be staying in my room tonight.'

Cane tilted his head. 'But where will Furi stay?'

Jay's eyes met Yeeran's.

'She's staying in the palace. Now go and get ready for bed, I'll see you soon.' Jay turned to Yeeran. 'How are you feeling?'

'Sore. I hear I have twelve stitches.'

Jay laughed.

'Sorry about Cane, he gets so excitable when Furi's around. He wants to be *just like her*.' They gave Yeeran a sad smile. 'But I'm glad he has her to look up to . . . he lost his ma, my partner, five years ago.'

As Jay spoke, Yeeran could see the grief etched into the creases in the corners of their eyes.

'I'm sorry.'

'So am I, but those are the perils of going topside.'

Yeeran swallowed. Jay's partner was killed by elves, though they didn't seem to hold it against her. Yeeran was glad of it, she wasn't sure she could face any more vengeance that day.

Jay rolled back the covers of the bed and carefully checked the stitches. 'They look clean, no sign of infection yet, but I'd like you to stay the night here. You lost a lot of blood, but the dagger missed everything that would have killed you. Somehow.'

'We were taught it.'

'What?'

'We were taught how to twist our bodies in order to receive the least amount of damage from an attack.'

Jay let out a horrified 'oh' before pulling back up the covers.

'This tincture next to the bed is made of snowmallow flower, so if you get any pain in the night sip this.'

'Thank you, Jay.'

Yeeran had lots of questions for the healer, namely: How long have you been Furi's lover? But she couldn't ask that, so instead she said, 'Why don't you work in the infirmary? Where I was before?'

Jay's charming smile slipped slightly. 'I am Lightless. Only those who are faebound can work in the infirmary.'

'Oh.'

Jay lingered in the doorway, sensing Yeeran wasn't finished talking.

'How long have you known Furi?'

Jay's eyes crinkled as if they knew what Yeeran was really asking.

'A long time. Though it's not what you think. We take pleasure in each other to sate our loneliness. But our love is one of deep friendship, nothing more.'

Yeeran told herself she didn't care either way, but she felt something ease in her chest.

'I think I'm going to rest now,' Yeeran said.

Jay nodded, but as they turned to leave something caught their eye and they bent down to pick it up.

'Is this yours?'

Jay held up a small conch. Yeeran recognised it as the shell she and Furi had used to train with on the beach.

Furi must have kept it.

'Yes, it's mine.'

Yeeran slept with the shell in her hand and a smile on her face.

CHAPTER TWENTY-SEVEN

Lettle

'I want to see her. Let me in.' Lettle hammered her fist against the wooden door.

It swung open, framing Furi in the last light of the fray. Her expression was thunderous.

'I will not tell you again, this house is small enough without you filling up space with your inane chatter. Let the healer *work*. Go back to your rooms, I will ensure word is sent when she wakes.'

With that, Furi shut the door.

A frustrated cry erupted from Lettle's throat.

'There's nothing we can do here, Lettle,' Rayan said. He held a wad of fabric to a shallow cut on his arm. Komi was sitting on the ground, a faint grin on his face. He barely looked ruffled.

'Furi won't let us in,' Rayan continued. 'I've already spoken to Berro—'

Lettle snarled at the fae's name, but Rayan didn't seem to notice.

'—and she has apprehended all of the fae who attacked us. She knows of Yeeran's condition and has assured me that the healer Furi has called on is one of the best.'

'If they're one of the best, then why isn't Yeeran *awake yet?*'

Pila let out a low whine behind them. The obeah had been prowling the doorway in Lettle's shadow.

The beast looked so forlorn Lettle wanted to cry. She let out a breath, the fight going out of her.

Rayan reached for her hand and squeezed it. She gave him a grateful nod.

'Let's go.'

Lettle headed straight to her bedroom when they returned. She turned on the gas lamps near her bed and pulled out some of the books she had brought back from the library.

For she had not forgotten what she had learned just this morning – Yeeran would die during initiation.

If she doesn't die now from her wound.

She felt her throat bob, but she swallowed the tears. Tears wouldn't help her escape Mosima. Tears wouldn't help Yeeran.

She had searched nearly two hundred books and had found only one reference to the boundary or Afa, the last human. She withdrew the fae dictionary Golan had given her a few weeks ago and began to transcribe another text.

Tap. Tap. Tap.

The knock at the door was light, careful.

'You can come in, Rayan.'

Maybe he had news of Yeeran. He entered with two plates of fried okra and bread.

'Can I join you? I don't really like waiting for news, so I thought company might help.'

She nodded and waved at the space next to her on the bed. 'Please don't distract me though.'

Rayan handed her one of the plates and she inhaled the bread before he had even settled down.

He laughed lightly. 'I'm glad I brought food. I thought you'd be too worried to eat.'

She looked at him gravely. 'We spent so many years being hungry, that I don't think there will be a time or place where I can't, or won't, eat.'

Rayan must have seen something in her gaze because he looked away.

'I'm sorry you had to go through that,' he said quietly. His hand twitched beside hers and she wanted him to reach for her. 'Did your father not work?'

It was Lettle's turn to look away.

Her nightmares about her father had all but stopped for the first time in years. She wondered if being this far from the Elven Lands had helped ease his ghost from her mind.

So often she had seen his lifeless body flash behind her eyes. But here she was more preoccupied with escape than her haunting memories of her father's death – no, murder.

'I don't want to talk about him.'

Lest he resurface in my dreams.

Rayan nodded and didn't speak again. Once he had finished his food, he reached for the prophecy journal that held all their notes. He added a few sentences to an extract and Lettle peered over to see what he had written.

'"The Flare Feast will happen next week during the waxing moon." How do you know the moon is waxing?'

He shrugged.

'Berro told me. She was with Furi topside.'

Lettle snatched the journal from Rayan's hands, sending her own books toppling to the floor.

'What is it?' he asked, but Lettle wasn't listening.

She flicked through the pages until she reached her last prophecy.

'Under a waxing moon that no one can see, when the sun flares and twilight reigns. A burdened partnership will die when poison passes their lips. One gilded, one pearl.'

She sat back on the bed.

'What does it mean?' Rayan asked.

'Two people are going to die on the day of the Flare Feast.'

Rayan shrugged. 'Does it matter if they lose two fae? Two less people to fight to escape.'

Lettle felt unsettled. She couldn't put her finger on it until she realised why. The prophecy didn't specify *fae*.

One gilded, one pearl.

Rayan shifted on the bed until his shoulder was touching hers. She let out a breath and reached for another book.

'Maybe you should take a break from reading. We might not escape Mosima tonight, but someday we will be free.'

That irritated her. 'Sometimes it feels like I'm the only one actually *trying* to leave here.'

'That's not true, Lettle. I spend every day collecting information, and Yeeran, she's been studying the boundary for hours each day. Even Komi has been making friends. I saw him with Nerad in a tavern just yesterday, plying him with drink to glean intelligence.'

'But none of it has worked. We're still no closer to getting out of here.'

'We will though.'

She felt the net of his body heat pull her closer.

'How can you be so sure?' she whispered into the space between them.

He closed his eyes and let out a breath. 'Remember how I told you that my mother gave Chieftain Akomido a prophecy he didn't like?'

'Yes, you said that no one knew the prophecy except the two of them.'

Rayan's mouth drew into a line.

'That was a lie.'

Lettle watched him and waited.

He reached for her hands and held them in his lap, 'She prophesied that I'd be the death of him. And because of that, because of what I would one day do, he murdered her.' His voice cracked.

'Rayan . . .'

'But don't you see,' he said, animated once more. 'We *must* leave here. Because one day, I'll kill the Two-Bladed Tyrant on the battlefield.' He had turned his pain into comfort and was using it to try and soothe Lettle's fears. She loved him for it. But she didn't have the heart to tell him that he could have already impacted the tyrant's death. Without a clearer foretelling, being the death of someone could mean myriad things.

He reached out a hand and cupped her cheek. Lettle found herself closing her eyes and leaning into the warmth of it.

'You don't need to worry, you see.' His breath hot, his voice rough. 'We'll be free in the end.'

'Rayan.'

He dropped his hand.

'I know, I understand you don't feel the same way as I do about you . . . but know that I do care, all right? I will always care.'

Lettle didn't trust herself to speak. She was watching his lips, the way they moved and dimpled in the corners. She imagined what it would be like to kiss them, to have his arms wrap around her waist, to have his bare skin mould into the curves of her body.

She became aware of the bed beneath them. It would be so easy to slip under the sheets . . .

'Lettle . . .' The way he said her name made her dizzy. She closed her eyes.

There was a bang as her bedroom door flew open.

'She's going to be fine,' Komi sang from the doorway. He brandished a letter.

Lettle was beside him in a blink. She reached for the paper and read aloud. 'It's from the healer. Yeeran's going to be fine. She had twelve stitches. The damage was minimal as it missed all major organs. She'll send her home in the morning.' Lettle let out a sob of relief.

Rayan folded her into his arms. It wasn't the comfort she wanted, but it was the comfort she needed.

CHAPTER TWENTY-EIGHT

Yeeran

Yeeran was assigned to bed rest for three days, which galled her. Now with Furi back she was looking forward to getting on with her training.

To learn how to use your magic? Or to spend more time with Furi?

Though the words had Pila's dry humour, they came from the depths of her own mind.

She shook the errant thought free. Everything was about getting back home. To the war.

To Salawa.

Her name was like a cold shower on a warm day. It sent painful tingles across her body, reminding her of the woman she'd left behind.

'Why are you frowning?' Lettle said as she swept into her bedroom. She held a mug of witch hazel and turmeric tea which she'd been brewing every hour since Yeeran had come back to their chambers.

'Again, Lettle? My veins are pure tea by now.'

'It helps stave off infection.'

Yeeran grunted but took the mug anyway.

Lettle settled down on the edge of the bed and waited for Yeeran to sip before asking, 'So? What were you thinking about?'

Yeeran tried to keep her face neutral as she said, 'Salawa.'

Lettle's nostrils flared and crinkled as if inhaling a bad smell.

'It will be hard to convince Salawa to stop killing obeah, you know.'

'She will. Once she knows it murders fae, she'll have to.'

Lettle's laugh was harsh. 'Salawa is not the woman you think she is, Yeeran. She does not deserve your loyalty.'

'She fights for the people we used to be. And a person like that will always have the beat of my drum.'

Lettle scoffed, her lips twisting her mouth into something ugly. 'Did you know she was the one who shot drumfire into the crowd the day you left? Did you know she was the one who knocked me out so I couldn't say goodbye?'

It was clear Lettle had been holding on to these thoughts for some time, letting them fester to withdraw when they'd hurt Yeeran the most. They hit their mark.

'She wouldn't do that,' Yeeran protested.

Lettle laughed and it was so bitter Yeeran winced.

'She exiled you, Yeeran, *exiled*. Something she knew that would be more painful than death because you were a *political threat*. Stop clinging on to the one image you have of her. There are more facets to that woman than you could ever imagine. And most of them are not good.'

Then she said something that chilled Yeeran's blood. 'When we're free, don't become a prisoner to her love again.'

With that, Lettle swept out of the room, tripping on the lip of the door as she did so.

Yeeran lurched out of the bed as if to help her, but Lettle was gone before Yeeran could reach her.

She dropped her chin to her chest and sighed.

I wasn't Salawa's prisoner, was I?

Her thoughts went to Furi, to the person who was truly keeping her captive. But as her face manifested behind her lashes, she felt something akin to exhilaration flutter in her chest.

I can't stay in bed for another minute. Pila, do you want to go for a run? I need to get out of here.

Yes, the obeah answered instantaneously. Since the attack, she hadn't ventured further than the palace. *We should ask for an escort.*

Though Yeeran hadn't seen Furi since she had woken in Jay's home, she had received a stern message from her that strongly suggested that none of the elves leave the palace without one of the faeguard.

No, we'll be fine, you and I. Unless you don't think you're the fastest obeah in Mosima?

Pila snorted in her mind.

I'm waiting in the courtyard.

They ran and ran until Pila's fur was slick with sweat and Yeeran's curls were wild and free.

Thank you, Pila. I needed that.

We should go back.

Pila could feel the echoes of Yeeran's own pain and so when exhaustion started to settle into her bones, Pila knew it was time to get her to bed.

As they made their way through the Royal Woodland, Yeeran spotted a familiar face sitting among the knotted roots of an acacia tree. Nerad had a collection of papers in front of him and as one lifted in the breeze, Xosa, his obeah, pounced on it.

She brought it back to the pile – with added bite marks – and rested her paw on them.

Nerad didn't even seem to notice.

Yeeran slipped off Pila and walked over, her footsteps heavy.

You should be resting, Yeeran.

I will, I just want to see Nerad. I haven't seen him since the attack.

She managed to get within a foot of the prince before he spotted her.

'Yeeran!' He reached for the papers, shuffling them together and moving them out of the way so she could join him on the ground.

She peered at the pages, only catching a few sentences here and there. It looked like a list of coordinates coupled with a map of some kind.

'What are you working on?' she asked.

Nerad handed the stack of papers to Xosa to take away.

'I'm tallying up the usable land across the blight. Seeing how much more crop we can grow now.'

Yeeran nodded and settled into the crook of the tree bark. Pila came and curled up by her feet.

'How are you feeling?' Nerad asked.

'Cooped up.'

Nerad gave her a crooked grin.

'Same.' His words sobered her. So easy it was to forget that the fae were prisoners too.

He continued, 'When we were younger, Furi and I used to swim out to the boundary from Conch Shore and pretend that if we just kept swimming, we'd find ourselves on the other side of Mosima.' He laughed. 'Really, we would just go in circles and imagine what topside was like. The obeah had told us what the world was like beyond, but it wasn't the same as seeing it ourselves.'

Yeeran felt a pang of sympathy for both Furi and Nerad. She could envision them floating on their backs looking up at the fray, sharing their fantasies of what topside looked like.

'How old were you when you first left Mosima?' Yeeran asked.

Nerad's expression was darkened by a memory. 'I was fifteen when my older cousin figured out how to open the boundary. He took Furi out first, though I was the elder . . . the two of them had fostered a relationship that had no room for me.'

'Why?' Yeeran gently probed.

Nerad's eyes flashed. 'I didn't fit the mould the Jani dynasty had for me. He sought to temper me.'

Temper him? He is the gentlest of his family, Yeeran said to Pila.

So too is a platypus, but their sting is venomous, she replied.

Yeeran was about to ask Pila where in the three gods she had ever seen a platypus, when Nerad spoke again.

'Anyway, enough lingering in the past. It must be nice to have a break from training.'

Yeeran let out a breath between her teeth and Nerad laughed.

'Don't tell me you miss it?'

'No, it's just that I still haven't mastered my magic. I'm yet to call on it. Even during the attack, I had nothing but my fists' – Pila huffed out a breath – 'and Pila of course.'

Nerad bobbed his head.

'It's difficult to master. You have to split your mind, focus with one and unfocus with the other. Use both magesight and tug on the spool of your power.'

Yeeran rubbed her brow in frustration.

'Those are just words. I can't actually do it.'

'Hmm. Do you know how to use a bow? Imagine it's like that. You must focus on the target, but also let all your other senses guide you.'

Yeeran felt the prickle of an idea crawl across her skin.

'Or perhaps drumfire . . .'

She leaned forward and clapped Nerad on the back.

'You're a genius.'

He coughed and she realised she'd been a bit too violent.

But he laughed and said, 'I don't know what I did, but I hope it works.'

Come on, Pila. We need to make a drum.

Yeeran waited on Conch Shore for Furi to turn up. Jay had begrudgingly given Yeeran permission to return to training the night before.

'But nothing too physical, all right?' Jay said, then added with a wink, 'I know it's the Flare Feast tonight, but you be careful when that fire gets doused. I'll tell Furi the same.'

Yeeran pretended not to understand her meaning, though the flush in her cheeks was enough to confirm it. Jay was still laughing as they left.

Now Yeeran was pacing across the wet sand, her rudimentary drum hanging from her shoulder. She told herself the excitement she was feeling was for the drum alone. But Pila set her right. *You missed her,* Pila said.

I did not.

But Yeeran couldn't deny the warmth Furi's presence brought as she rode towards her on Amnan. Like a sun ray through clouds, Furi's beauty burned Yeeran's skin and turned it flushed. The wind tore at the pale blue gossamer dress she wore, revealing the seam of her lace slip visible at the top of her thighs. Her hair was knotted at the top of her head, baring the freckled skin along her collarbone and neck.

As she jumped down, she gave Yeeran a tentative smile.

'Hello.' Furi's voice was a little breathy.

'Hello,' Yeeran replied. Her lips were numb, her eyes hungry.

Furi's smile slipped from her face. 'What's that?'

'It's a drum. I've been practising.'

Furi snarled and stepped away like a cat arching its back. Amnan recoiled, drawing a hiss from Pila in retaliation.

Yeeran held out a placating hand to both Furi and the obeah. 'It's made of old leather skin from the uniforms in the barracks.'

Yeeran spent all night scraping and carving the material until it was soft and supple enough to be stretched over a barrel. It wasn't much more than a cobbled-together imitation of a drum, but it would do.

'Why have you brought this?' Furi tilted her head to the right.

Instead of answering, Yeeran showed her.

She drew in a deep breath and opened her eyes to the magic. It wasn't quite like slipping into water, like it was for Lettle, or even Rayan. For Yeeran magesight required more effort, like climbing a staircase, or running a hill. But when she got to the top, she could see it bright and shining all around her.

Then she ran her ring finger across the edge of the drum, her wrists turned outwards. The gesture produced a simple tone, sharp and snappy, a higher note than she would normally use, but one whose magic was easier to harness. With intention, she drove the drumfire forward.

Instead of pulling on the magic from the obeah skin, Yeeran searched within and finally felt the tugging motion Furi had been explaining.

A shot of magic fired across the clearing.

Yeeran turned to Furi with a triumphant smile, but the other woman was frowning. 'How did you do that?'

You should have struck Amnan between the eyes instead of that tree. Pila was still smarting from the obeah's earlier hostility.

Yeeran ignored her and said to Furi, 'I combined the technique for drumfire with magesight and I did it, I pulled on the spool.'

Furi's mouth parted, awe crinkling the corners of her eyes. 'Show me again.'

Yeeran did so, but this time she drew out the sound with a drumroll, creating a long thread that she could manipulate once formulated.

Furi stood close to Yeeran, watching her fingers and the magic move. Yeeran could feel the heat of her. The silk from her dress wrapped around Yeeran's bare ankles in the breeze.

When Yeeran had finished the demonstration, Furi touched the hand that was resting on the drumskin. A jolt went through Yeeran at the contact.

'Can you show me?' Furi asked.

Yeeran tried to translate the motion of the drumbeat to Furi, but it was clear that she couldn't quite grasp the movement and the magic simultaneously.

'No, lighter, you don't need to hit it that hard.' Yeeran grasped Furi's wrist to guide her. It was small and delicate, though her hands were strong and broad. 'The sound is just a vessel for the magic, it doesn't truly draw it out, your focus does that.'

Furi sighed and Yeeran felt her breath on her cheek, tangy and sweet like the heart of a kiwi.

'It seems this doesn't work for me. It is good, though, that we have discovered a way to draw out your magic.'

Yeeran didn't realise her hand was still resting on Furi's until a silence pulled taut between them.

Furi's fingers twitched as if to grasp hers, but then the moment was gone and she snatched her hand away, snapping the thread of tension between them. Without Furi's grip the drum fell to the ground with a thud. Neither of them reached for the echoing sound between them.

Furi's eyes met hers. The golden core of them was hot and alluring. Amnan made a whine low in his throat.

Yeeran instinctively reached for him, brushing her hand along his hide. Furi lurched forward with a gasp, her eyes wide, her lips parted.

Yeeran snatched back her hand. 'Did I do something wrong?'

Furi seemed to be searching for the right words. Her mouth opened then closed, until she settled on, 'No.'

Yeeran wasn't sure that was quite true, and would have asked, but Furi had moved away.

There was a sound from the shore and they both turned to see Nerad walking towards them. It was time for her lesson with him already.

'Nerad.' Furi nodded curtly at her cousin before her gaze stuttered back to Yeeran's. 'I'll see you at the Flare Feast later.'

Yeeran had no time to say goodbye before Furi mounted Amnan and left.

Was his fur wirier than mine? It looks like black straw. Pila grumbled, her thoughts felt like grit between Yeeran's toes.

Yes, much wirier.

Pila settled her head onto her paws, content with Yeeran's answer.

Nerad cocked an eyebrow at her. 'Did I interrupt something between you and Furi?'

'No,' Yeeran said quickly. She turned to him. 'Can I ask, what is the etiquette when it comes to obeah?'

Nerad laughed. 'Oh, you didn't try to touch Amnan, did you? That's what's got her so annoyed.'

But Furi didn't *seem* annoyed.

Nerad lowered himself to the beach, and Yeeran settled next to him. 'Obeah are . . . the most sacred part of us.'

We are very special, Pila agreed.

'It is polite to acknowledge them, to respect them. Now *touching* an obeah.' Nerad chuckled. 'It's an act between lovers.'

Yeeran felt herself jerk upright.

'An obeah's connection is intimate.' He shook his head. 'I have friends who have been with their partners for years and have still not embraced their partner's obeah.'

Yeeran thought of Amnan and Furi, how she had reacted when Yeeran had touched Amnan.

How she hadn't told me to stop.

CHAPTER TWENTY-NINE

Lettle

'Well, did it work?' Lettle asked Yeeran when she returned from training. Rayan and Komi looked up from their positions on the sofa.

A small smile hung crookedly across Yeeran's lips, but when Lettle spoke she started as if she hadn't noticed that anyone was in the room.

'What?' Yeeran asked.

'The drum? Did it work?'

'Oh, yes. Just like drumfire.'

Komi cheered and Rayan murmured, 'Well done, Colonel, very well done.'

Lettle closed the book she was reading with a snap. 'Thank Bosome. We now have something we can fight the fae with when we escape.'

Something fleeting crossed Yeeran's features. Something akin to doubt. Lettle's stomach churned. 'You don't think we can do it.'

Yeeran lowered herself to the sofa next to Lettle. 'That's not what I said, Lettle.'

Lettle felt the fire of her anger begin to flicker beneath her eyelids. She clamped her mouth shut and tried to give Yeeran the benefit of the doubt.

But when Lettle didn't speak again, Yeeran opted to change the subject. 'Is everyone going to the Flare Feast?'

Komi clapped his hands together. 'Yes, I can't wait to see which mead they've brought in for the occasion.'

Even Rayan nodded and said, 'Berro told me it's the biggest night of celebration throughout the year, I don't think it's possible to avoid it.'

Lettle felt her rage surge and she stood up, books toppling around her. 'Why am I the only one trying to leave this godsforsaken place?'

The elves stiffened at the volume of her voice. Yeeran shook her head slowly but didn't respond.

'You,' Lettle pointed at Rayan, 'you spend your days with Berro, and yet we are no closer to knowing *why* the fae are preparing for war. You,' it was Komi's turn to be condemned, despite the wide-eyed look he gave her, 'are a drunk, whose only contribution to our plight has been collecting drinking songs.'

Lettle turned her wrath to Yeeran. 'And *you*. You have given up. I can see it. You don't think you're going to survive initiation, so you're simply biding time before the inevitable. Tell me it's not true.'

'Lettle . . .' Yeeran said her name like she was a disobedient child.

She didn't want to hear it. 'Each of you enjoy tonight. I will *not* be going. Because I for one have not forgotten our purpose.'

Then she stormed out of the room without a backward glance.

Lettle shut her bedroom door with a bang. Her heavy breathing filled the silence that followed.

She knew that both Rayan and Yeeran were trying, but they weren't trying *enough*.

Lettle closed her eyes in an effort to calm the anger that fizzed in her veins. When she opened them again, she looked to the window. The fray was dimming for the day, its colour turning from gilded yellow to the orange of glowing embers. She looked to the cavern ceiling and saw the small triangle of light where the sun would shine from topside for the only time that year. In an hour or so, its sunset rays would strike the Tree of Souls.

She repeated the prophecy in her mind:

Under a waxing moon that no one can see, when the sun flares and twilight reigns. A burdened partnership will die when poison passes their lips. One gilded, one pearl.

Somewhere out there two people were going to die. She had no way of knowing who. Only how.

Not that I could stop the prophecy either way.

Prophecies always came true, but she tried not to linger on that point. If she did, her thoughts would lead her back to Rayan.

And to love and death.

She shook the thought from her mind and tried to settle back to reading another book. But the sounds of the festival preparation below grated on her.

'I need to get out of here,' she said to herself.

Yeeran had impressed upon her that she shouldn't leave the palace without a faeguard escort. Even though Hosta and their crew had been captured it was likely that there were more fae who would happily murder Lettle.

She looked at the obeah hatch in her bedroom window that led down to a courtyard of fruit trees. It would be easy enough to slip through it and make her way down the staircase without Yeeran finding out.

Without hesitation she tucked her prophecy journal into her pocket and strode to the obeah opening. She pressed her palms against the pane of glass until it swung open. It was tall enough for an obeah to duck their horns under, so Lettle could walk through while still standing. The staircase on the other side was a little more precarious, it wasn't much more than protruding bricks with no rail to hold on to.

Lettle made it to the last few steps before tripping and stumbling to the ground.

'Ouch,' she groaned. She'd fallen on her left arm, causing the constant throb of pain there to spike.

There was a movement ahead of her and she looked up to see a cluster of obeah pause in their feeding. They watched her with curious eyes as she collected her limbs and strode away with an air of regality she had perfected over the years.

Crowds had already begun to pour into the streets. Cheers of merriment were sung from mouths glazed with mead and sugared cashews. Fae lounged on roofs and climbed up ladders. They were the unlucky ones who hadn't been invited into the Royal Woodland for the ceremony. Instead, they all hoped for a glimpse of the sunlight hitting the Tree of Souls from balconies or top-floor windows.

The presence of the masses did nothing to lessen Lettle's fears and she found herself almost running in the midst of the crowd. Her plan had been to go to the Book Orchard, but now it seemed too far away. And too isolated.

She felt like someone was watching her, but every time she swung around, she saw nothing. Once she thought she saw the flash of green eyes, but they were gone once she blinked.

Lettle was pulled roughly to the side by a tall woman. She started to kick at her until she realised the woman was trying to twirl Lettle around in a dance.

'A gift from the god who watches on high, a slice of the sun setting bright in the sky . . .' the woman trilled as she danced a jig.

Lettle spotted the purple sign of Seer Sahar's apothecary shop and dashed towards it, away from the reaching hands of the dancing fae.

'Hello?' She banged on the door, but the shop looked closed. She tried the door handle. Thankfully it gave way just as a group of fae riding their obeah cantered past, almost sweeping Lettle along with them.

She slipped into the shop and called out, 'Sahar?'

The door at the back of the room swung open and Sahar strode in clutching two steaming mugs of raspberry leaf tea. He had been expecting her.

'Hello, elf.' He handed one of the mugs to Lettle. It was made of purple clay, hand-painted with florals. She wondered if Sahar had made it himself.

'I've sweetened it with owen tree sap. I suspect you are out.'

She nodded gratefully and took a sip. She hummed as the pain relief surged to her left shoulder. 'Thank you.'

Sahar gave her a sly smile. 'Of course.'

They drank their tea in silence, Lettle's eyes running along the spines of the books that lined the shelf behind Sahar's head. She realised with a start that she could now read them. Her eyes snagged on one of the small volumes.

'*The Story of the Wheat, the Bat, and the Water*. What's that?'

'Exactly what it says.' Sahar reached for it and passed it to her. 'It's the story of the beginning of things. And the end of things, I suppose.'

Lettle reached for it. 'May I?'

Sahar met her eyes, then nodded once, sharply. 'Keep it.'

Lettle ran her hungry hands over it.

A new book that might have more to offer on how to escape this place.

She looked to the streets outside. Somehow, they had become even busier than before. There was no way she was making it through to the Book Orchard.

When she looked back at Sahar he was waiting expectantly. 'Can I stay here for a little bit? Just until it quietens?'

He nodded. 'I'll be out back if you need me. The Flare Feast has never been a festival I have enjoyed.' He shook his head sadly. 'Celebrating a piece of the sun is not celebration, but a reminder of our imprisonment.'

His slender shadow stretched as he shuffled back out behind the door.

Lettle pulled out the stool from the counter and began to read.

Only when Lettle's eyes began to droop did she realise so much time had passed. The fray had dimmed completely and, though she didn't remember it happening, Sahar must have come back into the room and turned on the gas lamps for her.

She sat up and stretched her shoulders. *The Story of the Wheat, the Bat, and the Water* was folkloric, full of more myth than truth. Some of it she recognised from tales told by diviners in the Elven Lands, but those had focused on Bosome, and not on all three gods.

She looked down at her notes.

Ewia granted the fae magic made of sunlight, Bosome gave the elves the magic of the Fates made of moonlight, and Asase bestowed on humans the language of the rocks and the trees.

Gold for fae, silver for elves, bronze for humans.

It made sense: the boundary's magic was burnished darker than the gold of the fae's power, and the Fates' magic had always shimmered in silver pearls.

Lettle felt the cold fear of dread slice like a knife against her throat. She flicked back to her last prophecy, her gaze stuttering to a stop on the final sentence.

A burdened partnership will die when poison passes their lips. One gilded, one pearl.

She'd dismissed the victims as inconsequential.

'A burdened partnership . . . gold and silver. Fae and elf.'

Furi and Yeeran.

That day in the forest she had asked the Fates about Yeeran, and they had told her. All this time she had foretold Yeeran's death and not known it.

Lettle jumped up, the stool falling out from behind her with a crash.

'What is it?' Sahar asked, appearing in the doorway.

'My sister . . . there's a prophecy . . . it's coming true today. I might be too late . . .'

Sahar looked to her book and read the words there. 'There's nothing you can do, Lettle.' His words were broken things brought forth from the rupture of grief, for tears had pooled in his eyes.

Lettle had no time to wonder why he was crying. All she knew was that she had to *find Yeeran.*

She burst out of Sahar's shop and into the foray of dancers. Her feet pounded on the tiled ground as she ran. But she was still too slow.

A figure pranced out of the shadows and into her path. It was the obeah she'd seen before, with the green eyes and a broken horn.

'Get out of the way,' she hissed at it, but it didn't move. She tried to skirt around it, but it lunged towards her, its front two paws bowed downwards.

'Move,' Lettle shouted.

It pounced again, not letting her past.

'Wait . . . do you want me to ride you?'

It tilted its head.

If Lettle wasn't so panic-stricken she would have stopped to question who was bound to this obeah. Instead, she jumped onto its back and clung onto the base of its mane like she'd seen Yeeran do with Pila.

'Take me to the Royal Woodland.'

Lettle's thighs burned as they galloped towards the palace. She was grateful for the owen tree sap that blunted the pain in her shoulder. The crowds were blurred by her tears as they lurched their way through them, not caring about who she offended. When they got to the woodland she was slick with sweat.

She jumped from the obeah's back and ran through the Royal Woodland. The fire had been doused, and so the fae had taken to the trees to seek their pleasure.

Every groan of bliss masqueraded as pain. She turned to magesight to help guide her to her sister.

'Yeeran!' she shouted, but no one was listening.

Then there was a scream. Panic burned down her throat as she ran towards the sound.

A cluster of people had gathered in a clearing up ahead. One of them had a gas lamp. Its light cast a shadow over two bodies on the ground. Lettle saw dark curly hair.

'They're dead,' she heard someone say and felt the darkness swallow her whole.

Lettle fell to the ground and sobbed.

CHAPTER THIRTY

Yeeran

Yeeran watched Lettle stride out of the room, her last words hanging heavy on all of them.

'I for one have not forgotten our purpose.'

It echoed like a guilty conscience in Yeeran's mind. She thought every day about escape, but the longer she spent in the world of the fae, the more she realised her magic alone wasn't going to be enough to save them. They needed to find another way.

Rayan stood up as if to go after Lettle, but he lingered in the doorway, his expression torn. Then he clenched his fists and strode away.

I wonder what happened between them, Pila mused. *I thought they were to be mates, but instead they circle each other with their scents.*

I don't know, but I think it has something to do with Berro.

Hmm, but he does not circle Berro in the same way?

'I'm going to go down early, get a good seat next to the . . . mead.' Komi's gaze was troubled. Lettle's words had hit their mark for all of them.

Yeeran and Pila were not alone for long.

Knock. Knock. Knock.

When Yeeran opened the door, she let out a surprised, 'Oh.'

Furi stood in the doorway, shifting from foot to foot. 'I have something for you.'

She withdrew a large circular object wrapped in cotton. She handed it over with a thrust of her hands and looked away, her gaze slipping to the ground.

Yeeran opened the parcel and smiled.

It was the mahogany drum that Salawa had gifted to her on her first day as a colonel.

'I had it reskinned, of course.' Furi's lips rose in distaste. 'I thought it would be better for you than the drum you made.'

It was that and more. In gifting back this piece of her, Furi had given her a semblance of the person she used to be. She felt herself stand straighter, her chin lifted upwards. She swallowed the knot in her throat.

'Thank you, this means a lot to me.'

Furi's eyes met hers and she smiled her rare smile. 'I have to go, I'm late for my dress fitting. I'm expected in the woodland in an hour.'

Yeeran didn't want her to go. 'Shall we test this out first?'

Furi cocked an eyebrow and stepped into the living room. 'Hit the painting above the fireplace,' she said.

Yeeran threw the drum strap over her head and focused on the target.

She harnessed her magesight and placed her wrist and palm on the drum in order to muffle the resonance. Then she tapped lightly with her index finger and thumb, rotating the groups of fingers to draw out a clear beat. She unspooled her threads of magic and let them fly.

Each hit the centre of the painting, tearing through the canvas to the stone wall beneath.

She turned triumphantly to Furi, pulling her into a hug before she realised what she had done. At first Furi stiffened in shock, and then she melted against Yeeran. When the embrace ended, Yeeran found herself wanting more than that brief touch. She wanted to taste every freckle on her skin. She wanted to explore every curve and shadow. As Furi's gaze made contact with hers, a thought came to her.

My initiation is in just over a month.

We'll figure it out, Pila said. The obeah was lying on the floor next to Amnan, and Yeeran noticed their tails were intertwined.

I thought you didn't like Amnan?

When did I say that?

You said his fur was wiry.

It is, but only because mine is the softest.

Yes, it is, Yeeran agreed, and she bent down to stroke Pila's head.

Furi walked to the doorway and lingered.

'The queens want to make sure you're in attendance tonight. It's to be a big celebration. With the blight ended, the threat to their rule is over.'

'I'll be there.'

Furi didn't speak for a while, and when she spoke her words were soft, tinged with the cobwebs of an old memory. 'My brother and I had come to terms with the fact the blight would have destroyed all of Mosima during the next royals' reign. It is strange to think that both him and it have now gone.'

Yeeran pressed her lips shut. This was the most Furi had ever spoken about anything that wasn't training, she wasn't about to ruin the moment by interrupting.

Furi continued. 'Before the curse, my ancestors lived in Lorhan, the capital of the Fae Lands. Nerad and I had dreamed of going back there again. Of leaving Mosima behind.'

'But doesn't Mosima die if the Jani dynasty leave?'

Furi looked at her sharply. The question came out before Yeeran could stop it.

'Did Nerad tell you that?'

Yeeran nodded, her lips an impenetrable line once more.

See, there's always a solution, Pila chimed in unhelpfully. *Kill all the Jani dynasty.*

Do you think we could do that? Kill Furi? Kill Amnan?

Pila didn't reply but her tail tightened slightly around Amnan's. It was answer enough.

Furi looked over to the painting Yeeran's drumfire had ruined. 'It's true, none of us can leave for long without the trees beginning to wilt. Remember, this may seem like a paradise to you, but it is not. It is our curse to remain hidden away from the world. It is our curse to never feel the rain on our faces or see the clouds in the sky. Mosima is wonderful, but all wonders cease to amaze when you realise their restrictions. We are trapped here, just as much as you are.'

She stepped into the hallway and Amnan went to join her. He clung to Furi's leg as she said, 'Don't be late, the queens won't like it.'

Yeeran sighed, annoyed to see the expression of the commander back on her face. Just like Salawa, Furi was her title before anything else.

But then Furi turned and said, 'Wear red. It suits you.'

Then she loped off on Amnan's back, her hair falling down from the knot it had been bound in. Ethereal and free. A goddess come alive.

Yeeran tugged on the waistline of her red shirt. It was lined in black leather with brassware buckles that tied around her ribcage like a harness. The skirts were adorned with the same leather detailing. The material was sheer, outlining the shadows of her muscular legs. She had painted her lips and fingertips blood red.

Her gaze roamed the crowd. The two queens sat on their thrones in the bark of the Tree of Souls. Both were dressed in magnificent gowns that frothed and flowed in lace and silk.

Queen Vyce wore a gold circlet across her head that fanned out into sun rays, whereas Chall's crown was far more ornate and speckled with pearls. Their obeah lounged in the bough of the Tree of Souls, their tails swishing in the cluster of star gliders that surrounded the queens.

Yeeran had arrived on time at the feast, but it was now past eight in the evening and still Furi hadn't shown up.

Pila, have you seen Amnan?

No, do you want me to find him?

It's all right.

Pila was lounging in a group of other obeah in the thick of the forest. The queens had harvested a mound of fruit and laid it out for the beasts to gorge themselves. Pila was sated and content.

'You choose that outfit yourself?' Golan said, walking over. He wore a green skin-tight dress that fell to the floor.

Yeeran smiled warmly. 'Yes, I did actually.'

'I think you might be learning more about style than your sister. Have you seen her, by the way?'

'She's not coming.'

Golan smiled and shook his head, 'She's taken a liking to studying fae.'

Because it could be the key to our escape, Yeeran thought but didn't say. Instead, she nodded vaguely.

There must be more I can do to get us out of here. Lettle's words were still clawing at her skin. Maybe by getting closer to Furi she could get her to advocate for the elves to the queens.

The idea of getting closer to Furi made her heart race.

'O holy Ewia,' Golan's words dragged her back to the present. His gaze snagged on someone in the distance. Yeeran was about to ask what had made his eyes go so very wide but then she saw them.

Nerad and Furi had arrived.

The music seemed to reach a crescendo, filling in the hushed silence that had rippled across the crowd. Both wore matching bronze corsets that fanned out behind them in a trail of fine chainmail. Upon their brow they wore crowns that replicated the shape of their obeahs' horns, twisting upwards like branches of a tree.

Their eyes were lined with liquid gold, and their lips shimmered with rouge so dark it was almost black. Amnan and Xosa, their two obeah, stood on either side of them.

They looked every bit like the future king and queen of Mosima.

'He looks incredible,' Golan muttered.

'They both do.' For a while Golan's gaze lingered on Nerad. Yeeran had not taken her eyes off Furi. How could she, how could anyone, when she looked like *that*?

Furi hesitated by the bottom of the steps while Nerad made his way to his mother. She seemed to be searching the crowd, looking for someone.

Yeeran waited for her gaze to land on hers and when it did, the whole world seemed to darken around her. For a moment she thought she might have slipped into magesight, but no, Furi simply shone brighter than anyone else in the woodland.

Furi's mouth parted, and Yeeran could see how shallow her breath had become. Then her expression became hard, her lips pushing together becoming bloodless, and she turned away to go and stand beside her mother. The four of them together cut a striking sight.

Yeeran let out an unsteady breath.

'The full force of the Jani dynasty, for all to see,' Golan said. 'Now the blight is over they are once more exerting their power and cementing Nerad and Furi as the next monarchs.'

Yeeran looked around. The crowds of fae were looking at their rulers with unconcealed admiration. Yeeran wondered if it wasn't half rubbing off on her.

'It seems to be working,' she said.

Yeeran looked over to Rayan. He was chatting to a few members of the faeguard that he'd become friendly with. He seemed at ease in their company and in turn, they didn't seem to treat him any differently. They spoke elvish to accommodate for his lack of fae, though Yeeran had noticed more than once that Rayan had picked up a few fae words here and there. He saw her looking and walked over.

'Are you all right?' Rayan asked.

'Yes, though I can't compete with Komi. It looks like he's having the best night of his life.'

They both chuckled as they looked his way. He was flirting with anyone who came within reach and dancing with everyone who dared ask him. His charms were harmless though effective; she wondered how much of it was driven by Lettle's harsh words and if he, too, was using the opportunity to collect information. She hoped so.

'There you are.' Berro appeared by Rayan's elbow. She wore a thin slip of silver material cut all the way down to her navel. Vines had been braided around her short white-blonde curls. Her obeah's horns had been similarly adorned.

'My eyes are up here, elf-boy,' she drawled to Rayan.

Rayan flushed and looked away. Yeeran muffled her laugh.

Komi was the one to save him in the end. He asked Berro to dance, 'Only if she didn't mind making it up as she went along.' Few people could say no to Komi, and so Berro found herself being led to the dance floor.

Yeeran was about to take her leave when she felt a prickle across her skin.

Furi was stalking towards her across the clearing.

'Incoming,' Rayan said under his breath. 'Go now, and I can make an excuse for you.'

'No,' Yeeran said quickly. Perhaps a little too quickly, as Rayan's eyebrows went upwards. 'I mean, it's fine. She'll probably want to introduce me to someone I haven't met yet.'

'Indeed. I, at least, can beg my leave,' Rayan said before ducking away.

Furi stopped a foot from Yeeran, her expression curiously neutral as she looked her up and down.

'You look . . .'

Yeeran waited.

'. . . Like fae.'

It wasn't the compliment she was looking for, but it was the highest one Furi would ever be able to give. But then Furi's lips pursed and Yeeran took a deep breath, bracing herself for whatever barbed comment was coming. She nearly choked on the exhale when Furi said, 'My mother thinks we should dance.'

'I don't dance.'

'Don't and won't are not the same. Dance we must.'

'Why?'

'Because tonight is a celebration and a show of our might. And you, elf, are the prisoner that we have not just stolen, but have made ours.'

Made ours.

Why did that sound so good on her lips?

'I don't know how.'

Furi snorted. 'I assumed. This dance, however, is an easy one. All you are required to do is hold my hand, and I will lead you through the movements.'

Furi's fingers were bejewelled with rings of silver and gold that glinted like starlight as she held out her hand.

Yeeran swallowed, then reached out. If she was going to make a fool of herself, at least it would be in the arms of the most beautiful woman in the woodland.

The fae made space for Furi as she led them onto the dance floor. Yeeran kept her eyes lowered and her chin dipped until Furi gripped her jaw between cool fingers.

'Head up, shoulders back, follow the sway of my hips.'

Yeeran felt Furi's other hand grip her waist and gently push her to and fro in time with the music. When the music changed an octave, Furi dipped backwards, her hair tipping down her back as she pushed Yeeran away, baring her neck to the sky.

Yeeran stood mesmerised, unsure what to do while Furi swayed with her head tilted backwards. She stole a glance at another couple and saw that one of them was holding the other's neck, supporting them as they curved their back.

She reached for Furi, her hand sliding around the nape of her neck behind her hair. Furi let the weight of her body grow heavy in Yeeran's grasp, her hip bones a breath from Yeeran's.

The music changed again and Furi straightened. Yeeran didn't drop her hand from Furi's neck. They stood flush together, the rhythm of the dance capturing them in a bind as they moved.

Why does it feel like you are running? Pila asked.

What do you mean?

Your heart, it flutters like a hummingbird. I can feel it buzzing in my chest. Maybe you should come and join me in the grass. It is cool and calm here.

I'm fine, Pila.

If you're sure.

Yeeran wasn't sure. Dancing with Furi felt like the currents of the ocean. The longer she fought it, the deeper she was pulled.

When the music stopped, they stood there, breathing heavily. Yeeran's hand slid from her neck to her collarbone. Furi's skin was hot and sheened with sweat.

Her mouth parted as if to say something, then she stepped away, her brow furrowed.

There was a commotion as the queens stood.

'It is time to douse the fire,' Furi said quietly, as if she were speaking to herself alone.

Yeeran felt her blood pump in her ears, and she watched the queens in a daze.

'We celebrate another festival of the flare, when the sun blesses our sacred tree,' Chall said with practised projection.

'Now the blight has ended, and prosperity has once more been restored. May the light bless, may the light cleanse. Children of Ewia we will always be.'

The queens raised the ceremonial chalice up to the sky before each sipped from the juice within. Once they had each drunk, they doused the fire with the remains.

Yeeran had never craved the darkness more.

Yeeran wasn't sure who reached the other first, all she knew was their lips collided with an urgency she had never felt before.

She reached her hands into Furi's hair, tipping her head back so she could expose the smoothness of her neck. She pressed kisses along her collarbone, letting her tongue savour the salt of her skin and linger in the hollows of her clavicle.

Furi trembled beneath her, her grip strengthening around Yeeran's waist like a flower clinging so desperately to its petals in the face of a storm.

For Yeeran was rain and thunder, her kisses unforgiving, her hands a tempest that roamed the curves of Furi's body.

'Yeeran.' A command. A plea.

Furi gasped as Yeeran's hand found the hem of her dress and slid upwards while Yeeran lowered herself to kneel in the dirt.

Yeeran's mouth and fingers met where Furi's desire grew hot and wet. Yeeran guided one of Furi's legs over her shoulder, her tongue coaxing sounds of pleasure.

Furi's feral panting joined that of many others in the twilight of the night and Yeeran drew back to see the wanton hunger on Furi's face.

She was flushed, her lips glistening and parted, showing the fierceness of her canines. Her eyes blazed like fire.

Yeeran didn't think she had seen anything so beautiful.

'More.' Her voice was cut glass, ragged and sharp.

Yeeran obliged, teasing the softness of her with her fingers before pushing inside. She lowered her lips down to the peak of her, parting Furi with her tongue.

Yeeran moved at a steady rhythm, rubbing her finger against the raised ridge inside Furi that made her quiver. With her other hand she pressed flat against Furi's navel, intensifying the build of ecstasy.

Furi's hands moved to Yeeran's hair and balled her fists in it.

'More.'

Again, Yeeran conceded to her demands, increasing in speed until Furi's breath caught and she went still.

Then Furi shuddered, bliss running through her like lightning. Her leg slipped from Yeeran's shoulder, and she sank to the ground.

Yeeran looked down at her.

'More?'

Furi gave her a wicked grin.

'More.'

Furi reached oblivion again before she turned her appetites to Yeeran.

And Yeeran let her.

Their clothes had long been shed, and now Yeeran lay back on the thick grass with Furi above her.

Instead of her tongue, Furi trailed her canines across Yeeran's neck, sending jolts of pleasure down her body. She cupped her breasts and pressed them to her lips before biting down.

Yeeran gasped and arched her back, enjoying the exquisite pain of it.

Her hand trailed across Yeeran's navel, lightly running over the small scar where Hosta had stabbed her.

Something like rage stoked the flames of Furi's golden eyes.

'Does it hurt?'

'No.'

It was true, in that moment all Yeeran could feel was desire.

Furi parted Yeeran's legs with her body, sliding her naked form up between them until her knee pushed into the curls that covered Yeeran's more sensitive part.

Then she began to move, rubbing and pressing down, Yeeran grinding with her, driving her own pleasure.

Furi's nails dug into her shoulders as she tilted her head to sate her desire from Yeeran's breasts. And when she bit down on her nipple, a cry tore through Yeeran as pain and pleasure collided in a heady mix.

Euphoria took her in its currents.

When she surfaced, Furi was lying on her side watching her. She trailed a hand along Yeeran's face. Yeeran sighed into her touch but stiffened as Furi reached Yeeran's slitted ears.

'Who did this to you?' Furi whispered.

'The chieftain of the Waning district, when I was exiled for insubordination.'

Furi laughed and Yeeran loved the sound of it. 'So, you're not only disobedient with me.'

Yeeran muffled her smirk with a kiss. When she withdrew, Furi had turned pensive again.

'I'll kill her, you know. For doing this to you.'

Yeeran believed it. 'No, she had to do it, it was the only way to let me live.'

'For that, she is in my debt then.'

Furi leaned forward and gently pressed her lips against the slits in Yeeran's ears. Yeeran could hear her breath, steady and sure. A juvenile star glider fluttered around her lashes, illuminating the affection in them. Where the first one joined her, another came, and then another, until star gliders spun in the air around her face, drawn to her Jani blood. As she lay among the leaves of the woodland in the sparkling whirlwind of their wings it was hard to see where the forest began, and she ended.

'You are exquisite.'

Furi laughed, reaching a hand towards a glider that had settled on her cheek. 'I used to hate them. They are pesky creatures, turning up where they shouldn't. When I was a child, they'd follow me through the woodland all the way up to my bedroom.' She laughed with the memory. 'But I've begun to see the beauty in them. They help to pollinate the plants of Mosima. Without them, many flowers would not bloom.'

Furi placed the creature in Yeeran's hand and closed her fist carefully around it. It illuminated the veins beneath her skin with its light.

'I always know if I follow the starlight, they'll bring me home,' Furi said. Then she kissed their clasped hands before releasing the star glider into the sky.

Yeeran's hand slipped behind her neck and pulled her closer.

'My starlight,' Furi whispered against her lips.

The sound of shattering glass cleaved the night air.

'Was that the staircase?' Yeeran murmured, more curious than worried. But all the blood had fled Furi's features.

The cacophony of crashing was followed by a scream. It was the sound of pure terror.

Pila, what has happened?

Come quickly, there has been a murder. Two of my kind are dead.

Yeeran was about to convey the message to Furi, but it was clear Amnan had already told her.

Furi jumped up and began to run. Yeeran was only a second behind because she had scooped up her clothing and attempted to dress as she followed.

Yeeran used magesight to find where the commotion was. The light of bodies was concentrated in the centre of the courtyard where the fire had been doused.

People were crying.

Yeeran looked around and saw a tear-streaked face she recognised. 'Lettle!'

Her sister ran at her, winding her with a hug.

'I did a reading, I thought it was you and Furi. It told me that two people were going to be poisoned, I just thought . . .' She was sobbing, and Yeeran couldn't understand half of what she was saying.

Furi pushed past them both and strode into the clearing.

Two dead bodies lay there.

A cry tore from Furi's throat, more animal than human. It was the sound of a heart breaking.

Furi sat in the dirt, her naked form shaking as she sobbed. Her hands cupped the cheeks of her mother and aunt, both unmoving and cold.

When she spoke, her voice was just as lifeless.

'The queens are dead.'

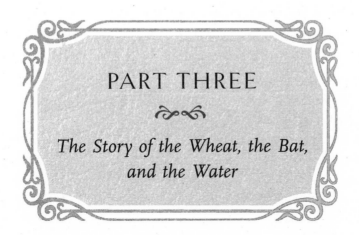

PART THREE

❧❧

The Story of the Wheat, the Bat,
and the Water

Three gifts were given to the children of the world. Carved from sunlight, the fae could pull and push. Grown from the earth, humans could create and mould. Chiselled by the tides, the elves could read the flow of the future. Three gifts from three gods, Ewia, Asase, and Bosome.

The fae used their magic to maim: pillaging and waging war against the humans. The humans used their magic to hinder: creating creatures of tooth and bone, weakening their strength. And the elves used their magic to warn the world what was to come.

They spoke of a prophecy:

Forever the war will rage, until united, the three shall die.
Humans made low, then fae made lower,
Then elves in ignorance, gone is their power,
Cursed to endure, cursed to survive.
All shall perish lest all three thrive.

The humans understood that their fate was to soon lie under the ground and, unaccustomed to the truth of prophecy, they waged wars like never before. But the fae, though weaker in magic, were greater in constitution; where one fae fell, ten humans fell first. And so, the fae reigned triumphant over the land.

It was with mercy that the fae left the last human alive. Afa was his name, left to wander the land until age stole his last breath. But like the lava of the fire mountains, Afa's vengeance grew hot. He used his final years to seek knowledge to amplify his power.

Then he returned to the Fae Lands.

'As the elves have spoken, so it will pass. Cursed you shall endure. Cursed you shall survive,' Afa said to the fae. Then he whispered the language of the trees and the earth and the rocks. Cracks split apart the earth that day, swallowing every fae that still lived. Binding them to an underground lair.

The gods in their grief retreated from the world, ending their wars. With the humans gone and the fae bound underground, only memories remained in the Elven Lands, fading with each passing day.

Until the truth was lost completely. And so too were the fae.

CHAPTER THIRTY-ONE

Lettle

There were no words to convey the relief Lettle felt at seeing the bodies of the two queens.

Once Yeeran and Furi arrived, everything became more frenzied. The faeguard were called in and crowds began to form around the bodies.

Nerad was sent for. His scream upon seeing his mother and aunt dead pierced Lettle's heart, the sound of it reverberating along her veins for some time.

Furi held him, her own tears drying on her face. The bitter expression Lettle had come to associate with her had returned, though today it was probably caused by shock.

At some point someone had given Furi a robe, which she'd accepted, but in her grief forgotten to tie. Now, she stood, stomach bare, barking orders at the faeguard.

Yeeran was watching her, concern filling her features.

'I can't believe the queens are dead,' Lettle said. 'Did you hear the staircase fall?'

'I think the whole of Mosima heard that.'

'Their connection to the curse, to the land, was holding the panes up.'

Yeeran nodded. The faeguard were already clearing the glass and had erected temporary ladders.

She turned to look at Lettle's tear-streaked face. 'What happened?'

'My last prophecy spoke of two people being poisoned . . .' Lettle couldn't keep the accusatory tone from her voice. 'I thought it was you. Furi and you. Gold and silver.' Lettle looked down to the ground where the two queens' crowns bore the signs of the foretelling. The burdens of their reign. 'Gilded and pearl,' Lettle added softly.

Yeeran nodded. Her shirt hung loose against her chest and her skirt was grass-stained.

'What were you doing?' Lettle asked.

Yeeran's eyes turned distant, and a small smile quirked her lips before she could stop it. 'Nothing.'

'Nothing looks a lot like something.'

They were interrupted before Lettle could ask further.

'What's going on?'

It was Rayan, he was a little out of breath and dishevelled. He must have come from a coupling with Berro. Lettle couldn't help the pit of jealousy that gnawed a hole in her gut.

'Where've you been?' she said, cold and accusing.

'I was about to go to bed when I heard the commotion.'

His jaw twitched. He was lying.

'The queens have been murdered,' Yeeran said. 'Poison they think, from the chalice that they doused the fire with. No one noticed until they came across their bodies.'

Yeeran was still watching Furi. Something had happened between them, Lettle was now sure of it.

Furi spotted the three of them and marched over, her face wan and severe.

'*You*,' the word was a growl from Furi's mouth as she rounded on Lettle. 'You knew it was poison. Guards, arrest her.'

In the time it took Lettle's mouth to fall open, ten of the faeguard had surrounded her. Rayan was swallowed by the crowd as the armoured fae marched forward.

Yeeran pushed Lettle behind her and stood firm.

'Furi, what are you doing? Lettle didn't do this.'

Furi met Yeeran's gaze. 'Did you know? Is that why you came to me tonight? To keep me away from the queens?'

Yeeran looked pained. 'You know that's not true.'

Lettle swung her head from Furi to Yeeran. There was something boiling here, it burned just beneath the surface.

'Furi, I didn't—' Lettle started.

Yeeran cut her off with a warning glare. A brief glance with magesight confirmed that the faeguard stood poised with magic between their fingertips. They were on the precipice of a cliff and once over the edge, the only way was down. If Yeeran could save them with words, then she would let her.

'Furi, you *know* Lettle didn't do this.'

'What I know is threefold. One: tonight, you came to me, distracting me from the queens. Two: your sister knew the killer's weapon was poison before we knew. And three: you are both trained in sleight of hand and so had the means to carry out this attack.'

Lettle's eyes snapped to Yeeran. She had dared tell Furi of their past? How had the fae earned that truth?

Then Furi spoke again, softer this time, her voice a shattered thing, 'There is a fourth, final thing I know. My mother and aunt are dead.'

Yeeran took another step towards her, drawn to Furi like a bee to nectar, but Furi flinched backwards. 'Come no closer, elf.'

It was Yeeran's turn to flinch.

'You called me your starlight just a moment ago . . . Furi . . .' Yeeran spoke so quietly Lettle wasn't sure she'd heard her right.

For a second Furi's eyes softened but then she glanced away and when she looked back her expression was hard and unforgiving.

'My name is *Queen* Furi.'

Yeeran's shoulders fell in defeat and her eyes turned glossy. Lettle wasn't sure what was happening, but she suspected her sister's heart was breaking.

The queen gave a signal to the waiting faeguard, whose magic whipped around Lettle's wrists a second later.

'Get off me. Lettle!' Rayan was pushing through the approaching guards.

Lettle felt the magic thread around her wrists tug her forward. She planted her feet and refused to move, but all that got her was a face full of dirt as she fell forward. Rough hands lifted her up and pulled on her left arm. The sharpness of the pain sparked a sudden realisation: she was being taken prisoner yet again.

'Rayan!' She couldn't see him any more. The crowd of revelers surged forward with the faeguard, pulling him backwards.

The fae who had tolerated them less than an hour before had now been given enough ammunition to turn their bigotry into violence.

And all because the elves were different.

'Filthy elves, lock them up . . .'

'Murderers . . .'

'Should have killed them all . . .'

'Primitive race.'

Lettle was dragged through the mob of fae who had, moments ago, been seeking pleasure in the forest. Rapture had so quickly turned to rage. Canines snapped and sharp nails clawed at her.

'You cannot do this!' Yeeran said, fighting the guard who was pulling Lettle along with his magic. Rayan appeared, his fists swinging, his nose bloodied from an earlier blow. The crowd turned their frenzied attention to the two of them, and Rayan went down under the weight of three fae.

Pila appeared by Yeeran's side and was using her horns to fling bodies left and right. Lettle spotted the obeah with the broken horn fighting by her side.

Yeeran had her fists by her ears, a blossoming bruise on her cheek as she fought off the mob.

Lettle looked around for Furi and saw her sitting on the throne, watching the chaos ensue with cold detachment. Nerad was sitting on her other side, his hand over his mouth in horror.

But neither of them moved. Neither put a stop to the violence.

She wants the elves to fight back. She wants the fae to have a pretext to kill us. The thought was a brutal reminder of who they were dealing with.

'Stop,' Lettle shouted, but no one was listening. 'Stop!' she screamed.

Yeeran and Rayan turned to her voice.

'Let them take me,' Lettle said, pleading. She hoped they could at least read her lips over the cacophony. 'I can prove my innocence later. Don't give them any reason to hurt you.'

'They don't need a reason.' The voice wasn't loud, but it cut through the clearing like an arrow. The faeguard parted as the person walked through. Whispers erupted in their wake.

It was Sahar, his bearded chin held aloft. He wore a robe of the deepest green. It hung over his thin frame, fluttering in the breeze as he strode forward with the presence of someone three times his size.

Furi stood up from the throne, her mask of passivity cracking just a little.

'Father,' she said, and stepped into his arms.

'Father?' Lettle murmured to Yeeran, but from her slack-jawed look she had not known Sahar was Furi's father either.

Once Sahar had embraced both Nerad and Furi, he stepped away, his face streaked with tears. It reminded Lettle of her own father, the last time he had been lucid. She had to look away in case she cried too.

'Daughter, nephew, this elf had no part in your mothers' deaths. She speaks to the Fates, like I do.'

Furi looked to Lettle, her nostrils flaring. 'How do you know?' she asked her father.

'The elf is my apprentice,' Sahar stated.

Lettle jolted in her captors' hands. *Sahar's apprentice? Since when?* But she kept her lips sealed.

'Tell them,' Sahar said to Lettle. 'Speak the words you foretold of this day.'

Lettle licked her lips, then spoke, 'Under a waxing moon that no one can see, when the sun flares and twilight reigns. A burdened partnership will die when poison passes their lips. One gilded, one pearl.'

Lettle blinked, and in that time Furi had crossed the woodland and stood a step from Lettle's face.

'You knew – and yet you stood by and let them die?' Furi's temper was as fierce as Lettle's.

Lettle recognised the heat of it and stood her ground. 'That is not how prophecy works.'

Sahar was slower at reaching Lettle. 'She speaks the truth, daughter. You of all people know that a foretelling cannot be changed.'

Lettle looked to Rayan. He held a hand over a wound in his arm. A wound he had got from trying to save her. How she loved him. The realisation was not timely.

Just like the queens' deaths, her own prophecy could not be denied. The acceptance of that fact was as blissful as a cold shower on a hot day.

'Why are you smiling?' Furi hissed at her.

'I'm not.' But Lettle was. She couldn't help it. She *loved* Rayan. Deeply, irrevocably.

One of the soldiers who was holding her pulled on the magic knotted around her wrists. It hurt, but she didn't feel it.

'Furi,' Sahar said gently. 'Send your faeguard to explore the vicinity. This murderer must be caught.'

Furi looked into Lettle's smiling face and bared her fangs. Lettle thought that she might lunge for her throat and tear it out, just like the fae in her stories. But she didn't. Instead, she turned away, giving the signal for the guards to drop her binds.

As the new queen stalked off, Yeeran ran after her.

'Are you hurt?' Rayan pulled her towards him, away from the dispersing crowd. His gaze travelled over her skin, searching for wounds.

Lettle laughed. He was the one bleeding. She pulled him closer, inspecting his bicep.

'That will need stitches,' she said.

It wasn't what she wanted to say. She looked deep into his eyes, where the brown of his irises turned gold.

'Lettle . . .' Her name was a tortured sound.

She looked at him and said simply, 'Kiss me.'

It was all the permission he needed.

His lips crashed like waves against hers, sending ripples of desire along her skin as his hands swept up across her back. She reached up and slid a hand into his hair, grasping on to it with the urgency of her own passion.

She bit down on his lower lip, and he groaned, his breath coming out hungry and gasping. She arched into him, feeling the hardness of his torso and more besides.

His wanton need was an intoxicating drug that made her mind hazy with all the thoughts of what she could do to him.

Or what he could do to her.

She moved her hand up his arm, and when she felt the warmth of his blood she broke away with a laugh.

'We really need to get that stitched up.'

'Why?' he whispered against her ear. 'Let me bleed to death. For I have reached nirvana.' His eyes danced with mischief.

'Pretty words, pretty boy,' she said, 'but I'd like you to stay alive. We've more to do, you and I.'

He made a pained sound as her nails scoured through his beard.

'I've never looked forward to getting stitches more.'

CHAPTER THIRTY-TWO

Lettle

Lettle left Rayan in the capable hands of a healer. The hospital smelled of snowmallow flower and nightmares.

'I'll see you soon.' She pressed a kiss to his forehead, and he hummed deep in his chest.

'Very soon,' he promised.

The healer tutted Lettle out of the way. 'Move, elf. If you want your friend here to stop bleeding, then I'll need some space.'

'I was already leaving,' Lettle said through clenched teeth. The little respect the elves had garnered in their short time in Mosima had disappeared the moment Lettle had been accused of the queens' murder.

Whispers followed her as she made her way through the streets. It was still early morning but the fae gathered in concerned clusters, shooting furious looks her way. But Lettle didn't mind them. It only strengthened her resolve to get out of this damn place. And to do so, she needed her skill of prophecy back.

It didn't take her long to reach Sahar's. He was waiting by the door for her.

'I didn't know you were Furi's father,' she said.

He ushered her inside and said drily, 'You never asked.'

Lettle scowled at him, and he laughed. 'It is common knowledge I was consort to Queen Vyce for many years, fathering both Furi and her brother. Though the title of seer superseded that of consort.'

'What does the title of seer mean exactly?'

'It is a role that has been part of the fae court since we learned the magic of prophecy from the elves, long ago. But Vyce . . . she could not accept the truth.'

Sahar walked past Lettle and rested his back against the wall of the apothecary. His eyes held little life as he looked back at her. 'I foretold the death of our son and in her grief, she banished me from court.'

Lettle understood how prophecies could tear apart families. 'Why did you share it? Why not keep the truth to yourself?'

'That was not my decision to make. My role was that of a conduit of the Fates,' Sahar said sharply. 'For years my son would come to me and ask, "Will this be the year I die?" Eventually he stopped asking and he learned to live life each day, without the fear of his death. We became close. I would have made him my apprentice if not for the fact Vyce would have objected. Though I had decades to mourn his upcoming loss, it is different when a prophecy actually comes true.' His smile turned bitter, tinged with grief.

Lettle gave him a moment before seeking the answer she had come for. 'Why do you call me your apprentice but refuse to teach me?'

Sahar tilted his head. 'Did I refuse to teach you, elf?'

'Lettle, call me Lettle,' she bit back.

Sahar's smile was a little crooked, his nod approving.

'Seven years ago, I foresaw that I would take an apprentice, a woman, an elf. And that on the day I proclaimed it so, I would save her from incarceration. For seven years you have been my apprentice, Lettle. Though only today was I able to voice it.'

Lettle swallowed, her mouth dry with disbelief. 'Will you teach me? How to do divination?'

Sahar clicked his tongue. 'You and I both know that what we do is a burden, not a boon. To seek the knowledge of the future but knowing it cannot be changed is a hardship. Why is it that you wish to listen to the Fates?'

The question felt like a test of some kind, so she answered just as vaguely. 'Who else will listen to them?'

Sahar barked out a laugh. 'That is not an answer.'

Lettle opted for the truth. 'I wish to learn divination again, so I can help us leave Mosima.'

Sahar narrowed his eyes. At any point he could call for the faeguard, or moon's mercy, tell his daughter what Lettle had just said.

He nodded once.

'Then let's get started.'

Sahar led Lettle through to his back room. She let out a yelp as two orange orbs looked back at her.

'Oh, don't be scared, that's just Cori, my obeah.'

The obeah raised its shaggy head before settling back down on the floor.

A door at the back of the room opened and a man with yellow hair walked in. He was carrying a basket of harvested roots. As he stepped into the fraedia light Lettle realised the yellow dye was to cover the silver of his hair.

The newcomer looked at Lettle. 'Is this her?'

Sahar nodded before approaching the man and pressing a kiss to his cheek. 'Will you look after the shop while she and I speak?'

The man looked to Lettle and smiled. 'He has been waiting very many years for you, Lettle.'

'Should I not know your name, if you know mine?' Unfamiliar environments made her prickly.

The man set the root vegetables on the table in the centre of the room. He pressed his hand against his chest in greeting. 'I am Norey, Sahar's partner,' he said sincerely.

Lettle pressed her own hand against her chest in response. Norey nodded once, his eyes twinkling, before moving through to the front of the shop.

'Sit.' Sahar waved her into a seat around a small wooden table. He lowered himself into the chair next to hers and withdrew a pouch from his pocket.

'Now, like all good lessons, I must start at the root of it.' He rested his hands on the pouch on the table but did not open it. 'Ewia, the sun god, granted the fae the forces of sunlight, to pull and push. Bosome, the moon god, granted the elves the ability to read the Fates. And Asase, the earth god, bestowed on the humans the language of the trees and rocks.'

Lettle nodded. It was as she had read in the folklore.

'To see, to listen, to speak,' Sahar said.

'What?'

'The three functions of conducting magic, fae could *see* and use the sun beams. Elves could *listen* to the Fates. And the humans, well, they could *speak* the language of magic.'

She thought of the boundary and the unusual script that covered it. 'Of course, it's a spoken language.' This was a key to their freedom. She was sure of it. 'How can I learn it?'

Sahar laughed. 'Do you think we would still be trapped down here if we knew that?'

Lettle felt deflated, but not entirely, as divination was still within her grasp.

Sahar went on. 'To listen to the magic, you must be able to read the dance of the Fates from the core functions of life.' He tipped the pouch upside down, and six tokens clattered onto the table. 'A seer's talismans are where their power comes from. Each must be carved from a being of magic to represent the six major organs of the body: lungs, heart, stomach, kidneys, liver, and intestines.'

Each token was intricately carved out of wood into small replicas of organs.

Sahar continued. 'Once carved, you can cast the talismans and then read the magic.'

It was the same as reading entrails. But instead of physical organs they were representations of them.

'You see? You do not need to cut open an obeah for such a task. Talismans will work just as fine.'

Lettle's mouth hung open. She closed it once her mouth grew too dry. 'What can I use that is a being of magic, if not an obeah?'

Sahar stood and stamped down on a flagstone. It sprang up like the entryways to the baths. But instead of hot steam, dust erupted. He bent down and drew out a small piece of wood. 'This is the last piece of the branch I harvested.'

Lettle took it from his outstretched hands. The magic that emanated from it reverberated up her forearms. It wasn't painful, but it wasn't pleasant either.

'What is this?'

'It's a branch from the Tree of Souls. Each assigned seer is granted a branch in order to carve their talismans. Now this last piece is yours.'

'Can't I just use your tokens?'

Sahar laughed, his eyes dancing a merry jig. 'No, if that worked, I'd be using my master's talismans. It is in the carving that you become the seventh and final organ. The brain.'

Lettle squeezed the piece of wood, no bigger than a pack of cards. She had her divination back, here in the palm of her hand.

'Thank you,' she said to Sahar sincerely.

Sahar's kindly expression fractured, and he looked away from her. When he turned back the expression was gone and Lettle thought she must have imagined it.

'Take this carving knife and make your own talismans.'

'You just expect me to be able to whittle this branch into a bunch of organs?'

'The art is in the making. The making is not the art. When you have finished, come back to me and we will begin your schooling.'

'Begin?' she said doubtfully. 'I've trained to read entrails for five years, I can read better than almost anyone I know.'

'I do not seek to teach you how to read the magic; it is clear from the queens' fates that you can read as well as I. It is what you do with the information that must be taught. Learning that a murder is going to happen is one thing, but then turning that truth into action? Had you had a clearer mind, you could have informed the faeguard of an impending death and put in place a plan to catch the murderer before they got too far.'

'You think they would have listened to me?'

Sahar inclined his head, acknowledging the truth of her statement. 'That is why you must join the royal cabinet as the new seer, once I have finished teaching you.'

'No,' Lettle said automatically. 'I told you, I'm leaving Mosima.'

Sahar pursed his lips. 'We must let the wind of change ease our flight, not hinder it, Lettle. Come back to me when you are finished carving. Then we will speak again.'

Lettle had the distinct feeling that Sahar knew far more than he was saying.

Rayan was waiting for her outside Sahar's. A star glider floated around his head casting little spotlights of gold across his face. He shooed it away before slipping his hand into hers.

'How was it?'

She showed him the branch of the Tree of Souls and told him what Sahar had said about the talismans. She was so animated she hadn't noticed he was staring at her.

'What?' She touched her face self-consciously. 'Stop staring at me.'

'You're just so passionate, about divination.' He smiled, dimpling his cheeks.

She pressed herself against him and whispered hotly, 'There are other things I'm passionate about too.'

Rayan stopped laughing, his eyes turning molten.

The moment was interrupted by the shout of a person moving through the street on their obeah. 'Get out of the way, elves.'

Rayan growled and began to tug her along.

'Where are we going?' she asked.

'You'll see.'

Lettle laughed when she saw the door they stopped at. 'Is this the cottage they housed us in that first night?'

Rayan pushed open the door. It was vacant and smelled of stale air. 'Yes, that was a difficult day.'

Lettle nodded. 'It was hard being separated from Yeeran.'

'No,' Rayan said quietly, leading her inside. 'It was hard because I wanted so badly to bring you pleasure.'

Lettle stumbled, then righted herself. The room was as they had left it. One bed, dishevelled.

'I ran by here sometimes when I was training with Berro. I have dreamed of this moment since.'

Berro's name was like a hot poker in Lettle's eye. She found herself letting go of Rayan's hand and sitting on the edge of the bed.

'What is it? What have I said?' Rayan asked.

'Nothing, I'm sorry.'

'Lettle?'

She stood and let out a slow breath.

'I . . . I know you've been with Berro these last two months.'

'Yes, training with her.'

'No . . . more than that.'

'What are you talking about?'

'You've been sleeping with Berro. Having sex with her. Making love. Doing the in and out. Whatever you want to call it.' Lettle wasn't sure why pain always made her raise her voice. She turned away from him.

'Lettle.' His voice was calm. It irritated her more. 'I haven't once slept with Berro.'

'But what about all those nights you've not stayed the night in our apartment?'

Rayan turned her round and ran a hand along her jaw. 'I have not and would not sleep with Berro. You are the one I want, you have *always* been the one I want.'

Lettle felt her legs tremble.

'Ask me again,' Rayan said.

She knew what he meant.

'Kiss me,' she said.

And he did.

Their coupling was fierce and brief. Both had waited too long to not sate their desires so readily. They had moved only a few inches from where they had first kissed, though their clothes had been flung to the far corners of the room.

'That was . . .' Lettle tried to find the right word but couldn't. Instead, her mind went to the fae word *haljina* which meant both exquisite and satisfying.

'*Haljina.*'

Rayan nodded. 'It was, wasn't it?'

Lettle was surprised he knew the word. She'd been learning the fae language closely for six weeks and still she had only grasped basic conversational fae.

She propped herself up onto her elbows to ask but he stole the words from her mouth by planting a kiss against it. It started off soft but then he drew her closer, rolling her onto his chest so that her breasts pressed against his body. His arms wrapped around her, one hand in her hair, the other roaming further to cup her buttocks.

'How about we use the bath?' he murmured against her lips.

She didn't answer him, instead she stood and took his hand, leading him down the marble steps where steam rose to meet them.

Lettle slipped into the water. Rayan stood looking down at her.

'What are you waiting for?' she asked.

'You're so beautiful, Lettle.'

She rose up from the water, so her wet torso was visible.

'Come and join me.' There was an edge to her voice that ignited something in the depth of his eyes.

Rayan entered the water. Lettle went to him and ran her nails along his chest, leaving him breathless. Her hands sank lower until she grasped the length of him.

He groaned, his head rolling back, his hips thrusting forward.

She lingered there, not moving, just holding him with a firmness that she knew would verge on pain.

Slowly she wrapped her legs around his waist but didn't ease herself onto him . . . not yet. She moved her hips up and down, rubbing herself along the hardness of his desire.

'Lettle,' his voice was ragged.

She moved faster, gaining her own gratification from the movement.

'Lettle.'

She arched her back, her nipples just out of reach of his lips.

'Lettle.'

She pressed herself down onto him. His answering moan was wordless. His hands went to her waist, pushing her deeper onto him.

Then she rocked her hips backwards and forwards. Rayan's lips found her breasts and bit down. She cried out in response.

'Too hard?' he asked.

'Not hard enough.'

His laugh was a rumble as he bent back down to worship her once more.

As the heat built between them, Rayan's hand slipped to where their bodies met and began to coax the pleasure from the most sensitive part of her, rubbing lightly and then with more pressure as she began to pant.

He moved faster, and she could feel the blurred edges of ecstasy take hold. Rayan felt the cadence of her movements change, and when she let loose so did he.

Their foreheads fell limp against each other, and they stayed like that, still joined, as the water lapped around them.

This man has my heart.

In the silence between each of their breaths a thought seared bright in her mind.

And one day I'll kill you.

CHAPTER THIRTY-THREE

Yeeran

Yeeran waited for Furi in the shadow of the Tree of Souls. This would not be the end of them. She wouldn't let it. Pila stood by her, watching Yeeran with concern.

The queens' bodies and their obeah had been removed from the clearing, the chalice taken away to be examined. Nerad had been sent to supervise the inspection of the poison. Furi ordered Berro to sweep the Royal Woodland and another batch of soldiers to interview any fae who had been near the fire at the time of the queens' deaths.

Slowly the woodland began to empty as dawn warmed the sky. Then Furi was alone.

'Go away, Yeeran,' Furi said without turning around. Yeeran slipped out of the shadows and into the fray-light, Pila at her heels. Furi was looking up at the Tree of Souls, her eyes glistening.

The two branches that represented her mother's reign had grown two new leaves. Beneath them two stems of new growth had begun.

'Those new branches will bind to you and Nerad?'

Furi didn't answer at first. She sniffed, wiped her eyes, and said, 'Yes, as they grow, so too will the magic, and in a day's time the curse will bind to the next rulers, Nerad and I.'

'Furi, I'm so—'

'Don't,' Furi shouted. 'Don't apologise for something you have no need to apologise for, especially as you must be rejoicing in their deaths.'

'That's not true, Furi. I have never wished for their deaths. And I am, I am truly sorry.' Yeeran reached for her, but Furi stepped back.

'You know I hated you? I hated you for taking him from me. And it was so easy to hate you again, tonight. When I thought you had—' She swallowed, looked away. 'Oh, it was so easy, Yeeran.' When she looked back, her eyes blazed with tears.

'Lettle had nothing to do with the queens' murders,' Yeeran said, sharper than she expected. Here was a wild animal hurting, and showing it the blade would do no one good.

Furi hissed through her teeth and stepped towards Yeeran, her knees bent. She looked like she was going to swing for Yeeran and part of her wanted her to.

Furi's arm drew back, and her muscles clenched. Yeeran waited for the impact. Hoping the blows would hurt less than her words. Yeeran saw her fist fly, but then Pila was between them. She drew back her lips in a snarl as Furi swung.

Furi released the force in her fist an inch from Pila's face. Her mask of anger slipped away as she seemed to realise what she had been about to do.

Pila, step aside, Yeeran said. *It's all right, I don't think she'll hurt me now.*

But Pila didn't move. Furi's hand was still hovering in front of her face. Pila leaned forward, towards her touch.

Pila . . . Yeeran warned, but her obeah wasn't listening.

Furi's clenched fist opened, and Pila nuzzled her. Furi's eyes widened, then tentatively, quietly, she moved her fingers, stroking the soft side of Pila's chin. Then her shoulders dropped, and she began to sob.

Yeeran was there in a moment.

'I have you.'

Furi had turned limp in her arms as grief wracked her body.

'I'll help find the murderer.' The words were a promise. But she did not say the rest of what she was thinking. *And in return, my love, you must set me free.*

Somehow Furi heard the words all the same.

'You know I cannot go against the queens' wishes, your initiation must go ahead, Yeeran.'

It shouldn't have felt like a betrayal, but it did.

Fresh tears were flowing down Furi's face and Yeeran wasn't sure if they were for her too.

'The politics of the cabinet are more tenuous than you'll ever know. I may be the next queen, but they can still revolt.'

Yeeran tried to look away but Furi cupped her cheek. She didn't say sorry. They stood like that for some time, so many emotions hanging between them. Not all of them good.

'Queen Furi.' It was Berro. 'The poison report is back from Nerad.'

Furi dropped her hand from Yeeran's jaw and sat back down on her throne.

Yeeran watched her for a little while longer before it hurt too much. Sleep beckoned.

Komi was the only one in their apartment when Yeeran got home. It was mid-afternoon and she hadn't slept for over thirty-six hours.

He was bent over their journal of notes, his thick brows knotted together. The frown dropped when he saw Yeeran, his mouth splitting into a smile. 'Bit of an exciting night, wasn't it?'

Yeeran was so tired her knees gave way before she fell to the sofa. 'Where did you go after the fire was doused? I didn't see you.'

Komi crossed his ankles and leaned back in the chair. 'I found myself in a tavern, only heard about it an hour after it happened. Then I went to bed.'

'I didn't see you cross the woodland?'

'It was a farce,' he spread his hands theatrically, 'I had to prove my identity before they'd let me into the palace. Not having any form of identification, I had to flash them my flat canines.' He curled up his lip and wiggled his jaw.

Yeeran didn't laugh because she knew Komi was lying. Yeeran had been in the Royal Woodland, she'd watched every single person come and go from the palace steps. It's true that she could have missed him, but she doubted it.

Komi didn't notice her unease.

'Who were you with? In the tavern?' Yeeran asked lightly.

Komi screwed up his eyes as he trudged back through his memory. It was a good performance, if that's what it was.

'I'm not sure, maybe his name was Donya? Donda? Who knows?'

Pila, did you see Komi last night?

Obeah assigned smells, feelings, and memories to people, rather than names, and as Pila thought of Komi, Yeeran got an insight into the ball of jumbled senses that constituted the older elf. He was the colour orange in a dark sky, a vine crawling up the bark of a tree, and he smelled like blood and iron. It reminded Yeeran of a battle-field, so unlike the gentle Komi she knew.

Did you see him come home last night?

Yes, Pila replied and Yeeran chastised herself for being so stupid. She must be tired if she was accusing her friends.

He went in here.

The image that Pila sent showed Komi entering a room on the lower floor of the palace. Pila's memory was from the base of the baobab tree, when Yeeran had been talking to Furi. Komi was looking over his shoulder, a cold expression on his face – as if he was some-where he shouldn't be.

Yeeran's stomach churned.

'You said you came back here? Right?' Yeeran asked.

Komi chuckled. 'Slept like a camel who had walked the earth, woke up an hour ago.'

Sleep. Yeeran needed it. She rose shakily from the sofa.

Pila, can you watch Komi while I rest? He's lying about something, but I haven't the energy to figure it out right now.

Yes, go and sleep. Dream of fields and freedom.

* * *

Yeeran did not dream of fields and freedom. She tossed and turned for hours until she couldn't stand it any more. At dinner time she got up. She had to confront Komi. There must be a simple answer as to why he'd been sneaking around yesterday. He'd never given her any reason to doubt him.

But how well did she know him *really*?

Where are you? Yeeran asked Pila.

Pila sent an image back of her lying by Lettle's feet in the living room. Rayan sat next to her, his hand draped over her shoulder. She was pleased to see that they'd finally succumbed to their feelings. Komi was no longer there.

He went to bed after dinner, Pila said.

Yeeran got up and made her way down the corridor to Komi's room.

She knocked a few times, and when no one answered she opened the door. A gust of wind swept through the room as she entered. Komi's bed hadn't been slept in and the obeah hatch that went down to the courtyard was open.

Why would he leave through there and not the front door? Pila asked. She found the idea of Komi going down the steps made for an obeah amusing.

He didn't want anyone to see him.

Yeeran left, closing the door quietly behind her. She made her way into the living room.

'Komi's not in his room.'

'You sure? After we ate, he said he was going to bed,' Lettle replied.

'He's not there. He left through the obeah hatch in his window.'

Rayan seemed unworried.

'Probably slipped out to a tavern and didn't want us to worry.'

Yeeran chewed over her thoughts for a minute before saying, 'Have either of you noticed Komi acting . . . odd?'

Rayan shook his head.

Lettle set down her carving tool. 'No, why?'

'Pila saw him enter a room in the palace last night.'

Lettle snorted. 'So?'

'He lied to me about it. Said he'd come back here to sleep.'

Lettle shook her head in disbelief. 'You think Komi had something to do with the death of the queens?'

Yeeran didn't respond. Because the truth was, she didn't have an answer.

I don't like him, Pila said.

I know.

She took a seat and rested her hand in the beast's fur and looked at Lettle.

How long has she been here?

A few hours, whittling wood.

Rayan's hand played in the edges of Lettle's braids, a small smile creeping across his features. His expression held in it so much love. Here was someone else who would protect and love Lettle as much as she, even after she was gone.

She pulled herself from her morose thoughts and turned to Lettle. 'Show me.'

Lettle sighed, throwing a look of betrayal to Pila before unfurling her arms to show Yeeran what she was doing.

The charms were small, and a little rudimentary, but it was clear they were on their way to being carved into the shape of organs.

'Lungs, heart, liver, kidneys, stomach . . .' Yeeran said.

'I'm just finishing the intestines.' Lettle held up a squiggle of wood. Lettle was not about to become a carpenter anytime soon. 'They're talismans. When I cast them, I'll be able to read the Fates without having to kill an obeah.'

'You went to Sahar?'

Lettle filled her in. Then she sat back and waited, watching Yeeran carefully.

'Do you think the Fates will help us get out of here, back to the Elven Lands?' Yeeran asked.

'You finally understand the benefits of prophecy, sister?'

Yeeran pressed the heels of her palms into her eyes. 'It's not that

I didn't understand it, Lettle.' She felt like they were on the cusp of an argument. 'I'm glad you've got your divination back, truly.'

Yeeran probably sounded too earnest, because Lettle's scowl returned. 'You don't think it'll work.'

'That's not what I said.'

I don't.

'You think I'm wasting my time.'

I do.

'I didn't say that either.'

'You know that the moon god, Bosome, gave elves the gift of divination to give them wisdom?'

'I would have preferred the fae's magic, if I'm honest. It's better in battle.'

Lettle didn't respond at first, though the irritation was clear in the set of her jaw.

'You remember the reading I gave you that day? To seek your glory to the east?'

How could she forget. Yeeran dipped her head.

'Do you recall the words that the queens said to you during your binding banquet? I didn't understand them at the time because I couldn't speak fae. But I've since understood it: "As bestowed by the god Ewia, we submit to the highest glory. Yeeran O'Pila, we welcome you. Faebound forever more."'

Lettle waited, but Yeeran wasn't sure what she was getting at.

'To become faebound is the fae's highest glory. You fulfilled the prophecy by coming east and finding Pila.'

The obeah's ears twitched at her name.

Yeeran made a face. 'It's a little tenuous . . .'

Lettle seethed, Yeeran could feel it from across the room. 'All right, all right. I believe you.'

Yeeran's words didn't make a difference and Lettle went back to whittling the wood. Her movements were violent and forceful. It was little wonder the end products were so crude. Her sister was not known for her light touch.

'Maybe Furi will cancel your initiation now she's queen, and you won't have to rely on prophecy,' Lettle said.

'Maybe.' Yeeran couldn't face telling her that the initiation was going ahead as planned.

Rayan looked up. 'How goes the investigation? Have they caught anyone?'

'No, but Nerad confirmed the poison was clammer squid ink, found in the bay. They're questioning the fishermen to see if there had been some unusual trades made.'

Yeeran looked to the window. A whole day had passed. It was night again.

'I miss the rain,' Yeeran said suddenly. 'And I miss the smell after the rain.'

Lettle's face took on a dreamy look. 'I miss eating meat, specifically Auntie Namana's grilled chicken.'

'I miss my comrades in the army,' Rayan said, his gaze going distant.

Pila whined into the silence.

The air is thick, it aches, she said.

Yeeran didn't fully catch her meaning, but she understood the sentiment.

'We'll all go home again,' Yeeran said.

Lettle continued to work on the talismans until the fray-light turned to gaslight.

'I really am quite good at this,' she murmured.

Yeeran had to hide her snort.

An hour later Lettle brandished the final carving at Yeeran. It cast a squiggle of shadows onto the wall across from her. 'Finished.'

'Looks perfect,' Rayan said, and he kissed her on the top of her head.

Yeeran peered over, examining the small piece. 'So that's it? You can do divination again?'

'Yes.' Lettle could barely keep the excitement from her voice, eager as she was.

'Can you ask the Fates about Komi?'

Lettle let out an irritated sigh. 'Why are you so suspicious of him all of a sudden?'

Yeeran wasn't sure. Something just wasn't sitting right. 'Please, just ask.'

'I've never done this before, so I don't know what's going to happen. And don't forget the Fates are wily and elusive, sometimes they answer, sometimes they do not.'

Lettle lowered herself to the cold flagstones and crossed her legs beneath her. She cradled the six carvings in her hands. She held them to her chest, clasped tight in her palms, before scattering them on the floor ahead of her.

Yeeran watched the proceedings in magesight.

At first the talismans shone a soft bronze, like the magic of the Tree of Souls that tied the Jani dynasty to the land. The magic of the humans. But then, as she searched in the space between them, she saw it, the pearls of silver that Lettle called the Fates.

Yeeran watched the magic coil and pulse over the charms. After ten minutes a headache began to blossom at her temples, and she withdrew from magesight.

A little while later, Lettle said, 'The journal, please.' Yeeran brought the notebook forward, now heavy with their knowledge.

Lettle wrote down the words she had gleaned while they were still fresh in her mind.

Yeeran read over her shoulder, spoiling the sanctity of the moment.

'*A king's vengeance sated. A prophecy fulfilled.*' Yeeran barked out a laugh. 'What does that even mean?'

Lettle frowned.

'Whatever Komi's doing, it has something to do with Nerad.' It wasn't the answer either of them wanted. All the prophecy did was plunge them deeper into murky water.

Lettle tried to cast the talismans a few more times that night, but the Fates didn't speak again.

CHAPTER THIRTY-FOUR

Yeeran

That next morning, Furi and Nerad laid their mothers to rest. Yeeran did not attend the funeral, but neither had she been invited. When dawn signalled the coming of the new day, Yeeran strapped her drum to her back and made her way down to Conch Shore.

She spent two hours practising with drumfire with Pila by her side. The training focused her mind, and she found her skill with her spool of magic was increasing with every drumbeat.

You can hold the magic longer each time, Pila noted.

Yes, it strains me, but I think I could hold a thread for half an hour if I needed to.

Will it be useful? For the war that ravages your home?

The beat of Yeeran's magic faltered. Home felt like a faraway thing. Less substantial than yesterday.

Her first home had been a little village on the southern edge of the Bleeding Field. No bigger than the shack on the beach. She'd shared it with her father and Lettle until the night she had left for the war.

Why did you leave? Pila was curious.

Lettle was getting weaker, the battle was moving further and further north, so it became difficult to scavenge. I was trained in nothing except hunting. I couldn't read or write.

Yeeran shook away the memories of the taunts from her fellow soldiers. She'd shown them by becoming the youngest colonel in history.

Until she wasn't.

Pila growled as she felt the depth of Yeeran's loss.

The war gave me a way to fight for all the children who had no one to fight for them. I miss that purpose more than my title.

Or Salawa.

Yeeran didn't acknowledge Pila's interruption. She tipped her head to the fray-light and thought of how just a quarter of the fraedia crystal would be enough to end the war. When she left Mosima she'd take with her as much as she could carry. She hoped it would be enough to soften the news that she would bring.

That we are not to be killed?

Yes, Pila. No more will elves kill obeah.

Pila lifted her head and rested it on Yeeran's leg. She could feel the echoes of the obeah's worry.

I won't let anyone hurt you, Pila. But if you would prefer, you can stay in Mosima.

Pila snapped her jaws. Her lips rising upwards.

No. We go together.

Yeeran laughed and scratched the underside of Pila's chin until she settled again.

'We go together.'

Yeeran went back to practising her magic.

Pila sniffed the air. *Someone is coming.*

Yeeran hoped it was the servant that usually brought her lunch at this time, and she didn't stop her practice. But as she shot a projectile of magic, her golden thread was joined by another's. Yeeran recognised the hue of it.

'Try and lead the thread around mine,' Furi said. She wove her magic up and under Yeeran's until they were interlocked like a braid. Yeeran kept the steady beat of her drum going as she manipulated the undulating thread of magic. 'Yes, just like that. Hold it. Hold it.'

They kept weaving their magic until a latticed form shone bright ahead of them.

But then Yeeran caught sight of Furi, and her concentration faltered. She was dressed head to toe in gold chainmail, her eyes lined with thick charcoal that had left streaks down her face.

'That was well done,' Furi said.

'What was that?'

'That was a threaded cage.'

Yeeran raised her eyebrows. 'That was how you trapped us?'

The fae's grin was mischievous, but it dipped a second later and she lowered herself to the ground. Yeeran joined her and reached for Furi's hand.

Furi looked down at their intertwined fingers.

Slowly, she broke away, folding her hands in her lap.

'The Tree of Souls has nearly finished growing the two new branches. The coronation will be in a few hours.' Furi closed her eyes. 'I can feel the tree's magic across my skin, it's getting stronger.'

Yeeran's hand was still lying open in the sand. She closed it into a fist.

'Is it only at night that you let yourself feel?' Yeeran said bitterly.

Furi looked to the sea. She let out a small sigh and said, 'All stars burn the brightest in the night.'

Yeeran wanted to shout at her, she wanted to scream, but she had known their love was untenable from the very beginning. She was an elf.

And Furi was a queen.

Yeeran looked away from her before Furi saw the tears that she refused to shed.

Pila, let's leave here. Take me to the boundary.

As Yeeran mounted Pila, Furi spoke again, just above a whisper.

'But all stars shine still, beneath the sun's radiance in the light of day.'

Yeeran wanted to ask her what she meant, but Pila had started galloping, taking her away from the woman who caged her heart.

Lettle said that the humans' magic was a spoken language, Yeeran said to Pila. She sat on Pila's back and leaned forward, running her hands along the boundary. The cursive script hummed beneath her fingers.

But who knows the language any more?

I don't know.

Yeeran inspected the boundary for a little longer before directing Pila back to the palace. As she entered the Royal Woodland she dismounted and let Pila head off to the orchard in the inner court-yard to graze.

The faeguard littered the forest, the investigation into the queens' murders made more urgent by the imminent coronation. Yeeran took a less travelled path to avoid the glares of the soldiers. As she turned left, she barrelled straight into the body of another fae walking towards her.

'Oh, I'm sorry.'

The fae had fallen backwards and Yeeran offered them a hand to help them up.

'Golan?' she gasped.

He looked wan, his skin clammy and feverish. What was perhaps most shocking was that he wore none of his usual make-up or jewellery and looked sparse without it.

'Oh, Yeeran, I'm so sorry. I wasn't looking where I was going.' He sniffed and Yeeran realised he'd been crying.

'I'm sorry,' Yeeran said. 'About the queens.'

Golan's red eyes widened. 'What?'

Yeeran frowned, unsure how to respond. Then the fear fled his eyes, and he rubbed his brow. 'Yes, an awful thing. An awful, awful thing.'

'Golan, wait.' The call came from the palace. 'You can't just run off.'

Golan flinched as Nerad appeared by his side.

'Oh, Yeeran, hello.' The momentary outrage that had painted Nerad's face was smoothed away when he noticed Yeeran.

'Hello, Nerad . . . or should I call you King Nerad now?'

He flashed his teeth. 'Not until tonight.' He turned to Golan and said with tight lips, 'Can we go and talk somewhere private?'

Golan raised his chin in an act of defiance.

'No, Yeeran asked me to help her with something . . . didn't you, Yeeran?'

'I . . .'

Golan widened his eyes in a plea. But before she could lie to the future king of the fae, Nerad said, 'Fine, I'll see you later then.' And turned on his heel and left.

Golan grimaced in the silence of Nerad's wake. 'I'm sorry.'

'What was that about?'

Golan ran a hand through his limp hair, which was usually so vibrant and tinkling with braided beads.

'It doesn't matter. None of it does.' Then he walked off, leaning heavily on his cane.

Yeeran recalled the event to Lettle when she got in.

'Three gods . . .' Lettle breathed. 'Golan's gentleman sweetheart is *Nerad*?'

'What?'

'He's been seeing someone in secret. Someone important who couldn't date him in public because he is Lightless.'

It could have just been a lovers' tiff, Yeeran supposed.

'But first Komi's foretelling and now this? Does it seem odd to you – like maybe Nerad's the crux of it all?'

Lettle laughed and cast her talismans again. 'You really are being very suspicious.'

Maybe she was. Or maybe the queens' murders had put her trust of people into peril. A trust that should never have been granted in the first place.

'Where is Rayan?'

Lettle's eyes took on a dewy look. 'He wasn't feeling quite right, so he decided to go for a walk. And before you ask, I don't know where Komi is, I haven't seen him all day.'

'The coronation of Nerad and Furi is in a few hours.'

Lettle nodded. She had already known. 'Sahar told me.'

'How did your training go today?'

Lettle gave her talismans a deathly stare. 'I'm yet to hear from the Fates again. Rayan thinks I'm trying too hard.' Then she smiled. Her love for Rayan made her so radiant, Yeeran couldn't help but smile in return.

If only Furi would look at me like that.

'Yeeran? Did you hear me?' Lettle dragged her out of her thoughts.

'No, sorry – what did you say?'

'Are you going to go to the coronation? Sahar says the magic of the tree binding is spectacular.'

'Maybe.' Yeeran hadn't yet recovered from her earlier meeting with Furi.

The door to their apartment opened and Komi strode in. He wore a deep blue skirt that fanned around him as he twirled into the room.

'What do you think?' he said. 'The weaver named the skirt, "royal blood runs thickest", which seemed fitting for the coronation.'

Lettle reached for his hand and squeezed it. Yeeran saw that the skin there was thin and leathery, revealing his age more so than his mind did.

'You look wonderful.'

Lettle looked to Yeeran.

'Yes . . . wonderful,' she added a little woodenly.

'Why are neither of you dressed yet?'

'Yeeran isn't sure if she's going, and Rayan isn't feeling great.'

'Well then, it'll be a party of two.'

That perturbed Yeeran. She didn't want Komi alone with Lettle until she felt she could trust him again.

'I'll come.'

Komi clapped his hands, his grin lifting his moustache to his plump cheeks.

'A threesome, my favourite.'

Lettle laughed. Yeeran didn't.

Yeeran regretted going to the coronation as soon as she arrived. The air was sombre, the crowds in the woodland thick.

'It's almost like we're at a funeral,' Lettle said, a little too loudly.

'We are, in a way,' Yeeran replied with a far more hushed tone than her sister.

As they moved to get a better view, the fae parted around them, whispers sprouting up like weeds.

'I heard the faebound one made a deal to free her sister . . .'

'They assassinated the queens . . .'

'Should have killed them all when we had the chance . . .'

Yeeran ignored it, but she could see how the whispers affected Lettle. Her lips had turned down at the corners.

I wish I could cheer her up a bit.

Tell Lettle her ears look pretty, Pila said, stretching into the empty space the fae had vacated.

What?

Do you not compliment each other's ears?

Is that what obeah do?

Yes, like with Amnan. I tell him I like his ears by licking them.

Pila, I'm not going to tell Lettle she has nice ears.

Well, if you won't tell her, lick them.

Yeeran opted to squeeze Lettle's hand instead. Her sister gave her a grateful smile.

'Over here.' Golan was a few rows ahead. He looked a different man than he had been a few hours ago. His make-up was back on, his eyes clear and shining.

Komi trumpeted out a sigh. 'It's like we're diseased or something.'

Golan patted him on the arm. 'You get used to it after a few years.' It was true, the fae had parted around him as well, all because he was Lightless. He waved at someone in the distance and Yeeran recognised Jay the healer who had stitched her up after her run-in with Hosta.

Furi's ex-lover.

Being Lightless too made it easy for Jay to slip through the crowd towards the elves, and as they joined the group they asked, 'Have you seen Cane? That boy is like an eel in water.'

'Here I am!' Cane jumped up from under the feet of a group of fae behind them. 'Hello, Yeeran. Can I see your scar?'

Jay tutted at their son and steered him away from Yeeran with an apologetic shake of their head. 'Sorry. He's excited to see Furi's coronation.'

'Queen Furi,' Cane corrected his mother. Jay rolled their eyes.

Yeeran smiled and turned away from them. She hated that envy coiled in her gut every time she took in Jay's beauty.

Lettle was chewing her lip beside her. Rayan hadn't returned from his afternoon walk and she was worried about him.

'He'll be fine,' Yeeran said to reassure her.

'He's probably gone to a tavern,' Komi added unhelpfully. The four of them were standing in clear view of the Tree of Souls. Furi and Nerad were sitting on their thrones, the words of the prophecy above them.

Cursed to endure, cursed to survive. All shall perish lest all three thrive.

But here, beneath the setting fray-light, neither one of them looked cursed. Star gliders tangled in their hair and rested in their crowns. The fire in the gilded vessel warmed the richness of their skin, making their brown eyes glow amber. Furi wore the same chainmail dress as she had that morning, but her make-up had been redone and fraedia jewellery hung from her ears.

Yeeran would have thought the fraedia jewellery extravagant and crass if it didn't look completely beguiling. Furi's jaw was set in an expression of pain, and Yeeran wondered what it must feel like to have the very essence of a land bound to your soul.

Yeeran slipped into magesight. Though it was difficult to see at first, she spotted the small filament of magic. A trickle of bronze flowed from one of the newly-grown branches to Furi, winding up her arm like a vine and settling deep within her chest.

It looks like an obeah binding, Pila commented. Yeeran shared her insight with Lettle.

'Oh, that's interesting. The magic is weaving in the most unusual way, it almost looks like a word.' Lettle's head was tilted to the right as she scrutinised the binding with a scholar's eye.

Yeeran tore her gaze away from Furi to Nerad. The king's magic was too fine to see. Yeeran worked her way backwards and looked to the branch, but the thread there wove out of her sight.

She blinked away the magic and looked to Nerad with clear eyes. His serene face had grown perplexed. He tilted his head up to the branch in confusion, before muttering something quietly to himself.

'Something's wrong. The magic isn't working for Nerad.'

Lettle nodded. 'It looks like the thread is weaving elsewhere.' Someone drew her attention on the edge of the crowd.

It was Rayan.

Lettle waved him over.

'Rayan?'

He was looking past her, his complexion feverish, sweat peppering his brow. His eyes rolled with a wildness Yeeran had never seen before, even in the heat of battle. He turned to the Tree of Souls.

'What is happening to me?' Yeeran could just make out Rayan's words.

'No,' Lettle whispered. 'It can't be.'

Other people were looking at Rayan now, the audience parting as he took shaking steps closer and closer to Nerad and Furi.

Nerad stood, his eyes bulging. His lips moved in wordless rhythm. It was one word over and over.

'No, no, no, no, no.'

Yeeran didn't need to slip into magesight to confirm the magic that wove up Rayan's hands. The Tree of Souls had chosen a king.

And it was Rayan.

CHAPTER THIRTY-FIVE

Lettle

Lettle snapped out of her state of shock and ran towards Rayan. 'Why has the Tree of Souls chosen you?' Lettle felt breathless, light-headed. This couldn't be happening.

'I-I don't know,' Rayan said. The magic that had him in his grasp grew brighter, and Rayan hissed, his muscles tensing. Then it dimmed, the binding made.

'Lettle, what just happened?'

'You are king.' The words were sharp and cold. Furi was there, Nerad a step behind.

'How dare you?' Nerad shouted. 'How dare you try to take what is rightfully mine.'

Furi stepped between them.

'Stop, cousin.' She widened her eyes at the surrounding crowd. 'Let us go and speak in private.'

Two of the faeguard had arrived on either side of Rayan, who appeared not to notice. They escorted him a step behind Furi and Nerad.

'Rayan.'

He turned at Lettle's voice.

'Leave them, this is not a time and place for elves,' Furi said. The faeguard moved to block Yeeran and Lettle from following. Komi had disappeared into the crowd, but Lettle had more important things to worry about than the older elf's welfare right now.

'No, I want them to come with me,' Rayan said.

The faeguard hesitated. Technically Rayan was now their crowned king. Furi saw this and knew that it wasn't a time to test the loyalties of her army.

'Come then.'

Lettle and Yeeran followed numbly. Pila a step behind.

'What just happened?' Yeeran asked.

'I don't know.'

'Did he tell you anything?'

'No.'

'But surely you must know why—'

'I don't know!' Lettle shouted. She felt her panic and anger bubble up at the same moment. She clenched her fists and breathed out.

Yeeran held her own hands in front of her as if Lettle might charge at her. It made Lettle even more furious.

'You don't know anything, I get it,' Yeeran said.

Furi and Nerad led them through the woodland and to a room in the back of the palace. It was clearly one of the cabinet chambers, as there was a desk in the centre, littered with maps and papers.

Furi swept them away as they entered. She dismissed the guards with her free hand.

'Who are your parents?' she demanded of Rayan.

Nerad scoffed, 'You mean to entertain the idea that he could be of our line? Clearly, they exercised some sort of elven magic we're not aware of. Perhaps Lettle could have done it.'

'I think we're done accusing my sister of things she *has not done*.' Yeeran stepped forward into the space between her and Nerad.

'Can everyone be quiet?' Furi barked. 'Rayan, who are your parents?'

'My mother, she was of the Crescent tribe. Her name was Reema. She died when I was young.'

'And your father?'

'I know not. My mother always said I was fathered by the storm's mist.'

'The storm's mist?' Furi whispered.

'No, he cannot be . . .' Nerad was shaking his head so violently that it seemed as if his neck might snap.

'What? What is it?' Rayan asked, dread thick in his voice.

'My cousin . . . his name was Najma.'

Lettle didn't need the translation, she understood it.

Born of a storm's mist.

'Najma, it means the mist before a storm in the fae language,' Lettle said softly.

Rayan swallowed.

'No, but it doesn't make sense,' Nerad hissed into the silence. 'Even if he is half fae, he cannot be king without being bound to an obeah.'

Rayan looked down at his feet.

'He is already bound to an obeah,' Lettle said. He looked up sharply at her. 'Isn't it true? The obeah with the green eyes and the broken horn?' Every night Lettle had thought Rayan had been visiting Berro – when he was visiting his obeah.

Rayan nodded. 'After Yeeran's binding banquet, after the fire was doused. Ajix, he found me.'

It was then that Lettle felt the first fracture in their trust for each other. If only he had told her about the obeah sooner. If only she had told him about the prophecy.

'We have been such fools.' A bone-weary tiredness settled on her.

'Fools, indeed,' Nerad said. He was looking at Furi.

Furi stepped forward now, her hands outstretched, to strike or embrace no one was sure. Then she did the most unexpected thing: she bowed. When she stood again, her eyes were shining and her lips trembling from emotion.

'Welcome to the family, King Rayan.'

Lettle looked at Yeeran. She looked horrified, her gaze swinging between Rayan and Furi as they embraced.

Pila was whining softly by Yeeran's side, but her sister didn't seem to notice.

Then Lettle heard Yeeran mutter, 'I . . . I killed Rayan's father.'

Guilt had her in its grasp. Lettle should have recognised the shape of it right away.

'It's all right, Yeeran,' she murmured. 'You didn't know.'

Yeeran turned her haunted gaze to Lettle's. 'But it doesn't dispel the facts. I murdered his father.'

Lettle looked back to Rayan. Furi held him at arm's length.

'My nephew,' she said, then laughed.

Rayan's shock had turned to raw emotion and Furi led him to a chair and said, 'Nerad, bring out the aged mead.'

But Nerad had fallen silent, his lips pressed together until they were almost purple. He sighed before marching out of the room altogether.

'He will come around. The monarchy was never his true calling. Just give him a little time.'

Furi turned to Rayan. 'Your obeah, are they near?'

Rayan smiled, his eyes going distant. A few moments later his obeah arrived. Pila leaned forward as the obeah passed, sniffing the air for his scent before settling back down on her hindquarters unconcerned.

'This is Ajix.' The obeah brushed past Lettle's leg with familiarity, and she reached out to scratch his ears.

Rayan hummed deep in his throat as he watched her. He seemed more at ease with his obeah in his sights and Lettle imagined him cantering through the fields under cover of darkness with just the light of star gliders to guide him.

A sudden thought came to Lettle. She gasped and everyone turned to her.

'The blight. Rayan, *you* caused the blight.'

Furi frowned, then took a step backwards.

Lettle continued, 'Isn't it true that if one of the Jani dynasty leaves Mosima, the land knows, and reacts? It's why you can't go too many weeks from home? And it started . . . around thirty years ago, when Rayan was born.' Lettle had stitched together meaning where the rest had seen only air.

'Then when we arrived, the blight, it stopped.'

Rayan swallowed. 'My birth meant that someone with the Jani bloodline was living outside of Mosima,' he said. 'And that's when the blight began.'

The four of them stood in silence, considering the impact of what Lettle had just discovered.

Furi said quietly, 'We will need to spin the tale of this in our favour. Rayan's return has healed Mosima and brought back prosperity. We cannot linger on the threat of famine that once was. We all must be united in this.'

Rayan nodded, though his gaze was troubled. 'Will you tell me about my father?'

Lettle walked towards Yeeran and took her by the elbow. 'We should let them talk.'

Yeeran merely nodded, still unsettled by the day's revelations.

The sisters didn't speak on their way back to their rooms. Both were preoccupied by their own emotions.

Komi was waiting for them, having spent the rest of the day at a coronation party in the south of the city.

He held a hand over his mouth in astonishment as Yeeran recounted the truth of Rayan's heritage. His gasps and glassy eyes would have seemed inauthentic on anyone else, but Komi simply felt more than other people.

That evening Rayan didn't come back to the apartment.

Yeeran retired early, her eyes heavy with the weight of the day. But Lettle was struggling to sleep.

One thought kept repeating over and over in her mind.

If Rayan is king, he can never leave.

The depths of her loneliness threatened to consume her, but eventually she fell asleep.

She dragged the bloated corpse of her father across the room in short bursts. Her tears splashed onto his unblinking eyes. His lips were parted as if saying her name. And she thought she heard it.

'Lettle, why did you murder me?'

Lettle awoke sobbing. Her nightmares were back. She didn't want to weather them alone, so she padded to Yeeran's door and knocked gently.

'Pila?' Yeeran called.

Lettle opened the door.

'No, it's me.'

Yeeran turned her bleary eyes to the door.

'Are you all right?'

Lettle hesitated, her shadow shimmering.

'Can I sleep here tonight?'

They hadn't shared a bed for many years.

'Of course.'

Lettle crawled under the covers. She felt the stable presence of Yeeran behind her. Her sister, her shield.

In a few breaths she was asleep.

Lettle could feel a gentle breeze on her arms. She shivered awake.

Yeeran was sleeping on her stomach with the blanket tangled up in her legs, her arm hung off the bed above Pila's sleeping form. She was snoring loudly, her mouth open.

Lettle rubbed the sleep from her eyes and stood. The window was open and the light from the fray warmed the flagstones beneath it. It was just past dawn.

She padded out of Yeeran's room, closing the door quietly behind her.

'I looked for you last night.'

Lettle jumped at the sound of the voice and put a hand to her heart.

'Moon's mercy, Rayan.'

He was sitting on the sofa, his eyes tired and red. 'I'm sorry, I didn't mean to startle you.'

Lettle hovered by the armrest, unsure whether to sit opposite or next to him. Thankfully there was a knock at the door and a servant arrived with their breakfast. Lettle went to get the tray before taking her seat at the dining table.

'I stayed up for you, but when you didn't come home . . . I didn't want to sleep alone,' she said, carefully avoiding his eyeline.

'Lettle . . .' He whispered her name, his mouth grasping for words, but they didn't come.

'Ajix, he rode me to the woodland that day.'

He dipped his head. 'Yes.'

'And he was there when Hosta threatened me, and when we fought them.'

'Yes.'

'So you've been watching me?'

Rayan flinched and pressed the heels of his hands into his eyes. 'I'm so sorry.'

Lettle felt a lump grow in her throat. 'Why didn't you tell me?'

'Our position here is tenuous . . .'

'So? You could have told me, we could have figured it out together.' Anger made her voice hard.

Rayan stood and came to her, he knelt by her feet and reached for her.

'You were the one person I was scared to tell the most. I see the way you hate them, the way they make you feel. I didn't want you to look at me that way.'

'Yeeran is faebound, I don't hate her.' A part of Lettle wondered if she did hate her sister, just a little.

Rayan squeezed her hand, but she did not squeeze back.

'I would have understood,' Lettle said. 'We might have been able to figure it out, realise who your father was beforehand.'

'How? If I didn't know, how would you?'

Lettle pulled her hand from Rayan's grasp and stood, facing the window.

'I-I did a reading a few months back, it was about you.'

Rayan didn't say anything, and she couldn't bear to look back and see the expression on his face. So, she continued, 'The words were "The one born of a storm's mist shall be your beloved."'

Now was the time to tell him the truth of it all. To tell him one day she would be the one to murder him.

'Is it true?' he asked.

She turned around. He was still there kneeling in front of her. His eyes shining, his jaw clenched as he gazed up at her, waiting for her to speak.

No, she could not tell him. Not today.

'Yes, it is true. You have my heart.'

He held open his arms and she went to him. His arms slipped around her waist as he let out a shaky breath.

'My heart is yours, always.'

She lowered herself until she was level with him. Her hand traced his jawline and brushed away the single tear that had fallen from his eyes.

'You can't leave Mosima now, can you?' she whispered. 'You are bound to the land.'

He broke her stare.

'No,' he said heavily. 'To do so would be to condemn innocent people.'

Lettle nodded.

She thought of her hopes of being shaman of the Gural diviners.

'We must let the wind of change ease our flight, not hinder it,' Sahar had said. He had known she was going to stay in Mosima.

Seer Lettle, it had a different ring to it than shaman, but she didn't dislike it.

She ran her hand through Rayan's beard. 'If we're staying in Mosima, I hope we get given bigger rooms.'

Rayan's smile was radiant as he brought her hand to his lips and kissed it. 'Thank you, I know how big a sacrifice it will be.'

Yeeran . . . she thought, then pushed her sister from her mind.

'A king of Mosima in love with an elf, what will the fae think?'

'I don't care what they think,' he said fiercely.

'They're your people now. Don't they deserve your loyalty?'

He stroked her forearm with his thumb.

'I was raised an elf, to reign as a fae king. I am both but neither.' He took a deep breath, 'But there is only one person who deserves my loyalty. You.'

Then she kissed him, and all was right with the world.

For now.

CHAPTER THIRTY-SIX

Yeeran

Yeeran woke up with a start, her hand reaching to the cold part of the bed where Lettle had once been.

'Lettle?'

She is in the living room with the king. Pila was by Yeeran's side, her eyes drowsy.

The king? Her dreams were still a thick fog in Yeeran's mind.

Rayan, the half elf.

Something occurred to Yeeran then.

Did you know? That Rayan was half fae?

Pila cocked her head.

I suppose.

Yeeran reeled upwards.

Why didn't you tell me?

I did, I told you he smells different.

That's not quite the same.

Pila let out a sigh.

It's not my fault you do not smell him like I do.

Yeeran rolled her eyes.

Next time, tell me, would you?

You want me to tell you every time I smell something? Because then I should really tell you that you need a bath.

Yeeran threw a pillow at the beast, who hissed through her teeth and scuttled backwards, her claws clattering against the flagstones.

'Breakfast first, then I might consider a bath,' Yeeran said.

Lettle and Rayan were sitting in the living room talking quietly with each other. Their hands clasped tightly.

Yeeran walked towards Rayan, her eyes burning, her chin low.

She paused in front of him and recited the apology she had concocted before going to sleep. 'Rayan, I will never forgive myself for killing your father. I do not ask for your forgiveness because no one can grant that for such a heinous crime. But know that it is written in the walls of my mind as a daily reminder: I owe you a blood debt.'

Rayan let out a long breath. 'Colonel.'

'Don't call me that.'

'Yeeran. I mourn the father I will never know, but know this: I do not blame you. How could I? In your position, I would have done the same. Our ignorance made victims of us.'

The relief Yeeran felt made her knees shake as she said, 'Ignorance has indeed made victims of us for too long.'

Rayan reached for her shoulder and squeezed it. Lettle stood and crossed the room, leaving Rayan and Yeeran to share a moment of unbreakable friendship.

But as Lettle moved away from them Yeeran saw her trip over a chair leg.

There was the sound of grinding stone and Yeeran saw the floor reach up and grasp Lettle's ankle. Rayan's hand was outstretched, but it wasn't him that held her. The flagstones had formed an arm like a stone statue and it held her in its grip. As Lettle regained her footing, the stone melted back to the flat surface that it once was. She rubbed her ankle with a frown.

'Did anyone else see that?' Yeeran whispered.

Rayan made a small, pained sound.

'Sorry. My new status . . . has changed me.'

'That was *you*?' Yeeran said,

'Yes, the palace, the plants, Mosima as a whole, reacts to me now,' he said with a frown. As if omniscient power was a mere irritation.

Lettle made a sharp inhale. 'How?'

'Furi says it's because I'm now bound to the land, to the curse. It'll get easier as I get used to it.'

Yeeran sat down, her mind reeling.

'Wait.' A thought occurred to her. 'You can let us out of Mosima. We can leave, today, now.'

'Yes, though Furi will not tell me the word that opens the boundary.' He turned to Lettle. 'You were right about the curse. My father discovered some of the human language for magic. But she cannot withhold the information from me for long.'

Yeeran growled low in her throat.

Was it always going to come down to this? Furi or her freedom?

'She will tell us,' Yeeran said and stormed out of their rooms.

A reckoning was coming.

Furi was not at the training ground, or in the woodland. When Yeeran tried to get access to her chambers she was escorted away by four of the faeguard. So, she went to Conch Shore and waited.

Her anger cooled to helplessness until sobs wracked her and she found herself gasping for air. She fell to her knees, her hands reaching forward into the sea foam.

Guilt and pain, love and lust swirled and rattled in her chest.

How could someone feel so much?

'Argh,' she screamed at the sea.

'Did that help?'

Yeeran leapt up and turned round.

It was Furi. Of course it was Furi.

'You.' The word was thunder in her heart. 'Tell Rayan the magic to let us out of here.'

Yeeran reached out and grasped Furi's throat. Furi let her.

'Why won't you let me go?' Yeeran said quietly. 'I want to go home. I want to leave here and never come back.' It felt like a lie because it was.

Still Furi stood limp, her eyes watering, her breath coming in pants as Yeeran's grip tightened and tightened.

Furi's lips curved up into a smile and she looked skywards. She was letting Yeeran kill her.

Yeeran's hand dropped from her neck, her head falling to Furi's shoulder.

'I hate you,' she cried. She sobbed harder, knowing it wasn't true.

Furi held Yeeran as she cried. She stroked her hair gently, soothing her. Then she whispered, 'I will tell him if that's what you want. I will tell him.'

Yeeran broke away from the embrace and looked at Furi. Her gaze held an openness that Yeeran had craved for so long.

'I'm sorry,' Furi said at last. 'For everything. Though I know an apology will never be enough.'

Furi's hand brushed her cheek, her thumb rubbing over the swell of Yeeran's bottom lip.

Yeeran shuddered and Furi's eyes turned hot and perilous. She felt herself lean forward until their lips brushed.

Yeeran enjoyed the moment of tension she could feel tightening within Furi. She was like a coil waiting to spring. Furi waited for permission.

But Yeeran wasn't ready to give it.

'Undress.' Yeeran said, and for a second Furi looked like she was going to say no, then she gave Yeeran a small salacious smile. Her clothes were shed a moment later.

Yeeran's gaze roamed leisurely over Furi's body, appreciating all the curves and contours.

Furi's eyes flashed, and she reached a hand down her navel to where Yeeran's gaze lingered. Her fingers moved against the fine curls between her thighs. Her brown eyes locked with Yeeran's, and the air seemed to crackle between them, charged with energy.

Furi's mouth parted, her breath shortening as she sought her own pleasure.

'Faster,' Yeeran said.

It was only when she was near the brink that Yeeran's hands slipped around her lower back and pulled her into an embrace.

Their kiss was hard, blistering, consuming. Neither one of them had time for gentleness. Too many thorns had grown between them.

It was Furi who pulled back first, only to turn her attention to Yeeran's neck, where she grazed her canines along the sensitive skin there. Yeeran hummed low and deep, her hands roaming across Furi's chest. Yeeran circled a nipple with her finger, then squeezed, drawing a gasp from Furi.

Furi's hands were at Yeeran's shirt, deftly opening each button one by one until the fabric slipped from her shoulders and her chest was bare. Furi turned to her trousers, tugging them down over her hips.

Yeeran stepped out of them, now cloaked only in her desire. Furi's gaze was hungry, and she made a feral sound in the back of her throat before reaching a hand out to push Yeeran's hipbone until she was lying on the sand.

But Yeeran wasn't ready to relinquish control just yet. She propped herself up onto her elbows and said, 'Come here.'

Furi shivered in response, her grin wicked.

Yeeran held out a hand to Furi and guided her until her knees were by Yeeran's ears. Yeeran's hands cupped Furi's buttocks and lowered her onto her mouth.

Yeeran teased out her sounds of pleasure until Furi was shuddering and spent.

Only then did Yeeran let Furi turn her attentions to her. She lowered her lips to Yeeran's breasts, her teeth unyielding. Her fingers slipped down to the warmth of her, kneading the knot of desire with her palm before exploring the centre of her.

When oblivion came, Yeeran welcomed it with a cry.

After they had sated their desire, they washed the sand from their bodies in the sea. It was then that Yeeran realised she was not quite yet done with Furi and lapped at the tides of her pleasure once more.

'*Aiftarri,*' Furi said.

She was lying in the crook of Yeeran's arm on a blanket they had found in the shed. Their clothes lay where they had left them as they waited for the seawater to dry from their skin.

'What?'

'It is the word Rayan needs to speak at the boundary. It will hold for as long as he stands across it.'

'*Aiftarri.*' Yeeran sounded out the unfamiliar word.

'When will you leave?' Furi asked.

Yeeran was drowsy, her eyes half closed. Content even.

Though Furi's question had disrupted that.

'Soon.' Now freedom was hers it didn't seem as urgent any more.

Yeeran's hands ran through Furi's hair as she watched her.

'I have no right to ask this,' Furi said. 'But I will ask anyway. Will you stay?'

'Here in Mosima?' Yeeran sat up, tipping Furi from her chest.

'Yes. With me, as my consort.'

Yeeran's heart pounded. She didn't know what to say. Was she prepared to turn on her country, her home?

No. Never. Not while children go hungry in the Waning tribe.

'Why don't you come with me? To the Elven Lands? The truth about the obeah needs to be known. Who better to tell it than the queen?'

Furi sifted through a handful of sand, but instead of falling the sand began to swirl around her, lulled by the strange curse that bound her to this place.

'My life is tied to Mosima now, Yeeran. I cannot leave it.'

Yeeran's mouth smacked closed. 'I could travel back and forth maybe. It would be a bit tricky with my shift pattern . . . but I could make it work.'

Furi pressed a finger against Yeeran's lips.

'I want you here, by my side, always. I know what I ask is a lot. Think on it, and tell me what you decide tonight. Now, I must go. Nerad has locked himself in his rooms and is refusing to acknowledge Rayan's title.'

Yeeran nodded. She wasn't really listening, because she had realised something: if Furi could never leave Mosima, neither could Rayan. And if Rayan wasn't leaving then . . .

Lettle wasn't leaving either.

CHAPTER THIRTY-SEVEN

Lettle

Lettle moved around her new chambers. Rayan's chambers. They were expansive, stretching over more rooms than she'd had a chance to explore yet. Two of the faeguard were stationed outside. She was alone, waiting for Rayan to return home.

Home.

Lettle tested the word out. It seemed strange to think of Mosima in that way. Without Yeeran.

She had yet to tell her sister she wasn't going with her back to the Elven Lands. How could she? Rayan could not leave, so neither could she.

Her hands slipped into her pockets where her talismans lay, and she smiled. She had her magic back, and she had Rayan. That was all she needed to make a life.

After breakfast that morning Rayan and Lettle had gone to see Sahar.

The seer stood behind his counter waiting, his eyes shining as Rayan walked in first.

'Grandson,' he said quietly, reverently. 'King.' He dropped his head to his chest.

Rayan crossed the room and folded the thin man into a crushing embrace.

'It is good to meet you,' he said.

'Did you know?' Lettle asked, cutting through the tenderness of the moment. 'Did you know Rayan was your grandson?'

Sahar shook his head, tears flowing freely from his brown eyes. Brown like Furi's. Brown like Rayan's.

'No, I did not know.' Then he turned to Rayan. 'Will you join me? For tea?'

Rayan nodded.

'I will go back to the palace,' Lettle said.

This was a moment for him alone, a chance to learn about the father he had lost.

And now, Lettle was waiting in their new rooms, their *royal* rooms. That evening Rayan was being formally introduced to the cabinet as the King of Mosima, and Lettle as seer.

A bell rang from the side of the double doors and a guard presented themselves. Lettle wasn't allowed to go anywhere unattended. There was still a murderer on the loose.

'Seer? Golan is here, shall I let him in?'

There was a light laugh from the corridor.

'It's fine,' Lettle said. 'Golan can come and go as he pleases.'

The guard nodded once before retreating back behind the door.

Golan walked into the room carrying a leather pack brimming with clothes.

'I come bearing gifts for the new seer of Mosima, and as I understand it, the consort of our king,' he said with a flourish, waving his cane like a conductor's stick.

Lettle chuckled. 'Stop that.'

'I will not. I see how far you have risen, my friend.' Golan smiled with sincerity. 'We on the outskirts rarely fly so far. It lightens my heart to see it.'

Lettle reached out and squeezed his hand. He squeezed back then broke away.

'Now shall we dress you in the most ridiculously ostentatious outfit ever?'

They laughed, but Golan was true to his word. He dressed her in a gown the colour of fresh milk with a fine silver pattern woven around the hem.

'This weave is called "light from a fallen tear",' he said.

'It's beautiful.'

'*You're* beautiful.'

Lettle looked at herself in the mirror and agreed. The colour of the dress made the deep colour of her skin seem almost glossy and the cinched waist accentuated her curves.

'Yes, I am, aren't I?'

'But can I make one suggestion? We replace that old necklace with something with diamonds.'

Golan pointed to the bead pendant that hung low on her chest.

'No.' She clasped her hand around it. The gift from Rayan meant more to her than any other possession she owned.

Golan laughed. 'OK, fine, I thought it was worth the ask. Now on to your make-up. It'd be better if we stained your brows, but I've run out of clammer squid ink, so we'll have to make do with eye shadow until a new order comes in.'

He got to work on her make-up.

'Do you think they'll accept me?' Lettle asked.

Golan tutted as she smudged the lip liner he was drawing.

'Do you want the truth?'

'Every time.'

'No, they won't. It'll be harder for you and Rayan than anyone else in this palace. But I also think you'll both bring the most change. Mosima is stuck, not just by the curse, but by our traditions. Lightless are treated no better than elves and I hope that your influence will bring about that change.' Golan's voice wavered.

Lettle sat up and looked into his eyes. She remembered what Yeeran had said about Golan and Nerad arguing.

'Are you OK?' she asked.

Golan looked like he was going to say something, but then he closed his mouth with a snap.

'Yes, I'm fine.'

'Trouble with your gentleman lover?'

Golan laughed and it sounded forced.

'All is well, Lettle. Though I should go. I feel a headache coming on. I fear I'll have to miss tonight's celebrations. Soar high, Seer Lettle, soar far.'

Seer Lettle. The title itched a little. She didn't feel like a seer. The Fates hadn't spoken to her since her last prophecy about Nerad and Komi.

A king's vengeance sated. A prophecy fulfilled.

But Nerad wasn't king. Rayan was.

Lettle felt the truth unravel and come loose in her mind.

No, it couldn't be . . .

Lettle had to hold the skirt of her dress as she ran across the Royal Woodland. Yeeran had said that Komi had gone into a door on the ground floor, behind the baobab tree.

Lettle had to know if her suspicions were right. She had to.

There were four doors that could have been the one Pila had seen Komi enter. The faeguard tried to stop her, but she used her title, feeling it suited her all of a sudden. The first two rooms were court offices of some kind. The third was a lavatory, and the fourth was a . . .

'War room,' Lettle whispered.

A map of the Elven Lands spread across the centre of a table. The battlefield was circled in the middle, but it wasn't labelled the Bleeding Field – it was called Lorhan. Lettle knew enough of the Forever War to know that the wooden tokens were military encampments.

Komi had been feeding the fae information about the Forever War. Komi of the Crescent tribe. Komi who had disappeared from the Elven Lands ten years ago.

Lettle could hear voices coming from the corridor that led into the heart of the palace. She was about to slip away, back out into the woodland, when she heard a voice she recognised. Golan.

She lowered herself to the floor and hid underneath the table.

'You cannot follow me wherever I go, Nerad,' Golan said.

A meeting with his gentleman lover.

'You gave me no choice. You won't answer my summons,' Nerad replied.

'We agreed to not see each other, for a few months, until everything dies down.'

'I just wanted to talk, I've got a new idea, a new plan . . .'

Golan stamped his cane. 'I am not interested.'

Lettle peered out to see their shadows merge into one on the back wall.

'I've missed you,' Nerad said with a sigh.

'Nerad, what do you want from me?' Golan said.

'I wanted to see you.'

'Well, now you've seen me.'

There was the sound of wet lips and a fumble. Then a cruel laugh.

'You no longer want me?' Nerad said.

'You are not yourself, Nerad.'

'*Prince* Nerad. You'd do well to remember that.'

There was a heavy exhale, then a sob.

'I'm sorry, I didn't mean that. You know I didn't mean that,' Nerad said.

'I'm leaving now.' Golan's voice sounded detached, devoid of emotion.

'Did you see him out there? On *my* throne?'

Golan sighed. 'It's not your fault. You couldn't have known.'

'But I did know. Najma wrote a letter and gave it to me on the day he died. It spoke of his son. But never did I think that, with his diluted blood, the tree would grant him the throne. If I did, I would have killed him along with the queens.'

Lettle felt her stomach churn with the knowledge of the truth.

'But I suppose . . . I wasn't the one to kill them, was I?' Nerad said.

Golan took a few shaking steps with his cane. Lettle clutched her elbows, her nails digging into flesh.

'I merely supplied the poison. You were the one to lace the chalice, don't forget that,' Golan said.

'Are you sure?' Nerad taunted. 'That's not how I remember it.'

Golan and Nerad killed the queens.

Golan and Nerad killed the queens.

Lettle made a sound in her throat.

'There's someone in here,' Nerad whispered.

Lettle held her breath. When nothing happened, she let it out.

Suddenly the familiar burn of fae magic wrapped around her throat, and she was pulled backwards out from under the table.

'Lettle.' Golan was by her side.

Nerad's sad eyes appeared above her.

'What were you doing in my study, little elf?'

'Let . . . me . . . go . . .' she wheezed out.

'Nerad, stop this. She is an innocent here,' Golan pleaded.

The fae prince knelt on the floor beside Lettle.

'Did you hear something you shouldn't have?' he asked her, and she shook her head.

Nerad's smile was sickly sweet. It was then Lettle knew she was going to die.

She accepted her fate and closed her eyes.

CHAPTER THIRTY-EIGHT

Yeeran

Yeeran made her way back to the palace, the scent of Furi still clinging to her skin.

Lettle has just entered the door that Komi went in, Pila said down their connection. She sent an image of Lettle's face, wan with worry, as she shut the door behind her. Yeeran recognised that expression – Lettle knew something.

Yeeran started to run.

Branches whipped at her arms as she ran through the woodland.

Pila, where are you?

Coming up to your left.

Yeeran felt her presence before she saw her and dived in the direction she knew Pila would be running in. The breath knocked out of her as she landed on Pila's side, but she was able to grab her mane and swing her leg over.

They flew through the forest, arriving at the door in moments.

Yeeran pulled it open and came face to face with her worst nightmare.

Nerad had strung magic around Lettle's neck and chest. Her sister was dying, right there in front of her eyes. Golan was by her side pleading at Nerad to stop.

Yeeran didn't hesitate. She swung her drum across her shoulder and began to shoot drumfire. Blossoms of red spread across Nerad's torso, and he released the magic restraining Lettle.

'He killed the queens,' she croaked before collapsing into Golan's arms.

Yeeran had no time for the truth to settle, all she knew was that Nerad had hurt her sister, and for that he would pay the highest price. She levelled another shot at his stomach, but he deflected it with his own magic.

'Don't kill him,' Lettle tried to shout as if her fear of Nerad had been replaced by her fear for Yeeran. If Yeeran killed another prince, they would not let her live. But Yeeran did not care.

Xosa, Nerad's obeah, appeared by his side, clashing horns with Pila.

Drive him out into the woodland, Pila. We need to separate Nerad from Xosa in case he tries to flee.

I'll try, was Pila's quick reply. Yeeran could feel the strain in Pila's muscles as she fought the larger obeah. But she didn't let Pila's efforts distract her.

She fired rapid hits at Nerad's feet, cornering him in the back of the room. Nerad whipped magic back at her, slashing at her arms, drawing them away from her weapon so her drumfire faltered.

Nerad dashed towards the door pushing a bewildered Rayan out of the way.

'What is happening here? I heard commotion—'

'Lettle,' Yeeran screamed at him. 'Check Lettle.'

In the seconds it took Yeeran to speak, Nerad had mounted his obeah.

Yeeran and Pila laid chase. They charged through the Royal Woodland. The cadence of the ride changed as another rider joined the hunt.

Yeeran looked to the side and saw Furi riding Amnan, her hair a waterfall of molten gold. She nodded grimly at Yeeran and charged Amnan on. The plants of the Royal Woodland parted from Furi's new connection with the land, giving them a clean pathway towards Nerad. But he had the lead and so they followed him through the streets of Mosima all the way to the boundary.

Nerad and Xosa scaled the steps that led to the tunnel where Yeeran had first entered the city.

'We can't let him leave. On my signal – bind our magic!' Furi shouted.

Yeeran waited for the call, and when it came, she held on to Pila with one hand and with the other rattled her drum to unravel a thread of magic. With intention she interlaced it with Furi's, who drove the force of their weaving up and over Nerad's head.

He tried to break the barrier, but he was no match for their combined strength.

'Let me out,' he spat.

'No,' Furi said.

Yeeran and Furi dismounted and walked towards the cage they had trapped Nerad in. They were above the city, the steps to Mosima behind them, the boundary ahead.

'Why did you do it?' Furi asked quietly.

Nerad deflated, his chest concaving. But when he looked up, he was smiling.

'Do you think we deserve this life, Furi?' he asked.

She didn't answer him.

'Do you think we deserve to be trapped here? For a thousand years. *A thousand years.*' His voice careened into a higher octave.

'You know I don't, Nerad.'

'I was glad when the blight came, it gave us a reason to leave. But then,' his lips curled, 'the blight improved and our queens gave up on all the work we had done with Crescent.'

What has Crescent got to do with anything?

Concentrate, Yeeran. Your magic is slipping, Pila warned her, and Yeeran tightened her threads around the cage.

'You should have talked to me, we could have figured it out, together,' Furi said.

'Talk to you? Your duty, no, your *obedience* has ever been my adversary, cousin. When I removed the queens from the throne, I did it for you, so you could finally think for yourself.'

Furi shook her head, flinging tears across her cheeks.

'Don't you dare say you killed our mothers in my name, *cousin.*' She twisted the word and threw it back at him.

Nerad laughed sadly.

'Let me leave. Let me join the extra troops we deployed to the Elven Lands yesterday.'

Furi's shoulders tensed, letting Yeeran know she was planning something.

'This was badly done, Nerad,' Furi said. She pulled out a dagger from a thigh strap under her dress. When she let go of her magic so too did Yeeran.

Xosa whined softly. Nerad slipped from her back and stood a few feet from Furi, his back to the city. He was crying.

'I wanted to see a storm. I wanted to feel the seasons change. I wanted to watch the sunset every day and feel its warmth on my skin. I wanted to go *home.*'

There was a grunt, and Amnan launched himself at Xosa at the same time Furi dived for Nerad. There was a deafening clap as the two obeah locked horns, but Amnan being the larger of the two, drove Xosa back until her hind legs skidded off the cliff and she fell backwards down the stairs.

Time seemed to slow. One second Nerad was lashing outwards with his magic, the next he was still. He let out a final breath, his eyes brimming, before falling backwards off the cliff to join the body of his obeah down below.

Furi's scream was anguished and broken. She fell to her knees and Yeeran went to her.

'All of them, all of them gone,' she murmured over and over, rocking back and forth. When she tilted her face to Yeeran's it had hardened. 'Nerad jumped.'

'Nerad jumped,' Yeeran agreed, committing to the lie.

Furi stood, her knees shaking, her eyes clouded with pain.

A few minutes passed in silence. Yeeran felt exhaustion follow the end of the hunt. She reached for Furi but the fae shrugged her off. Grief masked as anger.

'What did Nerad mean?' Yeeran said softly. 'All the work you had done with "Crescent"?'

Furi went to Amnan and stroked him tenderly. Pila stood by Yeeran's back, lending her strength always.

'When the blight began to accelerate, we started a campaign to reclaim our homeland,' Furi said, her head dipping to her chin. 'We became allies with the Crescent tribe.'

'What?' Yeeran's heart began to pound.

'In exchange for helping them win the war, they will acknowledge the Fae Lands as ours.'

'The Fae Lands?'

Something itched at the back of Yeeran's memory. Rayan had said he'd seen a map in the Book Orchard.

Furi released her pursed lips.

'Though your histories have forgotten that the land was once ours. The capital, Lorhan, is what you call the Bleeding Field.'

Yeeran shook her head.

'It doesn't make sense. They'd be in ruins – there'd be some kind of evidence that the land was once part of the Fae Lands.'

The truth unfurled in her mind. 'Of course, the fraedia mines . . .' Yeeran felt her stomach burn with acid. 'Lorhan was an underground city, just like Mosima.'

It is hard to see a leaf among the trees, there are many truths in the boughs still, Pila said.

'So you are going to fight for Crescent in the Forever War?' Yeeran pressed.

Furi looked away from her to the city below.

'We already are, Yeeran.'

Yeeran's head shook back and forth as the memory of her last day on the battlefield resurfaced. She found herself reliving the moment she told her archers to release their arrows against the oncoming attack from Crescent. How their attack had glanced off an invisible barrier.

Magic she had never seen before.

It was fae magic. The shield the Crescent tribe used that day.

How had she not realised until now?

'So, what was the scouting mission you were on when you found me?'

Furi lowered herself to the ground and placed her head in her hands.

Yeeran had torn the stitches of Furi's lies away, and the truth flowed freely now. Bleeding her dry.

But when she looked back at Yeeran, her eyes were clear and steady. 'I was attending a strategy meeting with the Crescent general.'

'How could you keep this from me?'

Furi's laugh was weak, but it still sounded harsh.

'Don't talk to me of secrets. I know of the journal you write in every night. Compiling the details of my race like we are your specimens. All to give to the chieftain of your tribe. A fine gift, I think.'

How did she know?

Pila growled low in her throat.

'It's not the same. Those are only words. These are people's lives,' Yeeran said.

'And what do you think your chieftain will do with your pretty words?'

Wage war against the fae for the fraedia crystal that grows in Mosima. The thought was cruel, but Yeeran realised it was true.

'No, this cannot be,' Yeeran said.

'It is,' Furi said heavily. 'The queens, they wanted to break off the alliance now that the blight has gone. Nerad did not want that.'

'And you?' Yeeran's voice was thick with unshed tears.

Furi averted her gaze and didn't answer.

'I heard what Nerad said. You went back on the queens' plans, didn't you? You sent more troops?'

Yeeran wanted to hear the betrayal from Furi's lips.

'I don't want to be hidden away any longer,' Furi said, the words staccato with frustration. 'I want . . . I want—'

'What do you want?' Yeeran stepped closer to Furi where the warmth of her skin soothed the sting of her betrayal.

Furi tilted her head and said softly, 'You know what I want.'

Yeeran looked away first, her eyes resting on the glow of the boundary. On the other side her own people were being killed by the fae.

Furi could let me out right now.

But she could not leave. Not without Lettle.

'Lettle,' she reached for Pila. An image of Lettle lying prone on the floor fluttered behind her eyelids, bruises around her neck, her skin purple and blotchy.

Take me back to her, Pila.

Lettle had been taken straight to the infirmary and diagnosed with a collapsed lung.

'The magic around her chest cracked a rib which in turn punctured the lung. Air then leaked into the chest cavity and . . . splat. The lung deflated,' the healer said, fanning out her hands.

Yeeran did not appreciate the healer's theatrics.

'What does that mean?' Rayan asked. He had carried Lettle the entire way. His face was bloodless and worried.

'We'll have to sedate her while we attempt to re-inflate it. I don't envision any complications, but I will say you being here won't improve matters. I suggest you both take your leave and return in an hour. Your presence is not conducive to working conditions.'

Yeeran looked around. Healers were watching Rayan with a mixture of awe and trepidation. Those not looking at Rayan were looking at Yeeran with suspicion. None of them were working.

'They're right, we need to go.' Yeeran squeezed Lettle's hand.

'Komi,' Lettle rasped suddenly. 'Komi, scheeftun akoomydo.' The words were nonsensical, her breathing heavily laboured.

'Please, do not speak,' the healer chastised her. 'Runi, bring the sedation.'

Lettle's mouth opened and closed as she tried in earnest to convey her meaning.

Rayan stooped to press a kiss to Lettle's brow.

'Rest now, we will see you shortly.'

Yeeran and Rayan left the infirmary.

It was the thick of night and they needed to use their magesight to get around. They walked silently through Mosima and back through the woodland.

It was then that Yeeran noticed that the trees were wilting.

'What is it?' Rayan asked.

'The trees, I think they're reacting to your mood.'

Rayan let out a sigh. 'This new power will take some getting used to.'

Yeeran reached for a nearby branch and snapped it.

'Did you feel that?'

Rayan frowned. 'No, the connection to Mosima is less tangible than a limb. It's more like . . . hair. Like I can manipulate it if I want to by just tugging.'

Yeeran's eyes widened as she watched the broken twig sprout new growth under Rayan's manipulation. But as soon as the leaves grew big enough, they wilted too.

She reached out a hand to Rayan's and squeezed it.

'Lettle will be OK, you know. You need to believe that, or half this forest is going to die.'

'I should have been by her side. I should be by her side now.'

'No,' Yeeran used her colonel voice. 'Going back there won't help her, and worrying yourself – and Mosima – sick won't help anyone.'

He nodded and Yeeran noticed the leaves perk up. 'Nerad . . . he's really dead?' Rayan asked.

'Yes. Furi chased him to the boundary. They fought at the top of the steps. Nerad . . . he fell.'

Yeeran hadn't allowed herself to feel grief for the friend she had lost. He was a traitor, a traitor to her and the Waning tribe.

'Why did he do it?'

Yeeran took a deep breath in. They had reached the Tree of Souls. An extra leaf had grown among the branches. She looked away. The door where Yeeran had found Lettle had been closed. It was guarded by two of the faeguard.

As she approached it, Rayan waved them aside.

Yeeran pushed open the door and blinked away the image of Lettle on the floor. There was a map on the table. She had been a little too preoccupied to notice its importance before.

'The fae are allying with the Crescent tribe,' Yeeran said.

Rayan stilled.

'No, that can't be possible.'

He looked over at the map, murmuring to himself, 'The northern bank, the eastern quarter, the Dying Hill . . .'

Yeeran told him all: about Nerad and his plans to continue the campaign, about the Crescent tribe and their deal with the fae, and how the queens had wanted to end the alliance and to stop their involvement in the war.

Yeeran placed her hand flat over the part of the map that was home.

'They've condemned them all to destruction,' Yeeran said.

Rayan nodded, his gaze distant. She wondered how he felt; the fae had partnered with the people he hated the most. The Two-Bladed Tyrant's tribe, the man who had killed his mother. The man he was destined to one day kill.

'What I don't understand is, how did this alliance come about? Why ally with the Crescent tribe?'

Yeeran shrugged. 'They are closest geographically to Mosima—' Realisation was as cold and sudden as a flash flood. 'A king's vengeance sated. A prophecy fulfilled,' Yeeran whispered. Who else but Komi could have told Furi of the journal. 'That's what Lettle was trying to tell us. Komi . . . he's Chieftain Akomido.'

Rayan looked up.

'What?'

'He's been helping them to broker this deal.'

Rayan shook his head, disbelieving.

'I would know.'

'Weren't you a child when you last saw him? The years have changed you both.'

Rayan screwed up his features and Yeeran imagined him peeling back the layers of years on Komi's face, shaving his face clean and removing ten years' growth of locs.

'He can't be,' he said, his voice heavy with dread.

'She's right,' the voice came from the doorway. Furi was there, shadows gathering in the rings beneath her eyes.

'No,' Rayan choked.

Furi looked pained. 'The Two-Bladed Tyrant has been our prisoner for these last ten years. It was Nerad who worked with him to make the deal with the Crescent tribe. Our prisoner, yes. But also our ambassador.'

'A political prisoner,' Yeeran breathed.

Furi nodded. 'He would have won his freedom when we won our land.'

Rayan growled low in his throat. It sounded like the roar of an obeah. A wind swept through Mosima, pulling leaves from trees and swirling in through the open door, his rage come alive.

Then he turned and ran.

Yeeran followed him as he thundered down the hallway to their rooms. Furi was on her heels.

'Wait,' she called. But it was no use. Rayan could not see or hear anyone.

Komi was reclining on the velvet sofas when they burst into the apartment. When he saw their expressions, he slumped, looking every bit his age.

'You killed my mother.' Rayan's magic lashed out with a spark, twisting around Komi's midriff.

'I've killed many mothers, and many fathers,' Komi said with quiet resolution as Rayan squeezed his essential organs with his magic.

'Reema, she prophesied your death by my hands.'

Komi's eyes widened. 'You?'

Rayan's expression was grim. 'Me.'

Yeeran stepped towards Komi, her hands shaking so she balled them into fists.

'You're the Two-Bladed Tyrant.'

Komi couldn't maintain eye contact with the intensity of Yeeran's gaze, and so he looked away. 'I hated the name the Two-Bladed Tyrant. It always made me seem worse than I was. Because all I am is what the war made me, a martyr to peace. All I ever wanted was to stop the war. And the fae will help do that.'

'By killing people with magic no one can compete with.'

Komi tried to shrug but Rayan's magic held him down.

'You use drums, I use fae. A weapon is a weapon.'

Yeeran drove her fist into his face until his nose bled.

'Stop this,' Furi hissed. 'You cannot kill him.'

Furi's own magic sparked, but Yeeran wheeled on her, her fingers bloody with Komi's blood.

'Don't,' Yeeran said. Furi's eyes met hers and Yeeran laid bare the bitterness of betrayal in her gaze. If Furi came to Komi's aid now, then this burning thing between them would turn to ash.

And she knew it.

Furi dropped her magic in defeat. Her shoulders slumped and grief etched into every crease and line on her skin.

Yeeran looked away from her and back to Rayan and Komi.

Rayan turned to Furi and smiled. 'He is already dead by my hand. He has been since the Fates spoke to my mother, and he killed her for it.'

There was the churning sound of boulders moving as the flag-stones rose up and smothered Komi's legs. The stone didn't move smoothly, it juddered and clawed its way over his thighs leaving the ground where the flagstones had been bare, revealing the wooden foundations of the palace.

Komi's scream curdled Yeeran's blood and it rose in volume as the stone grew up his chest, only going quiet when the stone encased his neck and he could scream no more. If Yeeran had thought his scream had been horrifying, the silence of Komi's last moments proved to eclipse it. His eyes bulged and rolled in their sockets as the stone grew up from his chin and smothered his whole face. He was gone. Entombed in death.

Rayan breathed heavily into silence.

'You don't know what you've done,' Furi said. 'You have brought us war after all.'

She shook her head sadly.

'You were working with a tyrant . . .' Yeeran hissed.

'All of them are tyrants, Yeeran, every single one of them uses the war as a means of power. He was just the nearest chieftain to our border.'

Yeeran felt her fists go slack.

Furi withdrew something from her pocket. She pressed it against Rayan's chest.

'We found this on Nerad's body. It was addressed to you from my brother.'

Then she walked away leaving Rayan, Yeeran, and the statue of Komi. His mouth parted in a scream.

CHAPTER THIRTY-NINE

Lettle

'Hello, sleepyhead.'

The words lulled Lettle into consciousness and she woke bleary-eyed.

'Golan?'

He sat in the chair next to her bed, both hands folded over the top of his cane. He looked haggard, but his smile was kindly.

'The healers tell me you'll make a full recovery.'

'What happened?'

'Your lung collapsed. But you'll be fine.'

He stood up and came to stand beside her. She reached for his hand.

'Where's Rayan? Yeeran?'

'The healers sent them away, their presence was causing quite a stir, but I'm sure they'll be here shortly.'

'And Nerad?'

'Dead.'

Lettle nodded but gasped as a dull pain reverberated around her throat.

'You have some bruising, but Sahar himself made the poultice that the healers used. He proclaimed the one they were using was less useful than camel dung.'

Lettle thankfully couldn't smell snowmallow flower.

'Lettle . . .' Golan paused, trying to formulate his words.

'I will not tell them of your involvement,' she said.

Tears brimmed in his eyes, and he looked away.

'I don't deserve you,' he said.

'You do.'

He smiled sadly.

'Mosima has never been a safe space for the Lightless. The queens . . . they weren't kind, they didn't fight for our rights. Nerad, he promised he would when he was in power. So I gave him the poison from my make-up kit and he—'

Golan stopped, his lips pressing together until they were thin quivering lines.

'Golan, I understand.'

And Lettle did. Sometimes, violence was the only way to make a change.

'Besides, I don't think you're Lightless. I think you shine brighter than anyone here.'

Golan smiled and Lettle added, 'Maybe we can be each other's obeah.'

He chuckled. 'I'd like that.'

Golan embraced her, careful not to twist her neck.

'I'll come and visit you soon.'

'Very soon,' she said.

As Golan turned to leave, someone nearly ran into him. It was Yeeran, breathless and carrying a pack.

'You're awake.' Yeeran hugged her with less care than Golan had, and she winced with the ferocity of her sister's love. 'The healer told me you'll be OK.'

'Yes, apparently I'll make a full recovery—' Suddenly Lettle remembered: 'Komi . . . he's Chieftain Akomido.'

Yeeran looked away, the grief of losing a friend written in her features.

'He's dead?' Lettle whispered, and Yeeran nodded. 'Oh, Rayan, I hope your vengeance is sated.'

The silence was heavy with grief and guilt. Tears flowing silently down their cheeks.

Then Lettle sniffed and sat up, pointing to the pack. 'What's that you've brought me?'

Yeeran took a step back, her eyes downcast. Lettle recognised her expression. She'd seen it before.

'You're leaving.'

'Yes, I have to. The fae, they've been working with the Crescent tribe to end the Forever War.'

Lettle balled her blanket between her fists.

'The fae have sent troops to join the Crescent army. I have to warn Salawa,' Yeeran said.

'So, you're choosing the war over me. Again.'

'Thousands of our tribe will die, Lettle.'

'It is a *war*, thousands are always going to die.'

'I have an opportunity to broker peace.'

Lettle scoffed and Yeeran shook her head sadly.

'Don't make this about you, Lettle. Not now, not like this.'

If Lettle had the strength she would have stood from her bed and slapped her sister.

'This isn't about me, Yeeran. It's about you. It has *always* been about you. You were the one who was so good at hunting, it was you who Father loved more than anyone else. Then you went and you broke his heart. You killed him when you followed in Mama's footsteps.'

'I did not kill him, Lettle, don't put that blame on me.'

Lettle nodded. 'You're right. That guilt is for me alone.'

Yeeran frowned.

'What?'

'Father's mind began to wander in his later years. One day . . . one day he forgot who I was. At first, I could draw him back to me, talk of stories of the past until he remembered me . . .' Lettle's voice dropped to a whisper. 'But though his mind had gone his body was still as lean and as strong as ever . . . sometimes he'd get angry, he'd lash out—'

'Why haven't you told me this before?'

'Because you were away in Gural, training. You didn't visit, so what else could I do?'

Yeeran laid a hand on Lettle's wrist.

'I should have been there.'

'Yes, you should have.' Emboldened by her anger, she went on, 'Perhaps you would have been able to stop me killing our father.'

Yeeran made a wordless sound in the back of her throat.

Lettle felt the shackles of the secret set her free. Tears flowed down her face as she spoke.

'I killed him, I killed our father.'

Yeeran took a step back.

'No, you didn't mean to, it was in self-defence.'

'You're not listening to me, Yeeran. It was my fault. One day I gave him some snowmallow flower in his food to keep him calm. Then a bit more to help him sleep. Then slowly, day by day, I increased it, eventually giving him enough to sleep forever.'

Lettle's hands were shaking from the memory. She clenched her fists harder.

Yeeran took another step back.

'I shouldn't have left.'

'And yet, here you are, doing it again.'

'Please, Lettle. Don't make me choose.'

'But it's not a choice, is it? I see you already inching your way backwards, closer and closer to your precious war. Go then. Let us part in anger, because I cannot part in love, it hurts too damn much.'

Yeeran saw the stubborn set of Lettle's shoulders. Thankfully she had come to recognise it over the years and knew when the battle was lost.

'I love you, Lettle. I forgive you for Father. But please, forgive yourself.'

It was only after Yeeran was gone that Lettle broke down in tears, mumbling, 'I'm so sorry, Father, I'm so sorry.'

CHAPTER FORTY

Yeeran

Yeeran's footsteps were heavy as she walked to the beach.

It was time to go home.

Furi was by the shore waiting for her. She didn't look up as Yeeran approached.

'You're leaving.'

'Yes.'

'To warn your chieftain.'

'Yes.'

'Who is this chieftain to you?'

It was a question Yeeran didn't know how to answer. Once Salawa had been her lover, but now Yeeran realised it was not love that had grown between them but something more placid.

'She has always been a symbol of what I was fighting for. Being close to her . . . eased the pain of the battlefield.'

Furi nodded, the sea spray shining as it ran through her hair.

'And me?'

'You are more.'

'More?'

'More.'

Yeeran folded her into her arms and Furi let her kiss her like she wanted, fiercely, with a need that could never be satisfied. When they broke apart, Furi turned away.

Amnan cantered towards her, and she jumped onto his back.

'You are my starlight, always,' Yeeran said, but Furi didn't reply. She loped away on her obeah's back, sea spray in her hair.

Yeeran watched her disappear, and when she could no longer see the gold of her hair, she slipped into magesight and watched the glow of her magic until she blinked out of sight.

Pila, it's time to go.

Rayan was standing at the boundary when they got there. She pulled him into a hug.

'Please look after Lettle,' she said.

'I promise, I will.'

Yeeran pulled the straps of the pack, made heavy by the journal in there.

'I'll do my best and try to get Salawa to draw up a new treaty to end the war. I hope the truth will give way to peace.'

'I hope so too.' Rayan rubbed his brow. 'There's something you should know. I went back to the war room and looked through Nerad's papers. He deployed two hundred of the faeguard to Crescent before the coronation – before he knew he wasn't going to be king.'

Yeeran felt shock slacken her jaw.

'Furi had said they'd sent troops, but I didn't realise it was that many. You need to recall them, you need to stop this, Rayan.'

His eyes flashed.

'I will, you know I will. Mosima will not ally with Crescent while I am king.' His words were rich with authority and Yeeran appraised him with a cocked brow.

Here is a king who will fight for what is right.

It is because he never sought power, and so he does not seek to wield it like a weapon, Pila said. And once again the obeah was right.

'You have come far, Captain Rayan.'

He gave her a tentative smile, but it dropped as he said, 'Furi thinks Crescent will retaliate after Komi's death. They may turn on our troops before I can get a message to them. Either way, war will come.'

'It never left.'

Rayan nodded, his expression stern, determined.

Yeeran looked to the boundary.

'I'll do everything I can from Waning, too,' she said.

'Give my best to my comrades. Tell them I'm a king now.' He laughed, shaking his head in disbelief. Then he stepped up to the boundary and said the word that Furi had gifted her, '*Aiftarri.*'

Yeeran slipped into magesight and watched the bronze words of the boundary swirl and curl to the sides leaving an opening that Yeeran could step through. Rayan whistled through his teeth.

'That felt strange, like the magic surged through my breath.'

'I'm glad it worked,' she replied.

She turned and gave Mosima one last glance.

The fray was dim in the thick of night. When Yeeran looked to the palace, she gasped.

Star gliders filled the space above it, hundreds of them, thousands.

'Furi,' Yeeran whispered. Because it could only be her with the ability to draw on the magic of all the beings of Mosima.

Furi had made her starlight.

Yeeran stepped through the boundary with hope swelling in her chest. Hope that one day she would see her love again. And hope that when she did, it would not be on the other side of the battlefield.

EPILOGUE

Rayan

Yeeran didn't look back at Rayan as she walked through the tunnel.

She is free now, Ajix said.

He smiled, his obeah always managed to warm his heart. He was currently eating wild raspberries from someone's garden.

I'll save you some, he said.

Thank you, but first I'm going to sit here a little while.

I might eat your portion then.

He laughed.

Please do.

Rayan slipped his hand into his pocket and withdrew the letter Furi had given him. They were the last words of his father that they'd found on Nerad's body. He opened it with shaking hands.

Son,

> *May the light shine bright, and your spirit shine brighter. I have known this day would come for many years, but I did not know that you would be by my side when it did, or rather Hudan's side, my obeah. Through him I am able to see the man you have become. And what a gift that is.*

> *But to linger near a hunter is to welcome death, and I welcome it to spend another moment with you.*

> *I cannot lie and say your mother was my true love. My coupling*

with Reema was brief, its purpose a comfort to both of us, and nothing more. I had become brazen with my newfound freedom and did not know you existed until Hudan scented you on the breeze these last few weeks. All I hope is that you will come home to Mosima and find the family I will have left behind.

I burden you with one more thing other than my death. Many years ago, Hudan discovered a grimoire in Afa's tomb, east of the Wasted Marshes, and brought it back to me. It is in those pages where I gleaned the secret of my ability to leave the boundary. It has taken me many years to translate what I could, but I'm afraid I will not be able to break the curse while I still live. I do not trust everyone here, including some of my family. So instead, I choose to trust you, my halfling son, whose eyes may see more than I could ever.

I have hidden my research where the earth's teeth grow, once a river flowed.

My love eternal,

Najma

Rayan slid the letter back into the envelope and clutched it to his chest. He didn't try to contain his tears.

It was nearly dawn when he returned to the palace. His steps lighter with the gift his father had given him.

He had a curse to break.

TURN THE PAGE FOR
A FAIRYLOOT EXCLUSIVE
BONUS CHAPTER

Pila

You are startled by the crunch of a fallen leaf and rush towards where the shadows flicker like a moth's wing.

You are waiting.

There, you drink from the river water and savour the sweet taste of earth. The bank is scented with the hides of those who have come before.

The chirp of a mawbill tells you it is nearing dusk, and you feel the stirrings of hunger.

You are waiting.

You grip the dirt between your claws as you run through the forest following the trail of fruit left by your brethren; a strawberry seed, an apple pip, the drip of saliva mixed with pulp.

The vibrations of the earth change as another of your kind falls into cadence with your step. Their fur is as black as a raven's beak.

You dip your tail low and angle your body in respect. You know they deserve it, but you do not know why. They are different. Whole.

A litter mate nuzzles you as you enter the orchard. From their touch you know where the quieter feeding spots are.

When you find a fruitful branch, you sate your appetite. But still – you are waiting.

You leave the quiet smells of the orchard and stroll through the centre of the woodland.

Then you see a light in a glade.

You tilt your head and watch the light speak.

'Yes, I am the person who killed your cousin. Though I did not know that was the consequence of killing the obeah.'

You do not understand the words.

Then the light sees you and you feel a jolt like the snap of a spring twig, dry and brittle.

The trees shiver from the anger pressed deep into the bones of the woodland where the souls who feed the land reside.

You are scared by that anger. So you leave.

Only to return again soon. You need to see. Will the twig snap again when you look upon the light?

Not a twig this time, but the crack of an eggshell beginning to hatch.

The light smiles and you feel something unravel within you.

Then there is a scream and the light dims, their attention drawn to another, their brethren, in the crowd.

But you do not leave, for the time for waiting has ended.

You have chosen.

They try and take the light from you with magic that binds their neck, but your magic is stronger.

Older.

You feel your own binding begin. It feels like a word, it feels like a song. But you will not remember it.

For you are no longer you. You are Pila.

Pila felt the cage in her mind shatter and release the being that was her. Awareness flooded her senses, and her fur rippled as if a breeze blew through it, changing the colour from brown to black. She shifted her paws, feeling the earth on the pads of her feet. Though it felt the same as it did a moment ago, all was infinitely different as well. Before, she was a beast waiting, and now . . .

She let her silver gaze settle on the person ahead of her. The light that had drawn Pila to them no longer blinded her like it had before.

Now she could see the person's features, pinched tight in confusion.

Confusion was a new emotion for Pila, but she understood it through the feelings of her bonded half.

Her partner's eyes found hers and widened. Pila dipped her horns in their direction to ease their discomfort. Then words came to her, like falling leaves, and she branched them together to form meaning.

Hello, I'm Pila. I have been waiting for you for a very long time.

Lettle's

~~Prophecy Journal~~

Notes on Mosima

One quarter of the group who are compiling these notes — Y

❧ ELVES ❧

YEERAN Colonel of the Waning Army. *She/her*

LETTLE Diviner pledged to the Gural diviners, and sister of Yeeran. *She/her*

The person whose notebook you're all using — L

Former captain   *Do we need to include that? — R*

RAYAN ~~Captain~~ in the Waning Army, <u>defected from</u> Crescent as a child. *He/him*

KOMI Elf captured by the fae ten years ago and kept prisoner in Mosima. *He/they* *I'm using a pen, can you believe it! — K*

SALAWA Chieftain to the Waning tribe, and Yeeran's lover. *She/they*

IMNA A Gural diviner who now resides in the infirmary due to illness of the mind. *He/him*

MOTOGO General of the Waning Army. *They/them*

❧ FAE ❧

FURI Commander of the faeguard and daughter of Queen Vyce of Mosima. *She/they*

NERAD Prince of the Jani dynasty, son of Queen Chall. *He/him*

VYCE Queen of the fae, ruling in tandem with her sister Chall. *She/her*

CHALL Queen of the fae, ruling in tandem with her sister Vyce. *She/her*

GOLAN Stylist to the fae's elite. *He/they*

HOSTA One of the faeguard who escorted the elves from the Wasted Marshes. *They/them*

Wants to kill us
- L

BERRO Faeguard. Furi's second-in-command. *She/they*

SAHAR Former seer in the fae court. Father of Furi. *He/him*

I didn't know that, did you know that, Rayan? —L

NO —R

JAY Healer and ex-lover of Furi. *They/them*

NAJMA Prince of the Jani dynasty killed by Yeeran. *He/him*

↣ OBEAH ↢

PILA Bonded to Yeeran. *She/they*

XOSA Bonded to Nerad. *She/they*

AMNAN Bonded to Furi. *He/they*

HUDAN Bonded to Najma. *He/they*

SANQ Bonded to Berro. *She/they*

MERI Bonded to Chall. *She/they*

ONYA Bonded to Vyce. *She/they*

Pila wants me to write down that she has the softest fur of everyone in the list —Y

⮞ HUMANS ⮜

AFA Name attributed by the fae to the last living human. Believed to have cursed the fae to Mosima. *He/him*

Also known as the 'Wandering Human' in elven lore - R

⮞ GODS ⮜

ASASE The earth god who came into being as a grain of wheat. Created humans and bestowed on them the magical language of the rocks and trees. *They/them*

EWIA The sun god born as a bat with two heads. Created the fae and granted them the gift of sunlight magic. *They/them*

BOSOME The moon god, who resides as a drop of water in the sky. Created the elves with the power to read the Fates. *They/them*

Praise merciful one - L

❧ TERMS ❧

BINDING BANQUET A party that marks the binding of a fae to their obeah. It includes drinking, dancing, and merriment.

Also known as Yeeran's worst nightmare - L

Lettle, can we leave the dramatics out of this, I have to give this to Salawa one day - Y

CONCH SHORE A beach that runs the length of the bay situated west of the Royal Woodland. It is fed by an estuary on the eastern coast of the continent.

I tried swimming to the boundary and there is no means of escape through the sea. The waves grew rough near the cavern wall. I won't be doing it again - Y

Sounds dramatic - L

DRUMFIRE The magic predominately used by the Waning tribe in warfare. Obeah skin is used to adorn drums, which is then harnessed to create magical projectiles.

FAEGUARD The soldiers who protect and police the citizens of Mosima. The faeguard ranking system is numerical ranging from one to three, except the commander who exists outside and above the ranks.

Berro's role is a One, the highest position bar Furi. Her role is mainly strategic, supporting that of the commander. Twos work offence and Threes defence, knitting their magic to create shields. But who is the enemy? - R

You seem to know a lot about Berro, Rayan - L

Maybe the weakness of their laws has allowed defiance to grow, and the enemy is in their own ranks - K

FLARE FEAST A yearly festival celebrating the annual moment that sunlight strikes the Tree of Souls.

And the fae have yet another party - L

FRAEDIA A crystal that mimics the properties of sunlight which can be used to grow plants and warm homes. The most valuable elven commodity.

It is the largest reserve I have ever seen – Y

FRAY The fray is a cluster of fraedia crystal that grows from the ceiling of the Mosima cavern.

I can hold my magic for up to half an hour if I need to, but I feel my power strengthen day by day. It will be of great benefit on the Bleeding Field – Y

FAE MAGIC The fae can summon a magical thread, only seen through magesight. It can only extend as far as the height of the fae who wields it. Strength and duration varies per person.

LIGHTLESS Those unbound to an obeah.

They are treated poorly in Mosima, as if they are not whole – L

Can land ever be owned? Or is it borrowed by those whose roots run deepest in the soil? These are the questions I wonder – R

Deep – L

LORHAN Capital of the Fae Lands that used to reside on the Bleeding Field.

MAGESIGHT The ability to see magic through a sixth sense. Diviners call this 'becoming heedless'.

It only took Rayan a few minutes to learn it, and Yeeran a week – L

It didn't take me a week, Lettle. Just a few days – Y

MOSIMA The underground cavern where the fae have been cursed to live.

SONG OF SACRIFICE A song sung in taverns in Mosima. At the end of the chorus everyone must finish their drink.

It goes like this:

Blessed are we, to live this life
The Jina dynasty's sacrifice
To reign this day, today, tomorrow
Mosima's heart in the earth below
– K

That's lovely, Komi – Y

FAE LANGUAGE The fae language comes fully formed to those who become faebound. The sounds are difficult to master if you are Lightless. Therefore, all fae are first taught the universal tongue, that elves refer to as elvish.

Riyahisha is the fae word for home. But it is also the word for a warm embrace. Therefore, it is possible to receive riyahisha and also perceive it. How I miss my home - L

THE FATES The Fates allow diviners to parse the future. They are believed to be part of the god Bosome's many influences in the world.

The prophecy I read in my most recent research rings of truth, I cannot shake it from my mind.

Forever the war will rage, until united, the three shall die.

Humans made low, then fae made lower, Then elves in ignorance, gone is their power, Cursed to endure, cursed to survive. All shall perish lest all three thrive

-L

No one knows how or why obeah choose the people they do. I often wonder why Pila chose me, an elf who has murdered her kin. Though I am grateful — Y

OBEAH Creatures that bind to fae, enabling them to come into both the fae language and fae magic. They are beasts of magic, which has made them vulnerable to overhunting by elves.

It started thirty years ago, diseasing the land and soiling crops. Nothing grows there — Y

THE BLIGHT A large agricultural district, three fields wide, that has been pockmarked by acidic soil.

STAR GLIDERS Small lizards with translucent scaled wings. Often seen around those with Jani blood. Their bulbous heads are bioluminescent and light up the Royal Woodland at night.

They have many fauna and flora with the same bioluminescent properties. I wonder if it is a result of evolution under the light of the fray — L

MEAD A fermented honey drink favoured by the fae.

The whipped honey mead from Tola's tavern is my favourite. She spices it with cinnamon — K

ACKNOWLEDGEMENTS

This book is dedicated to my sister, and so I'd like to acknowledge her first. Sally, thank you for your support over the years and being an ardent reader of my work. Thank you for all the baked goods, the long evenings playing Mario Kart and the phone calls listening to every mundane detail of my life. None of my stories would have been written without you wanting to read them.

Juliet, my agent and superwoman extraordinaire. Thank you for always supporting my crazy timescales and fostering my ambition. Especially when most conversations start with 'I've had another book idea'. You are the best co-conspirator and collaborator. Rachel, thank you for manning the helm in Juliet's absence, and huge gratitude to the whole team at Mushens Entertainment: Kiya, Catriona, and Liza. My co-agent, Ginger, you're a class act, and I'm so lucky to have your support, advice and friendship on the other side of the pond alongside the team at Ginger Clark Literary.

Thank you to Natasha Bardon, who spearheaded the acquisition of this new trilogy at Harper Voyager UK after I mentioned the idea back in March 2022. Your relentless championing of my work is the foundation of my success. Shoutout to Amy Perkins for helping to bring this novel to fruition, and Rachel Winterbottom for being the best addition to the team I could ask for. Thank you to the incomparable Tricia Narwani, who jumped in with both feet when Faebound landed on her desk. I will always be grateful for your editorial guidance and for giving my stories a home at Del Rey in North America.

And thank you to the wider publishing team whose efforts are the reason this book is a book. From the Del Rey team: Ayesha Shibli, Ashleigh Heaton, Tori Henson, Sabrina Shen, Scott Shannon,

Alex Larned, Keith Clayton, David Moench, Jordan Pace, Ada Maduka, Ella Laytham, Nancy Delia, Alexis Capitini, Rob Guzman, Brittanie Black and Abby Oladipo. And the Voyager UK team: Elizabeth Vaziri, Chloe Gough, Vicky Leech Mateos, Robyn Watts, Terence Caven, Susanna Peden, Montserrat Bray, Ellie Andre, Sian Richefond and Roisin O'Shea.

To the whole team at FairyLoot, I cannot thank you all enough for sprinkling your fairy dust on Yeeran and Lettle. You made my special edition dreams come true. And a big thank you to the wonderful people at Goldsboro who have continued to be a supporter of my work from the very beginning, you have a very special place in my heart.

The writing community continues to foster my imagination, and there are a few shoutouts I want to make: Karin, thank you for taking every call, for reading my early work and for being the bedrock of support I need to keep writing. Tasha, unfortunately we're family now, there's no turning back. And Sam, your support has kept me buoyed when sometimes I felt like I was drowning. Hannah, Lizzie, Amy, Rebecca, Cherae and all the other writers who have offered a shoulder to lean on, or an ear to listen: you are the best.

Thank you to the long-suffering friends who have been there from the beginning of every trashy draft I have ever written: Rachel, Juniper, Richard, David.

And thank you to my families; the Dinsdales and the El-Arifis and all the extended branches who continue to support this wild career I've chosen.

Then there's Jim, no words will be able to express how grateful I am, so two will have to do: thank you.

And finally, if you've read my previous work, then you know who I dedicate the last words of my book to. You. Yes, you. To the readers and dreamers, it has been the greatest honour creating these stories with you. I just write the words, you bring the characters to life.

We're making magic, you and I. And for that, I will always be thankful.